NETTIE'S SECRET

London, 1875. Thanks to her hapless father, Nettie Carroll has had to grow up quickly. While Nettie is sewing night and day to keep food on the table, her gullible father has trusted the wrong man again. Left with virtually nothing but the clothes they stand in, he's convinced that their only hope lies across the English Channel in France. Nettie has little but her dreams left to lose. Even far from home trouble follows them, with their enemies quietly drawing closer. But Nettie has a secret, and it's one with the power to save them. Does she have the courage to pave the way for a brighter future?

DILLY COURT

NETTIE'S SECRET

Complete and Unabridged

MAGNA
Leicester

First published in Great Britain in 2019 by
HarperCollins*Publishers*
London

First Ulverscroft Edition
published 2020
by arrangement with
HarperCollins*Publishers* Ltd
London

A catalogue record for this book is available from the British Library.

ISBN 978–0–7505–4789–5

Published by
F. A. Thorpe (Publishing)
Anstey, Leicestershire

Set by Words & Graphics Ltd.
Anstey, Leicestershire
Printed and bound in Great Britain by
T. J. International Ltd., Padstow, Cornwall

This book is printed on acid-free paper

For my great-granddaughter,
Marcy Charlotte-Ann Avant.

1

Robert Carroll appeared in the doorway of his attic studio, wiping his hands on his already paint-stained smock. A streak of Rose Madder appeared like a livid gash on his forehead. 'Nettie, I want you to go to Winsor and Newton in Rathbone Place and get me some more Cobalt Blue, Indian Yellow and Zinc White. I can't finish this painting without them.'

Nettie looked up from the garment she had been mending. 'Do you need them urgently, Pa? I promised to finish this for Madame Fabron. It's the opening night of her play at the Adelphi, and she must have her gown.'

'And I have to finish this commission, or I won't get paid and we'll find ourselves homeless. We're already behind with the rent, and Ma Burton isn't the most reasonable of souls.'

'All right, Pa. I'll go, but I thought we didn't have any money, which was why we had nothing but onions for supper last night.' Reluctantly, Nettie laid her sewing aside.

'Food is not important when art is concerned, Nettie,' Robert said severely. 'I can't finish my work without paint, and if I don't get this canvas to Dexter by tomorrow there'll be trouble.' He took some coins from his pocket and pressed them into her hand. 'Go now, and hurry.'

'I know you think the world of Duke Dexter, but how do you know that the copies you make of old masters' works aren't passed off as the real thing?' Nettie pocketed the money. 'You only have Duke's word for the fact that he sells your canvases as reproductions.'

'Nonsense, Nettie. Duke is a respectable art dealer with a gallery in Paris as well as in London.' Robert ran his hand through his hair, leaving it more untidy than ever. 'And even if he weren't an honest dealer, what would you have me do? Commissions don't come my way often enough to support us, even in this rat-infested attic.'

'I still think you ought to check up on him, Pa.'

'Stop preaching at me, Nettie. Be a good girl and get the paint or we'll both starve to death.'

'You have such talent, Pa,' Nettie said sadly. 'It's a pity to squander it by making copies of other people's work.' She snatched up her bonnet and shawl and left her father to get on as best he could until she returned with the urgently needed paints. Everything was always done in a panic, and their way of living had been one of extremes ever since she could remember. When Robert Carroll sold one of his canvases they lived well and, despite Nettie's attempts to save something for the lean times to come, her father had a habit of spending freely without any thought to the future.

Nettie made her way down the narrow, twisting staircase to the second floor, where the two rooms were shared by the friends who had kept her spirits up during the worst of hard times. Byron Horton, whom she thought of as a much-loved big brother, was employed as a clerk by a firm in Lincoln's Inn. Nettie had been tempted to tell him that she suspected Marmaduke Dexter of being a fraud, but that might incriminate her father and so she had kept her worries to herself. The other two young men were Philip Ransome, known fondly as Pip, who worked in the same law office as Byron, and Ted Jones, whose tender heart had been broken so many times by his choice of lady friend that it had become a standing joke. Ted worked for the Midland Railway Company, and was currently suffering from yet another potentially disastrous romantic entanglement.

Nettie hurried down the stairs, past the rooms where the family of actors resided when they were in town, as was now the case. Madame Fabron had a small part in the play *Notre-Dame, or The Gypsy Girl of Paris*, at the Adelphi Theatre, with Monsieur Fabron in a walk-on role, and their daughter, Amelie, was understudy to the leading lady, Teresa Furtado, who was playing Esmeralda. The Fabrons were of French origin, but they had been born and bred in Poplar. They adopted strong French accents whenever they left the building in the same way that others put on their overcoats, but this affectation obviously went well in the theatrical world as they were rarely out of work. Fortunately for Nettie, neither Madame nor her daughter could sew, and Nettie was kept busy mending the garments they wore on and off stage.

She continued down the stairs to the ground floor, where sickly Josephine Lorimer lived with her husband, a journalist, who was more often away from home than he was resident, and a young maid-servant, Biddy, a child plucked from an orphanage. Nettie quickened her pace, not wanting to get caught by Biddy, who invariably asked for help with one thing or another, and was obviously at her wits' end when trying to cope with her ailing mistress. Not that she had many wits in the first place, according to Robert Carroll, who said she was a simpleton. Nettie knew this to be untrue, but today she was in a hurry and she was desperate to avoid their landlady, Ma Burton, who inhabited the basement like a huge spider clad in black bombazine, waiting for her prey to wander into her web. Ma Burton was a skinflint, who knew how to squeeze the last penny out of any situation, and her cronies were shadowy figures who came and went in the hours of darkness. Added to that, Ma Burton's sons were rumoured to be vicious bare-knuckle fighters, who brought terror to the streets of Seven Dials and beyond. It was well known that they were up for hire by any gang willing to pay for their services. It was best not to upset Ma and incur the wrath of her infamous offspring and their equally brutal friends.

Nettie escaped from the house overlooking the piazza of Covent Garden and St Paul's, the actors' church, and was momentarily dazzled by the sunshine reflecting off the wet cobblestones.

4

She had missed a heavy April shower, and she had to sidestep a large puddle as she made her way down Southampton Street. It would have been quicker to cut through Seven Dials, but that was a rough area, even in daytime; after dark no one in their right mind would venture into the narrow alleys and courts that radiated off the seventeenth-century sundial, not even the police. Nettie stopped to count the coins her father had given her and decided there was enough for her bus fare to the Tottenham Court Road end of Oxford Street, and from there it was a short walk to the art shop in Rathbone Place. She must make haste — Violet Fabron would expect her gown to be finished well before curtain-up.

Nettie spotted a horse-drawn omnibus drawing to a halt in the Strand and she picked up her skirts and ran. The street was crowded with vehicles of all shapes and sizes, and with pedestrians milling about in a reckless manner, but this enabled Nettie to jump on board. As luck would have it, she found a vacant seat. One day, when she was rich, she would have her own carriage and she would sit back against velvet squabs, watching the rest of the population going about their business, but for now it was the rackety omnibus that bumped over the cobblestones and swayed from side to side like a ship on a stormy ocean, stopping to let passengers alight and taking on fresh human cargo. Steam rose from damp clothing, and the smell of wet wool and muddy boots combined with the sweat of humans and horseflesh. Nettie closed her mind to the rank odours and sat back, enjoying the freedom of being away from her cramped living quarters, if only for an hour or so.

★ ★ ★

Two hours later, Nettie returned home with the paints and two baked potatoes that she had purchased from a street vendor in Covent Garden.

Robert studied the small amount of change she had just given him. 'The price of paint hasn't gone up, has it?'

Nettie took off her bonnet and laid it on a chair in the living room. 'No, Pa. I bought the potatoes because we need to eat. I'm so hungry that my stomach hurts.'

'There should be more change than this.'

'I had a cup of coffee, Pa. Surely you don't begrudge me that?'

Robert shook his head. 'No, of course not. I'm hungry, too. Thank you, dear.' He took the potato and disappeared into his room.

Nettie sighed with relief as the door closed behind her father. She reached under her shawl and produced the new notebook that she had purchased in Oxford Street. It had cost every penny that she had earned from mending a tear in Monsieur Fabron's best shirt, and she had supplemented it with a threepenny bit from the coins that her father had given her for his art supplies. Perhaps she should have spent the three-pence on food, but she considered it money well spent, and paper, pen and ink were her only extravagance. Writing a romantic novel was more than a guilty pleasure; Nettie had been working on her story for over a year, and she hoped one day to see it published. But she dare not reveal the truth to Pa — he would tell her that she was wasting valuable time. No one in their right mind would want to pay good money for a work written by a twenty-year-old girl with very little experience of life and love. She knew exactly what Pa thought about 'penny dreadfuls' and he would be mortified if he thought that his daughter aspired to write popular fiction. It was her secret and she had told nobody, not even Byron or Pip, and Ted could not keep a secret to save his life. Poor Ted was still nursing a broken heart after being jilted by the young woman who worked in the nearby bakery; he wore black and had grown his hair long in the hope that he looked like a poet with a tragic past. Nettie had met the love of his life, Pearl Biggs, just the once, and that was enough to convince her that Ted was better off remaining a bachelor than tied to a woman who was no better than she should be.

Nettie hid the new notebook, along with two others already filled, beneath the cushions on the sofa, where she slept each night. She was in the middle of her story, and the characters played out their lives in her imagination while she went about her daily chores. Sometimes they intruded in her thoughts when she was least expecting it, but occasionally they refused to co-operate and she found herself with her pen poised and nothing to say.

She put the potato on a clean plate and went to sit on a chair in the window to enjoy the hot buttery flesh and the crisp outer skin, licking her fingers after each tasty bite. When she had eaten the last tiny morsel, she wiped her hands on a napkin and picked up her sewing. She concentrated on Madame Fabron's gown, using tiny stitches to ensure that the darn was barely visible. Having finished, she put on her outdoor things and wrapped the gown in a length of butter muslin. She opened the door to her father's studio.

'I'm off to the theatre, Pa.'

'The theatre?'

'Yes, Pa. You remember, Madame Fabron needs her gown for the performance this evening.'

'Oh, that. Yes, I do. Wretched woman thinks she can act. I've seen more talented performing horses. Don't be long, Nettie. I want you to take a message to Duke. You'll need to make full use of your feminine wiles because this painting won't be finished today. He can come and view it, if he so wishes.'

'Yes, Pa. I'll be as quick as I can.'

Once again, Nettie left their rooms and made her way downstairs. She was tiptoeing past the Lorimers' door when it opened and Biddy leaped out at her.

'I heard you coming. I need help, Nettie. Mrs Lorimer's having one of her funny turns.'

'I'm sorry, Biddy. But I'm in a hurry.'

Biddy clutched Nettie's arm. 'Oh, please. I dunno what to do. She's weeping and throwing things. I'm scared to death.'

'All right, but I can only spare a couple of

minutes.' Nettie stepped inside the dark hallway and Biddy rushed past her to open the sitting-room door. The curtains were drawn and a fire burned in the grate, creating a fug. The smell of sickness lingered in the air. It took Nettie a moment to accustom her eyes to the gloom, but she could see Josephine Lorimer's prostate figure on a chaise longue in front of the fire. She had one arm flung over her face and the other hanging limp over the side of the couch. Unearthly keening issued from her pale lips.

'What's the matter, Mrs Lorimer?'

Josephine moved her arm away from her face. 'Who is it?'

'It's me, Nettie Carroll from upstairs. Biddy says you are unwell.'

'I'm very ill. I think I'm dying and nobody cares.'

Nettie laid her hand on Josephine's forehead, which was clammy but cool. 'You don't appear to have a fever. Perhaps if you sit up and try to keep calm you might feel better.'

'How can I be calm when I am all alone in this dark room?'

Biddy shrank back into the shadows. 'Is she dying?'

Nettie walked over to the window and drew the curtains, allowing a shaft of pale sunlight to filter in through the grimy windowpanes. 'Mrs Lorimer would be better for a cup of tea and something to eat, Biddy. Have you anything prepared for her luncheon?'

'There's soup downstairs on the old witch's range, but I'm scared to go down there. She'll put me in a pot and boil me for her dinner.'

Josephine groaned and turned her head away. 'Have you ever heard such nonsense? I'm supposed to be looked after by that stupid girl.'

'I'm not stupid, missis,' Biddy muttered.

'Come with me,' Nettie said firmly. 'We'll go down together. Ma Burton may be an old witch, but she doesn't eat people.'

Biddy backed away, but a fierce look from Josephine sent her scurrying for the door. 'All right, I'll go, but you must come with me, miss.'

'We'll be back in two ticks.' Nettie lowered her voice. 'She's just a child and she's scared.'

Josephine's lips trembled. 'I need someone like you — someone capable and caring, not a silly little girl.'

Nettie gave up her attempt to reason with the irritable patient and followed Biddy from the room.

★ ★ ★

Ma Burton was tucking into a bowl of soup with evident enjoyment. Nettie suspected that Ma had helped herself from the Lorimers' saucepan, but it would cause trouble if anything was said. Biddy kept so close to Nettie that she might have been mistaken for her shadow, but Ma Burton was too busy eating to make a fuss. To Nettie's astonishment, she allowed them to take the pan and leave without adding anything extra to the usual charge of one penny for use of the range.

'There, you see, she's not so bad after all,'

Nettie said as they climbed the stairs to the ground floor.

With the hot pan wrapped in her apron, Biddy was careful not to spill a drop. 'The missis will probably throw the soup at me — that's what she did last time. I had bits of carrot stuck in me hair for days afterwards.'

'I'll make sure she behaves better today.' Nettie struggled to keep a straight face. She could understand the frustration on both sides: Biddy was a child, taken from the orphanage because she was cheap labour; Josephine was the unhappy wife of a neglectful husband, with no recourse other than to play on her delicate constitution in order to gain attention. Nettie resigned herself to taking charge of the situation until Josephine was fed and comfortable, and, Nettie hoped, in a better mood. Biddy would no doubt improve out of all recognition if someone took her in hand, but that was unlikely to happen in the Lorimer household.

If Josephine was grateful for the food and Nettie's undivided attention, she hid it well. She complained that the soup was too hot, and that it was too salty. She nibbled a slice of bread and butter Nettie prepared for her and then threw herself back on the cushions, complaining of a headache.

'Fetch my medicine, girl,' Josephine said feebly. 'I need laudanum. Hurry up, you silly child.'

Biddy stood on tiptoe to reach the brown glass bottle set up high on the mantelshelf. 'I'm doing it as fast as I can.'

'There, you see what I have to put up with,

Nettie.' Josephine held her hand out. 'Give me the bottle, girl, and pour me some water. Not too much.'

Nettie took the laudanum from Biddy. 'Has the doctor prescribed this, Mrs Lorimer?'

'Mind your own business and give it to me.'

'I have a better idea,' Nettie said, glancing out of the window. 'The sun is shining so why don't you come for a walk with me? I'm delivering this gown to Madame Fabron at the theatre. Wouldn't you like to see them in rehearsal?'

Josephine clutched her hands to her bosom. 'I haven't been outside these rooms for over a year.'

'But you can walk,' Nettie said firmly. 'You aren't in pain.'

'I have pain everywhere, and I am so tired, but I can't sleep at night.'

'She is always saying that,' Biddy added, nodding vigorously. 'She is always complaining.'

'Be quiet,' Josephine snapped. 'Who asked you, girl?'

'It isn't far to walk to the stage door of the Adelphi. Why not make an effort, Mrs Lorimer? The fresh air will do you good, and maybe you'll feel a little better. You might even see Miss Furtado rehearsing, if you're lucky.'

Josephine raised herself to a sitting position. 'I saw Teresa Furtado perform at Drury Lane. We used to go to the theatre often before I became ill.'

'If Biddy will fetch your outdoor things, we'll see if you can manage to get that far. You won't know unless you try. We'll help you.'

It took twice as long to get to the stage door than it would have done had Nettie been on her own, but between them, she and Biddy managed to cajole, bully and half-carry a reluctant Josephine Lorimer to the theatre. Once inside there seemed to be a minor miracle and Josephine was suddenly alert and smiling. She walked unaided to the dressing room that Madame Fabron shared with all the minor female characters, and when Amelie Fabron appeared and offered to take them into the auditorium to watch the dress rehearsal, Josephine accepted eagerly. Her cheeks were flushed and her eyes alight with excitement. It was a complete transformation, and she sat in the front row of the stalls, gazing in delight at the stage.

'I have to do an errand for my father,' Nettie said in a low voice.

'Shhh!' Josephine held her finger to her lips.

Nettie sighed and turned to Biddy, who seemed equally thrilled with the rehearsal. 'Will you be all right if I leave you here?'

'Isn't Miss Furtado beautiful?' Biddy breathed, dreamy-eyed.

Nettie could see that she was getting nowhere and she left them enraptured and in a world of their own. She would happily have remained with them, but she needed to find Duke Dexter as a matter of urgency. It was fortunate that Ma Burton had, for once, been more interested in her food than in demanding the rent arrears, but that situation would not last, and Ma's boys used methods of persuasion that were brutal and very effective. As Pa said, 'What use is an artist with a broken hand or missing fingers?' They were not in that position as yet, but that could change.

★   ★   ★

Dexter's gallery was in fashionable Dover Street, patronised by the rich and famous. Nettie hesitated before entering, smoothing her creased gown and straightening her bonnet. The fashionably dressed ladies and gentlemen looked at her askance as they strolled past, and she felt dowdy and out of place. Then, out of the corner of her eyes, she saw a man lurking in a doorway further up the street. His battered top hat and oversized black jacket both had the green tinge of age, and his lank hair hung loose around his shoulders. Nettie observed all these details in the brief moment before he ducked out of sight, but his appearance had disturbed her and her active imagination had him marked as someone up to no good. She took a deep breath and let herself into the gallery.

The elegant interior was furnished with antique chairs and Persian carpets, and the walls were adorned with gilt-framed paintings. Bowls of spring flowers scented the air and clients were greeted by Pendleton, a thin, balding man dressed in a black frock coat, neatly pressed pinstripe trousers and a dazzlingly white shirt. The lack of hair on his pate was compensated for by a wildly curling ginger moustache, the waxed tips of which quivered every time he spoke.

Nettie found herself mesmerised by his facial hair, which seemed to have a life of its own.

'How may I be of service, Miss Carroll?' Pendleton raised his hand to twirl his moustache with delicate twists of his long fingers.

It was a routine they enacted each time Nettie entered the gallery. 'I'd like to see Mr Dexter on a matter of business.'

Pendleton's tea-coloured eyes met hers with a condescending smile. 'Are you a purchaser or a vendor today, Miss Carroll?'

She was tempted to tell him to mind his own business, but that would only make matters worse. Pendleton was in his own little kingdom and, if he so wished, he could prevent her from seeing Dexter even if his employer was on the premises.

'I have something that Mr Dexter wants, Mr Pendleton.'

'I'll see if he's in his office. Excuse me, miss.' Pendleton bowed and walked away at a leisurely pace.

Nettie glanced round anxiously. She was even more conscious of her shabby clothes and down-at-heel boots, and she was aware of the curious glances of the well-dressed clientele who were wandering about, studying the works of art that were presented on easels or hanging from the walls.

Pendleton reappeared after what felt like an eternity. 'Mr Dexter can spare you a moment or two, Miss Carroll.'

'Thank you, I know the way.' Nettie hesitated. 'It may be nothing, Mr Pendleton, but I saw someone acting suspiciously just a few doors down from here. He seemed to be watching the gallery.'

Pendleton was suddenly alert. 'Describe him, if you please.' He listened intently. 'Wegg, he said tersely. 'Samson Wegg — he's a private detective — a police informer with a long-held and very bitter grudge against Mr Dexter. Don't have anything to do with him, miss. Wegg is a nasty piece of work.'

'I'm not likely to speak to someone like that, Mr Pendleton.'

'Quite right. Wegg is trouble, so I suggest you leave now, miss.'

'But I must see Mr Dexter. I won't take up much of his time.' Nettie pushed past Pendleton and headed for a door that led downstairs to the basement. It was here that Duke Dexter stored the most valuable works in his collection, and the copies that he sold to art lovers who could not afford to purchase the originals. Nettie negotiated the narrow stairs, ending in a room below street level where some daylight filtered in from a barred window set high in the wall, but the main light source in the room came from a gasolier in the centre of the ceiling. Duke was using a magnifying glass to examine an oil painting in minute detail.

'Come in, Nettie, my dear.' He turned to her with the smile that she had seen him use on his wealthy patrons when he wished to charm them out of large sums of money. His dark eyes set beneath winged eyebrows gave him a saturnine look, which vanished when a slow smile curved his lips. He was a handsome man, who knew how to use his looks and fine figure to best advantage when it came to charming prospective customers, but Nettie could not rid herself of the nagging suspicion that he was secretly laughing at her and her father. 'It's always a pleasure to see you, my dear, but you seem to have arrived empty handed.'

'You know very well that I couldn't carry a wet oil painting through the streets, let alone climb on board an omnibus with it in my hands.'

He placed the magnifying glass on a table nearby and turned to her with eyebrows raised. 'The canvas ought to have been delivered to me three weeks ago. I suppose that's why Robert sent you to brave the lion in his den. More excuses, I suppose?'

Nettie put her head on one side. 'I don't think of you as a lion, Duke. You're more of a panther, sleek and dangerous and best avoided. I wish my father had never met you.'

'I'm only dangerous to those who attempt to deceive me or do me harm.' He pulled up a chair. 'Won't you take a seat?'

'Thank you, but I'd rather stand.' Nettie faced him with a defiant stare. 'Pa is still working on the painting. He sent me to tell you that it won't be finished for another day or two.'

'Your father has let me down several times and it won't do.'

'He's an artist, and he's a brilliant one. He's too good for this sort of thing, and you could help him more if you set your mind to it.'

Duke's eyes narrowed and his winged brows

drew together over the bridge of his nose. 'I didn't ask for your opinion, and I don't take kindly to criticism when, in fact, I've saved your father from bankruptcy several times over.'

'Then why don't you hang his original works in your gallery? Why are you encouraging him to make copies?'

'The truth, if you want to hear it, is that your father is a second-rate painter, but a first-rate copyist. My wealthy clients are prepared to pay handsomely for works that they believe are original. It makes them happy and we all benefit.'

'I thought as much. You take their money under false pretences,' Nettie countered angrily. 'You give Pa a small fraction of what you take and, he doesn't realise it, but he's risking imprisonment and ruin if he's found out.'

'I have the contacts and I am a businessman first and foremost.'

'You are a criminal and a trickster.'

'I dare say you're right, but Robert is in this too deep to stop now. Or perhaps you'd rather see your father lose everything, including his reputation?'

'No, of course not,' Nettie said angrily. 'I'm going to tell him what you're up to.'

Duke moved closer so that she could feel the heat of his body, and the scent of spice, citrus and maleness filled her head with dizzying effect. He leaned towards her so that their faces were inches apart. 'You can't prove it and I will deny everything. Robert will believe me because he needs me. Either you accept the situation and do your best to keep him out of trouble, or you face the consequences brought about by your father's frailty. It's your choice, Nettie. What's it to be?'

She looked into his dark eyes and knew that he had won this time, but she was not beaten. 'What do you want me to do?'

He backed away, smiling. 'That's better. That wasn't too difficult, was it?' He picked up the magnifying glass and turned away to study the painting. 'Tell Robert to bring it to me when he's satisfied that it will pass the closest scrutiny, but I want it soon or there's no deal, and I'll find someone who will work faster.'

'Why don't you tell him yourself?' Nettie faced him angrily. 'You could come to our rooms and see the painting as it is now. You know very well that it will take weeks, if not months to dry.'

'Which is why I want to have it and keep it safe.' Duke leaned towards her, narrowing his eyes. 'Your father is paid to do as I say. He'd do well to remember that, and so would you.'

'One day you'll meet your match, Duke.' Nettie walked away without waiting for a response.

2

'Don't take it to heart, Nettie,' Robert said calmly when she finished recounting her experience in the art gallery. 'Duke is like that with everyone. I wouldn't normally associate with someone like him, but he pays well.'

'He's a criminal, Pa. He's exploiting your talent for his own ends. He gives you a pittance for your work and makes a fortune for himself. I don't agree with what you're doing.'

Robert put his palette down and sighed. 'You're wrong, my dear. Duke has kept us out of the workhouse and he pays well. One day I will get one of my original paintings accepted by the Royal Academy and I'll never have to make another copy.'

Nettie sighed and shook her head. 'Do you know a man called Samson Wegg? He was hanging around outside the gallery. Pendleton said he's a police informer.'

'I don't know the fellow personally, Nettie. Duke has upset a great many people in the past, and I suspect that Wegg is one of them. It's nothing to do with us.'

She knew that it was useless to argue. 'I'll leave you to get on, Pa. Just remember that Dexter wants the painting urgently.'

'It's nearly finished, and I'm going to the Lamb and Flag for some refreshment.'

'Must you, Pa? We owe Ma Burton three weeks' rent.'

'I've been working hard, Nettie. A pint of ale won't bankrupt us.'

Nettie bit back a sharp retort. There was no reasoning with Pa when he was in this mood. 'What shall I do about supper?'

Robert stripped off his smock and reached for his jacket and hat. 'Don't worry about me, dear. I'll get something at the pub. You should have enough change from the paint to buy yourself a pie.' He kissed her on the cheek and sauntered from the room.

Nettie stared after him, shaking her head. Duke Dexter was undoubtedly a ruthless criminal who had led her father into a life of crime, and Pa was both feckless and easily duped, but she herself must take some of the blame for the fact that she had no money for food. She should not have spent so much on the notebook, and she could have walked from Piccadilly in order to save the bus fare. Yet again she would go to bed hungry — unless there was good news from the publishing house. It was some weeks since she had submitted the manuscript of her first novella, *Arabella's Dilemma*, a gothic tale of passion and revenge, which was as good, she hoped, as anything that Ann Radcliffe had penned in *The Mysteries of Udolpho*, or Mary Shelley's *Frankenstein*. Nettie had changed her style since writing about Arabella's adventures, but if the story was accepted it would give her a measure of independence, and relieve the pressure on her father to become ever more involved with Duke. There was nothing for it but to put on her bonnet and shawl and venture out again, although this time it was on an errand of her own. She set off for Soho and the small publishing house that had been her last resort. All the major publishers had rejected her manuscript, but Dorning and Lacey were yet to reply.

★ ★ ★

Nettie left the office in Frith Street with the manuscript tucked under her shawl. The clerk behind the desk had been sympathetic, but was obviously practised in dealing with disappointed authors. The rejection letter was similar to the others she had received for previous attempts at writing fiction, giving her little hope of furthering her ambition to see her work in print. It had begun to rain, and although it was probably just an April shower, it was heavy enough to soak her to the skin in a few minutes, adding to her frustration, and she was hungry. Perhaps this was her punishment for squandering money instead of putting it towards the rent arrears.

She arrived home at the same time as Byron. He took one look at her and his smile of welcome faded. 'Good Lord, Nettie. Where've you been? You look like a drowned rat — I mean,' he added quickly, 'you don't actually look like a rat — it's just an expression, but you are very bedraggled.'

'You don't have to tell me that,' Nettie said ruefully. 'I got caught in a shower.'

He opened the door and held it for her. 'You'd better get out of those wet things before you catch cold.'

She put her finger to her lips. 'Tiptoe or Biddy will leap out and ask for help. I've been caught once like that today.'

Byron followed her, treading as softly as was possible for a tall young man who looked as though he would be more at home on the cricket pitch or playing a game of tennis than working in the city. However, despite his boyish appearance, he was the person Nettie trusted the most.

They managed to get past the Lorimers' door without being waylaid, and Nettie could only hope that the outing to the theatre might have done sickly Josephine some good. They continued up the next flight in silence, but when they reached the second floor and Nettie was about to say goodbye to Byron, he caught her by the hand.

'Before you go upstairs, I wanted to ask you to join us for dinner tonight, Nettie. It's my birthday and I'm treating the chaps to dinner at the Gaiety Restaurant — I'd be honoured if you'd come, too.'

The mere thought of a decent meal made Nettie's mouth water, but the Gaiety was expensive and she knew that Byron earned little enough without making extravagant gestures. 'That sounds wonderful, but can you afford it? I mean, dining there isn't cheap.'

He winked and tapped the side of his nose. 'Ask no questions and you'll be told no lies,' he said, laughing. 'Don't look so worried, Nettie. I had the winning ticket in a sweepstake at work. I can't think of a better way to spend the money than to treat my best friends.'

★ ★ ★

Nettie put on her best gown of pale blue silk with a modest décolleté. Four years ago her father had had a run of good fortune. He had promised to take her to Paris to see the works of art in the Louvre and had even gone to the trouble of obtaining passports. Added to that, in a sudden fit of generosity, he had taken her to a fashionable salon and had chosen the outfit himself, but styles had changed subtly since then. Nettie had had to use all her sewing skills to bring the garment up to date, but when they entered the smart Gaiety Restaurant she felt like a sparrow amongst brightly coloured birds of paradise. She was dowdy in comparison to the elegant ladies present, but if Byron, Pip and Ted were not as smartly dressed as the other gentlemen they did not seem to know or to care. Their appearances passed largely unnoticed, whereas Nettie could feel the patronising and sometimes pitying glances from other women. They would know almost to the day when her gown had been bought, and probably the very salon from which it had been purchased.

Despite her discomfort, Nettie held her head high as Byron led the way past a table where several young men in evening suits were enjoying themselves noisily.

'Students. More money than sense.' Ted

moved on swiftly, but one of the party had apparently overhead his remark and the young man staggered to his feet.

'What did you say, sir?'

'Sit down, Rufus.' One of his friends caught him by the arm. 'We'll get thrown out if you don't behave.'

'The fellow just insulted us, Percy.' Rufus steadied himself, and his belligerent expression was wiped away by a slightly lopsided smile as he spotted Nettie. 'A thousand pardons, most beautiful lady.'

'Shut up, Norwood. You're drunk.' Percy tried to stand but fell back on his chair.

'Drunk or sober, I'm honoured to make your acquaintance, ma'am.' Rufus Norwood seized Nettie's hand and raised it to his lips. 'Will you and your party join us, fair lady?'

She met his gaze and realised with a shock that he was not nearly as drunk as he made out. His lips were smiling but his hazel eyes danced with amusement. She snatched her hand away and hurried on before Byron had a chance to intervene.

'Do you know that fellow?' he asked in a low voice. 'If he upset you I'll go and sort him out.'

'I've never met him before in my life,' Nettie said hastily. 'Ignore them; they're all tipsy.'

'I may be a trifle inebriated,' Rufus said with a courtly bow, 'but I would never insult a lady.'

'Sit down and stop being such a bore.' Percy tugged at his friend's coat-tails.

Nettie walked away and took her seat at the table with her head held high; she had no intention of letting anything or anyone spoil the evening, and it was Byron's birthday — he was the most important person present.

But her enjoyment was short lived. Just as they were about to finish their main course, who should walk through the door but Duke Dexter, and the young woman who clung to his arm, laughing and flirting outrageously, was none other than Amelie Fabron. They were accompanied by two other couples, who were equally loud and very drunk. It was obvious that Duke was a regular customer as the waiters fawned upon him, rushing around to clear a table in the centre of the restaurant, pulling up chairs and wafting clean napkins in the air before laying them on their patrons' laps.

'Who the hell is that?' Pip demanded, chuckling. 'You'd think that fellow was a royal.'

'He's an art dealer,' Byron said in a low voice. 'One of our clients tried to sue him and failed. Everyone knows he's a criminal, but so far the police haven't been able to pin anything on him. He's as slippery as an eel.'

'And twice as ugly,' Pip added. 'I'd call him vulgar. Look at the gold rings he wears on both hands.'

Ted sighed heavily. 'It doesn't seem to worry that young lady — she's beautiful. What does she see in him?'

'What's the matter with all of you?' Nettie leaned forward, lowering her voice. 'You must have seen her often enough. That's Amelie, the Fabrons' daughter. She's in the play at the Adelphi, or rather she's an understudy, so I don't

26

know what she's doing here.'

Byron turned his head to take another look. 'By Jove, so it is. I've only seen her in passing and she always puts her head down and scuttles by as if she thinks I'll bite. Look at her now.'

'I've a good mind to tell her father,' Ted said angrily. 'That fellow is up to no good. Look at the way he's running his fingers up and down her arm. I ought to go over there and give him a piece of my mind.'

Nettie reached out and laid her hand on his clenched fist. 'It has nothing to do with us, Ted. She's not like your lady friend from the bakery — Amelie is her parents' problem, not yours.' She glanced at Duke and felt the blood rush to her cheeks as their eyes met. Even worse, he rose to his feet and was coming towards them. Nettie looked around for a way of escape, but there was none.

Duke came to a halt beside her. 'Well, well, I wasn't expecting to see you here this evening, Miss Carroll.'

Byron rose to his feet. 'Do you know this man, Nettie?'

'Of course she does,' Duke said smoothly. 'How would I be aware of her name if we weren't acquainted?'

'This is Mr Dexter who has an art gallery in Dover Street,' Nettie said stiffly. 'I've visited it with Pa.'

'Of course you have.' Duke took her hand and raised it to his lips. 'I'm delighted to see you again after all this time, Miss Carroll. Please remember me to your father and tell him that I look forward to seeing his latest work — sooner rather than later.' He bowed and strolled back to his table.

Amelie turned to stare at them and looked away quickly, but not before Nettie had seen panic in the girl's eyes, giving her the appearance of a startled fawn.

'Someone ought to tell her father,' Ted insisted sulkily. 'She's too young for him, and he's obviously a libertine.'

'She is young,' Nettie said slowly, 'but she was brought up in the theatre. I'm sure she's got his measure, but I'll speak to her if it will make you feel better, Ted.'

He shrugged and pushed his plate away. 'I suppose it's none of my business, but I don't like the look of that man.'

'Neither do I,' Pip added with feeling. 'I've met his ilk often enough when they need someone to represent them in court. They think their ill-earned money can buy anything and anyone.'

Byron picked up the wine bottle and refilled Ted's glass. 'Drink up, everyone. It's my birthday, so let's enjoy ourselves. Who's for pudding?'

Pip smiled and raised his glass. 'Here's to you, Byron. Happy birthday, and I'd love something sweet.' He nudged Ted, grinning widely. 'I'm sure you would, too, if only you'd stop drooling over young Amelie. Anyone would think you'd never seen a pretty girl before.'

'I've never seen her looking like that,' Ted muttered.

'Don't tease him,' Nettie said, smiling. 'He's just being protective.'

28

'That's right, I am,' Ted murmured. 'Women need to be protected.'

'That's very gallant, Ted.' Nettie raised her glass. 'Let's remember that we're here to celebrate Byron's good fortune and his special day. Happy birthday, Byron.' She sipped her wine but she was aware that Duke was staring at her, and she looked away quickly.

'Are you enjoying yourself, Nettie?'

She turned to see Byron leaning close and smiling. 'Yes, of course,' she said hastily. 'It's a lovely restaurant and delicious food.'

'You looked so far away just now.'

'I was just wondering how I was going to convince Amelie that Duke Dexter is not the sort of man she should associate with.'

'What do you know about him, Nettie?'

She lowered her voice. 'I think he passes off the copies Pa makes as originals, although I can't prove it. I've mentioned it to Pa, but he refuses to believe ill of Duke, and he says he has to sell his work wherever he can. It's hard enough to find commissions, never mind worrying about the dealer's reputation.'

'If that's the case, Mr Carroll would be well advised to steer clear of Dexter. You ought to be firm with him, Nettie.'

She twisted her lips into a smile. 'You know my pa, Byron. He won't listen.'

'Here comes the waiter,' he said cheerfully. 'What are you all having?'

The rest of the meal passed off uneventfully, and they were all in good spirits as they prepared to leave the restaurant, but when Nettie passed the table where the young men were behaving even more badly than before, she could not resist a quick glance in Rufus Norwood's direction. Once again their eyes met, but it was a fleeting encounter and she left the restaurant accompanied by her friends.

★　★　★

For the first time ever Nettie came home to find her father had returned from the pub early. He was seated by the fire, reading in the light of a single candle. He looked up, scowling. 'Where have you been? I didn't give you permission to go out.'

Nettie took off her cape and hung it on a peg behind the door. 'I'm twenty, Pa. Surely I don't have to ask you if I can go out for dinner with my friends.'

'What friends? Of course I should know where you're going and with whom.'

She crossed the floor and took a seat opposite him, resting her booted feet on the fender. 'It was Byron's birthday. He treated us to a meal at the Gaiety, and very nice it was, too.'

'Well, you should have told me. I was imagining all sorts of things.'

She studied his face and realised with a jolt of surprise that he meant what he said. 'What's brought this on, Pa?'

'I should have gone to see Duke myself, Nettie. He has a certain reputation when it comes to women, especially young and pretty ones like yourself.'

'How could you think that I would have anything to do with someone like him?'

'I know he's waiting for the painting, and he can be ruthless when it comes to getting his own way.'

'Put your mind at ease, Pa. Duke isn't interested in me. We saw him in the restaurant this evening, and he had Amelie Fabron on his arm. I intend to warn her about him.'

'That would be courting trouble, my love. She would be sure to tell Dexter and then we would be in an even worse position. Don't underestimate him, Nettie. He's charming when it suits him, and he's always been good to me, but I know that Duke can be vicious if he's crossed.'

'Why do you continue to work for him then, Pa?'

'We have to pay our way, Nettie. All I'm saying is, take care.'

Nettie rose to her feet and kissed him on the forehead. 'I'll be very careful, Pa. I'm really tired, so if you wouldn't mind, I'll make myself ready for bed.'

'I'll have an early night and be up first thing, ready to complete the painting, and I'll take it to Dover Street myself. Good night, my dear.'

'Sweet dreams, Pa, and don't worry about me. I have Duke's measure.'

★　★　★

Several days passed, and despite her best efforts, Nettie was finding it almost impossible to have a quiet word with Amelie, but she felt compelled

31

to warn her against getting too close to Duke Dexter. Madame Fabron had nothing for her in the way of mending or alterations, which made it difficult to approach the family without raising their suspicions, and Amelie was always accompanied by one or other of her parents. Besides which, Nettie had problems of her own. Her father had finally taken the completed work to Dover Street and she waited anxiously for his return. He had been gone for three hours, and she could only hope that was a good sign. Despite her misgivings, the money from Dexter should be enough to see them through the next few weeks, and it would give Pa the chance to produce a work of his own. Such talent as his must surely be recognised eventually. Nettie had faith in him, if only he would apply himself instead of waiting for inspiration or a lucrative commission to fall into his lap.

She opened the new notebook and sat with her pencil poised above the blank page, but her thoughts strayed and she found it impossible to concentrate. Her young heroine, the daughter of a country parson, had fallen in love with a wastrel and was on the brink of leaving home to run away with the man her parents had forbidden her ever to see again, but Nettie was having difficulty picturing the scene between father and daughter. She closed her eyes, attempting to bring her characters to life, and failing miserably.

All she could think of was her empty belly and the fact that Ma Burton had threatened them with eviction if the arrears in rent were not forthcoming. Just that morning she had given them until six o'clock to come up with all or part of the money owing. She had not needed to elaborate on what would happen if they could not pay.

Nettie jumped to her feet as the door opened. 'How did it go, Pa? Did he pay you?'

'You'd best start packing, my dear. I'm afraid we have to make a move and do it quickly.' Robert rushed into his studio. 'We'll have to travel light, so take only what you need.'

Nettie stood in the doorway, watching helplessly as he began tossing his paints and brushes into a leather bag. 'What happened? What's wrong, Pa?'

'You were right all along, Nettie. Duke has been selling the reproductions as originals and Wegg has reported his dealings to the police. Duke has cut and run and, according to Pendleton, I'd do well to follow suit unless I want to go to prison. I swear I thought what I was doing was legitimate — at least I did until you put doubts in my head.'

'I know you were taken in by him, Pa. You were always convinced that Duke Dexter was an honest art dealer.'

'I still find it hard to believe that Duke misled me deliberately. I keep thinking it's all some horrible mistake, but Pendleton was in the middle of telling me all this when the police arrived. I was questioned by a big burly sergeant, who didn't seem to believe a word I said. He took my name and address and told me not to leave town.'

'I did try to warn you, Pa.'

'I know you did, my love. I didn't want to think ill of Duke, and I made those copies in good faith, but it seems that Wegg has done his worst. He was determined to ruin Duke and it seems that he's succeeded.'

'Think hard, Pa,' Nettie said urgently. 'Is there any way the police could prove you were the artist concerned?'

'I had to leave my painting behind. An expert would soon realise that there are other works in the gallery made by the same copyist, and it won't take long before the police put two and two together. I'm afraid if I don't make a run for it, I'll end up in prison. But you're innocent and you don't deserve to be dragged down by me.'

'That's nonsense, Pa. We're in this together.'

'You've stood by me even though you suspected that what I was doing was illegal,' Robert said with a wry smile. 'But it's time you made a life for yourself. I want you to go to your aunt Prudence in Wales. You'd be safe there.'

'I'd rather be on the run with you, Pa. Aunt Prudence lives on a mountain surrounded by sheep. Anyway, you need me to look after you.' Nettie went to the dresser and began searching the drawers. 'Where did I put the passports you obtained for us last year? You remember, Pa. It was for the trip to Paris we never made because we couldn't afford it.'

Robert pulled a face. 'Don't remind me of my past misdeeds, Nettie. That horse was a certainty, or so I thought. We would have visited the Louvre and Montmartre, the artists' quarter, if that animal had won.'

'Never mind that now, Pa. I've found them.' Nettie closed the drawer and tucked the documents into her reticule.

'You're a good girl, Nettie. I don't deserve you.'

'There's one problem, though. We haven't any money.'

'Duke must have a conscience of sorts: he left payment for my last canvas. As luck would have it, Pendleton handed it over before the police arrived.'

'But you didn't sign the copies,' Nettie said slowly. 'Even experts could be mistaken. If you had a good solicitor you might be able to prove that you knew nothing of Duke's business deals.'

'Everyone in the art world knows that I've been involved with Dexter for years, and I don't trust Pendleton to keep his mouth shut. He'll tell the police anything they want to know in order to save his own skin. I'm afraid there's no alternative but to leave the country until all this blows over.'

'Where will we go, Pa?'

'We'll head for Dover and catch the ferry to Calais. I don't know where we'll go from there. We'll take it day by day.'

'I must tell my friends. I can't leave without saying anything to Byron and the others.'

'You mustn't do that, Nettie. It's not fair to involve them. The less they know, the better. You can see that, can't you?'

'I suppose so.'

'Good. Now pack your things. We'll leave the

rent money on the table. I'm not so dishonest that I'd rob an old woman, even a harridan like Ma Burton.'

Nettie experienced a moment of panic as she packed a valise with all her worldly possessions, starting with the manuscript of her rejected novel. Moving in a hurry was nothing new, and leaving rented accommodation had often involved a moonlight flit, but it was the friends she had made in Ma Burton's house that Nettie would miss the most. She wondered who would help young Biddy when she was at a loss to know how to cope with her invalid mistress. Who would have the patience to mend Madame Fabron's torn garments? Who would spend hours listening to Ted agonising over his broken romance? Who would play cards with Pip when he was feeling bored, and who would laugh at Byron's terrible jokes? Leaving Byron was the hardest thing of all.

'Come on, Nettie. We must leave now.'

Nettie fastened the leather straps on the valise and took one last look around the room that had been home for almost three years. The hunger and cold were forgotten and she could only remember the good times, and the bonds of friendship that she had made and shared. She would miss these two attic rooms in Covent Garden more than she could ever have thought possible. She had made a home wherever they happened to be in the past, whether it was a smart town house or a leaky attic in Hoxton, but leaving here hurt her heart, and going without saying goodbye to those whom she had grown to love was the most painful part of the whole sorry business.

She followed her father downstairs, tiptoeing past the closed doors, but when Robert let them out into the street they came face to face with Byron and Ted.

'What's going on?' Byron demanded.

'Keep your voice down,' Robert said in a stage whisper.

'I'm so sorry.' Nettie reached out to grasp Byron's hand. 'We have to leave.'

'Why?' Ted asked. 'If it's the rent, we could help out.'

'Yes, of course,' Byron added hastily. 'We'll chip in, Mr Carroll.'

Robert shook his head. 'Thanks, but the rent is the least of our problems. Say goodbye, Nettie.' He strode off, leaving Nettie little alternative but to follow him.

'Where are you going?' Byron fell into step beside her. 'What's happened?'

'Victoria Station,' she said breathlessly. 'You don't want to be involved in this, Byron. Please keep out of it, for your sake if not for mine.' She hurried on, but Byron kept pace with them.

'I'm not giving up until you tell me what's happened.'

'I can't tell you.' Nettie broke into a run in an attempt to keep up with her father's long strides, but she was hampered by the weight of her case.

'Let me have that.' Byron took it from her hand, but Robert had come to a halt as he reached the Strand, and he stood on the edge of the kerb.

'Leave us alone, Horton.' Robert waved frantically at a passing cab, but it passed by. 'We have to leave London and that's all you need to know.'

'Now I know there's something seriously wrong.' Byron laid his hand on Nettie's shoulder. 'I'm your friend. If you're in trouble maybe I can help.'

She shook her head. 'I don't think so, but thank you anyway. Please go away and forget about us. We're leaving the country.'

'Nettie!' Robert turned to her, scowling. 'What did I tell you?'

'I'm sorry, Pa, but Byron deserves an explanation.'

'He works for lawyers. He would feel bound to tell the police everything he knows about us.' Robert raised his hand again and this time a hackney carriage drew to a halt at the kerb. 'Get in, Nettie.' He tossed the cases in after her. 'Victoria Station, cabby.' He leaped into the cab and slammed the door.

Nettie peered out of the window, raising her hand in a final farewell to Byron.

'Did you have to treat him like that, Pa?'

'Yes, I did. And I hope he doesn't tell anyone where we're headed, because if the police find out they'll know we're trying to leave the country. I wasn't supposed to leave London.'

'But you're not implicated yet,' Nettie said slowly. 'It will take some time for the law officers to work out that you made the copies, and it's Dexter they're after, not you. Couldn't we simply move to another town, as we've always done, and wait until all this blows over?'

'This time it's different, my love. Our previous moves have been to escape my creditors, and the sums owed were relatively small. The police were never involved, but once this gets out I'll be ruined. No one will ever buy my work again.' He leaned forward to take her hand in his. 'But you can still go to North Wales. I'll give you half the money that Dexter paid me, and you can start afresh with Prudence. She's not a bad old thing when you get to know her, and she'll look after you. I know she will.'

'No, Pa. That's out of the question. I'll go wherever you go. Maybe you'll find your work more appreciated in France. I believe they love artists there.'

'Let's hope so, Nettie.'

★ ★ ★

The last train had left the station some hours ago, and there was nothing they could do other than take a seat in the waiting room. According to the timetable the first train for Dover left early in the morning, and they made themselves as comfortable as was possible on hard wooden benches. One of the cleaners took pity on them and brought them cups of tea, for which Robert tipped her handsomely.

Nettie stretched out and managed to get some sleep, but it was not the most comfortable bed she had ever slept on, and when she awakened to the sound of movement outside it was a relief to stand up and ease her cramped limbs. A train had just pulled into the station, emitting great gusts of steam, and slowly the station came to life. Porters pushed their trolleys along the platform, loading and unloading the guard's van, and bleary-eyed passengers stumbled towards the barrier, fumbling in their pockets for their tickets.

Nettie shook her father by the shoulder and he awakened with a start. 'What time is it?'

'I'm not sure. I can't see the clock from here, but a train has just pulled into the station. Would it be ours?'

Robert sat up slowly, taking the silver watch from his waistcoat pocket and peering at it in the half-light. 'It's half-past five. Our train leaves at six. I'll go to the ticket office and hope that it's open.' He stood up, adjusting his clothing and brushing his tumbled hair back from his brow. 'Wait here, Nettie. I'll be as quick as I can.' He shrugged on his overcoat and made a move towards the door but it opened suddenly and Byron rushed into the waiting room, followed by Pip and Ted.

'What the hell is this?' Robert demanded angrily.

'We've come to beg you not to involve Nettie in this, sir.' Byron faced him with a stubborn set to his jaw. 'We won't stand by and see her life ruined because of something you've done.'

'That's right.' Ted stood behind Byron, and Pip leaned against the door, preventing anyone from entering or leaving.

'Get out of my way,' Robert said through clenched teeth. 'This has nothing to do with you.

Nettie is my daughter and she's a minor. She does as I say.'

'So you'll drag her into a life of poverty in a foreign country, will you? Is that what a good father would do?'

Nettie stepped in between them. 'Stop this, both of you. I choose to go with my father, Byron. What sort of daughter would I be if I abandoned him now?'

'I'd say you were being sensible.' Ted laid his hand on her shoulder. 'Come back with us, Nettie? We'll sort something out between us.'

'Ted's right,' Byron added earnestly. 'You don't have to do this.'

3

'Nettie, are you going to allow these three idiots to dictate to you?' Robert edged past Byron and Ted, but Pip folded his arms across his chest and refused to move from the doorway.

'Stop this, all of you, and that includes you, Pa.' Nettie reached for her cape and wrapped it around her shoulders. 'I appreciate your concern, but I intend to see this through. I love my father and I'll stand by him, no matter what trouble he's in. I care for all of you, but I know what I must do, so I'm asking you to let us leave without causing a fuss.'

Byron and Ted exchanged weary glances and Pip moved away from the door.

'Do you know what you're letting yourself in for, Nettie?' Byron asked in a low voice. 'You'll be in a foreign country, unable to speak the language, trying to eke out an existence on what your father can get for his paintings. If he can't earn his living honestly in London, how do you think you'll manage abroad?'

'I've had enough of this,' Robert said impatiently. 'Don't listen to them, Nettie. I'm going to buy our tickets and I want you to take the luggage and wait for me on the platform. Our train will be in soon.' Robert swept past Byron and Ted, elbowing Pip out of the way as he left the waiting room.

Nettie faced them with a tremulous smile.

'Don't think I'm not grateful, but you must see that I have no choice. I've been looking after Pa since I was a child, and he needs me even more now.'

'He's using you, Nettie,' Byron said urgently.

'Maybe, but that doesn't alter the fact that he's my father and I have to stand by him.'

'If you say so.' Ted gave her a hug. 'But I'll miss you, Nettie. Who's going to listen to me when I get so miserable that I feel like crying?'

'You'll get over her in time.' Nettie returned the embrace. 'You deserve someone much nicer than Pearl. I won't forget you, Ted.'

'We'll all miss you.' Pip managed a smile. 'Look after yourself, Nettie.' He picked up Robert's luggage and took it out onto the platform, leaving Nettie and Byron facing each other.

'I suppose nothing I say will make you change your mind?'

'Don't make this even harder than it is, Byron.'

He brushed her cheek with a kiss and turned away. 'I'll go now. I hate goodbyes. Take care of yourself, Nettie.'

She followed him out of the waiting room and watched him stride away, passing Robert, who was returning with the tickets clutched in his hand. He waved to Nettie.

'Our train leaves in five minutes. We'd better hurry.'

★　★　★

It was still early morning when they arrived in Dover, and after making enquiries, Robert

43

announced that the next ferry was due to sail at midday. This gave them time to have breakfast in a hotel close to the harbour and to rest before the crossing. Nettie sat on the terrace enjoying the warm spring sunshine with only a slight breeze to ruffle the feathery tops of the pampas grass that towered over the neatly kept flowerbeds. The air was so fresh and clean after the soot and smoke of the city, and the scent of spring flowers was sharpened by a salty tang from the sea. Nettie would have been happy to remain here all day, but she had to face the fact that they would be leaving soon and might never return. It was a disturbing thought. She sat back and closed her eyes — the sound of birdsong and the mewling of seagulls was a pleasant change from the clatter of boots on cobbled streets and the rumble of cartwheels, the shouts of costermongers and the porters bellowing at each other in Covent Garden as they went about their work. She was slipping into a deep sleep when she was awakened by someone shaking her shoulder.

'Is it time to leave, Pa?' she asked sleepily.

'It's me, Nettie.'

She opened her eyes and sat up straight. 'Byron. What are you doing here?'

He pulled up a chair and sat down. 'I'm coming with you.'

'You don't mean it.'

'Yes, I do. I hate my job at the law firm. It's not what I want to do for the rest of my life, and I don't trust Mr Carroll to take proper care of you.'

'But I don't know where we're going, or how we'll live.'

'All the more reason for coming with you. I'm strong and I can earn money doing manual labour, if necessary. I won't allow your father to drag you into poverty, and I've always wanted to travel, so this is a good opportunity. Besides which, there's something you don't know about me.'

Nettie gazed at him in amazement. 'What is it, Byron?'

'My mother was French. She left home when I was very young and I never saw her again, but my first language was French.'

'Why didn't you tell me this before?'

'It didn't seem important. When I was younger I tried not to think about the mother who'd deserted me, but recently I've been considering going to France to look for my French relations. I even have a passport.'

Nettie gazed at him, too stunned to put her thoughts into words. 'That's so strange, but how did you know we were here?'

'The cabby who picked me up at the railway station had taken a fare to this hotel, and when he described the pretty, dark-haired young lady and a much older man, I knew it must be you — or at least I hoped it was — and I was right. Here I am and here I stay. I've paid for my passage and I'm ready to go.'

'I don't know what Pa will say about this, Byron.'

'There's not much he can do about it. I'm free to do as I like, and I intend to travel to France.'

45

He hailed a passing waiter. 'A pot of coffee, if you please, and some bread and cheese. I didn't have time for breakfast.'

Nettie waited until the food arrived. 'I think my father is in the hotel lounge. I'm going to tell him you're here, Byron. If he comes upon us together he'll be angry and the last thing we need is a scene. If the cabby remembers dropping us off here it won't be hard for the police to trace us and, if Pendleton talks, I don't think it will take them long to associate Pa with the forgeries.'

Byron had just bitten off a chunk of bread and cheese and he nodded wordlessly. Nettie would have gone anyway, regardless of anything that he might have said. The main thing was to keep her father behaving in a manner that would not draw attention to them, which was difficult for someone who loved being the centre of attention.

★　★　★

It was sad to stand on deck watching the white cliffs fade into the distance, but in some ways it was also a relief, and Nettie began to relax. Her father had been angry at first, but he had been quick to admit that having Byron with them might prove advantageous. Nettie did not enquire further, but she suspected that her father would happily devote himself to his art, leaving Byron and herself to support him.

'A penny for them?' Byron appeared at her side.

'I was just thinking that we've done it now. We're on our way to goodness knows where. It's not the first time I've been homeless, but at least everyone at home speaks English.'

'Then it's just as well I decided to join you.' Byron leaned on the railings, staring at the rapidly disappearing shoreline. 'I'll translate for you.'

'Tell me about your mother. How did your parents meet?'

'Father was a medical student, and he went to Paris to attend a series of lectures. He was out one evening with friends and they saw a man beating a young girl. They intervened and took her back to her lodgings in a poor quarter, but Father was concerned for her welfare and he returned next day to make sure she was all right.'

'And they fell in love at first sight. How romantic,' Nettie sighed and closed her eyes. 'It sounds like a fairy tale.' She could see it all in her imagination; it would make a wonderful start to her next story.

'Not really. It didn't have a happy ending,' Byron said with a wry smile. 'I was only four when my mother left home. I remember her putting me to bed one night, and I can still smell her perfume when she kissed me and told me to be a good boy. She was gone next morning and I never understood why she had deserted me.'

Nettie reached out to lay her hand on his. 'Byron, that's so sad. It's amazing that you still remember how to speak her native tongue.'

'We always spoke in French together, and when I went to school I told my teacher that I

47

wanted to learn the language. She loaned me the books and I studied French on my own. It made me feel closer to Maman.'

'How brave of you, Byron. It must have been such a difficult time.'

'I don't think my father ever really got over it. He never remarried and he devoted himself to his patients in one of the poorest parts of the East End.'

'He sounds like a very good man.'

'He was, but he passed away five years ago. I think he died of exhaustion, because he gave so much to others.'

Nettie slipped her arm around his shoulders. 'I am so sorry, Byron. I wish I could have known him.'

'It's all in the past, but you can understand why I have no ties in London, which leaves me free to accompany you and see that you're kept safe.'

'And you might find your mother's family.'

'Yes. I doubt if I'll ever see my mother again, but I'd like to learn more about her and why she left us like she did.' He glanced up at the darkening sky. 'Let's go to the saloon. I'm hungry and a cup of coffee wouldn't go amiss.'

'I expect Pa's there already. He'll probably have found an audience to impress with his tales of his life as an important artist. He likes to tell people that he's been all over the world, although, in fact, he's never been any further south than Dover.'

'Let's hope there aren't any off-duty police-men on board,' Byron said, chuckling.

48

★ ★ ★

As Nettie had predicted, they found Robert seated at a table in the saloon, surrounded by an admiring audience.

'Nettie, my dear. Come and sit down. You, too, Byron. I want you to meet my new friends. I've been telling them of our plans to take Paris by storm. I intend to have an exhibition of my latest works somewhere in Montmartre. I haven't decided the exact location as yet, but I hope you will all come.'

Nettie sat down beside him. 'Pa, we need to have a serious talk.'

'I fear that I'm in trouble, ladies and gentlemen,' Robert said, smiling. 'As you see I am under petticoat government. I submit, Nettie. What have you to say?'

Nettie felt the blood rush to her cheeks, but the onlookers rose to their feet and shuffled off to their respective tables. 'Pa, how could you?' she whispered. 'That was very embarrassing.'

'You simply don't know how to enjoy yourself, my love.' Robert raised his glass and sipped the wine. 'What did you wish to discuss?'

Byron took a seat beside Nettie. 'We'll be in Calais soon, sir. Have you any plans from there?'

'We will go where the wind takes us,' Robert said airily. 'We're free now, my boy. Free from the restraints of living in London, and we can live as we please.'

Nettie stared pointedly at her father's empty wine glass. 'How many of those have you had, Pa?'

'Not enough, my darling.' Robert leaned towards Byron, grinning tipsily. 'Get me another, dear boy. My throat is dry.'

'No, Pa,' Nettie said firmly. 'This isn't a holiday. We're on the run,' she added, lowering her voice. 'We need a plan.'

'I can't be bothered with details like that. I'll set up a studio somewhere and make a good living. The French appreciate art.' Robert leaned back against the padded seat. 'Wake me up when we get there.' He closed his eyes and his head lolled to one side.

'He's drunk,' Nettie said crossly. 'Would you believe it, Byron?'

'Did you expect anything else? You ought to be used to your father's ways by now, Nettie.'

'I suppose so, but I keep hoping that one day he'll stop acting like a ten-year-old and take some responsibility for his actions. Who knows what sort of bother he'd get into if I deserted him?'

Byron gave her a long look. 'Your father wants to stay the night in Calais, although if it were left to me I'd suggest we went on to Paris. It would be easier to lose ourselves in the crowded city street, but we need to make a plan and we can't do that until your father sobers up.'

'Will you stay with him while I get some fresh air?' Nettie rose to her feet. 'It's so stuffy in here.'

'You mustn't worry, Nettie. We'll sort something out.'

She flashed him a grateful smile as she left the saloon and went out on deck. The wind whipped around her, dragging strands of hair from beneath her bonnet and tugging at her skirt. The sea was choppy and the paddle steamer ploughed through the waves, churning up the water and sending plumes of spray into the air, drenching the unwary. People hurried for the shelter of the saloon or down the companionway to the lower deck where cabins were available for those who could afford to pay extra. Nettie staggered as the vessel pitched and she collided with someone who had come up behind her.

'I'm sorry,' she said breathlessly as she attempted to stand unaided, but the ship yawed and she would have fallen if he had not grasped her firmly.

'Well, then. I didn't expect to find you here, Miss Carroll. Least of all being thrown into my arms.'

Nettie reached out and grabbed the ship's rail. 'Duke!'

'Hush! Not so loud, Nettie, my dear. I'm incognito for reasons that you will appreciate.'

'You're on the run from the police and so is my pa, thanks to you.'

'Now, now, that's not fair. I didn't force Robert to work for me. He was eager to earn money and I put him in the way of several decent commissions. I was informed on by a man who has a personal grudge against me and will stop at nothing until he sees me ruined.'

'What you did was illegal,' Nettie countered. 'You used my father's talents to make money for yourself.'

'That, my dear, is business.' He eyed her

curiously. 'What I don't understand is why you chose to accompany him. Haven't you any relations who would take you in and look after you?'

'I'm not a child, Duke.'

'Quite.' He shrugged and turned away. 'Well, good luck. That's all I can say.' He turned back to give her a quizzical smile. 'But what will you do when the money runs out? Will you beg on the streets or sell yourself in order to keep your feckless father in comfort?'

'Neither,' Nettie said angrily. 'We'll find a way.'

He hesitated, frowning. 'I suppose I do bear some responsibility for what has happened to you, although it pains me to say so. I must be getting soft in my old age.'

Suddenly curious, Nettie gave him a searching look. 'You can't be more than thirty-five.'

'As a matter of fact, I'm thirty-four. Riotous living must be starting to mar my good looks.' He put his hand in his breast pocket and took out a silver card case. He flicked it open and produced a gilt-edged visiting card. 'This is the one I use when in Paris. You will see that I go by the name Gaillard when in France. I have many identities, Nettie, but if you are in trouble you can find me at this address. I might even have work for your father, if he's so minded.' Duke walked away, adapting to the movement of the ship as if he had spent his life at sea.

Nettie tossed the card overboard, but the wind caught it and deposited it at her feet. Despite her misgivings, she bent down, picked it up and tucked it in her reticule. Duke Dexter was on the run just the same as they were, but Marc Gaillard, the Parisian art dealer, might be useful, if they were desperate.

She felt a sudden change in the tone of the ship's engine and she caught sight of land. She hurried back to the saloon to tell her father and Byron that they were nearing Calais, but she would keep Duke's presence on board a secret.

★   ★   ★

Robert had changed his mind about staying the night in Calais, or perhaps Byron had changed it for him, but in the end they took the train to Paris. It was an uneventful and reasonably comfortable journey, and when they reached their destination Robert insisted on hiring a fiacre to take them to Montmartre, where he was convinced he would meet like-minded people and his talent would be recognised. He seemed to be happy to sit back and allow Byron to do all the talking, and Nettie was quietly impressed by her friend's fluent French as he told the cab driver where they wanted to go. They were dropped off in a quiet backstreet close to a small square filled with flower stalls, fruit sellers and cafés where people sat at small tables in the shade of trees, which were bursting into leaf.

Byron paid the driver. 'He says we can get cheap lodgings here,' he said as the fiacre pulled away from the kerb.

Robert held out his arms, smiling as he took deep breaths of the air scented with French tobacco, wine and garlic, which barely masked the smell of drains and overflowing privies.

'I am in my spiritual home,' he said gleefully. 'It is here, in Paris, that I will do my best work. I was duped by Duke Dexter, but now I am free from his demands, and I will start afresh.'

Nettie said nothing, but the cab had driven along the street named on Duke's visiting card and she was uneasy. The last thing she wanted was for her father to get involved with the man who had led him into crime in the first place. It would be all too easy for him to go that way again when their money ran out, but she decided to talk it over with Byron at the first opportunity. Their most pressing need was for somewhere to stay, and Byron was making enquiries at the door of a house with a sign in the window advertising vacancies.

'Byron is a handy chap to have around,' Robert said grudgingly. 'I wouldn't have chosen him as a travelling companion, but he's proving useful.'

'We would be in a pickle without him, Pa. I can't speak a word of French, and neither can you.'

'I know how to communicate with people, Nettie. But we'll put up with him for a while and then he can go on his way. I don't want you getting too close to a fellow who has little or no prospects.'

Nettie stared at him, speechless. It was on the tip of her tongue to remind Pa that he was the fugitive from justice and Byron was here to help them, but she knew it would be futile. Once her father had an idea in his head it was almost impossible to make him see reason.

'She has two rooms,' Byron said as he hurried back to them. 'They're in the attic, but she says there's another couple who are interested so we have to give her an answer right away.'

'The woman is probably bluffing.' Robert was about to walk away when Nettie caught him by the sleeve.

'It's getting late, Pa. We need to have somewhere to sleep.' She turned to Byron. 'How much rent is she asking?'

'About twice as much as we were paying Ma Burton.'

'Daylight robbery,' Robert said, frowning. 'We'll look elsewhere.'

Nettie tightened her grip on her father's arm. 'Think about it, Pa. If we can't find somewhere quickly we'll have to pay for three hotel rooms. What would that cost?'

'All right.' Robert gave in graciously. 'We'll take the rooms for a week, and in the meantime we can look for something more reasonable.' He picked up the bag containing his paints and brushes, leaving Byron to carry his case. 'Lead on. I want to see what you've let us in for, Mr Horton.'

'I'd remind you that you are the one fleeing the law, Mr Carroll. And since you cannot speak the language you are at a definite disadvantage.' Byron dropped the suitcase at Robert's feet. 'I came as a friend, not as a servant.' He took Nettie's valise from her hand and led the way into the house.

'You asked for that, Pa,' Nettie said softly.

'Don't underestimate Byron, and remember that we need him if we're to get on in this country.'

'When I want your opinion I'll ask for it.' Robert stomped past her and followed the landlady up the stairs.

Madame was not a young woman, but she was obviously used to negotiating five flights of steep stairs and she was barely out of breath when they reached the attics. Robert, however, was red in the face and gasping for breath. Nettie's knees were aching, but she could see that her father was genuinely suffering.

Madame unlocked the door and ushered them into the room. She addressed Byron, speaking rapidly and waving her hands about as if conducting an invisible orchestra.

'She wants a week's rent in advance and she's put the price up,' Byron said hastily. 'I think she suspects something, so it might be as well to pay her and keep her happy.'

'Blackmail is the same in any language.' Robert took a leather pouch from his pocket and handed it to Byron. 'Pay the old hag, but we won't be staying here for long. That I promise you.' He glanced around the low-ceilinged room with bare floor-boards and the minimum of furniture.

All smiles now, Madame left them, closing the door behind her.

'I get the feeling she's had the best of that deal,' Byron said grimly.

Nettie examined the iron bed with a thin flock-filled mattress, and the washstand with a cracked basin and a jug with a chipped handle. A single chair and a low table were the only other items of furniture, and it was much the same in the larger room, although it boasted a double bed and two chairs. She was quick to notice that one of them had a broken leg.

'How am I supposed to work here?' Robert demanded. 'I suppose I will have to let you share with me, Horton, unless you can persuade Madame to supply another bed.'

Nettie turned on him, frowning. 'Stop complaining, Pa. At least we have a roof over our heads, and it gives us time to look round for something better. I don't know about you, but I'm starving.'

'Yes, of course,' Robert said apologetically. 'I'm sorry, Nettie. I am being selfish and thoughtless. Let's try that café we saw in the square. Maybe I can drum up some custom for sketching portraits in charcoal. That means cash on the nail.'

Nettie shook her head. 'Pa, you're unbelievable.'

'I'll take that as a compliment, my dear,' Robert said, smiling. 'Lead on, Horton. No hard feelings, old man. We're in this together now and I'm very grateful to you for using your linguistic abilities to our advantage.'

Nettie and Byron exchanged amused glances, saying nothing. Nettie was used to her father's mercurial temperament, and she was relieved to see that Byron did not take him too seriously.

'Let me wash my hands and face first,' Nettie said hastily. 'I need to brush my hair and make myself presentable.'

'Very well.' Robert sighed heavily. 'If you must.'

Nettie took off her gloves and laid them on the single bed before going to the washstand, but the pitcher was empty.

'I thought there would be water in the jug, but it's empty.'

Byron stuck his head round the door. 'Madame said we have to fetch it from the pump in the back yard. I'll go, Nettie.'

'Don't worry, Byron. I'll wash later. Let's get something to eat first.'

* * *

It was almost dark when they reached the café in the square, but it was packed with customers, and they were lucky to find a table outside.

'We must have wine to celebrate our first night of freedom,' Robert said grandly. 'A good claret, I think. You can order it, Horton, and I'll have a steak. I don't want any of their foreign food.'

'We have to budget our money, Pa,' Nettie said in a low voice.

'I have to eat, dear girl. I cannot produce my best work if I am hungry, and a man needs red meat. I don't suppose they do chops or steak-and-kidney pudding. Order plenty of food, Horton. We won't be short of money once I become established, and you're a big strong fellow, I'm sure you'll find gainful employment soon.'

Nettie glanced anxiously at Byron, who had managed to attract the attention of a waiter and was passing on the order. She leaned towards him.

'I'll have the dish of the day or whatever is cheapest, Byron.'

'Too late,' he said as the waiter hurried off into the café. 'I've ordered steaks all round. You heard your father, Nettie. He's going to earn a fortune with his sketches and paintings. We'll be dining like this every evening.' He sat back as another waiter arrived with a bottle of wine, and he sampled it like an expert, nodding his approval.

Nettie raised her full glass to her lips and gulped down a mouthful of the ruby-red wine, and a warm glow spread throughout her body. Suddenly her worries seemed quite trivial. After all, Pa had once been a famous artist in his own right — he could compete with any foreign painter on equal terms. The night air was relatively mild, compared to the chill in England, and the sound of chatter in a foreign language, together with gusts of laughter, made her feel as if she was a guest at a party. The savoury aroma of cooking emanated from the café, laced with wine and garlic, and everyone seemed to be smoking the exotic-smelling tobacco, even the women. Nettie felt as though she had entered another world.

'I think I might like it here,' she said, smiling. 'Maybe we could discover something about your mother's family, Byron.' She turned to her father, who was already on his second glass of wine. 'Did you know that Byron's mother came from Paris?'

'Really?' Robert sipped his drink. 'I wondered

how you came to learn the lingo.'

'Will you try to find your family?' Nettie asked eagerly.

'I doubt if I'll have much luck,' Byron said slowly. 'They were what are commonly known as water gypsies — never in one place for very long. I know very little about them.'

'That's even more of a reason to look for them.' Nettie rarely drank alcohol and now she felt pleasantly relaxed, and perhaps she understood a little why her father enjoyed a glass or two of wine. 'We could make enquiries, Byron. What was your mother's maiden name?'

'She was called Lisette, but I never knew her maiden name. It wasn't mentioned.'

'Maybe we can find someone who remembers the family.'

'It was a long time ago, nearly a quarter of a century. My grandparents might be dead, for all I know.'

'Ah! That smells good.' Robert brightened up as the waiter appeared with their order. 'Let's eat and enjoy our meal. Forget relatives, forget London.' Robert raised his glass. 'Here's to Paris, and a new beginning.'

Nettie joined in the toast, but even under the mellowing influence of the wine, she had a feeling that starting afresh in a foreign country was not going to be easy.

4

Nettie's fears grew as the days passed and her father earned very little money despite his efforts to promote himself. He was not the only artist attempting to make a living by touting for business in the square or on the steps of the great cathedral, and those who were there before him were not particularly welcoming. The fact that he could not speak a word of French also went against him, and the only people who paid to have their likenesses executed in charcoal were English visitors to the city, who were delighted to find someone with whom they could carry on a conversation. Nettie accompanied her father for the first few days, posing as an enthusiastic subject while he sketched her portrait, but even that failed to draw in an adequate number of clients eager to part with their money.

Byron went out daily, seeking work and returning each evening with very little to show for his efforts. They dined at the café each evening, but now they chose the cheapest food and wine, and during the day they ate almost nothing. Robert continued to be optimistic, but Nettie knew in her heart that they could not afford to live in Paris. At the end of the first week, with the rent due, she was tempted to go to the address that Duke had given her and ask for his help. After all, he was responsible for their being in this dire state, and he might be able to offer some good advice. He owed them that at least.

After a particularly bad day, when a sudden downpour soaked them to the skin and ruined a pad of expensive paper, Robert retreated to the café and ordered a glass of brandy and a pot of coffee. He had been quick to learn the French for what he considered to be the necessities in life. Nettie stood beside him with rainwater dripping off her straw bonnet, which was almost certainly beyond saving, and her wet clothing was causing her to shiver even though the day was relatively warm.

'Did you have to do that, Pa?' she demanded crossly.

'I need something stronger than coffee. Where would you be if I sickened and died?'

For a brief moment Nettie was tempted to tell him that she would be far better off without him, but she knew that was not true. Despite his faults she loved her father and she would do her best to protect him from a world that was proving indifferent to his undoubted talent. 'We have to be careful with money, Pa,' she said, making an effort to be reasonable.

'I should remind you that it is my money, Nettie. I have to look after myself. I have a great talent that must be nurtured. They'll acknowledge it here, eventually.'

Nettie could see that she was getting nowhere. 'I'm going back to the room to change into something dry. Perhaps you should do the same.'

'That's it, run along, my love.' Robert greeted the waiter with a smile. '*Merci*.' He grabbed the

62

glass of brandy and sipped it with obvious pleasure. 'I'll be quite all right, Nettie. I'll see you later — and bring a fresh supply of paper, please. We'll try again this afternoon.'

Nettie hurried back to their rooms, narrowly avoiding Madame, who was standing outside a door on the fourth floor, hammering on it with both fists. She was shouting volubly and she neither heard nor saw Nettie, making it possible for her to slip past and race up the narrow staircase to the attics. Safely inside, she stripped off her wet garments and hung them over a rope that Byron had stretched from one side of the room to the other, which served as a clothes line. When the sun shone the rooms beneath the sloping roof were like an oven, but at night the temperature dropped noticeably, and Nettie could barely imagine how cold it must be in midwinter.

She dressed quickly, choosing her best gown and mantle and her only other bonnet. Assuming that Byron had not found any work that would earn him a few centimes, there was only one path open to them now. She opened the door and tiptoed downstairs. They had one more day in which to find next week's rent, and she was ready to sup with the devil, if necessary.

The address that Duke had given her proved to be an elegant town house, set back from the street with a small paved front garden. It looked surprisingly respectable for a man who earned his living by fraud. She tugged at the doorbell and heard its peal echoing around what she imagined to be a large entrance hall, probably marble-tiled with a sweeping staircase and elegant furniture. She was expecting a uniformed maidservant, or even a smartly dressed butler to answer her knock, but to her surprise it was a young woman who opened the door. Her fair hair was taken back from her oval face and piled high on the top of her head, cascading around her shoulders in silky curls, and her striped dimity gown was the height of fashion.

Nettie had not been prepared to meet the lady of the house, or perhaps this was the daughter, judging by this person's youthful appearance. Had it been a servant, Nettie would have shown them the visiting card and indicated that she wished to see Monsieur Gaillard, but now she was at a loss. She took the visiting card from her reticule, holding it up for the young woman to see. 'Monsieur Gaillard?'

'You are English?' The young woman spoke with a charming French accent.

Nettie could have cried with relief. 'Yes, I am. A gentleman I know gave me this visiting card and told me to contact him if I needed his assistance.'

'You'd better come in.'

Nettie stepped over the threshold and found herself in an entrance hall not unlike the one she had imagined. 'My name is Nettie Carroll,' she began shyly.

'I'm Constance Gaillard. Perhaps I can help.'

Nettie stared at her in disbelief. 'You have the same surname as the person who gave me this card.'

'Marc Gaillard was my father, but sadly he is

deceased. You must be speaking of Monsieur Dexter,' Constance said with an infectious giggle. 'Duke and my father were business partners. Come into the parlour, where we can talk in comfort.'

Nettie followed her into an elegant room where a fire burned in the grate beneath a white Carrara marble fireplace. Bowls filled with hyacinths filled the air with their scent, the delicate colour of the flowers fitting in well with the pastel theme of the soft furnishings and the matching curtains. The walls were hung with exquisite watercolours of rural scenes, and the highly polished antique side tables were set beneath elegant gilt-framed mirrors that reflected the sunlight as it streamed through tall windows.

'How lovely,' Nettie breathed, soaking up the luxury with a heartfelt sigh. She had almost forgotten what it was like to live in a house like this. Once, when she was much younger and her father had been painting the portraits of fashionable ladies, they had lived in a comparable style. That was before Pa's style of painting went out of fashion, and the gradual decline in their fortune.

'Won't you sit down, please?' Constance perched on the edge of the sofa. 'You said that you needed help, but Duke was in London when I last heard from him. How do you know him?'

'My father is an artist. He had some dealings with Mr Dexter.' Nettie sank down onto a chaise longue, leaning back amongst satin-covered cushions. 'Duke was on the cross-channel paddle steamer heading for Calais when he gave me his card.'

'And you are in need of his help?'

'It's a long story, but yes.'

'You look a little pale, would you like some coffee, or perhaps you'd prefer tea?'

'Thank you. I would love some coffee. I didn't have time for breakfast this morning.'

Constance rose gracefully and rang for a servant, who appeared as quickly as if she had been standing outside the door.

'We don't get many visitors.' Constance resumed her seat, having given the maid her instructions. 'I think you are the first person to call this week.'

'Do you live here alone?'

'I have a companion, but she is old enough to be my mother and we do not have much in common. I like theatre and ballet, and I would love to go to parties, but Mademoiselle Menjou likes to play cards and gossip with her friends, who are all old and very dull. There are the servants, of course, but they keep to themselves.'

Nettie was so interested in Constance's plight that she had almost forgotten the reason for her visit. 'I can sympathise wholeheartedly.'

'You have a similar problem?'

'Not exactly. I live with my father and he's having difficulty in finding work. I was hoping that Duke might help him to get established in Paris.'

Constance was about to answer when a timid tap on the door and the rattle of cups on saucers announced the arrival of the maid, who edged her way into the room carrying a heavy silver tray, which she placed on a low table.

'*Merci, Berthe,*' Constance said, smiling. '*C'est tout, merci.*'

Berthe hesitated in the doorway, taking one last look at Nettie. No doubt she would rush back to the kitchen and relay everything to the servants below stairs. Nettie smiled at her and Berthe scurried from the room and closed the door.

Constance sighed. 'That girl is so nosy. One day I will have to speak sharply to her.' She picked up the coffeepot and filled two cups, passing one to Nettie. 'I didn't want to say anything in front of her because it will go straight back to the other servants, but I haven't seen Duke for months. He comes and goes as he pleases. However, he sent me a telegram from Dover, saying he's on his way to Paris, so I expect he will call on me quite soon.'

Nettie sipped the coffee. 'He seems quite young to be your guardian.'

'I suppose it is unusual, but I've known him since I was a child. My papa owned an art gallery in Paris, and he wanted to open one in London. Duke was a young man, half my father's age, when they first met, and eventually they went into business together.'

'You must have been just a child at the time.'

'I was only seven when we left Paris and went to London, and I remember the house we lived in overlooked a large park. The gallery prospered and Mama wore beautiful gowns and we had our own carriage, and servants to look after us.'

Constance's violet-blue eyes darkened and she turned her head away. 'We were all so happy — and then my parents were killed in a train crash. Duke took care of me and became my guardian. He brought me back to Paris and set me up in this house, and he saw to it that I had a good education. He's always made sure that I have everything I need.'

'Even so, you must have been very lonely at times. Haven't you any relatives who would have taken care of you?'

'My grandparents died some time ago and my mother was an only child. I know nothing of my father's family, but I am very fortunate to have a nice home and a kind guardian.' Constance replaced her cup on its saucer, eyeing Nettie curiously. 'But you are obviously troubled. Is there anything I can do to help?'

Nettie stared into the dark liquid in her cup, seeing her own worried reflection. 'It's rather complicated, but you could let me know if Duke contacts you. We're in lodgings at the moment.'

'I will, of course.'

'Thank you.' Nettie managed a smile but she was disappointed and desperate.

'Maybe we could meet again?' Constance said eagerly. 'I would like to get to know you better. I have so few friends.'

Nettie would have liked to hug Constance and tell her that of course she would be her friend. Her heart went out to the lonely young woman, but she was wary of getting involved with someone who was close to Duke Dexter. 'That would be lovely, but I'm not sure what I'll be doing.' She could see that this was not the answer that Constance had hoped for. 'What I meant to say was that I have to help my father. We had to leave London in a hurry and we're rather short of money.'

'You're obviously in some kind of trouble or you wouldn't be here now. I'd like to help, if I can.' Constance's hand flew to her throat and she rose to her feet. 'You'll hardly believe this, Nettie, but I've just seen Duke walk past the window.'

She ran from the room and Nettie realised that she would have to be careful what she said in front of Constance, who quite obviously had no idea that her guardian was a criminal. She sat very straight, sipping her coffee and straining her ears in an attempt to hear what they were saying.

Constance burst into the room, her face alight with smiles. 'Isn't this the most incredible good luck? You wanted to see Duke and here he is.'

Nettie put her cup down and rose slowly to her feet, turning to face Duke Dexter with a carefully controlled expression. 'How do you do, sir?'

He greeted her with an urbane smile. 'How do you do, Miss Carroll? To what do I owe this pleasure?'

She met his mocking gaze with a steady look, and for a moment she was tempted to shame him in front of his ward, but that would be cruel and serve no useful purpose. Nettie knew that she would have to play along with his game, whatever it was. 'My father is in Paris and we need your help, Mr Dexter.'

'Robert Carroll is one of my favourite artists. How may I be of service?'

Nettie clenched her hands behind her back, digging her fingernails into her palms. She wondered how Duke could stand there, looking as if butter wouldn't melt in his mouth, when he had brought them to a state of near destitution. 'He's having some difficulty in finding a studio and suitable accommodation. I wondered if you might be able to help.'

Dexter smiled. 'I'd be only too happy to assist in any way I can, Miss Carroll. I'll be at the gallery for an hour or so tomorrow morning, between nine o'clock and ten o'clock, if you and my friend Robert would like to call on me. I'll see what I can do.'

'How splendid,' Constance said eagerly. 'And how fortunate that you came to see me today, Duke. You will stay awhile, won't you?'

'Of course I will, Connie. I couldn't come to Paris without spending some time with my favourite ward.'

Constance's eyes widened. 'You have another?'

'It's a manner of speaking — an English eccentricity. Miss Carroll will understand.'

'I understand a great deal,' Nettie said, rising to her feet. 'But I must go now. My father will be wondering where I am.'

'I'll see you out.' Constance followed her to the front door. 'You will come again, won't you?'

'I'll try, but it depends on what we're doing. We might have to leave Paris if we can't find more suitable accommodation.'

Constance clasped her hand. 'I'll speak to

Duke. If anyone can help you, he can. He pretends to be world-weary and cynical, but he's a kind man at heart.'

Nettie left the house, trying hard to equate her vision of Duke Dexter with that of his adoring ward, and failing miserably. Duke was a skilled confidence trickster, a purveyor of forgeries, and behind that urbane smile she suspected lay a heart of solid stone.

★   ★   ★

'Where have you been?' Byron demanded. 'Robert didn't know where you'd gone and we were both worried that something might have happened to you.'

Nettie laid her shawl on the bed and took off her bonnet. 'I need to find Pa. Do you know where he is?'

'He was sitting at a table outside the café when I last saw him, but you haven't answered my question. I was worried about you, Nettie.'

She met his angry gaze with a smile. 'I'm not a child, Byron. I can look after myself, and I've been taking care of my father ever since I can remember.' She took the visiting card from her reticule and handed it to him. 'I didn't tell you or Pa, but Duke Dexter was on board the ferry. I met him by chance and he gave me this card. I went to investigate.'

Byron studied it. 'This says Marc Gaillard. Who is this person?'

'It's Duke using an alias.' Nettie glanced at the bare table beneath the skylight. 'Have we

71

anything to eat? I'm starving.'

'Nothing, I'm afraid. I haven't eaten all day.'

'Have you any money?'

'I've got enough to buy us a meal tonight, but after that I'm broke. I tried to find work again today, but there was nothing.'

'We need to catch my father before he spends what little he has left, and I have something to tell Pa. He won't like it and neither will you, but I don't think we've any alternative other than to ask Duke for help. I've arranged for us to meet him at the gallery tomorrow morning.'

'Is that wise, Nettie? Dexter is nothing but trouble.'

'And we're fugitives from the law with little or no money, and no prospect of earning anything legally — unless you can come up with a brilliant solution, Byron, because I can't think of anything.'

He slumped down on the rickety chair. 'This is the time when I wish I knew how to find my mother's family. The life of a water gypsy is becoming more and more attractive.'

Nettie eyed him thoughtfully. 'Have you made enquiries?'

'What's the point? It's over twenty years since my mother ran away from her bullying father. I expect the old man's dead or in prison, from what my father told me about him. She had a brother, but I doubt if he'd want anything to do with me.'

'I don't know,' Nettie said, giggling. 'If you find them and tell them you're wanted by the Metropolitan Police for aiding and abetting a criminal, they'll probably welcome you with open arms.'

'I'm glad you think it's funny.' Byron spoke severely, barely disguising a chuckle. He rose to his feet. 'If we can persuade your father to forgo wine this evening, I've just enough money for two bowls of soup and two cups of coffee. We'll worry about tomorrow when it comes.'

As Nettie wrapped her shawl around her shoulders and picked up her one decent bonnet, she could not help thinking of Constance living in her grand house. If only she had eaten more of the delicious cake that had been served with the coffee, she might not feel so weak and lightheaded now, but she had not wanted to appear greedy.

'I'm coming,' she said stoutly. 'And I suggest that we go for a walk along the river bank after we've eaten. If we make enquiries we might find someone who remembers a family of bargees who had a daughter called Lisette.'

★ ★ ★

They found Robert at the café, and, as usual, he was the centre of attention, chatting volubly in English, regardless of whether his audience could understand him or not. He illustrated his life story with charcoal sketches, and Nettie was horrified to see that he had used up almost a whole pad. Paper was expensive and charcoal was not cheap, but he was using it as if the supply was inexhaustible and free.

Nettie waited for the audience to disperse

73

before she sat down next to her father and told him how she had met Duke on board ship. Robert studied the visiting card and tossed it back at her.

'Marc was a fool,' he said casually. 'I knew him well, but he was no businessman. He loved art but he would have been bankrupt if Duke had not taken him in hand. I know now that Dexter is a crook, but he's a clever fellow.'

'Not so clever that he didn't get found out.' Byron emptied his pockets of money and laid it on the table. 'This is all I have left, Mr Carroll. What about you?'

Robert leaned forward, putting his finger to his lips. 'Not so loud, boy. I'm travelling incognito. My name is not unknown, even in Paris.'

'I doubt if the people here are very interested in art,' Nettie said hastily. 'Anyway, Pa, I've arranged for us to meet Duke at the gallery in the morning.'

Robert sat back in his chair, a stubborn look masking his handsome features. 'I'm not going.'

'But, Pa, we need help. Can you think of any other way to raise money, or to find alternative accommodation? Madame will throw us out the moment she discovers we can't pay next week's rent.'

'Do you want me to spend the rest of my life working for that criminal? I believed in him, Nettie, and he betrayed my trust.'

'I'm just trying to keep us from ending up in the gutter,' Nettie said angrily.

Robert eyed Byron with a calculating smile.

'You're a strong young chap, surely you can find work, even if it isn't scribbling away in a lawyer's office.'

'I've been trying,' Byron snapped, 'which is more than I can say for you, Mr Carroll.' He snatched up a pile of discarded sketches. 'Is this what you've been doing all day? Have you spent all your money on drinking with your friends?'

'Well, I was hoping to sell some of my work,' Robert said sulkily. He put his hand in his pocket and produced a handful of coins, which he threw onto the table. 'Here, this is all my worldly wealth. Spend it on food and tomorrow we'll go hungry.'

'Tomorrow we'll go cap in hand to Duke Dexter and ask for his help. It's that or we end up on the streets, Pa.' Nettie snatched up the money and handed it to Byron. 'Is there enough for a decent meal?'

'Soup and bread all round,' he said, signalling to a waiter.

'And a bottle of cheap red wine,' Robert pleaded. 'I must have something to calm my shattered nerves.'

'No, Pa. We'll ask for water. I don't think there's even enough for coffee.'

Robert buried his head in his hands. 'What have I come to?'

★ ★ ★

Madame was standing outside the door to her quarters when they returned to their lodgings, and she started shouting at them before they reached the top step. Even though Nettie could not speak her language, the woman's meaning was obvious. Byron waited until she slammed the door to her apartment, but his translation was quite unnecessary.

'Amongst other things she said we're to be out of here first thing in the morning, unless we can find the rent, in which case she wants two weeks' money in advance. I don't think the good lady trusts us.'

'I wonder why,' Nettie said grimly. 'It looks as if she has our measure.'

Robert shrugged. 'Don't worry, my love. Duke will give me the money. He owes me some recompense for the trouble he's caused us.' He sauntered off in the direction of the stairs.

'I don't know how you've stood him all these years,' Byron said, shrugging. 'Your dad is impossible.'

'I agree, but at least he's come round to the idea of asking Duke Dexter for help. I can't see any other way out of this predicament. Let's hope tomorrow brings us better luck than today.'

★　★　★

The gallery was in the fashionable rue de Rivoli, but when they arrived at just after nine o'clock next morning they found it closed and shuttered. They waited for an hour, pacing up and down outside, but no one appeared.

'I'll have more than a few words to say to Duke when I next see him,' Robert said angrily.

'It was a bad day for me when I fell in with that fellow.'

'Something must have happened, Pa.' Nettie glanced up and down the street, but there was no sign of him. 'I think we ought to visit Constance. She may know where he is and he might have left a message with her.'

'We've got nothing to lose,' Byron said grimly. 'I don't fancy sleeping on the river bank tonight. Lead on, Nettie.'

'It's really not good enough,' Robert grumbled. 'I deserve more respect. I'm a celebrated artist. People used to pay good money for my work.'

'Come on, Pa.' Nettie slipped her hand through the crook of her father's arm. 'You'll like Constance. She's a really nice person, but just remember that she knows nothing of Duke's criminal activities. She thinks he's wonderful and it would be a shame to ruin her trust in him.'

'She'll get to know about him soon enough when the police turn up at her door,' Robert muttered. 'I hope he's there, and the least he can do is to buy us a decent breakfast.'

They walked on, stopping every now and then to ask the way, and eventually they reached the street where Constance lived. Nettie knocked on the door, but after what seemed a long wait it was opened by a middle-aged woman dressed in black. Her grey hair was scraped back into a tight chignon and her eyes were reddened, as if she had been crying.

'I've come to see Miss Gaillard.' Nettie spoke

slowly, hoping that the woman would understand, but she waved her hands and raised a sodden handkerchief to her eyes.

Byron stepped forward to translate, although it made little difference and her tears flowed freely.

'Ask her if she's Mademoiselle Menjou,' Nettie whispered.

Byron repeated the question in French and Mademoiselle nodded, but whatever she said was punctuated by sobs and unintelligible. Nettie was at a loss, but her father stepped forward, and to her surprise he put his arm around Mademoiselle Menjou's shoulders, making sympathetic noises until she grew calmer.

'Take over, Nettie. The damned woman is ruining my best jacket,' Robert said in a stage whisper.

Nettie took his place and guided the distraught woman into the parlour. Mademoiselle Menjou sank down on the sofa, raising a tear-stained face to Byron. She spoke volubly, gesticulating to emphasise her words.

'What's she saying?' Nettie demanded. 'What's happened, Byron?'

'She says that Dexter turned up late last night and the next thing she knew Constance was throwing things into a valise, and Dexter paid off most of the servants. She is to remain here and keep house with the minimum of help.'

'Tell her we'll take care of things,' Robert said eagerly. 'We could stay here until something better turns up.'

Byron shook his head. 'She mentioned the

gendarmerie, Robert. The police are involved. It seems as if they've been here, making enquiries about Duke's whereabouts.'

Nettie gave Mademoiselle Menjou an encouraging smile. 'Tell her I'm sorry, Byron, and ask her if Constance left a message for me.'

In answer to his question Mademoiselle shook her head, and her eyes brimmed with tears. She buried her head in her hands and her plump shoulders shook.

'The police might be watching the house even now,' Nettie said urgently. 'I think we should get away from here as quickly as possible.'

Just as they were about to leave, Mademoiselle Menjou caught hold of Nettie's arm. 'Château Gaillard,' she whispered. 'Beauaire-en-Seine.' She scuttled off before Nettie had a chance to ask Byron to question her further.

Nettie turned to him. 'Did you hear what she said?'

Byron nodded. 'I think she was trying to tell you where Duke had taken Constance. If I remember my geography lessons at school, Beauaire is a small river-side town, north of Paris.'

5

They stood on the bank of the River Seine with their worldly goods piled at their feet. A hurried departure from the lodging house had left them homeless and slightly breathless. Madame had demanded extra money for the inconvenience of having to chase them for the next week's rent, which Robert refused angrily, but their raised voices had caused a stir amongst the other tenants. They had left the building with abuse being hurled at them, and someone threatening to call a gendarme. It seemed that wherever they went they were to fall foul of the law.

Nettie gazed into the gunmetal waters of the river as it reflected the grey of the clouds that threatened yet another April shower.

'If only we had a boat,' she said, sighing. 'If Duke saw fit to leave town I think that's what we should do, before we get into any more trouble, and if we could get to Beauaire we might be able to find Constance. It doesn't sound as if she wanted to leave with Duke.'

'You ought to abandon me.' Robert moved to the water's edge. 'Perhaps I should fling myself into the river and set you free, Nettie dear.'

'Don't be silly, Pa.' Nettie knew that he was bluffing, but even so she moved closer to him, placing her hand on his shoulder. 'Perhaps we could find somewhere quiet in the country where no one has heard of you.' She turned to

Byron. 'But you don't have to stay with us. You could return to London and no one would be any the wiser.'

Byron grasped her free hand. 'We're in this together, and I'm not quitting now just because things are difficult. It's not totally unselfish, anyway. I want to use this opportunity find my mother's family.'

Robert eyed him gloomily. 'You said yourself that it's more than twenty years since your mother left Paris. I doubt if you'll find anyone who knew her.'

'I've been asking around and one of the older men remembers a barge called *La Belle Lisette* and the family were called Joubert. Even if there's a connection, they could be anywhere after all these years.'

'We can't just give up,' Nettie said firmly. 'And I, for one, do not intend to sleep in a shop doorway or under a bridge. I'm going to start asking the boat people if they will take us anywhere away from Paris. You two can stay here and guard our things.' She marched off in the direction of the quay where barges were being unloaded. Glancing over her shoulder, she saw her father slumped down on his case, but Byron had gone off in the opposite direction and she could hear him calling out to a boatman downriver.

She walked for miles, stopping to speak to everyone she met who worked on the river, whether it was bargees, fishermen or the men who unloaded the boats, but all her enquiries, in halting French, were met with negative responses. It seemed that none of the owners of small vessels were able or willing to take passengers. Nettie suspected that some might have been more amenable had there been a generous offer of payment, but that was out of the question.

It was late afternoon when she made her way back to the place where she had left her father, and her clothes were still damp after being caught in several showers with nowhere to shelter. She was cold, hungry and exhausted, but a small flame of hope still burned within her heart. Giving up was not an option, but if they could not find cheap transport to get them away from the city, they would have to set off on foot. Tonight, however, they would need to rest, and already she could feel blisters the size of grapes forming on her heels. When she reached the spot where she had parted from Byron and her father, they were nowhere to be seen, and it had started to rain again.

'Nettie.'

She turned at the sound of Byron's voice, saw him emerge from a shack further along the river bank, and she hurried to join him.

'I was wondering where you'd gone,' she said breathlessly. 'Did you have any luck?'

He shook his head. 'No, unfortunately, but I found your dad in the boatmen's café, drinking wine with some of the locals. He was sketching their portraits to pay for his food and drink.'

'How like Pa. Here we are, doing our best to save him from being arrested, and all the time he's enjoying himself.'

Byron tucked her hand in the crook of his arm. 'Come on, Nettie. It's not so bad. As a matter of fact he's done what we set out to do. He's been chatting to a bargee who remembers my grandfather and he thinks my family moved north to Beauaire, the town Mademoiselle Menjou mentioned.'

'That's marvellous, Byron. But how will we get there?'

'Monsieur Durand, the bargee, has agreed to let us travel with him, providing we work our passage, and your father will be kept busy making sketches of the old fellow and his precious steam boat. Apparently Robert has met an art lover at last.'

'Thank goodness for that,' Nettie said wholeheartedly. 'I don't feel as though I can walk another step.'

'Take my arm. The café is just over there. I'm sure your father can wheedle a cup of coffee for you. He seems well in with all of them, even though he can't speak much French.'

Arm in arm they made their way to what was little more than a wooden shack, but when Byron opened the door Nettie was enveloped in a warm fug laced with the heady aroma of coffee, wine and the inevitable hint of garlic. Her father was seated at a long table with several others, and she could tell by his expression that he was enjoying himself. His pad of paper, slightly crumpled after its soaking, was propped up before him and he was using charcoal to sketch the proprietor. An empty cup and wineglass suggested that his artistic talents were being appreciated in the most practical way. Nettie moved to his side, greeting him with a tired smile.

'You look comfortable here, Pa.'

Robert looked up at her, beaming. 'I've made some wonderful friends, and I've been treated with the greatest hospitality.' He signalled to the barman, pointing to Nettie and making a drinking motion with his hand. 'Cafe, please, Monsieur. For my daughter.' He glanced up at Byron. 'What's the French for 'daughter'?'

Byron went to the counter and translated. He returned to the table moments later bringing a steaming cup of coffee for Nettie.

'They think you're very pretty,' he said, smiling. 'They show good taste.'

Robert tugged at Nettie's sleeve. 'I want you to meet Monsieur Durand, the gentleman who appreciates art and who is going to take us to safety.' He turned to the man seated on his left. 'Aristide, my friend, this is Nettie, my daughter.'

Aristide took Nettie's hand and raised it to his lips. Such a gallant gesture seemed oddly out of place from a man more used to working the river than mixing with polite society. Aristide was dressed, like his fellow bargees, in baggy trousers and a coarse linen shirt, open at the neck. A bright red and white spotted neckerchief added a splash of colour, and a battered peaked cap lay on the bench beside him. He smiled and his shrewd blue eyes twinkled irresistibly beneath shaggy grey eyebrows. Nettie knew at that moment that she was going to like Aristide Durand and she had a feeling that he was a man to be trusted.

'It's a pleasure to meet you, Monsieur,' she said, smiling.

★ ★ ★

Later, when Aristide took them to where his vessel was moored, Nettie experienced a *frisson* of excitement. She had grown up within yards of the River Thames and she was accustomed to seeing vessels of all types, but there was something solid and appealing about the craft that bobbed gently on its moorings, rocking like a baby's cradle. Aristide boarded first, followed by Robert and then Byron, who held his hand out to steady Nettie as she bundled up her long skirts and stepped onto the deck. The planking was scrubbed to bone whiteness and Aristide showed them round like a proud housewife showing off a much-loved home. The cargo was stowed in the hold beneath vaulted hatch covers on either side of a single funnel, which smoked gently like an old man seated on a park bench with a pipe clenched between his teeth.

Aristide said something to Byron, who nodded and patted him on the back. 'Monsieur Durand says this was one of the first steam barges on the Seine.'

Robert nodded vaguely. 'Yes, that's all very well, but where will we sleep? Ask him that, Byron.'

After a brief conversation Byron translated yet again. 'The accommodation is very small so we'll have to sleep on deck.'

Nettie could see that her father was about to protest. 'That will be exciting,' Nettie said hurriedly. 'Please tell Monsieur Durand that we're very grateful to him.'

'I need a comfortable bed, but I suppose beggars can't be choosers,' Robert said gloomily. 'I just hope that the fellow doesn't expect me to swab the decks.' He wandered off to sit in the bows with his pad and charcoal and began sketching the view.

Nettie shrugged and sighed. It seemed that nothing would ever change her father; he would go through life oblivious to the chaos he caused along the way. Perhaps all creative people were like that. She could only be glad that she had not inherited her father's artistic temperament, and she thought longingly of the blank pages in her notebook that begged to be filled with her next attempt at the novel. Maybe she would set it in Paris, or it might be a story about life on the river — that was a chapter just waiting to be told. She dragged her thoughts back to the present, wondering what Aristide was saying to Byron. They were having a long conversation, and it was obvious that Byron struggled at times in his attempt to understand Aristide's rapid French. Then they shook hands and Aristide strolled off to speak to Robert.

'What did he say?' Nettie asked eagerly. 'How are we going to pay our way? We can't expect him to provide transport and feed us for nothing.'

'Aristide had a youth who crewed for him, but the boy became ill and he had to send him home to his parents. I told the old man that I know nothing about sailing a barge, but he says he needs someone to stoke the boiler and work the locks. He said we can all help in one way or another.'

'I'll be happy to cook or clean, but doing hard physical work is a bit different from sitting in a law office copying dull documents,' Nettie said, frowning. 'Do you think you're up to it?'

'It's true that I've never done manual labour, but we need to get away from Paris and I want to find my mother's family, so this seems to be the best solution all round.'

'I'll do what I can to help,' Nettie said, smiling. 'Pa will do what he always does, which is as little as possible, but I suppose I shouldn't grumble. It was his gift with people that made Monsieur Durand offer to help us.'

'And it was your father who got you into this mess in the first place.'

'Yes, I know, and it's a shame that you've been dragged into our affairs.'

Byron took her hand and held it in a firm grasp. 'I knew what I was getting into, and I wanted to come to France. It was my choice.'

'I hope we find your mother's family, but meeting them for the first time might not be easy. After all, they turned their backs on her.'

'I've thought it through and I want to find out where I came from, whether it's good or bad. I just need to know.'

'I understand, or at least I think I do.'

He smiled and squeezed her fingers. 'We're in this together, Nettie.'

'Byron, *mon ami*.' Aristide was suddenly active, marching towards them, waving his arms and shouting instructions.

Byron leaped to attention. 'We're off, Nettie.' He caught the mooring line that was thrown to him from one of Aristide's friends on the river bank. He was attempting to coil the rope when Aristide hurried up to them, and showed him how it was done. He spoke rapidly and Nettie had no idea what he was saying, but it was obvious that she was the subject of the conversation.

'He wants to show you where he does the cooking,' Byron said at last. 'I think you're to take over.'

'That's one thing I can do.' Nettie nodded to Aristide, who grinned in response and headed off in the direction of the accommodation in the stern of the vessel.

Every effort had been made to use the available space, from the bench seat that pulled down into a bed, to the rows of pots and pans that hung above the tiny stove. Talking volubly and miming with dramatic gestures, Aristide managed to demonstrate what he wanted her to prepare. A large soot-blackened pan was already on the stove and when he lifted the lid the aroma of onions and garlic wafted round the cabin, but when he produced a bucket filled with live eels Nettie had to clamp her hand over her mouth to stifle a cry of horror.

Aristide seemed to find this hilarious and his round belly shook with laughter. He pulled down a flap, which suddenly became a table, and he took a cleaver from the drawer and snatched a wriggling eel from the water.

Nettie backed away, shaking her head. 'No, Monsieur. No, I can't do that.' She reached the door and stepped up onto the deck, gasping for air.

'What's the matter?' Robert hurried towards her. 'You've gone green, girl. Are you ill?'

'No, Pa. He wants me to kill an eel and cook it.'

'Is that all? I used to do it all the time when I was a boy. We used to set eel traps in the Thames at night and have fried eel for breakfast next morning.' Robert pushed past her and stepped down into the accommodation. 'Hold on, Aristide, my friend. You must forgive my daughter, she's been brought up to be a lady, but this is something I can do.'

Nettie remained on deck until her father reappeared, wiping his hands on a bloodied cloth. 'How satisfying. I feel like a man of the river now.'

'I couldn't do it, Pa. What's happened to the eels?'

'They're skinned and cut up and stewing nicely in the liquor. If only he had some parsley to add to it and some mashed potato. We'll have to do with bread. Luckily Aristide bought some fresh this morning. I'll leave the rest to you, dear.' He patted her on the cheek and sauntered off, edging past the smoke stack, which was now puffing clouds of black smoke into the atmosphere as the engine creaked and groaned into action. Aristide erupted from the cabin, giving Nettie a cheery wink as he returned to take over the tiller from Byron, who was looking distinctly nervous.

Nettie was equally apprehensive and she returned to the stove, but the debris had been cleared away and the eels were simmering gently in the pan. She had to brace herself in order to taste the liquor for seasoning, but it was surprisingly pleasant and the slimy eels had been transformed into meaty white chunks. She set the table, sliced the bread and waited for the eel stew to finish cooking.

$\star \quad \star \quad \star$

That night Nettie, her father and Byron slept on deck beneath the stars. Aristide supplied them with blankets, pillows and a tarpaulin in case it rained, but Nettie was so tired that it would have taken a violent thunderstorm to rouse her. She awakened next morning to a chorus of birdsong and the gentle plashing of the water against the hull. It had been dark when they tied up for the night, but now in the gentle light of dawn she could see that they had left the city and were in a rural setting. Trees were just bursting into leaf and cattle grazed on lush green grass, while fluffy white lambs frolicked, jumping and leaping as if for joy. Born and bred in the city, Nettie was enchanted to find herself in the countryside with air that smelled fresh and sweet, in complete contrast to the noxious, smoky fumes in the city. She scrambled to her feet, taking care not to disturb her father and Byron, who were still sleeping peacefully. Her gown lay neatly folded on top of a hatch cover and she slipped it over her head. If they were to travel far on the waterways of France they would need to make better sleeping arrangements, especially in the way of cover in case of bad weather. She buttoned her bodice and sat down to put on her boots. If Aristide was up and about she could put the kettle on and make coffee, although she would have loved a cup of tea, and perhaps she could toast what was left of yesterday's bread. She made her way towards the stern, but came to a sudden halt at the sight of Aristide, naked as the day he was born, apart from his peaked cap, boots and a red and white spotted neckerchief. He was standing on the deck, staring out over the fields with a plume of tobacco smoke rising above his head. He turned to look at her and smiled, taking the pipe from his mouth.

'*Bonjour, Mademoiselle.*'

'Er, good morning, Monsieur Durand.' Nettie averted her eyes. 'Breakfast,' she said tentatively. 'Coffee.'

He said something in rapid French, laughed and strolled off towards the cabin. Nettie followed at a distance, trying not to look at the vast expanse of pink flesh wobbling along in front of her.

'Byron,' she called in a hoarse whisper. 'Wake up, please.' But there was no sound from where her father and Byron were sleeping and she had little choice other than to follow Aristide into the accommodation. She hung back as long as possible, and when she eventually set foot in the

91

cabin she was relieved to see that he had pulled on a pair of baggy trousers. He indicated the stove, and she could feel the heat from the doorway. A kettle was bubbling away and he pointed to a coffee grinder and a bag of beans. Nettie knew then what she must do, and she edged past him to make a start on the coffee.

He was talking to her as if she understood what he was saying and, to keep him happy, she nodded in what felt like the right places and shook her head when he paused, eyeing her expectantly. It seemed to work, and he tapped the dottle from his pipe, refilled it from his tobacco pouch and lit it with a spill from the fire. He sauntered out on deck, slipping on his shirt and leaving a trail of smoke in his wake. Nettie heaved a sigh of relief and concentrated on making a pot of coffee, and toasting the bread left over from last night's supper on the hob. The aroma of toast and coffee must have filtered out on deck as Byron was the first to appear, followed by Robert. Both looked bleary-eyed, but Nettie suspected that it was due to the rough red wine they had consumed rather than a lack of sleep.

Nettie sat on the bench, sipping the strong black coffee. 'We've left Paris and we're headed north, is that right, Pa?'

Robert bit into a slice of dry toast and pulled a face. 'I want some butter and marmalade.'

'You haven't answered my question.'

'Yes, dear. You know we had to leave Paris.'

'Of course, and we're trying to find Byron's family as well as making sure that Constance is happy to be with Duke, but what then?' Nettie looked from one to the other. 'When we reach Beauaire, where do we go from there? Are we going back to England, or are we going to become water gypsies and go on to Le Havre with Monsieur Durand?'

'I haven't quite decided,' Robert said vaguely. 'It depends on whether the police have given up the chase. I can't think that they would waste their time hunting for someone like me. It's not as if I've committed murder or treason.'

'So we might be going home?'

Robert picked up his cup and drank thirstily. 'We'll see.'

'I'd better go back on deck.' Byron made a move towards the doorway. 'According to Aristide, we're nearing a lock and that's where I have to leap into action. I haven't the slightest idea what to do, so it should be interesting.'

Nettie followed him out into the warm spring sunshine. 'Everything moves so slowly on the river. We might be on this barge for weeks, so will you teach me to speak French? It will make things much easier.'

A slow smile lit Byron's eyes. 'Of course I will, and I'm sure that Aristide will co-operate fully. He's not a bad chap when you get to know him.'

Nettie stifled a giggle. 'I saw rather more of him that I wanted to this morning. He was standing in the bows, smoking his pipe and staring at the view with nothing on.'

'You mean he was undressed?'

'Exactly, although he was wearing his neckerchief and his cap.'

Byron's lips twitched but his brow was creased in a frown. 'I should speak to him. It's not the done thing when there's a young woman on board.'

'You can't tell him what to do on his own barge.'

'He would be mortified if he knew you'd seen him naked.'

'He saw me and he wasn't at all embarrassed. I'll just try to avoid him tomorrow morning. Anyway, I know now what to do for breakfast, and maybe we might have the opportunity to go ashore at some point. He must buy food from somewhere and there's precious little in any of the cupboards.'

Nettie was about to return to the cabin when Byron caught her by the hand.

'You don't have to trail around after your father. Say the word and I'll take you back to England. You're not involved in Robert's crimes.'

'He's my father, Byron. You've seen how he is, and heaven knows what would happen to him if I went home. I can't desert him.' Nettie withdrew her hand, giving him an apologetic smile. 'You're a good friend, Byron. I'm so glad you came with us.'

'I do care about you, Nettie,' he said slowly. 'You must know how I feel about you.'

This time her smile was wholehearted. 'I do, and it's wonderful to have such a good friend.' She stood on tiptoe to brush his cheek with a kiss. 'Oh, heavens,' she added, sniffing the air. 'Someone has burned the toast and we were already low on bread.' Without giving Byron a chance to respond Nettie returned to the cabin to find her father staring glumly at a slice of charred bread.

'That's the last of the bread, Nettie. Remind Aristide to buy some when we go ashore, although heaven knows when that will be. The fellow chatters away, but I haven't the slightest idea what he's saying.' Robert took his pad and tin of charcoal from the shelf where he had placed them the previous evening. 'I'm going out to sketch the view. Charming countryside — I think I could quite happily live in France for the rest of my days.' He hesitated in the doorway. 'I believe Aristide has a consignment of wine in one of the holds, and grain in the other. This is the life, my dear. I might have been born to it.'

He wandered out onto the deck, leaving Nettie to clear away the mess he had created.

Having tidied the cabin, swept the floor and the deck, Nettie found herself with nothing to do other than sit and admire the scenery. Aristide was at the tiller and Byron was kept busy stoking the boiler and cleaning the hatch covers, while Robert sat in the stern, sketching and sometimes dozing in the warm sunshine. Nettie found a secluded spot and took out her notebook. She sat for a while, chewing the end of her pencil as she tried to think of a suitable title for this new novel, and in the end she simply wrote *Belinda*, which was the name of her wayward heroine. Then she started to write.

Writing about the trials of the beautiful but headstrong young woman, Nettie lost track of time, but was brought back to reality by a sudden jolt as the barge bumped gently against the river bank.

'This isn't the time to be writing your diary,' Robert said impatiently. 'I'm going ashore with Aristide. Are you coming?'

Nettie tucked her book and pencil down behind a sack filled with grain and jumped to her feet. 'Yes, Pa.' She hitched up her skirts and reached out to take Byron's hand as he leaned over from the top of the river bank. It was muddy and difficult to find a foothold but eventually she reached safety. The heroine of her book, Nettie decided, would break with convention and wear men's breeches when she travelled by barge. The story would mirror her own experiences and therefore would be much more believable than a gothic fantasy. She was determined to make the publishers sit up and take notice of her. The adventures of Belinda Makepeace would captivate readers, and the public would queue up to buy her books.

'Where are we?' Nettie shielded her eyes from the sun, but they seemed to be on the edge of a wood and straight ahead there were fields filled with grazing cattle, stretching as far as she could see. They were in the middle of the country with no sign of habitation. 'Why have we come ashore here, Pa?'

'I don't know.' Robert scratched his head. 'I need a straw hat. If we were near a town I could purchase one to protect my head and neck from the sun.'

Nettie turned to Byron. 'There doesn't seem to be anything here.'

Byron held up his hand. 'Listen. That sounds like music.'

'Music?' Robert put his head on one side, closing his eyes. 'Sylvan sounds. It might be fairy folk.'

'Pa!' Nettie said, laughing. 'You've been drinking too much of the wine that Aristide hands out so liberally.'

Aristide had been standing a little apart from them, but he became animated, shouting instructions to Byron, who leaped back onto the boat and pulled back the hatch covers.

The music grew louder. Nettie could hear singing and the voices sounded very human. A flight of startled birds erupted from the wood and the music swelled, twigs snapped underfoot, and, one thing was certain — the newcomers were not fairy folk. Nettie waited, barely daring to breathe as the hubbub rose in a crescendo . . .

6

Aristide stood with open arms as the crowd burst from the darkness into the bright sunshine, their costumes ablaze with colour, curls flying, hands clapping in time to a fiddler and the beat of a drum.

'What on earth is going on?' Nettie whispered into her father's ear. 'Where did all these people come from?'

Robert grasped her hand. 'I've no idea, but Aristide seems to know them. Smile, Nettie. Stop looking scared.'

She bared her teeth in an attempt at a grin. 'I'm not frightened, Pa. I'm amazed to think that these people knew we were here, but I don't understand why they are so pleased to see us.'

'It's Aristide they love,' Robert said in a low voice. 'We'd best keep out of the way.' He stepped aside as the crowd of men, women and children converged on the river bank.

Aristide was at the front, holding up his hands for silence. Then, with a surprisingly athletic move for a man of his age and build, he leaped on board, and, in answer to their names being called, the onlookers stepped onto the barge, laying their contributions on the deck in return for a large bag of grain and as many bottles of wine as they could carry.

Nettie watched in awe as the gifts of bread,

vegetables, meat, fruit, cheese and milk piled up on deck, and then the party began. Bottles were uncorked and Nettie found herself being offered a drink by a burly, bewhiskered French farmer. She refused at first, but realising that she had offended him, she took the bottle and held it to her lips, sipping just enough to be sociable. This seemed to be the sign that she was willing to dance with him and he whirled her around in time to the music. Soon everyone was dancing, even the small children, and the older men and women sat round chatting like old friends who had not seen each other for some considerable time.

Byron had come ashore and Nettie made the excuse of being too breathless to keep dancing, miming in a desperate attempt to convince her new beau that she needed to rest. She moved swiftly to Byron's side, and the frolicking farmer seized another girl round the waist and danced off with her into the wood.

'What's going on?' Nettie had to raise her voice to make herself heard over the noise.

'Aristide visits here once a month, so he told me. These people come from outlying farms and it's quite a social event.'

Nettie chuckled and nodded. 'Yes, I can see that. But I thought he was transporting the wine from a vineyard to a wholesaler. That's what Pa told me, and the grain is for a distillery in Le Havre.'

'They'll get what's left after Aristide either drinks or barters it away. It seems to be the accepted way of life, or the way he runs things.

99

Right or wrong, they're all having a wonderful time.'

'I think that pretty girl with the scarlet blouse is eyeing you, Byron. It looks as though you've made a conquest.'

He backed towards the edge of the bank. 'Maybe I'd better get on board and put some of that food away before it goes off in the heat of the sun.'

'I thought you'd be flattered,' Nettie said, chuckling. 'She is very attractive, Byron.'

'I'm not a lady's man,' he muttered. 'I've never known what to say to women.'

Nettie stared at him in surprise. 'But you've never had a problem with talking to me.'

'You're different.' He lowered himself onto the deck and began scooping up the perishable goods.

Nettie was about follow him when another young man tapped her on the arm. He was a year or so her junior at a guess, but he smiled shyly and she could not disappoint him by refusing to dance. As they galloped around, clapping in time to the beat of the drum, and kicking up their heels, Nettie could see that her father had taken advantage of the situation. He had retrieved his pad and charcoal and was sketching the villagers as they drank, danced and enjoyed themselves. One elderly farmer sat for his portrait and paid for it in tobacco, and another, emboldened by his friend, had his likeness sketched in exchange for his straw hat.

Nettie danced with her young admirer, but the

language barrier made communication difficult, and then she was claimed by an older man with straying hands. His breath reeked of garlic and he was very drunk, but she managed to put him in his place without creating a scene, and by that time people had begun to drift away. Nettie took this as her cue to say adieu to the ageing Lothario and she joined Byron on board the barge.

'That was a surprise,' she said, chuckling. 'I wonder if this will happen every time we set ashore.'

Byron picked up a sack of potatoes and slung it over his shoulder. 'It seems to work for old Aristide, and Robert has got the hat he wanted, even if it is a bit battered.' Byron sniffed the air as a cloud of blue smoke wafted their way. 'But that tobacco your father is smoking smells terrible.'

Nettie glanced at her father, who was seated in his favourite place, the straw hat pulled down over his eyes as he smoked his pipe and sipped wine from a bottle. Aristide was still on the river bank, bidding a fond farewell to a voluptuous woman, who was obviously more than a passing acquaintance. With one last, lingering kiss, he released her and backed away, blowing kisses, while a youth, who bore a striking resemblance to Aristide, looked on with a disapproving scowl. Aristide stepped on board the barge, turning to wave as the boy grabbed his mother by the hand and dragged her away.

Nettie's fertile imagination was hard at work as she tried to imagine a young, handsome

Aristide falling in love with the raven-haired country girl. Perhaps their families had opposed the match, like the Capulets and Montagues in *Romeo and Juliet*, but Nettie abandoned the idea almost immediately. Aristide was not a romantic hero, and, from what she had just witnessed, he was illegally bartering the goods he had been entrusted to deliver. Aristide, she decided, was just as much on the wrong side of the law as Pa, and if the French police were to take an interest in his activities, Pa, Byron and herself would be in even more trouble. She glanced at her father, who looked happier than she had seen him in a long time, and she knew that he would laugh off her worries.

'We're leaving now, Nettie.' Byron stepped ashore to release the mooring rope and he tossed it to her, jumping on board as the barge started to drift towards mid-channel.

Drunk as he was, Aristide took the tiller and Byron went to stoke the boiler. The engine chugged into life and, once again, they were headed downstream.

Nettie picked up the last of the food they had been given and stowed it away safely before starting to prepare the evening meal. The meat and vegetables would make a savoury stew that would cook slowly all afternoon, ready to eat in the cool of the evening. She would have time to find a secluded spot and concentrate on the trials of Belinda, her wilful heroine, and her search for true love.

★　★　★

A routine developed, with each day more or less the same. They all had their duties to perform, even Robert, whose job it was to sweep the deck, which he did in a half-hearted way before retiring to the bows to make even more sketches or snooze in the sunshine, his new hat pulled down over his eyes. In the evenings, when they were moored in a sheltered spot, Aristide and Robert sat and smoked their pipes after supper and drank wine, while Byron gave Nettie lessons in French. When it was fine they went ashore and walked along the river bank, but when it rained they either huddled in the cabin, or sat beneath a tarpaulin that Byron had rigged up over their sleeping area. Nettie was beginning to enjoy life as a bargee, but she could not rid herself of the nagging fear that one day the police would descend upon them and arrest both her father and Aristide.

There had been no repeat of the impromptu party that had caught Nettie by surprise, but Aristide continued to be himself, getting up early to commune with the dawn — stark naked apart from his usual accessories — and working the barge with the expertise gained from a lifetime on the river. They had to put ashore frequently in order to barter for bread and fresh produce from small farms. Aristide knew all the farmers and smallholders by name, and everyone seemed delighted to see him. The women in particular greeted him warmly, and some of the children who came to stare at them might easily be related to the amorous bargee. Nettie wondered how he had managed to survive without a jealous husband or lover taking the law into his own hands, but Aristide seemed to be universally popular. Acting as a go-between, he passed on messages from one family to another, together with titbits of gossip that made the farmers' wives curl up with laughter or fold their arms across their chests, pursing their lips and shaking their heads. Nettie and Byron always accompanied him on these visits, mainly to help carry whatever produce was on offer, and Nettie was eager to practise the French that Byron had taught her.

Life on the river was slow and leisurely, and the late spring weather seemed to add a touch of magic to the landscape. The sun sparkled on the water and birds sang in the trees, but the undercurrent of worry was never far from Nettie's mind, and her only escape was getting lost in Belinda's story. It had changed slightly in content, but her heroine had become like a second self, and the ancient castle where Belinda was held prisoner became Nettie's retreat from the world. Belinda's only way of communicating with the man she loved was a tame pigeon that flew in her window at night carrying a message from gallant Sebastian, who was an army officer fighting under the command of the Iron Duke. Nettie had to force herself to write slowly, even as her excitement grew with every twist and turn of the plot, and she tried to avoid crossings out, where possible. There had been vague praise for the novel that had been rejected, but a note in red ink had criticised Nettie's presentation, and she was determined not the make the same mistake again.

When she finished writing she stowed the notebook and pencil behind the sack of flour they used for cooking, safe in the knowledge that none of the men would think of attempting to make bread — although Aristide did admit to having a go, apparently with disastrous results. Byron was useless in the kitchen and Robert could barely make a pot of tea, let alone attempt anything more ambitious. Nettie had never made bread, but pancakes were her speciality, which she served with the honey that one of the farmers had swapped for two bottles of red wine.

The hours of daylight lengthened, but Aristide showed no sign of urgency in getting his cargo to its destination. He seemed to enjoy having passengers on board, and as long as his belly was full and he had enough tobacco to smoke, and plenty of wine to drink, he did not complain. Robert's career as creator of faked masterpieces had ended with the departure of Duke Dexter, and the longer he remained free from discovery the more confident Nettie became. Perhaps they had been granted a new start and maybe life on the river was for them. She could not speak for Byron, but she knew that he was still hoping to find his mother's family and he questioned everyone he met, although with little success. Sometimes his hopes were raised by someone who said they remembered the Joubert family, but their memories were always vague and inconclusive.

Then, suddenly, everything changed when

they reached Beauaire, a charming small town set beneath high chalky cliffs. Nettie was eager to go ashore and make enquiries about the château, which was clearly visible from the river, and Robert wanted to purchase more sketching pads and charcoal. Always on the lookout to earn money, he said he hoped to sell a few portraits. Nettie suspected that this would entail her father taking residence outside a convenient café so that he could drink wine while touting for business, and no doubt Aristide would join him. They made an odd couple, as different from each other as it was possible to be, and yet they had become good friends. They managed to converse using a mixture of sign language and odd words and phrases in French and English. To an onlooker it might appear like a comic double act, but Nettie knew that her father had found someone with whom he was completely at ease. Where they differed most was their attitude to women: Aristide was a philanderer, but Nettie had never known her father to show more than a professional interest in his female clients. She had realised as a child that he had suffered greatly when her mother died and had never looked to find a replacement for his lost love. For all his failings, Nettie would have loved him if only for his devotion to her dead mother, and to herself. Selfish, self-opinionated and easily led, Robert Carroll had a faithful heart, and to Nettie that meant everything. She knew she could never love a man who played her false.

Going ashore felt like a holiday, and, true to character, Aristide and Robert chose to take a seat outside the first café they came across in the market-place. This left Nettie and Byron to explore the narrow cobbled streets, lined with half-timbered buildings, nestling beneath a turreted castle. Nettie felt as though she had gone back in time or had landed in the middle of a fairy tale. She would not have been surprised to see characters from much-loved children's stories roaming freely amongst the burghers and their well-dressed wives, but what was even more astonishing was the small cobbler's shop they discovered in a back street with the name JEAN JOUBERT in bold black letters above the door.

Nettie clutched Byron's arm. 'Do you think Monsieur Joubert is one of your relatives?'

'There's only one way to find out.' Byron braced his shoulders and his knuckles whitened as he grasped the door handle.

'Fingers crossed,' Nettie whispered as she followed him into the dark interior. The smell of leather and glue was the first thing she noticed as she peered into the gloom, and then she saw a middle-aged man bent over a shoemaker's last. He looked up, peering at them over the top of steel-rimmed spectacles.

Nettie held her breath while Byron tried to make himself understood. The older man seemed to be a little hard of hearing, and perhaps Byron's accent was unfamiliar, but eventually the conversation became more animated, and Nettie was able to grasp a few words. It was only when the cobbler lifted the hatch in the counter and emerged to throw his arms around Byron that she was convinced that they had come to the right place.

Byron turned to her with tears in his eyes. 'Nettie, this is my uncle Jean — my mother's elder brother.'

Nettie bobbed a curtsey, which felt like the right thing to do in this town where dreams seemed to come true. '*Bonjour, Monsieur.*' The words had barely left her lips when she found herself hugged against a leather apron, with Jean Joubert talking so fast that she could not keep up with the flow of rapid French.

He released her and hurried back behind the counter, where he opened a door and beckoned to them. Byron went first and Nettie followed him into a small parlour, which was crammed with furniture and bric-a-brac on every surface, reminding her forcibly of the cabin on Aristide's barge. A kettle simmered on a small black-leaded range and Jean chattered volubly while he ground beans to make a pot of coffee.

'What is he saying?' Nettie asked in a low voice, during one of Jean's rare pauses to catch his breath.

'He is the only member of the family living in this town. He had to leave the river due to ill health.' Byron's eyes misted with emotion. 'He's been telling me about my mother, and why she left the barge and went to live in the city.'

Nettie thanked Jean as he handed her a steaming bowl of coffee. It was dark and bitter and she would have liked to ask for sugar, but she didn't want to appear rude, and she sat quietly sipping the hot beverage. Byron and Jean were deep in conversation and she waited until there was a brief pause.

'I think I should leave you to get to know your uncle,' she said in a low voice. 'You don't need me here.'

'I'm sorry, Nettie. We've been ignoring you.'

She rose to her feet, smiling apologetically at Jean. 'Not at all. I think it's wonderful that you've found your uncle. I'll explore the town and I'll meet you at the café where we left Pa and Aristide.'

'Are you sure you'll be all right on you own?' Byron asked anxiously. 'You've never been here before and you might lose your way.'

'I'm sure I can manage without too much difficulty, and I need to find a haberdashery where I can buy needles and thread.'

'All right,' Byron said reluctantly. 'But take care.'

'I will. Don't worry about me.' Nettie smiled and leaned over to kiss his tanned cheek. She turned to Jean. '*Au revoir, Monsieur.*' He responded in kind and Nettie made her way through the shop and let herself out into the street.

After the stuffy atmosphere of the parlour and the musty darkness of the shop, it was a pleasure to step into the sunshine and take deep breaths of fresh air.

Nettie set off in search of a shop that would stock what she needed, as her limited wardrobe had suffered during her time on board the barge, and now she had several tears to mend. In a sudden burst of generosity her father had given her some of the money that he had received for his sketches, and she might even treat herself to a ribbon or two. The prospect of shopping, even for something so simple, was exciting in itself, and as Nettie roamed the backstreets in the shadow of the great castle, she could imagine her novel's heroine, Belinda, gazing out from one of the towers, unable to enjoy such freedom. Eventually she found a shop that sold what she wanted and she managed to make herself understood with the smattering of French that Byron had taught her. When she left the shop the tempting smell of hot bread wafted from a nearby bakery, making her mouth water, and, as she returned to the square she came across market stalls laden with fresh produce. It was midday and she was hungry. She quickened her pace as she headed for the café where she had left her father.

As she had expected, Robert was surrounded by curious townsfolk, who were watching intently as he completed a sketch of a plump, well-dressed matron. He held it up for the woman to see and she put her head on one side, squinting short-sightedly at the drawing. For a moment Nettie thought the subject of the portrait was going to criticise Robert's efforts, but even at this distance Nettie could see that her father had flattered the sitter. Gone were the wrinkles around her thin lips, which he had made fuller, and he had erased the double chin. The woman in the portrait had a gentler, more pleasing and much younger appearance, and one of the onlookers began to clap, the others joining in. Madame rose majestically to her feet and took a purse from her reticule. She paid, if rather grudgingly, and marched off, clutching the likeness of herself as she might have looked a decade earlier.

Nettie made her way through the crowd and took a seat next to Aristide, who was smoking a cigarillo. On the table in front of him was a bottle of red wine and two glasses, one full and the other almost empty. He leaned forward to refill his glass, squinting through a spiral of tobacco smoke, but at that particular moment Robert leaped to his feet, tilting the table and sending the bottle crashing onto the cobble-stones. A puddle of red wine spread from the broken glass like a pool of blood, and Aristide uttered a string of words that were not in Nettie's vocabulary, although she did not need an interpreter to tell her that he was extremely displeased. But it was her father's startled expression that made her turn her head, and she stood up, hardly able to believe her eyes.

Robert rushed towards the familiar figure who had emerged from the crowd. 'Duke. You're the last person I expected to see here.'

Aristide looked up at Nettie, eyebrows raised, but she was lost for words in English or French, and even more so when she saw the young woman who walked a few paces behind Duke.

'Constance!' Nettie hurried towards her, arms outstretched.

'Nettie. I didn't think I'd ever see you again.' Constance grasped Nettie's hands, her lips quivering with emotion.

'Come and sit down. You're white as a ghost.

111

Why did you leave Paris without telling me?'

'It happened so suddenly.' Constance cast a wary look at Duke, who had his arm around Robert's shoulders, hugging him as if he were a long-lost friend instead of the business associate he had abandoned and left to take the blame for his crimes.

'Nettie, my dear girl,' Duke said, smiling. 'I can't tell you how delighted I am to see you and your father. What an amazing stroke of luck.'

'What are you doing here, Duke?' Robert's smile faded into a frown. 'You disappeared when I needed your help the most.'

Aristide rose to his feet, his bushy eyebrows drawn together over the bridge of his nose. He spoke rapidly to Robert, but it was Duke who stepped forward, holding out his hand and smiling as he answered in fluent French.

Aristide sank back on his chair, eyeing Duke warily.

'I don't know who your friend is, Robert, but he has a colourful vocabulary.' Duke summoned a waiter with an imperious flick of his fingers.

'Aristide Durand is a bargee who saved us from destitution in Paris after you abandoned us.' Robert's smile was replaced by a frown. 'You have a lot to answer for, Duke.'

Seemingly unabashed, Duke grasped Aristide's hand and shook it, speaking to him in a conciliatory tone, which seemed to have a calming effect, and even more so when Duke gave the waiter an order that brought a smile to Aristide's face.

Duke turned his attention to Constance. 'You

112

look unwell, my dear. Would you like to go back to the château and wait for me there?'

She shook her head. 'No, thank you. I want to talk to Nettie.'

'I've ordered coffee and those pancakes with chocolate that you like so much.' Duke patted her on the shoulder as if he were humouring a child. 'Look after her for me, Miss Carroll, while I talk to your father and his new friend. We have business to discuss.'

Nettie glared at him. She had suffered greatly, thanks in part to Duke Dexter, and she was not going to let him off so easily. 'Whatever you say to my pa concerns me, too, Duke. You left us to fend for ourselves in London and again in Paris. We were lucky that Monsieur Durand allowed us to travel with him, but where we go next is anybody's guess.'

'Leave us to talk this through, Nettie,' Robert said hastily. 'I need to have words with Duke in private.'

'Just remember that whatever you decide will involve me, too.' Nettie met Duke's amused gaze with a steady look. 'Don't try to involve my father in your schemes, because I won't stand for it.'

He shrugged. 'I'll be sure to ask you for your advice before I plan my next move, Miss Carroll.'

Nettie turned her back on him. At this moment she hated Duke Dexter and all he stood for. Life with her father before he had become embroiled in Duke's schemes had been far from perfect, and times had been hard, but now they were homeless and on the run from the police — and all thanks to the man who had greeted Pa like a long-lost friend.

She turned to Constance with a conciliatory smile. 'Let's sit down and we can talk.'

Constance moved to another table and a waiter brought the food that Duke had ordered. Nettie would have liked to refuse to eat it, but she was hungry and the aroma of warm chocolate and crisp pancakes was too tempting. She took a seat next to Constance, turning her back on Duke and her father. Aristide had not been taken in by Duke's seemingly effortless charm; she could only hope that he would provide a voice of reason if Duke suggested another nefarious scheme involving her father.

Constance picked at her food. 'I'm sorry that we left Paris without telling you, Nettie.'

'What happened? Why did you go with Duke?'

'He's my guardian. I didn't have much choice.'

'But Paris is your home. Duke spends most of his time in London.'

Constance pushed her plate away. 'I'm not hungry. Perhaps you could eat it for me.'

'No, thank you. It was delicious, but I've had enough.' Nettie leaned towards Constance, lowering her voice. 'Why did Duke have to leave Paris in such a hurry?'

'I don't know, Nettie. He doesn't tell me everything.'

Nettie glanced over her shoulder and saw her father and Duke with their heads together while Aristide looked on, glowering. 'He's up to something,' Nettie said slowly. 'And it concerns

114

Pa. I don't want him to get involved in crime again.'

'What do you mean?'

'Are you so naïve that you don't know how Duke makes his money?'

'He's an art dealer,' Constance said slowly. 'He buys and sells fine paintings.'

'Yes, he does, and he also sells forgeries. That's where my father comes in. He makes copies of paintings that even experts find it difficult to tell apart from the originals.'

'You must be mistaken,' Constance said in a whisper. 'Duke is a respected businessman.'

'If you take my advice you'll leave him and return to Paris. You don't want someone like Duke as your guardian.'

'You're wrong about Duke, Nettie. You don't know him like I do.'

'What are you keeping from me, Constance?'

'It has nothing to do with you, so please don't ask.'

'Why not?'

Constance was about to answer when Duke appeared suddenly at her side. 'We have to leave now.'

'Why?' Nettie demanded. 'What are you doing, Duke?'

He eyed her coldly. 'You'd better come with us. If you don't believe me, just look round.'

Nettie turned her head, but the sight that met her eyes made her leap to her feet. Aristide and Robert were being led away by two gendarmes.

'Pa!' Nettie was about to run after them, but

Duke caught her round the waist and dragged her into the crowd.

7

Despite her protests, Nettie was hurried through the marketplace and into a narrow, cobbled street that wound its way up the hill, ending abruptly at a postern gate set in a high stone wall. Duke opened it and ushered them inside.

'What's happening?' Nettie demanded breathlessly. 'Why were my father and Aristide arrested?'

'You'd better ask them that, if and when you next see them,' Duke said tersely. 'Be thankful that I was there to save you from the indignity of being taken by the gendarmes.'

'If they've traced Pa here, why are you still a free man?'

'You're upset,' Constance said gently. 'Come to the house and we can talk about it in comfort.'

'I should be with my father. What good can I do him here?'

'Constance is right. Asking questions I cannot answer will get you nowhere, Nettie. You're free to go if that's what you wish, but giving yourself up to the police won't help Robert. We're in a foreign country and we need to go about this with tact and diplomacy.' Duke strode off along a path set between flowering cherry trees. His boots crunched on the gravel, shattering the silence that had suddenly fallen upon the neatly ordered gardens surrounding the château.

Nettie remained where she was. Her feet felt like lead and her head ached as she tried to come to terms with the sudden change in their situation. One minute everything had seemed to be going well, but then Duke had appeared as if from nowhere and her father and Aristide had been dragged away by the local police.

'Byron,' she murmured. 'He'll come looking for me and he won't know where I've gone. I have to go and find him, Constance.'

'But you don't know the town, Nettie. You'll get lost.'

'He would have made his way back to the market-place. I can find that easily enough.'

'And walk straight into the arms of a gendarme? If they were looking for your father they must know that you were with him.'

'I've been afraid that this would happen, but it might be Aristide they were after. If the police traced us here they would know that Pa was working for Duke and have arrested both of them.'

'You're forgetting that Duke is known as Marc Gaillard here and in Paris,' Constance said urgently. 'You need to talk to him, Nettie. I'm sure he'll tell you that this is all a mistake. He's a wealthy man, but I'm sure he made his money honestly. I can't believe that he would trick people into buying forgeries.'

'Duke led my father astray. He uses people, Constance. I know you think well of him, and perhaps he's been kind to you in the past, but no good can come from you staying with him now. When he's discovered he'll end up in prison.'

'You don't understand,' Constance said urgently. 'I can't leave him.'

'You have that lovely house in Paris. Why did you follow him here?'

'We're married, Nettie. I'm his wife.'

Nettie stared at her in stunned silence and a sudden breeze showered them with petals like pink confetti.

'You're married!'

'It was very sudden. Duke came to my home and told me to pack. I thought we were going to stay in Honfleur, as we have done every year since my parents passed away, but then he told me that we were coming to the château. I could have refused, but I saw the sense of his proposition, so we came here and went through a marriage ceremony in the town church.'

Nettie shivered as clouds covered the sun, leaving them in deep shadow. 'Do you love him?'

'I don't think I know what that emotion feels like, Nettie. I've led a quiet life with very little chance to meet people of my own age, and Duke has always been kind to me. It was what my parents would have wanted.'

'But this isn't the Middle Ages,' Nettie said angrily. 'You're young and you have your whole life before you. You could have refused.'

'It's done now, and there's no going back.'

Constance walked off, heading towards the house, and Nettie was left with little choice other than to follow her. She could have let herself out into the street and gone in search of Byron, but there was no guarantee that he would be waiting in the market square. She could try to find the cobbler's shop, but it was unlikely that he would still be there, and if she made her way back to the barge it would almost certainly be watched by the gendarmes. She quickened her pace in an attempt to catch up with Constance, who was hurrying on ahead, and it was only when Constance stopped to let herself into the servants' wing of the ancient building that Nettie finally arrived at her side.

'I'm sorry,' Nettie said breathlessly. 'It's none of my business.'

'I expect it does seem odd,' Constance acknowledged with a faint smile. 'Duke is a lot older than me, but he could have had any woman he wanted.'

Nettie did not agree, but there were more important issues to consider and she needed Duke's help. 'I suppose I should call you Mrs Dexter now,' she said, changing the subject. 'Or is it Madame Gaillard?'

Constance smiled and nodded to a young kitchen maid who scurried past them carrying a large pan of water. 'Nothing has changed between us, Nettie. I hope we can be friends.'

'You can rely on me for as long as I'm here, but I really do need to speak to Duke and ask for his help. I can't abandon my father.'

'Duke will be in his studio by now. He spends hours there studying the paintings, which I find very dull.'

Nettie followed her through narrow flagstone passageways with vaulted ceilings, their footsteps echoing eerily and their voices coming back to them in ghostly whispers. She was beginning to feel as if she had walked into one of her own novels.

'This house must be very old.'

'I believe so. Duke told me it was a fortress in the thirteenth century, but I'm not particularly interested in history and, to tell the truth, I hate it here. It's always chilly, even in summer. It's very damp and it smells musty.'

The passage opened out into a vast hall with a huge fireplace at either end. Armorial shields had been carved into the stone, and the walls were hung with hunting trophies, tapestries, swords and ancient blunderbusses. Tall mullioned windows filtered the sunlight, creating patterns on the flagstone floor, which felt cold beneath Nettie's feet. The room was sparsely furnished with cumbersome wooden coffers, uncomfortable-looking upright chairs, and a refectory table that would sit at least forty. A door concealed beneath oak panelling led into another passage and at the far end they came to Duke's studio.

Constance knocked and entered.

'You shouldn't have walked away, Duke,' she said angrily. 'Nettie needs your help.'

Nettie stepped over the threshold and the familiar smell of linseed oil and turpentine was oddly comforting, but it was something of a shock to see easels with unfinished canvases and the usual clutter of paint tubes, palettes and pots filled with brushes. Large windows allowed the light to flood in and double doors opened out onto a terrace where spring flowers bobbed and swayed in the gentle breeze. She walked slowly round the large room, gazing at the paintings that hung on the walls, and she recognised several of her father's original earlier works. She spun round to find Duke standing behind her.

'What are you doing with these?' she demanded angrily. 'My father could have sold them.'

'I paid him for them,' Duke said coldly. 'Don't worry, he received a fair price and I bought them as an investment.'

'So you admit that my father has talent.'

'I do, most certainly, and he's been using it to great effect.'

Nettie glanced at the unfinished canvases. 'Pa didn't do those.'

'I had a very capable copyist here in France, but unfortunately the poor man sickened and died.'

Constance stared at him aghast. 'Did you really sell copies as original works of art, Duke?'

'How did you think I made my money, Constance? Your father almost went bankrupt, but I prospered. Didn't you stop to wonder why?'

She shook her head. 'No. I trusted you, Duke.'

'Well, now you know. I'm sorry if it offends your sensibilities, my dear. But you've enjoyed the benefits of my ill-earned profits, and continue to do so.'

'I'm sorry,' Nettie said, glancing from one to the other. 'I didn't mean to cause a rift between you.'

'And I'm sorry if I haven't lived up to your expectations, Connie,' Duke said, gently.

'I'm not a child, Duke.' Constance faced him

with a rebellious scowl. 'I just don't like being lied to. You should have told me everything before we were married.'

'There was no need for you to know.'

'That's not true,' Constance said angrily. 'If you're caught and sent to prison, where does that leave me?'

'You're a bright girl — you grew up in the art business and everything is in your name. I'm sure you could carry on where I left off.'

Connie's outraged expression melted into a wide smile. 'I'm sure I could, and I would probably do just as well as you, if not better.'

'My respect for you deepens the more I get to know you, Madame Gaillard.' Duke took her hand and raised it to his lips. 'I think we'll do very well together.'

'This is all very fine, but I hope you're not thinking of involving Pa again,' Nettie said angrily. 'We're in enough trouble as it is.'

Duke was suddenly serious. 'It had crossed my mind, but the gendarmerie seem to have put paid to that idea. I'll have to think hard about our next step.'

'But you're prepared to let my father take the blame for your failings. You must have made a fortune selling fakes, and yet the people who do the work live in poverty.'

Duke struck a pose, his eyes alight with laughter. 'Oh, come now, Nettie. You weren't starving in that garret — you weren't barefoot. If you were poor it was because your father is a spendthrift.'

Constance stepped in between them. 'Stop

teasing her, Duke. Are you going to help her, or not?'

Nettie stared at her in astonishment. This Constance seemed like a different person from the shy young woman she had met in Paris.

A dull flush coloured Duke's cheeks and he acknowledged her reprimand with a nod. 'You're right, my dear. Of course I'll do anything I can to get Robert out of trouble. For one thing, I doubt very much if our local police know of his involvement in the art world. I suspect that it was your bargee friend they were after.'

'What do you know of that man, Nettie?' Constance eyed her curiously. 'Why would the gendarmes arrest him?'

'I don't think he's a bad person, but he does make free with his cargo of wine and grain, and he seems to have a way with the ladies. Perhaps a jealous husband has made a complaint against him.'

Duke threw his head back and his laughter echoed round the studio. 'This is France, Nettie. We're not in hypocritical England where such things go on all the time but are brushed under the carpet.'

'What can we do?' Nettie looked from one to the other. 'And where could we go from here?'

'Where were you headed anyway?' Constance asked. 'Had your father decided to return to London?'

'We had very little money and nowhere to go — we were desperate and Aristide offered to take us on his barge; it was as simple as that.'

'And the young man who accompanied you,'

Duke said, frowning. 'Why was he travelling with you?'

'Oh, my goodness!' Nettie gazed at the large clock on the wall that would have looked more at home in a station waiting room than an art studio. 'Byron will be looking for us. He'll wonder what's happened.'

'You must do something, Duke,' Constance said firmly. 'It seems to me that you were at fault, and you should make things right for Nettie and her father.'

Nettie eyed Duke warily, expecting him to snap, but he smiled and nodded.

'I suppose I must admit some culpability, but Robert knew what he was doing when he agreed to work for me.'

'Duke!' Constance gave him a stern look and received a kiss on the forehead in return.

'All right, my dear. I'll send one of my men to find this fellow Byron and bring him here, and I'll go in person to the gendarmerie, and see what I can do.'

'I should go with your servant,' Nettie said hastily. 'He won't know who to look for, and Byron might refuse to accompany him. I dare say he'll return to the barge.'

'I'll go with you.' Constance drew herself up to her full height. 'Don't try to stop me, Duke,' she added. 'None of your servants speaks English and Nettie has very little French.'

He nodded reluctantly. 'Very well, but come straight back. I don't want you wandering about on your own.'

'I grew up in London and in Paris,' Constance

said smugly. 'I think I can look after myself in this small town.'

'Even so I'll send Henri with you, but don't linger. It's possible that we might have to leave suddenly.' Duke left them staring after him and his footsteps faded away until they were left in silence.

Nettie gave Constance a searching look. 'What did he mean by that?'

'I don't know, but this is so much more exciting than being stuck in Paris with Mademoiselle.'

'I was worried that Duke might have forced you to marry him,' Nettie said, smiling. 'But it seems to me that you can handle him very well.'

'It's easy enough in my position.'

'I don't understand.'

'It's a marriage of convenience, Nettie. I doubt if you would understand.'

'I might, if you can tell me why you agreed to such a thing.'

'My father was an expert when it came to art, but no good with money. It was Duke who saved Papa from bankruptcy, and Duke put the house in Paris and the gallery in my name. It was part of his promise to look after me should anything happen to Maman and Papa.'

'But surely that needn't involve marriage? Duke Dexter made his money by defrauding the people who bought the paintings that he passed off as originals.' Nettie shook her head. 'Don't look at me like that, Constance. I know my father is equally to blame, but you're married to a man who might at any moment be arrested and sent to prison.'

'I didn't know that when I agreed to marry him, although Duke told me there might be problems, but everything was signed over to me so I would always be safe.'

'I still don't understand what either of you would gain from a loveless marriage?'

'I have the protection of being a married woman, and I'm a woman of property. I didn't go into this lightly, Nettie. I'm neither clever nor beautiful, and I'm certainly not rich — hardly a good match. I thought about it carefully before I agreed to his proposition, and this way my future is assured.'

'But, Constance, what happens if you meet someone else and fall in love?'

'If and when that time comes, the marriage will be annulled, which was part of our agreement. I will keep the house in Paris and return the business to Duke.'

Nettie struggled to think of a suitable comment. Constance might appear to be fragile and inexperienced, but she had the unsentimental, pragmatic approach of a true businesswoman.

'I think you're wrong in your opinion of yourself, Constance.'

'Really? In what way?'

'I'd say you are very clever, and you're very pretty.'

'If you say so,' Constance smiled as she headed for the doorway. 'I'll get my bonnet and shawl. I expect Henri will be waiting for us. The servants fall over themselves to please Duke, which is very annoying because they treat me like a child.'

★ ★ ★

Henri was a dour, middle-aged man who clearly disapproved of his young mistress venturing into town on foot. He marched on ahead with a large stick clutched in his hand, as if expecting to be attacked by footpads, but the local population were obviously used to his eccentricities and ignored him. Constance had never heard of the cobbler Jean Joubert, but Henri knew where to find him and they went to the shop, only to discover that Byron had left an hour ago. Nettie suggested that they try the market square and then the barge. Henri said nothing but led on, glancing over his shoulder every so often as if to make sure they were following him.

The market square was still busy, but there was no sign of Byron and so they headed for the river. As expected, they found the barge guarded by a gendarme, who eyed them suspiciously as they walked past for a second time.

'Keep going,' Constance hissed when Nettie hesitated.

'All my worldly goods are on the barge. If I leave them I'll have nothing but the clothes I'm wearing now.'

'We're about the same size. I have more gowns than I can ever wear. My allowance has always been very generous.' Constance smiled at the gendarme as they strolled by, and he responded with a broad grin.

'He likes you,' Nettie said urgently. 'You could explain that I was just a passenger on the barge. There's something on board that I value more than gowns and shoes.'

Constance came to a halt, staring at her in astonishment. 'Really? What could be more important than one's appearance?'

'Just a few notes I'd written,' Nettie said vaguely. 'But I'd like to keep them.'

'Is it a journal? Do you write down everything that occurs daily?'

'No, it's not that.' Nettie walked on. 'It doesn't matter. This must get sorted quickly. I expect Aristide will talk himself out of trouble, and Pa, too. I just need to find Byron — he'll be worried about me.'

'What does he look like?' Constance tugged at Nettie's arm. 'Is he tall with a mop of fair hair and bright blue eyes?'

'That sounds like him,' Nettie said vaguely as she turned to follow Constance's gaze. 'Yes, you're right.' She broke into a run. 'Byron. Where have you been?'

'Where have *you* been?' he countered. 'I've been searching for you for hours.'

'Do you know what happened to Pa and Aristide? Have you been to the gendarmerie?'

He shook his head. 'No, I thought it best not to get involved, at least until we know what the charges are. Even when we know, there's precious little we can do. We haven't the funds to hire a lawyer.'

'Do you think it's that serious?' Nettie asked urgently, but Byron was gazing over her shoulder. 'Who is that?'

Constance glided up to them, smiling and fluttering her eyelashes. 'So this is Byron.' She held out her hand. 'I'm Constance.'

'I'm very pleased to make your acquaintance.' Byron shook her hand. 'I've heard a lot about you.'

Henri was standing close behind Constance and he cleared his throat noisily. She turned on him, frowning, and issued an abrupt order that made him back away.

'This isn't helping Pa and Aristide,' Nettie said impatiently. 'And I need to collect some of my things.'

Byron shot a wary glance at the gendarme. 'Maybe they'll let us stay on board.'

'There's plenty of room at the château,' Constance said calmly. 'We would enjoy your company and Duke will find a good lawyer to speak up for Mr Carroll and Aristide.'

'Thank you, you're very kind, but I'll have a word with the guard before we do anything hasty. I think my French is up to it.' Byron walked off without waiting for anyone to comment, and he greeted the gendarme with a pleasant smile.

Nettie waited anxiously. 'At least Byron hasn't been arrested.'

'He's still smiling. That's a good sign.' Constance laid her mittened hand on Nettie's arm. 'You must stay with us until this business is settled. Byron, too, if he wishes. I've been trying to persuade Duke to return to Paris, but for some reason he's decided to remain at the château for the foreseeable future. I'd be glad of your company.'

Nettie gave her a searching look. 'Are you sure that Duke won't mind?'

'I'll get my own way in the end — I always do.' Constance glanced over Nettie's shoulder. 'Your friend is returning and he doesn't look too pleased.'

Byron strode back to them, his expression grim. 'I'm sorry. I did my best, but we're not allowed on the barge until after the magistrate's hearing tomorrow, and maybe not even then if the case goes against Aristide.'

'So it's just Aristide who'll be in the dock?'

'It's all to do with him selling off the cargo. Someone has reported him to the owner of the vineyard, and Robert is involved simply because he was said to be helping Aristide.'

'So it's nothing to do with Pa's work?'

'No, apparently not.'

Nettie breathed a sigh of relief. 'Thank goodness for that.'

'And you will stay at the château until everything is sorted out?' Constance asked eagerly.

'I will,' Nettie said hastily. 'But I can't answer for Byron.'

Byron raised Constance's hand to his lips. 'I'd be honoured, ma'am. The prospect of sleeping in a proper bed and eating meals at a dinner table is too tempting to refuse.'

Constance linked arms with him. 'It's the least we can do.'

Nettie was about to follow them, when out of

the corner of her eye she spotted a man lurking in the shadows. There was something familiar about him that she could not pinpoint, but a shiver ran down her spine and she quickened her pace.

8

Duke returned from the gendarmerie later that afternoon and joined them in the wainscoted drawing room.

'I saw Robert briefly, and he said he was being treated well enough, but his lack of French was making life difficult for him. I advised him to say as little as possible and I found an English-speaking lawyer to represent him. Aristide can look after his own affairs.'

'Was Pa all right in himself?' Nettie asked anxiously.

'Yes, as far as I could tell. He's worried that the French authorities might have been warned to look out for him, but I told him that wasn't the case. He's being held because of Aristide's liberal attitude to the cargo that doesn't belong to him. In any event, I am the person the Metropolitan Police are looking for.'

'The police did question my father,' Nettie said angrily. 'But you are Marc Gaillard now. Would anyone in this town know your true identity? Apart from us, of course, and Constance.'

Duke shook his head. 'I've taken great care to protect my alias, but one can never be complacent. It might be time to move on.'

'What does that mean, Duke?' Constance asked eagerly. 'Are you thinking of returning to Paris?'

'Maybe not Paris. But if my old adversary Samson Wegg has traced me here, we might have to move on. Wegg isn't the sort to give up.'

'What did you do to make him hate you?' Nettie asked, unable to contain her curiosity any longer. 'Mr Pendleton told me that there was some kind of feud between you.'

Duke shrugged and shook his head. 'Wegg thinks I seduced his younger sister and abandoned her. The girl died in childbirth, the baby also.'

Constance gazed at him in horror. 'It's not true, is it?'

'Wegg thinks it is, and that's all that matters.' Duke leaned over to drop a kiss on Constance's forehead. 'Don't worry, my dear. We will take a long sabbatical, somewhere warm and sunny.'

Nettie and Byron exchanged anxious looks, but Constance smiled like an excited child. 'How lovely. Where will we go?'

He smiled reluctantly. 'Who knows?'

'I'm not leaving without my father,' Nettie said firmly. 'Your lawyer will get him acquitted, won't he, Duke?'

'We must hope so.' Duke turned to Byron. 'There's not much we can do for the moment. I'll show you round the château, if you're interested. It has a gory history that isn't for the faint-hearted.'

Byron sprang to his feet. 'Thank you, I'd like that. I've never been in a château before.'

They strolled off together, leaving Nettie and Constance seated by the fire. Despite the heat from the blazing pine logs, Nettie shivered. It might be warm and sunny out of doors, but inside the thick stone walls of the château there seemed to be a permanent chill.

'I wish Duke would treat me like a grown-up,' Constance said moodily. 'I might be young, but I'm not a delicate flower. I don't want to be cosseted and protected.'

'In that case you can help me,' Nettie said firmly. 'I want to get my things from the barge. I could find my way there, but I need an interpreter. Will you come with me?'

Constance jumped to her feet. 'Yes, of course. How exciting! We'll slip away without telling anyone, and then we won't have to put up with Henri following us like a lapdog.'

⋆   ⋆   ⋆

They reached the water's edge without mishap and Constance kept the gendarme talking while Nettie retrieved her notebook from behind the flour sack. She tucked it under her shawl and climbed back onto the landing stage. Constance was flirting outrageously with the young policeman and Nettie walked off slowly, allowing Constance a chance to catch her up.

'I haven't had so much fun for a long time,' Constance said breathlessly. 'Did you get what you wanted?'

Nettie clasped the book tightly as they hurried back towards the château. 'I did.'

'What have you written? Will you let me see it?'

'It's a novel, but I've only done a couple of chapters.'

'Even so, I'd love to read your story.'

'All right, but only if you promise not to tell anybody. I haven't even told Pa that I write romances.'

'How exciting. You might become famous one day.'

'I'd just like to be able to earn my own living so that I'm not dependent on Pa, or any man, come to that.' Nettie shot her a sideways glance. 'I didn't mean that as a criticism, Constance. You did what you had to do in the circumstances.'

'I admire your spirit — I really do. But you can't change the way the world is, Nettie.'

'No, but there's no harm in trying.' Nettie quickened her pace. 'Come on, we'd better get back before we're missed.'

'We'll be in time to change for dinner. Maybe later this evening you'll let me read your story so far.'

* * *

The room that Nettie had been given at the château was luxurious beyond all her expectations, and every effort had been made to make her feel comfortable, from the bowls of spring flowers that brightened even the darkest corner, to the fire that crackled and sizzled as resin oozed from the sweet-smelling pine logs. It was a relief to go there after dinner and sit quietly on the window seat that overlooked the knot garden, while Constance perched on a chair by the fire, reading Nettie's novel.

'I love it,' Constance said, closing the notebook and laying it on a table at her side. 'You definitely have a talent, Nettie.'

'It's my secret. You must promise not to tell anyone.'

Constance rose to her feet and crossed the floor to where Nettie was sitting. 'I won't tell a soul.' She clasped Nettie's hands in hers. 'I'll say good night, and thank you for letting me read your story. I can't wait to find out how it ends.' Constance leaned over to drop a kiss on Nettie's forehead. She left the room, closing the door softly behind her.

Nettie was exhausted, but her thoughts were with her father as she gazed out into the darkness. Everything here was so different from the life she and her father had led in London. They had done many moonlight flits and had lived in a variety of different locations, but nothing like this strange and eerie château on the banks of the River Seine. The lights of the town twinkled in the distance and bats flew in crazy circles, swooping and diving against the deep blue of the night sky. Nettie rested her head against the windowpane, praying silently that the next day would see the release of her father and Aristide. Nothing was certain — their future depended on the expertise of Duke's lawyer — and then, as she gazed into the purple darkness, she remembered where she had seen the man who had been loitering near the landing stage. She leaped to her feet, and forgetting that she was wearing a borrowed night-gown and robe, she headed for the stairs. Her feet hardly touched the treads in her haste to find Duke, but the drawing room was in darkness apart from the glowing embers of the fire, and she made for his studio, her bare feet making soft slapping sounds on the flagstone floor. Her breathing was ragged as she burst into the room to find him standing in front of a particularly fine painting. He looked round, staring at her in amazement. 'Nettie? What's the matter?'

'Samson Wegg,' she gasped, clutching her hands to her bosom as she struggled to catch her breath. 'I saw him in Dover Street and I'd swear he was down by the landing stage earlier.'

'What are you talking about?'

'I went to the barge to collect something that is important to me. I saw someone in the shadows and I didn't think much of it at the time, but it came to me suddenly — I'm certain it was Wegg.'

'Are you sure? This could be serious?'

Nettie nodded vigorously. 'I couldn't see his face clearly, but I'm convinced that it was him, and if he's followed you here it won't take him long to realise that my pa is involved in your shady dealings.' She felt the cold strike up from the floor and she wrapped her arms around herself in an attempt to stop her teeth chattering.

Duke strode across the floor and took her by the arm. 'You're shivering. I've got a bottle of cognac in my study. You look as though you need a drink.'

'I don't want brandy,' Nettie protested. 'I want you to take me seriously. Why would a nark have followed you to France, if he wasn't working for the police?'

'You might be mistaken. You say the man was in shadow — it could be anybody.'

Nettie shook her head. 'It was the way he was standing with his shoulders hunched, and a battered top hat tilted to the side. I didn't think anything of it at the time, but then it came to me.'

'Come with me, and don't argue.' Duke led her from the studio to a small, book-lined room where he lit candles and pulled up a chair for her.

Nettie took a seat and sat primly with her bare feet tucked under the material of her robe. 'If it was Wegg you could be in trouble — my pa also.'

'I'm very well aware of that.' Duke took a bottle from a side table and poured two generous tots of brandy into cut-crystal glasses. He handed one to Nettie. 'Drink this — it will calm your nerves.'

Nettie did not argue. She was chilled to the bone, but she knew it was fear making her blood run cold. 'Thank you.' She took one sip and then another.

'Why were you down by the river?'

'I told you just now. I wanted to get something from the barge.'

'It was a foolish thing to do. Did you go alone?'

'You're not my keeper, Duke.'

'You're my responsibility while you're under my roof. I repeat, did you go alone?'

'Constance chose to accompany me. You can't keep her locked up. It isn't the right way to treat anyone, let alone your wife.'

Duke drained his glass and set it down on the desk. He perched on the edge, arms folded. 'I suppose Constance has told you everything.'

'I wouldn't say that, but she did confide in me to a certain extent.'

'Very neat,' Duke said drily. 'You would make a good lawyer, Miss Carroll.'

Nettie took another sip of the brandy. 'I wouldn't take you as a client, Duke. I think you're using Constance to protect your own interests, and I doubt if you've ever considered her feelings.'

'You know nothing about me, or about her, if it comes to that. I've watched Connie grow from a child to a woman and I would never do anything to hurt her. Does that satisfy you?'

'A little, but this isn't about Constance, is it? If Samson Wegg has traced you here, he will almost certainly have passed information about you to the French police. If you attend the court tomorrow you might be walking into a trap.'

Duke eyed her with an amused twist to his lips. 'Don't tell me that you care what happens to me.'

'I don't,' Nettie said coldly. 'But I do care about Constance. I think she deserves better than to be tied to a criminal like you.'

'So what do you want from me, Nettie?' Duke walked round the desk and sat down in a padded leather chair. 'What would you have me do?'

'I want you to make sure that my father

doesn't go to prison, and we need money to get away from here.'

He eyed her thoughtfully. 'I'll do what I can, but if you're right — if that was Samson Wegg you saw down by the river — we are all in trouble.' He straightened up and poured himself another drink. 'I suggest you go to bed, Nettie. There's nothing to be done until morning.'

★   ★   ★

Nettie slept surprisingly well that night and awakened early next morning. She dressed in a plain grey gown, borrowed from Constance, and confined her hair in a neat chignon at the back of her head before going downstairs to the dining room. Duke was just finishing his breakfast and Byron was also at the table. He put his coffee bowl down.

'What were you thinking of, Nettie? Duke tells me that you and Constance went down to the river yesterday afternoon.'

'Yes, we did,' she said calmly. 'And I saw someone who might cause trouble for all of us, including Duke.'

'I'd have gone with you, if you'd asked me.'

'Thank you, but we managed very well on our own.' Nettie sat down next to him and reached for the coffee pot. 'You weren't around, anyway.'

'I was being given a tour of the dungeons, and then I spent some time with my uncle, but you only had to ask and I'd have gone with you.'

'Did your uncle tell you anything more about your family?' Nettie asked, sipping her coffee.

'I don't want to talk about it now.' Byron bowed his head and a lock of fair hair flopped over his eyes.

Nettie stared at him in surprise. 'That's not like you, Byron.'

'Leave the fellow alone. He'll tell you when he's ready.' Duke rose from the table. 'I'm going to meet my lawyer and we'll go straight to the court house. We'll have to hope you were mistaken about seeing Wegg, Nettie.'

'I'd like to come with you,' Nettie said cautiously. 'I promise I won't interfere.'

He shook his head. 'It's best if you stay here. I'll let you know when there is any news.'

She was about to argue, but a warning look from Byron silenced her. 'All right. I suppose I'll have to do as you say.'

'You can trust me, Nettie,' Duke said solemnly. 'I know it will be difficult, but I don't want to see Robert sent to prison any more than you do.' He hesitated in the doorway. 'Just in case things go wrong, I suggest you make ready to leave in a hurry, but don't alarm Constance.' He walked off, leaving Nettie with a dozen questions buzzing around in her head.

She bit her lip, understanding his meaning only too well.

'I don't know how to take that fellow,' Byron said slowly. 'We know he's a criminal, but he seems to be the lord of the manor here, if they have such a thing in France. And why would a young woman like Constance tie herself to someone like him?'

Nettie was tempted to tell him, but she could

not break a confidence and she merely shrugged. 'Who knows what attracts people to each other? That's their business, anyway, but what concerns me is the outcome of the trial. What will I do if Pa is locked up in a French prison?'

'We'll meet that when we come to it.'

She smiled. 'You don't have to stay with us. You're a free man and you don't have to share our exile.'

'That's just it, Nettie. I received some disturbing news from Uncle Jean.'

Alarmed by his sombre expression, Nettie laid her hand on his arm. 'What did he say?'

'I suppose I should be overjoyed, but I hardly slept last night for thinking about the lie that I'd grown up with.'

'I don't understand.'

'Neither do I. Why would my father make up such a story?'

'You're talking in riddles. It must be something very bad to have upset you so much.'

'All these years I've believed that my mother abandoned me — it wasn't true. At least, that's what my uncle told me. He said that she could not settle down to life as a doctor's wife, and she went back to working in the theatre. My father threw her out and forbade her ever to see me again.'

'I'm so sorry, Byron. That's very sad. Did your uncle tell you anything else?'

'He said that she returned to her family on the river.'

'Does that mean she's living here, in France?'

Byron shook his head. 'Apparently she grew

bored with the life of a water gypsy, and she went back to Paris and earned her living as a songstress. The last he heard of her she was in Spain, living in a small town on the coast of Catalonia.'

'Why didn't your father tell you the truth?'

'I don't know, and it's too late to ask him now. It was a cruel lie to tell a child. I thought she had left because of me. Uncle Jean said that leaving me in London broke her heart.'

'She must have loved you very much.'

'You'd think so, wouldn't you? But she's never tried to contact me.'

Nettie clasped his hand. 'What will you do?'

'I have to find her. I want to hear her side of the story. Can you understand that, Nettie?'

She nodded. 'Yes, of course. You must do what you have to do, Byron.'

'I won't leave until I know that you and your father are safe.'

'I can't rest until I know what's happening at the trial.' Nettie released his hand and rose to her feet. 'I'm going to the court house, regardless of what Duke had to say.'

'Are you sure that's wise?'

'Probably not, but I can't stay here and do nothing.'

'Then I'm coming with you.'

'No, I don't think that's a good idea, Byron. Perhaps you could stay and tell Constance where I've gone. If things go wrong I don't want her to be involved.'

★ ★ ★

144

With her shawl wrapped around her head and shoulders, Nettie edged her way into the crowded court room, taking a seat at the back where her presence would be least likely to cause comment. Duke was seated at the front, together with a man she assumed must be his lawyer, but they had their backs to her, which was a relief. She knew that Duke would be furious if he discovered that she had disobeyed his instructions to remain in the château. She realised that she was attracting covert glances, and she was beginning to doubt the wisdom of her decision as the proceedings began and she could not understand a word. However, she tried to look as though she was following the case and she stood when everyone else rose to their feet and sat down again when they did. Aristide was brought before the magistrate, but a latecomer edged onto the bench beside her and she moved along as far as she could in an attempt to make room for him.

The rank smell of unwashed maleness made her want to retch, but when she turned her head to glance at her neighbour she stifled a gasp of dismay. Her first instinct on recognising Samson Wegg was to leave the building, but such a move would draw even more unwelcome attention to herself and might even interrupt the proceedings. She could hear Aristide blustering and probably proclaiming his innocence, but the prosecuting lawyer produced a list, and she had seen for herself how generous Aristide had been with the cargo entrusted to his care. Then Duke's lawyer stood up and with much gesticulating and theatrical intonation of his plummy voice, he put his case. Nettie was impressed by his performance: she might not understand much of the language, but in a theatrical manner he managed to give the impression that Aristide was a much maligned man.

'I dunno what the toff is saying,' Wegg whispered, 'but I've sent a cable to London informing the police that Dexter and your dad are here. They'll both end up in the clink, and good riddance.'

Heads turned and people hissed angrily. Wegg subsided on his seat, but the self-satisfied grin remained on his face. Nettie sat as if turned to stone. She had little option but to remain where she was while the case dragged on. Her father was brought before the magistrate and Nettie was quick to notice that he was unshaven and his clothes were creased. He looked pale and tired, and she hated to see him in such a state, especially when he had always taken such trouble over his appearance. He might be weak, but he was not a bad man, and if his talent had been truly appreciated he would never have become involved with Duke Dexter, and she would not be sitting in a foreign court room next to Samson Wegg. In any event, her father had nothing to do with Aristide's racket, and she could only hope that Duke's lawyer was hammering home that point.

Suddenly everyone rose to their feet and it appeared that the session had ended, although Nettie was still none the wiser. She glanced at

Wegg and felt a twinge of satisfaction when she realised that he was equally baffled. Everyone was talking, people had begun to leave, and Nettie took the opportunity to slip past Wegg and escape outside into the warm spring sunshine. She headed up the hill to the château, glancing over her shoulder every so often in case he was following, but there was no sign of him.

★　★　★

Byron was waiting beneath the flowering cherry trees in the château garden. 'Well? What happened?'

'I don't know exactly, but I was right about Wegg. He sat next to me in the court room, and he said he'd informed the police in London that we're here.'

'You should have let me come with you. I'd have dealt with that fellow.'

'Thank you, but it's probably just as well you weren't involved. Anyway, the case didn't seem to be concerned with Duke's swindles, it was Aristide who was in the dock.'

'Constance will be relieved, although she was a bit put out because you didn't ask her to go with you. Anyway, she calmed down when I explained why you went on your own.'

'I don't think she's quite grasped the fact that Duke is a criminal. She's known him since she was a child, and she still thinks of him as her protector. I don't know what she would do if he went to prison.'

'She has all this,' Byron said with a sweep of

his hand. 'She can be miserable in comfort.'

'Trust you to say something like that, but I wouldn't want to live here on my own,' Nettie said with a reluctant smile.

'She has a small army of servants to look after her.'

Nettie glanced over his shoulder. 'She's coming. What shall I say to her?'

'Tell her the truth.'

Constance hurried up to them. 'You should have told me you were going to the court, Nettie. I've as much right to be there as anyone.'

'I'm sorry, but I knew that Duke would be angry with me for disobeying him, and he would be furious if you'd been there, too. The case was all about Aristide.'

Constance tossed her head. 'Of course it was. Now maybe you'll believe me when I tell you that Duke is an honest art dealer.'

'You're deluding yourself, Constance. Samson Wegg was there today, and he told me that he's informed the police about Duke and my father. It's not safe for us to stay here.'

'If what you say is true, I've been taken for a fool,' Constance said wearily. 'If Duke had been honest with me in the first place I doubt if I'd have agreed to marry him.'

'It didn't sound as though you had much choice. Duke can be very persuasive, as my father has found out to his cost. I don't care what happens to Duke Dexter, but I do care about my pa.'

Byron laid his hand on Nettie's shoulder. 'I'll go into the town and find out what's happening.

I need to speak to my uncle anyway.' He walked off along the tree-lined avenue and let himself out into the street.

'I wish I'd stayed in Paris,' Constance said, sighing. 'I should have stood up to Duke and refused to leave my home.'

'I think he tried to do what's right for you.' Nettie made an effort to sound positive, but she could see that Constance was on the brink of tears. Wegg had made a difficult position even worse, but Nettie had experienced many catastrophes brought about by her father's inability to live within his means. Enduring a precarious existence had toughened her, to an extent, but that did not make her oblivious to the feelings of others. She could see that Constance was struggling to come to terms with the sudden turn of events, and she linked arms with her.

'We can't do anything until we know what the magistrate decided about Aristide and my pa. Duke will know how to handle Wegg, so we'll just have to wait and see what he says.'

Constance dabbed her eyes on her handkerchief. 'I don't want him to go to prison, Nettie. And it's not purely for selfish reasons. I am fond of Duke in my own way, and he can be very kind and amusing when he wants to be. But if he should be caught and sent to prison in England, I'll be forced to live here in seclusion like a grieving wife. I'm too young to be shut up within these stone walls. I'd be just as much a prisoner as Duke.'

'Maybe it won't come to that,' Nettie said hopefully.

'Well, I'm not staying here. Duke must learn that I have a mind of my own, and if he chooses to run away he'll have to take me with him. I'm ready for an adventure.'

The carpet of pink petals from the cherry trees swirled around their feet as they walked towards the château and prepared to wait for news.

★ ★ ★

Constance had been pacing the floor impatiently while Nettie sat on the window seat, but she rose to her feet as the door opened and Byron burst into the room, followed by Duke, Robert and Aristide.

'Well?' Constance demanded, standing arms akimbo. 'Is it true that you lied to me about your past, Duke?'

He kissed her absently on the forehead. 'I'm afraid it's only a matter of time before the police arrive from London. Wegg has done his bit, although I dare say he regrets it now.'

'What happened?' Nettie looked from one to the other. 'What did you do to him?'

Byron flexed his knuckles. 'I've never been much of a fighter, but that chap got what he deserved.'

'Have you killed him?' Constance asked eagerly.

'No, but he'll have a sore head for a day or two.' Byron shot a wary glance in Nettie's direction. 'I'm not normally a violent man, as you know, but I made an exception in Wegg's case.'

'He's a hateful character,' Nettie said with feeling. 'But there's one thing that puzzles me.' She turned to Duke, fixing him with an enquiring gaze. 'What did you do to make Wegg hate you so much? Is it true about his sister?'

'It was all a ridiculous misunderstanding.' Duke strolled over to a side table and poured himself a tot of brandy.

'Go on,' Nettie said determinedly. 'Tell us more.'

'Yes,' Constance added. 'I want the truth, Duke.'

He shrugged and looked away, sipping his drink. 'Wegg's sister was a servant in my household. I had to dismiss her because of her behaviour, and Wegg hasn't forgiven me.'

'That doesn't sound like a good reason to pursue someone and try to ruin them,' Robert said thoughtfully.

'It's true that the girl died in childbirth. Wegg is convinced that I was the father — utter nonsense, of course. He's an idiot, but a dangerous one.'

'It wasn't true, was it?' Constance asked anxiously. 'I must know.'

'You know me better than that, my dear. Would I treat a woman in that way? Have I ever behaved badly to you?'

Constance shook her head. 'No, Duke, of course not.'

'I'm glad we have that settled.' Duke tossed back the remains of his drink. 'Thanks to Wegg's interference I have to leave immediately, but you'll be safe here. I've put money in the bank to

151

keep you in comfort for the foreseeable future.'

'No, you don't, Duke,' Constance said angrily. 'You're not abandoning me to live alone in this creepy château. I'm coming with you.'

'You'll have Nettie to keep you company,' Duke said hopefully.

'You'll look after each other.' Robert slipped his arm around Nettie's shoulders. 'I have to go as well, my dear. I hope you understand.'

'I agree with Constance,' Nettie said firmly. 'You got yourselves into trouble, but it affects us also. We're both coming with you.'

'But, Nettie, we don't know where we're going. It might be dangerous.'

'I've accompanied you on all your flights from angry creditors and landlords. I'm not going to let you abandon me now, Pa.'

Aristide sank down on the nearest chair. 'Thanks to the duke I am a free man and my barge is at your disposal, although it will be rather crowded.' He looked from one to the other, grinning widely. 'It is the least I can do for my friends who have stood by me in my time of trouble.'

'Thank you, Aristide.' Duke moved to a side table and picked up a decanter. 'You're very kind, but I think we might be caught too easily should we take up your offer.' He poured a measure of brandy for each and handed them round. 'We'll leave immediately. Pack your bags, taking necessities only,' he added, staring pointedly at Constance.

'You mean I can come with you?' she asked eagerly.

'I don't seem to have much choice.' Duke smiled and raised his glass. 'We're all in this together, thanks to Wegg and a quirk of fate.'

'Here's to freedom.' Byron joined in the toast. 'I don't know where you're going, Duke, but I'm headed for Spain.'

'Are you sure that's where your mother is living now?' Nettie asked anxiously.

'It's all I have to go on, but find her I will.' Byron reached out to take her hand in his. 'Will you come with me, Nettie?'

9

The idea of travelling to Spain fired Nettie's imagination. Duke decided that it was an ideal place to lie low, and he was convinced that the Metropolitan Police would not venture that far. Virtually penniless and dependent on Duke's charity, Robert was not in a position to argue, and Constance seemed eager to move on.

The only person who had been openly disappointed by Duke's decision was Aristide, who said that he could not simply abandon his barge and the people who depended upon him. He grew quite tearful when Nettie said goodbye and kissed him on the cheek. Robert slapped him on the back, promising to return to Paris one day in the not-too-distant future, when they would share a bottle of cognac in the bargees' café. Byron added his thanks and they piled into Duke's carriage. Nettie leaned out of the window, waving until Aristide disappeared from view, and she wiped away a tear. Aristide had been good to them and she would miss him, but now they were heading back to Paris and the start of yet another long train journey.

★ ★ ★

Despite the fact that they were supposed to be keeping a low profile, Duke insisted on travelling first class. At the start they were all tense and

154

found it difficult to relax, but gradually the mood changed and their journey took on the spirit of a holiday rather than a desperate escape from the law. Nettie sat in the corner of the railway carriage and watched the countryside flash past the windows with a feeling of relief. Every mile travelled put more distance between them and the police, and Wegg in particular. She could only hope that, having done his worst, he had returned to England and was pursuing another victim.

The sky darkened and Nettie slept fitfully, her head resting against Byron's shoulder. The clickety-clack of the iron wheels drummed in her ears even as she slumbered, and in her dreams she was flying low over the railway tracks like a bird. She awakened at first light and her whole body was cramped and aching, but it was the beginning of a new day and the start of an adventure into the unknown. She experienced a *frisson* of excitement: anything could happen.

They changed trains at Avignon and began the last leg of their journey to Perpignan. After almost twenty-four hours of rail travel it was a relief to be back on solid ground. Duke booked them into a small hotel in the town, and that night they had a decent meal followed by a bath in a tin tub. Constance demanded to go first, and Nettie waited patiently for her turn. Tomorrow they would set off once again and the long and arduous journey would continue.

★ ★ ★

Duke had warned them that it was going to be hard going, and it was. He had hired a guide and horses to take them over the Pyrenees into Spain, but Nettie and Constance were not experienced riders and their progress was slow. Robert had once owned a horse and knew how to ride, but Byron had only ever travelled by omnibus or hansom cab, and he struggled at first to control his mount. They stayed at small wayside inns and on one occasion they had to sleep in a goatherd's hut, but after several days of constant travel, they reached the small coastal town where Byron's mother was said to reside.

Tired, dusty and with every muscle in her body aching from the long ride over rough terrain, Nettie shielded her eyes against the brilliant light and the dazzling reflection of the sun on the ultramarine sea, studded with tiny islands. Nets were laid out to dry on the silver sand, and fishing boats bobbed gently at anchor. It was mid-afternoon, the small town seemed to drowse in the heat, and there was no sound apart from the gentle lapping of the waves on the shore. It was all so different from the greyness and general filth that clad the streets of Covent Garden. The town square was quaint and quiet at this time of day. Bougainvillaea tumbled down the stark white walls of the civil offices in a vivid splash of purple blossom. An old man slept on a wooden bench beneath a stand of trees, his hat tipped over his face, his gnarled hands resting on his faded smock, and his mongrel dog curled up at his feet.

Nettie felt as though she had been transported

to another world far removed from the dusty streets of London or Paris. Here, in this quiet coastal town, the road and beach merged into one long strip of silver sand, and a narrow side street wandered up the hillside and disappeared into a pine forest. Directly ahead was a terrace of stone cottages, an inn and a small white church with a bell tower. Duke left them to make enquiries at the inn and returned moments later with the news that he had booked the only three rooms available.

'I'll have the smallest one,' he said importantly. 'Robert, you and Byron will have to share.'

Robert shrugged. 'I hope you won't snore as you did on the train, Byron.'

'I can't promise anything.' Byron slid from the saddle and stretched, yawning. 'I don't care where I lay my head, just as long as it's clean and reasonably comfortable.'

'I'm sure you won't mind sharing with Nettie,' Duke said, giving Constance an encouraging smile. 'You must be exhausted, both of you.'

'I'm not too tired. I was just beginning to feel at home in the saddle.' Nettie dismounted and stroked the horse's neck, and the animal nuzzled her affectionately. 'We've become good friends, haven't we, boy?'

'I'm so stiff I can hardly move.' Constance held her arms out and Duke lifted her to the ground.

'I can't guarantee a warm bath, but the rooms are clean.' Duke handed the reins to a young boy who had emerged from the stables at the side of the inn. 'They don't speak English or French, but the landlord seems a friendly sort of fellow.'

'I don't know how I'm going to find my mother if no one can understand me.' Byron surrendered his horse to the boy, who had summoned a friend to help him lead all the animals to the stables.

Nettie glanced round at the sound of footsteps and was surprised to see a priest running towards them with his soutane flapping around his skinny ankles. He was waving frantically with one hand and holding on to his biretta with the other.

'*Hola*,' he cried breathlessly. 'They tell me you are English.'

Duke welcomed him with a smile. 'Did the angels send you here, Father?'

The priest grinned and shook his head. 'This is a very small town. We do not get visitors very often.'

'But you speak excellent English,' Nettie said, eagerly. 'How fortunate for us.'

'I studied at a seminary in Surrey for a year. I do not very often get the chance to use my language skills. I am Father Ignatius.' He shook Duke's hand.

'Marmaduke Dexter,' Duke said solemnly, 'and this lady is my wife, Constance. Miss Carroll is my wife's companion, and this gentleman is Miss Carroll's father.' Duke beckoned to Byron. 'And this young man is the reason for our visit to your town, Byron Horton. He has reason to believe that his mother is living here.'

'My mother is Lisette Horton,' Byron said

eagerly. 'But she might be using her maiden name, Joubert.'

Father Ignatius eyed him curiously. 'We have a French lady living in the castle, but she is Condesa Talavera, and you are English.'

'My mother is French. My father was English.'

'She's a *condesa*,' Nettie said slowly. 'Does that mean countess?'

Constance clapped her hands. 'How exciting. We must visit this lady, Byron.'

'You are correct,' Father Ignatius said solemnly. 'The French lady married the late *conde* and came to live in the castle many years ago.'

'Do you know any more about her, Father?' Byron was clearly moved and Nettie slipped her hand into his, giving it a gentle squeeze.

'The *condesa* is something of a mystery. I know no more about her past.'

'How wonderful if it were true and she is your mother, Byron,' Nettie said enthusiastically. 'You have to see her and find out.'

'The *condesa* lives alone in the castle, apart from the servants, of course, and she has many visitors,' Father Ignatius said importantly. 'The *conde* died a year or so ago, but we seldom see the lady in the village, or,' he added darkly, 'at Mass.'

'I've come a long way to find my mother. Where is this castle?'

'High up on the rock, overlooking the sea.' Father Ignatius waved his hand to encompass a large area of the pine-clad cliffs. A beautiful but lonely place.'

'How would I get there?' Byron asked eagerly.

'You would need a guide. It could be arranged, but you look weary. Perhaps a rest before you travel on.' Father Ignatius smiled benevolently at Byron before turning his attention to Duke. 'I will be pleased to act as your interpreter. Our church is sadly in need of repair,' he added pointedly.

Duke nodded and put his hand in his pocket. 'A worthy cause, Father. Will you accept French francs?'

'The Lord is not particular,' Father Ignatius said, chuckling. 'We are quite near the border, which has caused conflict in the past, but not today. Shall we go into the inn? I have worked up quite a thirst, as you English say.'

He strode off without waiting for an answer, his sandalled feet sending up eddies of dust and sand as he headed towards the inn, Duke and Constance following in his wake and Robert not far behind them.

Nettie fell into step beside Byron. 'Are you all right? You're very quiet.'

'I don't know how I feel,' he said softly. 'None of this seems real.'

'What will you do now?'

'The priest said he could find a guide. I'd like to go as early as possible tomorrow.'

'Can I come with you?' Nettie asked tentatively. 'I won't be offended if you'd rather see her on your own.'

'I'd be grateful for your company. I might not know what to say when I meet her for the first time.'

'That's not like you, Byron Horton. You've never been at a loss for words since I've known you.'

Robert beckoned to them from the inn doorway. 'Come on, you two. Stop gossiping and let's sort out our accommodation. I'm afraid Duke will put us in the cow shed if it means he has a better room.'

'Constance will make sure we're comfortable. She knows how to handle Duke.'

Byron hesitated on the doorstep. 'Why is she sharing with you, Nettie? Duke and she are married, aren't they?'

Nettie glanced over his shoulder, hoping that no one had heard. 'I'll explain later. It's a delicate matter, so please don't say anything to Constance.'

'As if I would.' Byron stood aside to allow her to enter first. 'Always a gentleman, Nettie. You should know that.'

Nettie smiled as she walked past him, but she came to a halt as her eyes grew accustomed to the dim light. The shutters were closed in an attempt to keep the large room cool, and gradually she could make out several tables, laid with white cloths, a bar lined with bottles of wines and spirits and a wooden staircase that curved up to the first floor with a galleried landing. Father Ignatius had already taken a seat at the bar, together with Duke, and Robert hovered expectantly as the landlord filled their glasses with wine.

'I want to go to my room, Duke,' Constance said plaintively. 'I need a bath. I suppose they have tubs here, or do they bathe in the sea?'

'The Catalans are a civilised people,' Father Ignatius said huffily. 'You will find them eager to please you.' He snapped his fingers and a young maidservant hurried to his side. He rattled off instructions and the maid beckoned to Constance.

'Come with me, Nettie,' Constance whispered. 'I don't trust these foreigners.'

'I expect the maid feels the same as you,' Nettie said, laughing. 'All right, I'm coming,' she added hastily as she followed them upstairs.

Their room was bright and airy with a view of the bay. A salty breeze ruffled the net curtains and fluttered the white cotton coverlet on the double bed.

'It looks like we'll have to share,' Nettie said in a low voice.

Constance slumped down on the bed. 'I don't care. I think I could sleep on a bed of nails I'm so tired. But I would like a bath.'

The maid said something unintelligible and hurried from the room. She returned moments later dragging a large wooden tub, which she left in the middle of the floor, explaining with an elaborate mime that she was going to fetch water. Nettie went to sit by the window, gazing at the view in wonder. The sea was purple at the horizon fading through shades of ultramarine to turquoise, and the sun shone from an azure sky. Her only previous experience of visiting the coast, apart from her brief time in Dover and Cherbourg, had been many years ago when her father took her to Southend. It had been winter then, and the North Sea had been uniformly grey, merging with dark cumulus clouds at the horizon. This was another world and Nettie was entranced, but Constance seemed oblivious to her surroundings. She stretched out on the coverlet, ignoring the maid, who hurried in with a pail of water and slopped it into the tub before rushing off to fetch a refill.

'The bath will be cold at this rate,' Constance said with a sigh. 'But at least I can wash off the dust. You may have the water after me, Nettie.'

'I feel like running into the sea,' Nettie said, smiling. 'It looks so beautiful and inviting. I wish I could swim.'

'If we're to stay here for any length of time you might be able to learn. I prefer to stay on dry land, myself.' Constance shifted about on the bed, pulling a face. 'This mattress is stuffed with hay or something similar. Duke will have to find us a proper house soon, or I'll want to know the reason why.'

'I'm sure he will, especially now he has Father Ignatius to interpret for him. The old priest probably knows everyone for miles around.'

'I wish the maid would hurry up,' Constance said gloomily. 'I want to get undressed and take my stays off. It's so hot I can hardly breathe.' She lowered her voice, glancing at the door as if expecting the maid to burst into the room. 'I don't think that girl was wearing corsets. Wouldn't it be wonderful to be like that? Just imagine being able to breathe deeply and to eat a meal without feeling faint.'

'Maybe we'll start a new fashion.' Nettie rose

to her feet. 'I can hear the maid coming. Let me help you to undress and then it's my turn. I'm so hot and sticky I feel as if I'm melting.'

The maid was red in the face and perspiring freely when she arrived with the last bucket of water, which she emptied carefully. Constance waited until she had left the room before climbing into the tub and lowering herself to a sitting position.

'That's better,' she said, closing her eyes. 'I'll just wash my hair and then you can have your turn, Nettie.' She curled up and ducked her head beneath the water, and Nettie passed her the cake of lye soap.

'You don't want to get suds in your eyes, Constance. Keep them tight shut and I'll rinse the soap off your hair.'

'It's all right, just pass me a towel.' Constance ducked her head beneath the water before rising to her feet. She grabbed the towel from Nettie and, dripping water on the floorboards, she padded over to the window seat.

Nettie slipped off her gown and undergarments and stepped into the tub. The water was cooling rapidly and she spent as little time as possible over washing, but she felt refreshed and reasonably clean when she stepped out and dried herself on a coarse huckaback towel.

Constance was lying on the bed, wearing only a thin silk wrap, and a gentle snore confirmed that she was sound asleep. Nettie went to sit by the open window, combing her hair and allowing it to dry in the warmth of the sun. It was too late in the day to think about travelling on, but tomorrow they would go to the castle on the cliff and find out if the mysterious *condesa* was Byron's long-lost mother.

★ ★ ★

There was much discussion over breakfast next morning, but in the end it was decided that they would all accompany Byron to the castle, and Duke ordered their horses to be saddled. Father Ignatius arrived on a stocky mountain pony, together with a man whom he introduced as Pedro, their guide, and they set off for the long ride into the forest. It was still early morning and the air was fresh with the resinous scent of pine trees as the narrow, tortuous lane climbed to the top of the cliffs. It was cool in the shade, but the heat was intense when they reached the summit and found themselves outside tall wrought-iron gates.

Pedro dismounted and tugged a chain, which set a bell clanging so loudly that Nettie put her hands over her ears, but it had the desired effect and a man emerged from the gatehouse. After a brief conversation, the gatekeeper set off along a dusty avenue that ended with another pair of gates, behind which the stone walls of the castle gleamed like silver in the sunlight.

Pedro muttered something to Father Ignatius, who translated eagerly. 'Pedro said that his cousin Mateo, the gatekeeper, has gone to find out if we will be admitted.'

Nettie had the feeling that Father Ignatius was enjoying the drama of the occasion, but she sat back to await events. Byron had said little that morning, but she felt the tension building up in him, and she wished she could do something other than offer mute sympathy.

'What will you do if she isn't your mother, Byron?' Constance demanded impatiently.

'Let's wait and see, shall we?' Robert said sharply. 'No point surmising, Constance.'

'It's a perfectly reasonable question.' Constance urged her horse to move closer to Nettie's mount. 'It's all very well coming to a place like this, but what will we do here? How will we live?'

'That's for me to worry about. You needn't concern yourself with such matters, Connie.' Duke smiled condescendingly and Constance's cheeks reddened.

Nettie glared at Duke, irritated by his attitude. 'I think it matters to each of us. We're not just part of your entourage, Duke. You may be the one with the money, but there's no reason why Pa has to remain with you. In fact, we'd probably be better off on our own.'

Duke's eyes narrowed and his lips tightened. 'And how would you live? Tell me that. A second-rate artist fleeing from the English police, and a girl whose only asset is a pretty face and a neat figure.'

'Hold on, Duke.' Byron wheeled his horse round so that he faced Duke. 'That was uncalled for. Leave Nettie out of this.'

'I'm not a second-rate artist,' Robert protested. 'You made a lot of money from selling my original works, Duke. Admit it! And if I'd been aware that you were passing my copies off as

166

originals I would have refused to work for you.'

Duke curled his lip. 'You must have had your suspicions, Robert. I can't believe you're that naïve, or are you terminally stupid?'

Pedro leaned against the gates, looking from one to the other as he rolled a cigarette and held it between his lips while he struck a match on the sole of his boot. He muttered something under his breath and exhaled a plume of blue smoke into the still air.

Father Ignatius held up his hands. 'Gentlemen, please. This is not the time for an argument. You need to talk your problems over in a civilised manner, but not here and certainly not now.'

'Look,' Constance said urgently. 'The gatekeeper is coming back. I hope he'll let us in. I really want to see inside the castle.'

Nettie reached out to pat Byron on the shoulder. 'Fingers crossed.'

He gave her a half-smile in return, but she could tell from the rigidity of his spine to the white lines at the corners of his mouth that he was desperate to learn the truth, and yet afraid of the answers he might find within the walls of the stone fortress.

Pedro took a last puff on his cigarette before tossing it to the ground. '*Hola, Mateo.*'

The gatekeeper produced a ring heavy with large iron keys and unlocked the gates, which he opened wide enough to allow them all to enter. They rode slowly along the avenue and, at Pedro's command, they dismounted outside the second set of gates, which were opened by a

167

couple of male servants, who took their horses across a cobbled courtyard to a stable block.

The small party were left to stand and stare at the crenellated building, which looked to Nettie as if it had been built in the time of the Crusaders, and, as if reading her thoughts, this was confirmed by Father Ignatius.

'Castillo Talavera was built by a member of the Knights Templar in the twelfth century,' he announced grandly. 'The Crusades had ended, but the Templars continued to fight for what they believed in. The castle has seen many bloody battles, murders and struggles for power within the family. Some say it is haunted, and very few of the villagers ever come here.'

'Very interesting,' Duke said in a bored voice. 'I take it that the lady of the house is willing to grant you an audience, Byron. Good luck, my boy.'

'Yes,' Robert added hastily. 'I hope this turns out well for you.'

Byron opened his mouth to reply but at that moment the studded oak door was opened by a manservant resplendent in knee breeches and a tail-coat frogged with tarnished gold braid.

'The *condesa* welcomes you to the castle,' he said in halting English. 'Please to come this way.'

Nettie grasped Byron's hand. 'Good luck,' she whispered, as they followed the servant into a large, echoing stone entrance hall, which was reminiscent of the château, except that it was cool and dry and did not reek of damp and mildew. The walls were hung with old-fashioned weapons, shields and banners, more reminiscent of a military museum than a home, but the servant marched on and they all trooped after him, with Father Ignatius at the fore.

Nettie had no preconceived notion of what the interior would be like, although having entered the fortress she would not have been surprised had the rest of the building been as grim and forbidding as the ante-chamber. It came as a pleasant surprise when the long, dark corridor opened out into an inner hall giving the impression that they had stepped into another century. The walls were painted a delicate shade of green with panels outlined in ornate plasterwork in which hung gilt-framed oil paintings. There were portraits — presumably of the Talavera family — going through the centuries, landscapes and seascapes, all of which attracted Robert and Duke, who broke away from the party to examine them more closely.

The servant came to a halt beside an elaborately carved plant stand, which supported a silver urn overflowing with roses, lilies and trailing greenery. He made an announcement, which Father Ignatius repeated in English.

'You will all please wait here, except for Mr Horton. He is to come with me.'

'I want Nettie to accompany me,' Byron said hastily. 'Tell him that, please, Father.'

Father Ignatius translated once again and after a brief discussion he turned to Byron and nodded. 'You may take one person with you.'

Nettie squeezed Byron's fingers. 'Now for it. I hope the *condesa* is your mother, I really do.'

Byron said nothing, but his hand was

169

trembling and she held on tightly, willing everything to turn out as he had hoped. They followed the servant through double doors into a wider passage, lit by candles in wall sconces, and their feet sunk into the thick carpet. At the end of the corridor the servant flung open another pair of double doors and light flooded in from a series of windows overlooking the sea. The air was scented and fresh, and the large room was furnished with beautiful antique sofas, chairs and tables. Tall mirrors reflected the light and there were numerous vases filled with flowers. Nettie let go of Byron's hand as she gazed round in wonder. It was by far the most beautiful room she had ever seen, and for a moment she forgot why they had come to this extraordinary residence. It was not until a voice from a chaise longue set by an open window brought her back to reality and she found herself staring at the woman who rose to her feet in a swish of silk, sending a waft of expensive perfume across the room. She dismissed the servant with a wave of her hand and beckoned to Byron.

Nettie gazed at her in astonishment. The motherly figure she had imagined was so far from the truth that she would never have thought this exotic beauty could be old enough to have a son in his early twenties, and then it occurred to her that perhaps this was not the woman who had abandoned her child. Maybe their journey was in vain and Byron was going to suffer disappointment and humiliation. Nettie clutched her hands at her sides, hardly daring to breathe.

10

'Welcome to the Castillo Talavera.' The *condesa*'s voice was deep, mellifluous and strongly accented. She eyed Byron curiously. 'You are very like your father.'

Nettie stifled a gasp of dismay. It was hardly the warmest welcome from a mother to the young man whom she had abandoned in childhood. She moved closer to Byron, willing him to be strong, but he seemed to have his emotions under control as he bowed over the *condesa*'s outstretched hand.

'Thank you for seeing me,' he said humbly.

'What brings you here, Byron?'

'I wanted to find out why you abandoned me, Mother.'

'I have no excuse to offer, except that you were better off without me.'

Byron shook his head, apparently lost for words.

'That was unkind, Condesa,' Nettie said angrily. 'Byron has travelled a long way to find you.'

'Won't you introduce me to your companion?' the *condesa* said silkily.

Nettie could see that Byron was struggling and she stepped forward. 'My name is Henrietta Carroll, but my friends call me Nettie.'

'How do you do, Nettie Carroll?'

'How do you do, Condesa?'

The *condesa*'s laugh was deep and throaty.

'Oh, please, let's not be so formal. My name is Lisette. Only the servants and the fawning priest call me Condesa.' She shot a sideways glance at Byron. 'You may also call me Lisette. I haven't been a mother to you in the true sense of the word — it isn't in my nature — but perhaps we might be friends now that you're a grown man.'

Byron nodded mutely.

Lisette sank elegantly onto the chaise longue, her luminous brown eyes sparkling with amusement. 'Come now, Byron. You sought me out. What did you expect?'

'I don't know exactly. Although I did want to ask why you left me with my father. How could you do that?'

'Your father is a good man, but dull. He bored me.' Lisette reached for an onyx box, flicked it open and extracted a cigarillo, which she lit with a match, exhaling with obvious enjoyment. 'Look at me closely. Can you imagine me with small children, let alone a fractious three-year-old?'

'Perhaps I should leave you two to talk,' Nettie suggested hastily.

'No,' Byron said firmly. 'I want you to stay. It seems that I wasted my time coming here.'

'I'm sorry you're disappointed.' Lisette reclined against satin cushions. 'But as you have come all the way from England to find me, it seems a pity to leave right away.'

'We came from France. It was your brother, Jean, who told me where to find you.'

'Jean was the best in our family. He was the only one who didn't try to change me. How is he?'

172

'He's well.'

'I'm glad, but as to the rest of my relations, they can rot in hell, as far as I'm concerned.' Lisette's frown was replaced by a bright smile. 'Now, sit down and tell me all about yourself, Byron. You, too, Nettie Carroll. I think you will turn out to be an interesting young woman, and I am a good judge of character. I have had to be — my life hasn't been easy.'

Nettie could see that Byron was at a loss for words and she sat down, fixing Lisette with a steady look. 'I think your son is entitled to know why you deserted him.'

'What you really want to know is how I met Talavera and became the *condesa*. Am I correct?' Lisette's fine brown eyes gleamed like topaz and her full lips curled into a wry smile.

Despite her reservations Nettie found herself warming to her. 'Yes, I suppose it is. Did you return to your family when you left London?'

'I knew that they wouldn't welcome me, and so I went straight to Paris, and took a job as a waitress in a café where I sang to entertain the customers. A theatrical impresario happened to hear me one evening, and that was the beginning of my career. Talavera saw me on stage and that was how we met.' Lisette stubbed out her cigarillo. 'We were married shortly afterwards.'

'But you were still married to my father,' Byron said angrily.

'Is he well? For all I said, Geoffrey is a good man, too good for me.'

'He died some time ago.'

'I'm sorry for your loss, Byron.'

173

'Is that all you can say?'

'Your father deserved better than me. I was hoping he might have met and married someone else.'

'He was faithful to you until the end, Mother.'

'Lisette,' she said firmly. 'That's enough about me for now. Tell me about yourself, and if you are going to be a sulky boy, then I'm sure Nettie will oblige.'

Nettie rose to her feet. 'I think I ought to leave you two to talk.'

'I've heard enough,' Byron said, sighing. 'I'm sorry to have bothered you, Condesa. I can't call you Lisette. It doesn't seem appropriate.'

Lisette threw back her head and laughed. 'You are so like your papa, Byron. You and I will converse later, but I would like to meet the people who accompanied you. My servant tells me that one of them is a duke.'

'Not a duke as such,' Byron said with a glimmer of a smile. 'I'll go and fetch them and you can see for yourself.'

'No need. I have servants to do that sort of thing.' Lisette reached for a silver bell but Byron was already at the door, with Constance and the others peering over his shoulder.

'He is stubborn, like his papa,' Lisette said with a chuckle. 'You must introduce your companions, Nettie.'

The words had barely left her lips when the rest of the party entered the room. Lisette beckoned to Constance, who was looking round the elegant room with a rapt expression. 'You, young lady. Who are you?'

Constance took a step forward, but Duke moved quickly to stand between them.

'Condesa, this is such a privilege,' Duke said, raising Lisette's hand to his lips. 'I am Marmaduke Dexter, dealer in fine art, a very successful one, I might add in all humility, and this lady is my wife, Constance.'

'Can she not speak for herself, Marmaduke?'

'My friends call me Duke, Condesa.'

'Why do Englishmen think that women lose their ability to speak for themselves the moment the band of gold goes on their finger?' Lisette demanded. 'I was not speaking to you, Marmaduke. I addressed myself to the beautiful young lady.'

'I have a voice,' Constance said boldly. 'My name is Constance, and I'm delighted to make your acquaintance, Condesa. You have a beautiful home.'

'It's taken years to make it so, but thank you, Constance. We will have a chance to talk later.' Lisette turned her attention to Robert. 'You must be Nettie's father. I see the likeness.'

'Robert is a fine artist,' Duke said determinedly. 'I discovered him and made him famous.'

Nettie spun round to face him. 'That's not true. Pa was well known before he became entangled with you and your crooked schemes.'

'How delightful! Do I sense discord amongst your party, Byron?' Lisette looked from one to the other with an expectant smile. 'This promises to be most entertaining.'

'It is very good of you to see us, Condesa,'

Father Ignatius pushed past Robert in an attempt to get closer to their hostess.

'I'm sure you have better things to do, Father,' Lisette said sweetly. 'You will be needed elsewhere.'

Father Ignatius opened his mouth as if to protest, but Lisette was too quick for him. She rang the silver bell and the door opened so promptly that Nettie suspected the servant had been listening at the keyhole.

'Thank you, Father,' Lisette said firmly. 'We will not be needing your services from now on. Diego will show you out.'

Father Ignatius glanced at Diego's set expression and bowed. 'I hope to see you at Mass, Condesa.'

She inclined her head slightly and turned away, leaving the priest little option other than to shuffle dejectedly from the room. There was an awkward silence and Nettie glanced anxiously at Byron, who was staring at his mother with a bemused frown. Then, before anyone could think of a suitable subject for discussion, the door burst open and a tall, handsome young man strolled into the room. He came to a halt, staring at Nettie with a bemused expression.

'Good grief. I'm sure I know that face. We've met before, haven't we?'

Nettie recognised him instantly, but Lisette spoke before she had a chance to answer his question.

'Percy!' Lisette said crossly. 'What are you doing here?'

'I'm sorry, Ma. There was no way of letting

you know that I'd been sent down, so I thought it best to come and tell you in person.' Percy spoke with only the slightest trace of an accent.

Lisette swung her legs over the side of the chaise longue and sat up straight. 'Your timing, as ever, is perfect. What did you do this time?'

Nettie eyed the newcomer in disbelief, and a quick glance in Byron's direction confirmed her suspicions.

'You were in the Gaiety Restaurant,' Byron said slowly.

'I don't remember you, but who could forget such a lovely young lady?' Percy bowed to Nettie, who was seized with the desire to laugh.

Lisette rose from the chaise longue in a rustle of silk. She embraced the young man and then slapped his face. A startled gasp echoed round the room, and she laughed.

'Why am I not surprised to hear that you were dining out in London when you should have been at your studies in Cambridge?'

'A chap must have some recreation, Ma. The question is, why are these people here? Who are you?'

Lisette slipped her arm around his waist. 'This is a day for surprises. You, my boy, have terrible timing. I don't know why you were sent down, but now you are here you might as well meet Byron.' She held her hand out to Byron. 'This bad fellow is your brother, Percy.'

Byron and Percy eyed each other suspiciously.

'I don't understand,' Byron said slowly.

'I never knew who my father was,' Percy added, frowning. 'What are you saying, Ma?'

'I wish you wouldn't use that awful word. I tried to teach you to say *maman* but you were your father's son, stubborn and self-willed.'

'So who are you?' Percy demanded, glaring at Byron. 'Are you really my brother?'

Byron shook his head. 'I don't know. I've only just found my mother, and now it seems I have a brother who is reluctant to acknowledge me.'

'You just need time to get to know each other,' Nettie said hastily. She held her hand out to Percy. 'I'm Nettie. How do you do?'

A slow smile spread across Percy's handsome features, and he kissed Nettie's hand. 'How do you do, Miss Nettie?'

Constance slipped in between them, smiling up at Percy. 'My name is Constance. How exciting to find that Byron has a brother who lives in a castle.'

'And I'm Constance's husband,' Duke said firmly. 'I'm Marmaduke Dexter, art dealer, and my friend Robert Carroll, Nettie's father, is a well-known artist.'

Robert stepped forward to shake Percy's hand. 'How do you do?'

'Really, this is becoming tedious.' Lisette moved to a side table and began filling glasses from a carafe of red wine. 'Do help yourselves. This isn't the time to bring the servants into our private affairs. Heaven knows, my reputation is already in shreds locally. I don't need to make matters worse.' She took a sip of wine and resumed her seat. 'You were both born in wedlock, if that's what's worrying you boys. I left Horton before I knew that I had conceived

178

again, and he never knew he had a second son. No one knew, except Talavera and now he's dead. I am twice widowed.'

'You were married to him bigamously,' Byron said angrily. 'My father was still alive.'

'It hardly matters now. It's all in the past, anyway.' Lisette drank deeply. 'Do please join me in raising a glass to my boys. They will get used to each other, or not, as the case may be.'

Percy handed the wine round. 'At least finding her firstborn has taken Ma's attention away from me,' he said in a low voice as he gave Nettie a glass. 'Do you know my brother well?'

'We're friends. I hope you aren't going to make trouble for him.'

'Me?' Percy said with mock humility. 'As if I would.'

'I don't know you, but I think you are as unpredictable as your mother. Byron is a good man and all he wanted was to discover why his mother abandoned him.'

'Don't look at me like that,' Percy said, grinning. 'It wasn't my fault. I wasn't even born.'

'You're obviously her darling boy; don't use that against Byron. That's all I'm saying.'

Constance moved closer. 'What are you two whispering about? I think this is all so thrilling.' She put her head on one side, giving Percy a calculating look. 'Why were you sent down? What did you do?'

'I set fire to the cricket pavilion, quite by accident, you must understand. I was enjoying a quiet drink and smoking a cheroot when my tutor came looking for me. I thought I'd put the wretched weed out, but it transpired that I was mistaken. The wooden building burned to the ground.'

Nettie stifled a giggle but Constance threw her head back and laughed, earning a frown from Duke.

'Won't you share the joke?' He moved swiftly to her side, and laid his hand on her arm in a possessive gesture.

Constance shook free from his grasp. 'It was nothing, Duke. Go away and leave me alone.'

'Stop acting like a spoiled child.' Duke strolled off to join Robert, who was seated beside Lisette, listening to her with a rapt expression on his face.

'Do I detect a marital rift, Mrs Dexter?' Percy asked with a mischievous grin.

Constance shot him a sideways glance. 'Would you care if that was the case?'

'What were you studying at the university?' Nettie said, changing the subject hastily. It was obvious that there was mutual attraction between Constance and Percy, and Duke was not amused.

'Dashed if I know,' Percy said, chuckling. 'I'm not a good student, although I excel at fencing, shooting and riding. The English appreciate a good sportsman.'

Constance smiled up at him. 'Why didn't your mother send you to study in France?'

'Perhaps she thought Cambridge was far enough away to keep me out of trouble. I knew that my father was English, but she omitted to mention her other son.' Percy glanced at Byron, who had come to join them. 'Who would have thought it, brother?'

'Who indeed?' Byron said stiffly. 'It seems that neither of us knew that the other existed.'

They turned their heads as one, staring at their mother, who was in animated conversation with Robert and Duke.

'Ma does exactly as she pleases.' Percy slapped Byron on the back. 'Welcome to Castillo Talavera, brother.'

Nettie grasped Constance by the sleeve. 'Perhaps we should let them get to know each other.'

'There'll be plenty of time for that,' Percy said cheerfully. 'I, for one, am delighted to find I have a brother. What about you, old boy?'

Byron cleared his throat. 'I'm just getting over the shock.'

'You just need to get to know us. Anyway, has Ma invited you all to stay? We've got dozens of rooms and the servants laze about, for the most part, unless Ma has one of her parties that go on for days and nights.'

Nettie could see that Byron was struggling with a maelstrom of emotions. 'We couldn't impose on her like that,' she said hastily. 'There are too many of us and we're quite comfortable at the inn.' She could see that Duke was about to interject, but Percy had taken over the conversation.

'Nonsense,' he said airily. 'Ma loves company.' He leaned over to kiss his mother's soft cheek. 'I know I'm not your favourite son at the moment, Maman, but I'd like to get to know my brother. I

181

think we should invite him and his friends to stay for a while.'

Lisette took a sip of wine. 'Excellent idea, Percy. You are all welcome. I'm sure you will get on splendidly with my other guests.'

'I hope there aren't too many of them,' Percy said resignedly. 'Who have we here now?'

'The usual crowd.' Lisette turned to Duke. 'I assume you must be staying at the local inn as it's the only one within miles.'

Duke nodded. 'We are, but I wouldn't want to put you to any trouble, Condesa.'

'Lisette,' she said, smiling. 'I'll ask Mateo to have your luggage brought here.'

'But we need to pay for our accommodation.' Robert glanced anxiously at Duke. 'You have the money.'

'Don't worry about that. It will be taken care of.' Lisette rang the bell and, as before, Diego answered promptly. She sent him off with such a long list of instructions that Nettie wondered if the poor man would remember half of them.

'Excellent,' Percy said, gleefully. 'Now I suggest I might take the young ladies on a tour of the old ruin. Sorry, Ma. I mean the Castillo Talavera.'

'Stop interfering, Percy.' Lisette spoke severely, but her eyes were smiling. 'Just remember that luncheon will be served in half an hour.' She held her empty wine glass up for Duke to refresh from the carafe he had in his hand. 'You may go with them, if you wish, Duke.'

He inclined his head. 'I would prefer to stay and talk to you, Condesa — I mean, Lisette.'

Robert hesitated and Nettie could see that her father was torn between wanting to explore the castle and wishing to remain with the fascinating countess. He cast a withering glance in Duke's direction. 'I'll stay here, but perhaps you ought to accompany your wife, Duke.'

'No need. I'll look after her.' Percy proffered an arm to Constance. 'I can't pretend to be good at the history of the old pile, but I can show you the wonderful view from the battlements.'

'I have no head for heights,' Constance said coyly. 'I will have to hold on tight to you.'

'How long have you been married, Duke?' Lisette asked drily. 'Your wife is very young, is she not?'

Nettie did not hear his reply, but as she looked up at Byron she could see that he was thinking along the same lines. 'This should be interesting,' she said softly as they followed Percy and Constance from the room. 'Constance has led such a sheltered life, until now.'

'Duke will get his comeuppance one day,' Byron said, chuckling. 'He's spent his life swindling people out of their money, but I wouldn't be surprised if Constance got the better of him.'

'Do you really think so?'

'I think that young lady has a will of her own.'

'Come on, you two,' Percy called over his shoulder. 'Keep up, or you'll find yourself lost in the maze of passageways.'

Nettie and Byron quickened their pace, taking care not to fall behind. As Percy had indicated, there were parts of the building that had yet to be renovated, but these seemed to be uninhabited by anyone or anything other than bats, which hung from the rafters in gloomy silence. Nettie shuddered at the thought of what it must be like on the top floors after dark, and she could only hope that their rooms would be in the comfortably furnished and well-decorated living accommodation. As they climbed towards the ramparts she could imagine what it must have been like centuries ago when the occupants were at odds with their neighbours. But when they reached the top and looked over the parapet, the view was even more stunning than it had been from the inn. Constance forgot that she was afraid of heights and leaned over, exclaiming loudly with Percy holding on to her hand. They were both laughing so much that it was infectious and Nettie found herself joining in, even though she had no idea what provoked such mirth.

Byron cleared his throat. 'We don't want to be late for luncheon. I think the *condesa* would be very offended if we were.'

'You're right, brother. Ma is the most easy-going woman alive, until it comes to punctuality for meals. Come along, Mrs Dexter, I'll take you back to your loving husband.'

Constance pulled a face. 'Don't call me that. My name is Constance, and my husband's interests lie purely in the art world, and making money, of course.'

For once, Percy did not seem to have anything to say, and he led them back the way they had come.

As she walked into the refurbished part of the castle Nettie felt as if she were stepping into another century, only this time they were in a wide corridor, its walls lined with oil paintings. She came to a halt in front of one she recognised as a Botticelli, and she moved closer, examining it in more detail. The truth hit her like a physical blow, and she clapped her hand over her mouth to stifle a gasp of dismay. It was a copy, a very clever one, but she remembered her father working on it for weeks. Duke had commissioned it, and her father had executed it in good faith, telling her that it was to go to a collector who adored Botticelli but could not afford an original. The tiny, heart-shaped mole on the cherub's left shoulder was an exact match to a similar birthmark she possessed. Pa had included it as a private joke, and it seemed now it might spell his downfall.

'What are you staring at?' Byron asked as he walked over to join her.

She turned with a start. 'I was just admiring the brushwork.' She could not bring herself to tell him the truth.

'Come along, you two,' Percy said cheerfully as he strolled past with Constance on his arm. 'You know what my illustrious mother said about being late for meals.'

'We're coming.' Nettie dragged herself away from the painting, but as she walked with Byron she could feel the fake Botticelli calling out to her, and it could only mean one thing — trouble.

★ ★ ★

185

The dining room was more like a banqueting hall than a cosy place where a family might sit round the table at mealtimes. Ornate metal chandeliers hung from a vaulted ceiling and the refectory table seemed to stretch into infinity as Nettie stared down its length. Lisette was holding court at the far end with Robert and Duke seated on her left, but they were not alone.

'Who is that man sitting next to your mother?' Nettie asked in a low voice.

'That is Don Julio Alvarez, my mother's lover,' Percy said casually. 'Ma collects admirers and keeps them until they bore her, then they are discarded without a thought. Don Julio has lasted longer than most.'

'Really?' Constance peered into the distance, her lips forming a perfect circle of surprise.

'Don Julio has been around off and on ever since I can remember,' Percy added, shrugging. 'Ma gets tired of him and sends him away, and then he returns and is welcomed into her bed.'

Byron shook his head. 'I don't think you ought to say things like that about our mother.'

'The English are such prudes,' Percy said, chuckling. 'I'm sorry if it offends your sense of decency, brother, but Ma doesn't abide by the rules. That's why she shuts herself away in the castle and lives in the manner of her choosing. Can you blame her?'

Lisette rose to her feet, beckoning to them. 'Stop gossiping and come and sit down. I'll make the necessary introductions later.'

'After you, ladies,' Percy said softly. 'But I

186

think you ought to sit next to your husband, *querida*. He is looking at you askance.'

Constance angled her head. '*Querida?* What does that mean?'

'It means for goodness' sake go and sit down,' Nettie whispered. 'And stop flirting with Percy. Duke looks like a thundercloud and you are married to him.'

'Poppycock,' Constance said airily. 'But I will oblige, this time. You can sit next to the *condesa*'s lover, but try not to look as though you're enjoying yourself or she might take one of those swords off the wall and run you through.' Constance marched off to sit next to her husband.

Nettie had little choice other than to take a seat next to Don Julio, who greeted her with a charming smile. 'The *condesa* tells me that you are from London,' he said in thickly accented English. 'I was there a few years ago. A fine city, but dirty.'

Nettie said the first thing that came into her head. 'The castle is very beautiful.'

'Just like its mistress,' Don Julio said gallantly. 'I think you ought to paint her, Mr Carroll,' he added, pointing his knife at Robert. 'I will commission you to do her portrait. She has the most beautiful body imaginable.'

Robert's face flooded with colour and he shot a sideways glance at Lisette. 'I would be honoured to paint such a lovely lady.'

She raised her glass to him. 'I fancy myself as Venus in the painting *Primavera*, which you will have seen in the gallery. I purchased the

Botticelli some years ago and it's my most prized possession.'

Nettie glanced anxiously at her father, but he was smiling, oblivious to the fact that one of his copies had been purchased by the *condesa*.

'It's a wonderful painting,' Robert said enthusiastically. 'I'd love to see it, Condesa.'

'And so you shall, Robert. In fact we enacted it as a tableau last Christmas.' Lisette leaned towards her lover, pouting playfully. 'I was Chloris, and you were pursuing me.'

'How could I forget? I was the Zephyr, but Percy refused to play Cupid.'

'I was never any good at all that Greek mythology stuff. Can we change the subject, Ma?' Percy said, yawning. 'Leave me out of your theatricals. I'd rather hunt wild boar than take part.'

Robert rose abruptly from the table. 'Might I see the painting, Condesa?'

'Sit down,' Duke hissed. 'You're making a fool of yourself, Robert.'

'It is a masterpiece,' Lisette said proudly, 'but it will still be there when you finish your meal, Robert.'

She turned to Don Julio with a wry smile. 'I adore artists, don't you?'

11

Nettie had lost her appetite despite the delicious food served by a small army of servants, and she could hardly wait for the meal to end before she had words with her father. She ran after him as he left the dining room, following in Lisette's wake as she announced that they would have coffee on the terrace.

'Pa, I need to speak to you.' Nettie grabbed him by the arm. 'Have you seen the painting?'

'Why are you so bothered, Nettie? I look forward to seeing the original.'

'You haven't seen it then?'

'What is all this about?'

'The Botticelli is a copy, and what's more, it's the one you did years ago.'

'Don't be silly, dear. It can't be, and even if it were — how would you know?'

'The birthmark on the cherub's shoulder,' Nettie whispered. 'I remember that.'

Robert's cheeks paled. 'It can't be. I sold it to Duke for a good price, but he wouldn't have been stupid enough to pass it off as the original.'

Nettie tightened her grasp. 'This is serious, Pa. If the *condesa* discovers that she's been cheated she'll inform the local police, and we'll be on the run again. I think we should leave right away.'

Duke swaggered past, his unsteady gait confirming that he had drunk too much of the *condesa*'s wine. 'Come along, Robert. We don't want to keep the lovely lady waiting. I could get used to living in luxury like this.'

'Wait here, Pa.' Nettie released her father and ran after Duke. She caught him up as he was about to go out onto the terrace. 'You must come with me,' she said urgently.

'What's the matter with you, Nettie?' he demanded crossly. 'Did you drink too much wine at luncheon?'

'I didn't touch a drop. Please keep your voice down and act naturally, but you must come with me now.'

Duke shrugged, giving her a tipsy smile. 'Anything to keep you happy, my dear.'

Nettie led him to the corridor where she had seen the painting. She came to a halt in front of it. 'Now, Duke. Do you recognise this?'

'Of course I do, child. It's *Primavera* by Sandro Botticelli. The *condesa* told us that she owns it, and I must say I was impressed to think she could afford such a masterpiece.'

'Examine it closely, Duke.'

'Is this some kind of game, Nettie?'

'I'm in deadly earnest.' She pointed to the cherub. 'Do you see anything unusual?'

He peered at the chubby little figure and his smile faded. 'This isn't the original.'

'I know that because of that birthmark. It was my father's little joke — he used to call me his little cherub when I was a child.'

Duke's cheeks paled and he took a step backwards. 'I sold the painting to a private buyer. This can't be the one.'

'You took advantage of my father's talent and

turned him into a criminal, just like you.'

'He's been happy to take the money without asking any questions. You, too, have benefited, so that makes you an accessory.'

'Not any more,' Nettie said firmly. 'We're going to move on. You can stay here and enjoy the *condesa*'s hospitality, if you wish.'

Nettie was about to walk away, but Duke caught her by the sleeve.

'Wait a moment. Think this through carefully, Nettie. If you stay while your father paints the *condesa*'s portrait Don Julio will pay handsomely, and you'll have the money to go where you will. Leave now and you'll be alone and penniless in a foreign country.'

Nettie regarded him with a frown. She knew that he was speaking the truth. Hitherto she had never known the identity of the people who believed that they were purchasing original works of art, but this was different; the *condesa* was a real person. She was kind and generous, and she had been cheated out of what had doubtless been a small fortune. Suddenly the murky world of the fraudster was threatening to swamp Nettie in guilt and shame.

She drew herself up to her full height. 'Perhaps it would have been better if the police had caught you both. This has got to end, Duke. I refuse to be a party to your swindles.'

'Don't be a fool,' Duke said between clenched teeth. 'If you tell the *condesa* that her painting is a copy we will all suffer, including your friend Byron. Do you want to drag him down with you, and all for the sake of your newly awakened

191

conscience? You are as guilty as the rest of us, Nettie Carroll. Make no mistake about that.'

Nettie met his fierce gaze with a toss of her head, but she knew in her heart that he was right. The deed had been done, and there was no going back. She nodded reluctantly. 'All right, Duke. I won't say anything to the condesa, but I will speak to Pa, and we'll be off as soon as he finishes the portrait. You'll never see us again.'

Nettie marched off to join the others on the terrace, leaving Duke to follow at his own pace. She was angry and distressed, but she had seen her father growing in stature after Don Julio had commissioned him to paint the condesa's portrait, and they were in desperate need of the money.

★   ★   ★

That evening Nettie was in her room overlooking the bay. It was large and airy, with floor-to-ceiling windows and a small balcony. The pastel shades of the decor emitted an aura of calm and tranquillity, and the muted watercolour paintings of flowers and rural scenes that hung on the walls added to the mood. The contrast between this elegant bedchamber and the attic room in Covent Garden could not have been greater and, not for the first time, she was amazed how quickly life could change. Even allowing for the ups and downs of living with her father, this was something completely different, and although she knew it could not last, she decided to make the most of the unashamed luxury of her surroundings. She was wondering what she was going to wear to dinner when the door burst open and Constance rushed in with an armful of garments.

'Look what I've got, Nettie,' she cried enthusiastically. 'I told the *condesa* that some of our luggage had been lost along the way. Well, it wasn't exactly a lie; I was forced to leave all my lovely gowns behind when we left in such a hurry. Lisette wants us all to wear fancy dress. Isn't that exciting?'

Nettie eyed the gauzy gowns with suspicion. 'Are those for the *Primavera* tableau?'

'Yes, of course. Lisette is going to be Venus, which I think very appropriate. I, of course, will be Chloris and you can be one of the Three Graces. There are other guests, apparently, and we'll meet them at dinner. I think it will be very jolly.'

Nettie took the gown that Constance handed to her. 'This is so flimsy you can see through it. Pa will have a fit if I wear this.'

'So will Duke, but I don't care. It's Greek mythology so it's perfectly respectable. I can't wait to see Percy's face when I walk into the dining room wearing this frock.'

'It's Duke you should worry about,' Nettie said grimly. 'He's not a man to be trifled with, Constance. I think you ought to be careful.'

'Nonsense. He says he's signed everything over to me, so I have the upper hand. I could run away and leave him with nothing.'

'You wouldn't! Would you?'

'I don't know, but it's wonderful to have a

193

feeling of power over a man. I've never had that before, and Percy is plainly smitten by my charms. I can't help it if men fall in love with me.'

'Are you sure we have to dress up?' Nettie said, changing the subject.

'The *condesa* was adamant, and I think it will be fun. Will you help me change, Nettie? I can't get used to coping without a maid?'

'Yes, of course. I never had that luxury, so I learned to do things for myself.'

'You poor thing,' Constance said sympathetically. 'Never mind, we're here now and when I get to know her better I'll ask Lisette if we could have the service of one of her maids.'

Nettie had no answer for this. It was obvious that Constance was in complete ignorance when it came to Duke's business activities.

Half an hour later they were dressed and ready to go down to dinner, but the gowns were semi-transparent and Nettie wondered what her father would say when he saw her. Constance admitted to being a little apprehensive, but was determined to show off her lovely figure and eager to pose in the tableau. They went downstairs together and were greeted by strains of music and laughter emanating from the dining room. The scent of warm pine needles met them as they entered, and it seemed that half the forest had been brought indoors to form a sylvan background for the performance.

Lisette was there already, holding court amongst a group of people who were wearing wildly differing costumes. Don Julio was at her side, dressed as a Greek peasant, and Percy was wearing a black cloak with a horned headdress, which made him look more like the Devil than the mythological god of the west wind. Byron, Robert and Duke were looking mildly embarrassed in their knee breeches worn with frilled white shirts, open to the waist. Nettie noted that Duke had a hairy chest, but Byron's body was smooth and surprisingly well muscled. She averted her gaze, blushing.

Duke flung a cape around his shoulders and went to sit at the table where he poured himself a glass of wine. He glanced behind him and leaped to his feet when he spotted Constance. He hurried to her side, shrugging off his cape and wrapping it around her.

'That garb is indecent,' he said angrily. 'Go to your room and change into something more suitable.'

Constance threw off the offending garment. 'No!' she said, stamping her foot. 'This is what Lisette wants me to wear. I am Chloris — a nymph of flowers, or something like that. It's perfectly respectable to be a Greek goddess.'

'And a beautiful one, too.' Percy strolled up to them, holding his hand out to Constance. 'I am a Greek god, or so Ma tells me. Let's do what she says and get this over — I'm starving.'

'Constance,' Duke said sternly.

'You look rather silly in that outfit, Duke,' she said pertly. 'Maybe it's you who ought to go and change into something more suitable.'

Nettie moved away quickly, not wanting to be caught up in a domestic dispute. She could see that Duke was fuming, and likely to explode in a volcanic eruption of temper. She had only witnessed such an exhibition once, and she did not care to repeat the experience. Byron was standing to one side and she went to join him.

'I think there will be trouble before the evening is out,' she said in a low voice.

'Never mind Duke, you look beautiful, Nettie.'

She felt the colour rise to her cheeks, but she eyed him suspiciously. 'How much wine have you drunk, Byron?'

He laughed. 'I'm quite sober. You should learn to take a compliment.'

'You and the boys were always teasing me, so I never know when you're serious.' She clutched his arm, staring over his shoulder. 'Look, that man is breathing fire.'

Byron turned his head just as the man, dressed like a medieval court jester, held a lighted torch in front of his face and blew a plume of flames into the air. Lisette clapped her hands and a cheer went up amongst the spectators, which turned into a cry of dismay as one of the pine branches caught fire. A plump woman wearing a wimple screamed and grabbed the hand of a man who had been capering around, playing a tabor pipe, while another man, dressed in a toga, beat time on a tambori. The music ceased abruptly and there were shouts for the servants, who rushed out to fetch water. Byron leaped forward and dragged the burning bough to the floor, where he stamped upon it accompanied by cheers from the excited onlookers.

Lisette rushed over to embrace him. 'Thank

you, *querida*. We might have burned to death had it not been for your quick thinking.' She turned to her guests, smiling bravely. 'No harm is done. We'll forgo the tableau and take our seats at the table.' She beckoned to Diego, who was standing stiffly by the door. 'We will dine now.'

The fire eater had retired to a corner and was sitting there with his head in his hands being scolded by one of the Three Graces, whose shrill voice sounded more like that of a fishwife than a celestial being. Lisette uttered a sharp rebuke and they took their places at the table.

Nettie sat next to Byron. He had distanced himself from his mother and brother, and she knew him well enough to understand why he was holding back. Putting herself in a similar position, Nettie could imagine how difficult it would be to find a long-lost family — to be a part of them and yet feel like a stranger in their midst. She gave his hand a comforting squeeze, and he responded with a grateful smile.

'Your pa has just edged Don Julio out of the way and has taken his place at my mother's side,' Byron said in a low voice. 'It seems that some men find her irresistible.'

'Don't judge her too quickly,' Nettie replied in a whisper. 'I think it's all a game to her. Anyway, Don Julio seems to have taken it in good part. He's concentrating on one of the Three Graces; she's been trying hard to attract his attention.'

'This place is a madhouse,' Byron said softly. 'I'm not sure I can cope with this sort of life. Maybe I should just move on.'

'I need to talk to you,' Nettie whispered. 'Meet me on the terrace after dinner.'

★   ★   ★

The meal was over but the guests were still seated round the table, drinking and laughing uproariously at jokes that Nettie could not understand. The lady with the wimple had dozed off over her dessert and the pointed hat had slipped over one eye. The fire eater had given up and left the room, leaving the woman who had harangued him to attach herself to Don Julio, who was looking distinctly bored. Nettie managed to slip away unnoticed and let herself out onto the terrace. It was cool beneath the stars and the breeze from the sea rustled the fronds of the palm trees, almost drowning out the song of the cicadas. It was a night made for romance as moonlight etched a silvery pathway on the dark waters of the Mediterranean, and the heady scent of flowers filled the air. Nettie sighed, shaking her head. The castle would have been a paradise had it not been for the past that had a habit of catching up with them wherever they went.

'Nettie.'

The sound of Byron's voice made her jump and she turned to see him emerging from the shadows. 'Did anyone see you leave the party?' she asked urgently.

'If you mean Duke, no, he was fully occupied. Percy doesn't seem to understand that Constance is a married woman, and I was expecting

198

Duke to challenge him to a duel at any moment. Is that what you wanted to talk about?'

'No, it's more serious than that.' She pulled up a dainty wrought-iron chair and sat down. 'The painting that Lisette values so highly is a copy. It's the first one that my father did for Duke, although he had no idea it was to be sold as the original.'

'Are you sure?' Byron leaned against the stone parapet. 'How do you know?'

'I just do. You'll have to trust me. Anyway, Duke agrees with me.'

'My mother obviously thinks it's genuine, so why worry? I mean, the deed is done and there's nothing you can do about it.'

'She's been kind to us and I hate deceiving her. How can Pa and I stay here, taking advantage of her hospitality when she's been cheated out of a fortune?'

'I can't leave yet. You do understand, don't you, Nettie?'

'I didn't mean that you have to accompany us. I just think that Pa and I should move on. I don't know where we could go, or how we will live, but we can't stay here for ever, and I want to get Pa away from Duke. He's a bad influence.'

'I can't disagree with that.' Byron moved to sit beside her. 'Nothing has changed except that you've discovered a fraud, which was committed some years ago. My mother loves that painting, and that's what matters. It would only be if she came to sell it that she'd realise she's been duped, and luckily she seems to be a very wealthy woman, so that eventuality is unlikely to occur. Why not stay and let your father paint her portrait? I'm sure that she'll pay him handsomely and you'll have had time to think about the future.'

'It doesn't alter the fact that she was cheated out of what was probably a small fortune. What would she say if she knew?'

'I can't speak for her.' He laid his hand on hers. 'Nettie, I want to stay here for a while at least. I need to get to know my mother and brother.'

'Of course you do, and I wasn't thinking of dragging you away from them, Byron. This is your home now. You've found the family you thought were lost to you for ever, and that makes me happy.'

'You mean a lot to me, Nettie.' He withdrew his hand hastily. 'I mean, we've been through so much together and we're good friends. I don't want to think of you and your father homeless and alone, which you will be if you keep on running from the law.'

'What do you suggest? Do you want Pa to return to London and give himself up?'

'I haven't got a clever answer. I don't know what the outcome will be; all I'm saying is that I want you to stay here while we try to work something out. Duke is the real culprit. He's the one who has made a fortune from deceiving wealthy clients. I doubt if Robert was the only artist he employed.'

'I know you're right, and he's one of the reasons why I think Pa and I ought to get away now. Duke has the ability to make people do what he wants, regardless of whether or not it's to their advantage.'

'I think he's met his match with Constance,' Byron said, chuckling. 'That young lady has a will of her own.'

'And he said that he's signed everything over to her in case he went to prison,' Nettie added, smiling. 'I think that was his first big mistake.'

'Stay for a while, Nettie. Maybe you and your father could return to London in a few months' time. I doubt if the police would think Robert Carroll a serious threat to society — it's Duke they really want.'

She nodded. 'I hope that's the case.'

'So you will stay at least until the portrait is finished?'

'If that's what Pa wants then I won't argue.'

Byron rose to his feet, holding out his hand. 'Let's rejoin the party before we're missed. We might as well enjoy ourselves while we're here.'

★　★　★

Robert was allocated a room to use as a studio. It was situated in the older part of the castle where the bare stone walls and flagstone floor kept the heat at a bearable level despite the soaring temperature outside. He worked on the portrait every day, requiring Lisette to sit for him for several hours at a time. She bored easily and insisted on being entertained, but this often involved the local band, until Robert complained that the reedy sound gave him a headache, making it difficult to concentrate. The lady who had worn the wimple for the tableau turned out to be an opera singer who had fallen on hard times, and Lisette asked her to perform. But Robert said that the high notes of the ageing soprano were painful to his ears, and she too was banished from the studio. In the end Lisette had the grand piano brought from the music room and, surprisingly, the fire eater turned out to be a talented pianist. Robert painted to the thrilling sound of Chopin's piano concertos, and Lisette was content to sit and listen until she became bored and walked out, leaving Robert to paint from memory. The fire eater went through his entire repertoire until he decided that enough was enough and he, too, left the room, but Robert kept working until the light faded or he was overcome with hunger and fatigue.

In the meantime Nettie grew used to the life of luxury. She had little to do other than to explore the castle and the grounds, or to take long walks along the cliff top. At other times she strolled through the scented pine forest to the beach, where she watched the fishing boats set sail. The small town was always buzzing with activity, and there was a street market once a week where country folk brought their produce to sell. Nettie and Byron wandered round the stalls, sampling the goods, making small purchases and practising the sentences they had learned in Spanish. Sometimes they were accompanied by Constance and Percy, although Duke refused to walk anywhere. He preferred to ride and went off on his own, leaving early in the morning and returning late in the evening.

Nettie wondered where he went, but Constance seemed unconcerned, and it was obvious that she and Percy were growing closer with every passing day. Lisette made no secret of the fact that she disapproved, but Duke looked on with a brooding intensity that made Nettie nervous. She could only hope that either Constance or Percy would grow bored and end the relationship. At least her father was gainfully employed and happy now that he was doing what he loved most. Nettie was the only one who was allowed to view his work, despite Lisette's constant demands to see the painting.

Robert chose to ignore his patroness's tantrums, and the only person who could calm Lisette when she flew into one of her frequent rages was Don Julio. He came and went at will, and Nettie discovered that he had an estate in Andalucia, and, as Father Ignatius told her on one of his frequent visits, Don Julio had a wife and children. The priest's attempts to reform Lisette failed miserably. She listened to him politely, offered him food and wine, and sent him on his way with a charming smile. Nettie suspected that Father Ignatius enjoyed his battles for Lisette's eternal soul, and, despite the fact that his attempts were doomed to failure, he was not going to be the one to give in first.

There had been no repeat of the theatricals they had endured at the beginning of their stay, and the guests who were there at first began to disappear one by one, to be replaced by an odd assortment of characters. Lisette's main criterion for those who came to stay at the castle was that they should be amusing, and they paid for her hospitality by entertaining the party each evening after dinner. There were recitations by errant poets, dramatic interpretations by out-of-work actors, and performances by a variety of musicians. Dancing was what Lisette seemed to enjoy the most and the nightly revelry usually ended with everyone joining hands in a sardana. Nettie was shy at first, but it was impossible to be a wallflower when all those present took to the floor; everyone, that is, apart from Duke.

One evening, after a particularly good dinner and a recital on the piano by the fire eater, who had not yet gone on his way, Lisette held up the proceedings, insisting that Duke must stand up with her and take part in the sardana. He refused, but Lisette was insistent, and eventually he was persuaded to take her hand and that of a plump poetess, who fluttered her eyelashes at him. Her attempts to cajole him into a good humour were met with a stony stare, and Duke executed the steps stiffly with a grim expression on his face, but Lisette had had her way, and she was clearly delighted.

Nettie watched them together with a puzzled frown. Duke largely ignored Constance, and he was clearly smitten by Lisette, but their arguments were heated, especially so when Don Julio was present. In any other circumstances Constance might have assumed the martyred expression of a wronged wife, but she was so involved with Percy that Nettie doubted if her friend had even noticed that Duke was openly flirting with the *condesa*. Lisette herself simply took the devotion of her admirers for granted, and she treated each of them with the same casual affection that she might have shown an amusing pet dog. When it came to her elder son she was guarded, almost indifferent, as if she were afraid to allow herself to feel any deep emotion for the young man whom she had abandoned as a small child. Nettie could see that Byron was hurt by his mother's attitude, but at least he seemed to be getting on well with Percy, and, despite the difference in their natures, the brothers shared a similar sense of humour.

It was Percy's involvement with Constance that continued to worry Nettie. She could see no happy ending for either of them, but she could not confide in Byron for fear of upsetting the delicate balance between him and his brother. Robert had distanced himself from the rest of the party while he concentrated on finishing the portrait, which he said was his best work yet. He even talked about exhibiting it, and brushed aside Nettie's concerns about protecting their anonymity. He seemed to think that the police in London would have given up the chase and that they could return home whenever they chose. Nettie was not so sure.

The days passed pleasantly enough and Nettie was never at a loss for a quiet corner where she could continue to work on her novel. Sometimes she wrote late into the night, sitting up in bed with the soft breeze from the open window caressing her cheeks and ruffling her hair. The story was progressing well enough, but Nettie felt that there was something missing. There was a certain amount of adventure in the tale, little touches of humour and there were descriptions of the landscape of which she was very proud, but somehow it lacked heart. She felt no emotion when she reread the pages that had come from her imagination and she decided to leave it for a while, and come back to it later. Perhaps she was succumbing to the idle life of luxury that the *condesa* obviously enjoyed. Away from the hurly-burly of London and the constant struggle to survive, Nettie had begun to relax, but she knew in her heart that this was merely an interlude, and it was only a matter of time before the past caught up with them. One day they would be on the run again — whether it was from creditors or the police, it made little difference — life with her father meant being forever on the move.

⋆　⋆　⋆

Nettie was heading for the dining hall one morning, when she realised that something was missing. The painting of *Primavera* had been taken down, leaving a shadow of itself on the whitewashed wall. Her heart jolted against her ribcage and she uttered a gasp of dismay. There was no one about and, for once, all was quiet. Many of the guests had left the previous day, although late in the evening Nettie had seen another carriage arrive at the gates. She had paid little attention to the passenger, thinking it to be just another of Lisette's odd friends, but now his arrival seemed sinister. Her imagination was running riot. What if the well-dressed gentleman was a dealer who had come to value the old master? Beads of perspiration stood out on her brow and her pulse was racing. There was only one way to find out and that was to face Lisette with the question.

Nettie hurried to the dining hall and she could have cried with relief when she spotted the Botticelli propped up against the wall. Lisette was standing beside it, and, with his back to her, was the stranger who had arrived earlier.

'Condesa,' Nettie said sharply.

Lisette turned her head and the man straightened up. Nettie's hand flew to her mouth as she stifled a cry of dismay.

'What's the matter, child? You look as if you've seen a ghost,' Lisette said, smiling. 'Did you want something?'

Nettie shook her head, at a loss for words. 'No, I mean, might I have a word with you in private, Condesa?'

'This isn't a convenient time, Nettie. Go away, there's a good girl. I'll speak to you later. I'm sure whatever it is can wait.'

'No, please. You don't understand. I need to tell you something urgently.'

12

'I'm sure it can wait,' Lisette said icily. 'Please leave us, Nettie.'

'No, you don't understand,' Nettie said, tugging at the *condesa's* sleeve. 'This man is a spy.'

'A spy!' Lisette stared at her in amazement. 'What nonsense. Mr Wegg is an art dealer from London.'

'Mr Wegg is an imposter,' Nettie said angrily. 'He's a private detective and he's been chasing after Pa and Duke since we left London.'

Lisette turned on Wegg, her eyes flashing. 'Well, sir. Is this true?' she demanded. 'Did you wheedle your way into my home under false pretences?'

Wegg shrugged. 'It would seem so, Condesa. But some of your guests are not what they seem. The Metropolitan Police are looking for Duke Dexter and Robert Carroll.'

'What crimes are they supposed to have committed?'

'Forgery, ma'am.' Wegg pointed to the Botticelli. 'You've been swindled. This here painting is the work of the said Robert Carroll.'

Lisette stared at him in horror. 'I don't believe you.'

'It's true. Ask this young woman — she knows full well that this is a fake. Tell her, Miss Carroll.'

Nettie shot a wary glance at Lisette, who was

staring at her, pale-faced and trembling. 'I'm sorry, Condesa. I don't know how the painting came into your hands, but I believe it is a copy.'

'What did you hope to get out of this, Mr Wegg?' Lisette said slowly. 'You claimed to be an art dealer who was interested in purchasing the painting.'

'A justified deception, ma'am. Some of the disgruntled art lovers who were duped by your friends are offering a generous reward for their capture and imprisonment.'

'How much would it cost to buy your silence, Wegg?'

Nettie shook her head. 'No, Condesa. You mustn't give this man a penny.'

Wegg threw back his head and laughed. 'That's rich. This woman, who pretends to be Spanish nobility, has hardly got a feather to fly with.'

'I don't know what you mean,' Nettie said slowly.

'I've been making enquiries, Nettie Carroll. The condesa has been selling off the contents of the castle for months. She's bankrupted herself by her lavish lifestyle and the money she's squandered on this old ruin.'

'That can't be true.' Nettie gazed at Lisette in horror. 'He's lying, isn't he?'

'Of course he is,' Lisette said angrily. 'I have had some unexpected expenses, and that necessitated selling off a few items, but — '

'That's rich.' Wegg pointed to spaces on the walls where pictures had once hung. 'There's the evidence. Ask Dexter, if you don't believe me.

What do you think he's been doing on his trips into the country? He's her puppet and now you and your pa are being duped by the pair of them, Miss Carroll.'

'Mr Dexter has been acting as my agent, it's true, but that doesn't make him a criminal, Mr Wegg,' Lisette said coldly.

'It don't make him a saint, neither.' Wegg took a step towards the Botticelli. 'I'll take this instead of payment, shall I?'

'How dare you come into my home, blackening the names of my guests and making threats? Get out, and don't let me see you again.'

'You are harbouring criminals, Condesa. I have only to go to the local police and they will contact their counterparts in London.'

'Leave now.' Lisette reached for the tasselled bell pull and yanked it hard so that the peal echoed off the high ceiling, and Diego rushed into the room, confirming Nettie's suspicions that he had a habit of listening at the keyhole. 'Escort Mr Wegg from the castle,' Lisette said firmly. 'Make sure that the gatekeeper knows he is not welcome here.'

'You'll be sorry for this, Condesa.' Wegg shook off Diego's restraining hand. 'I don't need your help. I'm leaving, but this isn't the end. It's just the beginning. Tell your father and Duke that their game is up, Miss Carroll. If they leave this place they'll be arrested.' He shot a malevolent glance at Lisette. 'As for you, Madame High and Mighty, you'll find yourself back on the streets where you came from. I know all about your history, so don't think you can fool Samson Wegg.'

'Take him out of here.' Lisette's voice shook with emotion as Diego seized Wegg by the collar and marched him from the room.

'Was he speaking the truth?' Nettie asked anxiously. 'Are you really in financial difficulties, Condesa?'

'You can stop calling me 'Condesa',' Lisette said wearily. 'I was never married to Talavera, not legally, anyway. I took his name, but I am still Lisette Horton. At least my sons were born in wedlock.'

'What happened to your fortune?'

'That dreadful little man was right. I spent lavishly, and I sent Percy to the best schools and paid for him to attend Cambridge University. I was so poor when I was young and living in Paris that I ate scraps of food thrown out for the birds. I was close to starvation when Byron's father found me, and I vowed I would never sink to that level again.'

Nettie listened in silence. She had suffered privations enough at the hands of her thriftless father, and she understood what it was like to go without. Wearing threadbare clothes and going hungry had been a way of life that recurred often enough when times were hard. She could sympathise with Lisette to a certain extent, but the condesa's extravagant way of living was beyond anything that Robert Carroll could have envisaged.

'What will you do now?' Nettie asked cautiously. 'You could hand the painting over to

211

the police and claim the reward when they arrest Duke and my pa.'

Lisette turned on her, eyes flashing and pink-cheeked. 'I am not that sort of woman, Nettie. I do not betray my friends, and the Botticelli was bought from a dealer in Madrid. Who knows how many times it had changed hands since Duke commissioned it from your father?'

'Aren't you angry with them for the deception?'

'My dear girl, I lived by my wits before I married Horton, and again after I left him. I've done things of which I am not proud, so I can hardly stand in judgement of your father and Duke. As I told Wegg, Duke has been selling off trinkets and small items of value on my behalf.' Lisette began to pace the room wringing her hands nervously. 'I know that I should have cut down on my expenditure. I should not have entertained so lavishly — there are so many things that I ought to have done, but did not.'

'But you still own the castle,' Nettie said earnestly. 'Couldn't you sell it and use the money to pay off your debts? You might live anywhere then, in comfort.'

Lisette threw back her head and laughed. 'You don't know the extent of my liabilities, Nettie. It sounds so simple when you put it like that, but the castle doesn't belong to me. Talavera died without leaving a will, and as we weren't married the whole estate will go eventually to some distant cousin, who's been trying to evict me for years. The crippling legal fees have added to my burden.'

'What about Percy? Isn't he entitled to the estate?'

'Percy has no more rights than I have, even though Talavera brought him up as if he were his own child.'

Nettie was silent for a moment, imagining how Percy would feel when he found out.

'But you allowed Percy to think he would inherit all this,' she said, shaking her head.

'I've made many mistakes in my life, Nettie, and that was one of them. Now I will have to break it to Percy that he will inherit nothing but debts.'

'I don't know what to say.'

'It's not your problem, *querida*. But I think that you and your father had best leave here. Duke can do as he pleases, and as to that girl he married, she will soon forget Percy when she discovers that he hasn't a penny to his name.'

'I think you are being very unfair to Constance.'

'Maybe, but that's the way I see it.' Lisette sank down on a chair, staring sadly at the fake Botticelli. 'I loved this painting. It was going to save Percy and myself from penury. Now I realise that it's worthless, but still I love it. How sad.'

Nettie opened her mouth to speak, but she realised there was nothing she could say that would comfort Lisette. She left the room quietly and went in search of Byron. He needed to know the truth about his mother's plight, and then she would break the news to her father. The money

213

they had been counting on for the portrait would not be forthcoming, and Wegg would probably be on his way to report to the authorities at this very moment.

★ ★ ★

Nettie found Byron in the grounds below the terrace. He was standing very still, looking out to sea and he turned with a start at the sound of her footsteps.

'I think I could get used to living here,' he said, smiling. 'It's so beautiful and so peaceful.'

Nettie sank down on a rustic seat. Above her the silver-grey stones of the castle wall were barely visible beneath a tumbling cascade of purple bougainvillaea, and scarlet canna lilies stood like sentinels in a narrow bed edged with terracotta tiles, but she was about to shatter the peace and tranquillity of the scene.

'Come and sit down, Byron. I have something to tell you.'

'What is it, Nettie? Why so serious on such a lovely day?'

'I've just learned something from your mother that alters everything. There's no easy way to say this, so I'll come right out with it. She doesn't own this place and she's in serious financial trouble. I'm so sorry, Byron.'

He sat down beside her. 'Are you sure?'

'Wegg was here on the pretext of being an art dealer. Your mother was so desperate for money that she was trying to sell the Botticelli.'

'How on earth did he find us?'

'I don't know, and I certainly didn't ask.'

'He must have realised that the Botticelli was one of the fakes that Duke passed off as the genuine article.'

'He seemed to be very confident. I think we've underestimated him and his hatred for Duke. It's as if he's allowed a personal grudge to get the better of him.'

Byron leaned back against the wall, frowning thoughtfully. 'You said that my mother doesn't own the castle. I can't believe it — she seemed so settled here.'

'I think you need to speak to her, Byron. It's a matter between you and your mother and Percy. You're all involved, and to be honest, it doesn't sound too hopeful.'

'What haven't you told me?'

'Your mother said that Talavera didn't leave a will, and the castle is entailed to a distant relation who's been trying to have her evicted for some time. She's virtually bankrupt and she faces losing her home.'

'I had no idea. It makes me realise how little I really know of her. Poor Percy, that means he has no claim on the estate.'

'It's hard on him if he's been expecting to inherit all this,' Nettie said sadly.

'Our mother has a lot to answer for, Nettie. All this has been much more difficult than I anticipated. I suppose I had some romantic notion that she would be overjoyed to see me, but she's not an easy person to get to know.'

'You just need time together,' Nettie said gently.

Byron rose to his feet. 'I'm going to look for Percy. I'm going to put him straight and we'll face our mother together. We need to find out the exact state of her affairs.'

'I think Percy and Constance went riding, but you could have a word with your mother. She would know best how to break the news to him.'

'You're right, as always.' Byron squeezed her hand. 'We'll get through this together, Nettie.'

⋆ ⋆ ⋆

That evening Nettie was dressing for dinner when Constance rushed into the room without knocking. 'Is it true? Percy and I have been out riding all day and we've only just returned.'

'Is what true?' Nettie said guardedly.

'Diego told us that the police have been here and Duke is about to be arrested.'

'Servants shouldn't listen at keyholes, but it's partly true. Wegg was here this morning and he might well go to the police. He was trying to get his hands on the Botticelli, knowing full well that it's a fake.'

Constance sank down on the bed. 'Why would he do that?'

'You'd better ask your husband,' Nettie said angrily. 'It's his fault that we're all here, including you, Constance. Wegg isn't going to give up until he sees Duke behind bars.'

'Then Duke must leave, but we can stay with Lisette.'

'That won't be possible. I'm sure she'll tell you all this evening, but it looks as though our

216

countess is as much of a fraud as the Botticelli.'

'What do you mean?'

'She told me she doesn't own the castle and she's virtually bankrupt.'

Constance stared at her in disbelief. 'But that can't be. She's a wealthy woman.'

'You'll hear it from her own lips, Constance. We'll be in serious trouble if we remain here much longer.'

Constance leaped to her feet. 'How can you be so calm about it?'

'I'm not, but panicking won't help. We'll discuss it when we're all together at dinner.'

'I must change into something more suitable.' Constance hurried to the door. 'Just as I was beginning to enjoy myself, everything is going to change. It's all Duke's fault and I will tell him so.' She left the door swinging gently on its hinges.

Nettie sighed as she finished doing up the buttons on the evening dress that Lisette had given her. Dinner was going to be an interesting meal.

★ ★ ★

The dining room was deserted and the table had not been set for the meal. Nettie was standing in the doorway, wondering whether she had mistaken the time, when Diego rushed into the room. He came to a halt and bowed. 'I am sorry. I didn't know that you were here.'

'Where are the other servants, Diego?'

'Gone.' He spread his hands in a theatrical

gesture of dismay. 'They learn that there is no money to pay them and they have all gone, except me. The last of the guests also departed.'

'Does the *condesa* know about this?'

'I have told her.'

'Is there anyone left in the kitchen?'

He shook his head.

'But there must be some food left, unless they have taken everything.'

'I would not allow such a thing.'

Nettie could see that she had insulted him and she managed a smile. 'Of course not. Will you take me to the kitchen? Perhaps I can find something that we can all eat.'

'You are a lady. You cannot cook.'

'We'll see, shall we? Lead on, I'll follow you.'

★　★　★

The main kitchen, with its high vaulted ceiling, was more like a cathedral than a place where tasty meals were cooked. The great open fireplace still had the ingenious smoke jack used to turn the spit, and a large bread oven, both of which must have been used by cooks from centuries past. The fire had burned down, but Nettie decided that there was enough heat in the embers to cook something simple. A quick exploration of the larder provided a tray of eggs, some herbs and a whole ham.

Diego was hovering nervously behind her. 'You are a guest in the castle. This is not the place for you.'

'It's exactly the right place at this moment.'

218

Nettie took an apron from a hook and tied it round her waist. 'If you can find plates and cutlery and set the table with glasses and wine, we will have a reasonable meal. Leave me to get on with it, please.'

Diego backed away, mumbling incoherently, and Nettie rolled up her sleeves. She was at ease in the kitchen, even though every movement she made echoed eerily round the room, as if several cooks were at work. She broke eggs into a large bowl, sliced ham and filled a basket with fresh figs and grapes that she found in the cold room. That done, she waited until Diego came to inform her that everyone was seated, and she quickly fried the ham and made a large omelette.

When everything was served onto a large silver platter she carried it up the winding staircase to the dining room, followed by Diego with the fruit and more wine. Nettie entered the room to a round of applause.

Percy stood up, raising his glass. 'A toast to Nettie, who has prepared a feast for us.'

Everyone cheered and drank more wine, and Nettie suspected that they were all slightly tipsy as she sat down amidst more enthusiastic clapping.

Lisette helped herself to the food. 'Let's eat and enjoy this delicious meal. It could be the last one we share together.' She passed the salver to Robert, who was seated beside her.

'Why do you say that?' he asked anxiously. 'I know that Wegg paid you a visit, but surely we're safe here?'

She shook her head. 'I wish that were true, my dear friend.'

'Damn Wegg to hell,' Duke said angrily. 'I thought we'd shaken him off.'

'He seems determined to do you harm.' Lisette sipped her wine. 'He couldn't have come at a worse time.'

'Really, Mama!' Percy glared at her. 'Will you please stop being so mysterious. I want to know what's going on.'

Byron nodded. 'I agree with Percy. I think you need to be honest with us, Mother.'

'What I will say, since you are all so eager to hear the worst, is that my position has become untenable. I cannot remain here any longer because the Castillo Talavera belongs to someone else. My financial circumstances are dire and I can no longer offer you my hospitality.'

Duke reached for the carafe of wine and refilled his glass. 'What happened to the Botticelli? You didn't let Wegg have it, I hope.'

Lisette met his gaze with a grim smile. 'He wanted to take it from me, for what reason I don't know, because he says it's a fake. I sent him on his way, but I think you will have to face the law sooner or later, Duke.' She picked daintily at her food, drinking more than she was eating.

Percy gulped a mouthful of wine. 'There must be some mistake, Ma. As Pa's widow you should be entitled to live here for the rest of your life.'

'I'll tell you everything later, Percy. Now we should do justice to the meal that Nettie has prepared for us.'

'Wegg is a devil,' Duke said angrily. 'I've had enough of his machinations. I'll make him regret that he ever met me.'

'Calm down, Duke.' Robert laid his hand on Duke's sleeve. 'This isn't the time or place for empty threats. We're in trouble, largely thanks to you.'

'You were pleased enough to accept the money for your work,' Duke snapped. 'You weren't so naïve that you thought you were simply making copies of the originals. You knew damn well that it was all a fraud.'

'I was desperate for money, and I didn't stop to think why you wanted me to make the copies. You took advantage of me.'

Duke pushed his chair back and stood up. 'You are a weak-spirited apology for a man, and a second-rate artist, Robert Carroll. I'm done with you and your daughter. You two can find your own way back to London. Don't ask me for help.'

Constance tugged at his coat-tail. 'Sit down. You're drunk and you're making a fool of yourself.'

He turned on her with a savage snarl. 'And you are nothing but a silly child. Do you think this is all a game? You've had that idiot boy hanging round you like a lapdog, but you're my wife and you can say goodbye to him and come with me. We're leaving right away.'

Constance eyed him coldly. 'You may go where you please, Duke. I don't wish to be married to a criminal who's on the run from the police. You married me under false pretences and

221

I intend to get an annulment.'

'We'll see about that,' Duke said through clenched teeth.

'You can't stop me.'

'We'll discuss this later.'

Constance rose from the table, glaring at him. 'No we won't. You are a wanted man and I have all the money. You can rot in hell, for all I care. Percy and I are in love and as soon as I'm a free woman I intend to marry him.'

'What?' Duke leaped to his feet, spilling his glass of wine so that it pooled like blood on the white damask cloth. 'You dare to say that to me?'

Lisette slammed her hand on the table. 'Silence! I won't have this squabbling. Take your marital tiffs to the privacy of your room.'

'That we will do.' Duke grabbed Constance by the arm. 'We'll settle this once and for all. When I'm done you won't have just cause for an annulment.'

'Let her go, Duke.' Percy was already on his feet and he skirted the table, making a lunge at Duke, who sidestepped neatly.

'Keep out of this, Talavera. Constance is my wife.'

Nettie could see a fight ensuing and she managed to get between Constance and Duke, prising his hand from her friend's arm. 'This isn't the way, Duke,' she said in a low voice. 'I would have thought you have more imminent concerns than a quarrel with Constance.'

Byron leaped to his feet. 'Wegg has probably telegraphed London as to your whereabouts by now. I'd say you have two or maybe three days to

222

get away from here, unless the Spanish police agree to arrest you.'

'They'll take Robert, too,' Duke said spitefully. 'I could deny all culpability and say that I bought the copies in good faith from him. He's the one who painted the fakes.'

Robert shook his head. 'I know now that what I did was wrong. I should have realised what you were doing, Duke, but I'm prepared to take my punishment.'

'What sort of man are you, Robert Carroll?' Lisette demanded. 'Do you lie down like a whipped dog simply because this man tells you to?'

'It wasn't your fault, Pa.' Nettie turned to him with tears in her eyes. 'You believed Duke when he said he was going to sell your work as genuine copies.'

'I'm sorry, my dear. I'm afraid I let you down badly. Perhaps I should have done something else, swept the streets or collected night soil — anything to keep food on the table and pay the rent.'

'No, Pa. You're a brilliant artist. Duke took advantage of you.'

'That's right,' Duke said, curling his lip. 'Blame everything on me.'

'Well, you are at the bottom of this. You persuaded me to marry you. I didn't want to, but you left me little choice,' Constance said bitterly. 'And you put all your money in my name because you knew that Wegg was after you. Well, Duke, it's mine legally and there's nothing you can do about it.'

Percy slipped his arm around her shoulders, ousting Duke completely. 'We're in love, Mama, and we're leaving, and I think you should come with us. I wouldn't want to leave you here to face bankruptcy.'

Duke backed away and snatched a sword from where it hung on the wall. 'You are going nowhere, Constance, unless it is with me.' He pointed it at her heart. 'Do you understand?'

13

Percy tried to grab the sword, but Duke turned on him. 'Get out of my way.'

Lisette rose from the table, lifted her glass and with a flick of her slender wrist she aimed the stream of wine at Duke's face. He dropped the weapon as he raised his hand to wipe his eyes, and Percy snatched it up.

'That's enough.' Byron stepped forward. 'On behalf of my mother and my brother I'm telling you to leave the castle immediately. Pack your things, take your horse and go.'

Duke wiped his streaming face on a napkin. 'I'm still her legal husband. Constance comes with me.'

'No.' Constance shook her head. 'We were never married in the true sense of the word. I might be your wife on paper, but that is going to change. I think you're forgetting that you signed everything over to me.'

Duke gave her a pitying look. 'Do you think I'm so stupid as to entrust my money to a silly child?'

'You said you put all your money and property in my name.'

'I lied in order to make you feel secure. In fact, I now own everything, including your father's former house in Paris and the gallery. Without me you have nothing — you are nothing.'

Constance raised her hand and slapped his face, leaving the reddening outline of her fingers on his left cheek. 'You are the worst type of libertine, Duke Dexter. I would rather die than go with you.'

'Very well. You've had your chance.' Duke bowed to Lisette. 'It's been a pleasure, but I must go. However, being a gentleman, I'll leave the Botticelli with you as a reminder of our time together.' He pointed at the painting, which was still propped up against a chair.

Lisette moved swiftly with cat-like grace, seized the canvas, and smashed it over Duke's head.

There was a horrified silence as everyone stared at the sight of Duke's shocked expression as he stood with the ruined painting hanging around his neck like a bizarre collar. With an angry roar he freed himself from the gilt frame and threw it across the room.

'Don't think for a moment that you'll get away with this. If I'm caught I'll make sure that you are all charged with aiding and abetting a felon.'

There was a moment of stunned silence as he stormed out of the room, and then Nettie began to laugh. 'Oh, dear,' she said breathlessly. 'He did deserve that, but your poor painting, Condesa. You loved it so much.'

Lisette resumed her seat and reached for her glass of wine. 'My friend Robert will make me another copy, but not yet.'

Robert moved to her side. 'You may depend upon me.'

She gave him a wan smile. 'Dexter was right

about one thing: we must all leave here as soon as possible. I don't know where I'll go, but I hope my two handsome sons will stand by me.'

'You should have told me that you were in difficulties, Mama,' Percy said slowly. 'I will sell the castle and we can buy something smaller and live quite comfortably.'

Nettie glanced anxiously at Byron, but his attention was fixed on his mother.

'Our mother has something to tell you, Percy.'

'What else could there be?' Percy's smile faded. 'Why so serious, Mama?'

'You know now that Talavera wasn't your father, Percy. All this will go to one of Talavera's relatives, or what's left of it after the creditors have been paid. The money might be gone, but you have a brother. That must count for something.'

'All these years I've been living a lie,' Percy said angrily. 'Why didn't you tell me the truth, Ma? And why did you allow Talavera to think I was his son?'

'I'm, sorry, Percy. It was a cruel deception, but I was afraid that Talavera would abandon us if he knew the truth.'

'He was a good man,' Percy said angrily. 'He didn't deserve to have another man's child foisted upon him.'

'You're right.' Lisette's bottom lip trembled. 'But you are a man — you don't know how hard life is for a woman on her own, and Talavera loved you as if you were his son.'

'But not enough to leave the castle to me. Now we're all but bankrupt. Is there anything

227

else you haven't told me?'

Byron slid his arm around his brother's shoulders. 'Steady on, old man.'

'I'm truly sorry, Percy.' Lisette dashed a tear away. 'I know I've treated both my sons badly.'

'When I started out on this venture I was looking for my mother,' Byron said slowly. 'I didn't know that I had a brother. I know how you feel, Percy, because it came as a shock to me too.'

Percy shook his head. 'That's putting it mildly. I don't know who I am now.'

'You are my brother and we're a proper family,' Byron said firmly. 'We might have nothing, but we have each other.'

Constance leaned over to caress Percy's cheek. 'I don't care if you are poor — so am I. We will be poor together.'

'Well said, Constance.' Robert rose to his feet, applauding loudly. 'I feel somewhat responsible for your present position, Lisette. You thought the Botticelli was genuine and all the time it was just a copy, but I will do my best to make things right. I will set up a studio somewhere else, and I'll work until my debt to you is paid in full.'

'We're all with you, Lisette,' Nettie said earnestly. 'But if we leave here, where will we go?'

'Somewhere that Wegg would never think of looking.' Robert sat down again and refilled his glass.

Nettie thought for a moment and then she smiled. 'We should go home.'

Her father gazed at her in surprise. 'To London?'

'Yes, exactly. That's the last place that Wegg or the police would think of looking for us. They'll think we're still hiding away on the Continent.'

'But I won't be able to work, Nettie. How can I sell my paintings without alerting the authorities?'

'I don't know, Pa. But has anyone a better idea?'

'Nettie's right,' Byron said, nodding. 'It's easy to lose oneself in the city, and I'm sure it's Duke that Wegg really wants to ruin, not you, sir. Even if you were arrested, a good lawyer might be able to convince a court that you were duped into making the copies, and you put your trust in Duke.'

'Maybe I should face up to what I've done. If nothing else, I was a fool.' Robert sighed, staring into the ruby-red wine as he swirled it around the glass. 'I do miss London.'

'What about you, Ma?' Byron eyed his mother doubtfully. 'What about all this?' He encompassed the room and all its trappings with a wave of his hands.

'It doesn't belong to me, my son. It never has, but I've enjoyed every minute of my life here.' Lisette sank back on her seat. 'I've been rich and I've been poor, but now I have my two sons with me. What more could I want?'

Percy eyed her suspiciously. 'You say that, Mama. You didn't give much thought to either of us until now.'

'I know I've been a selfish woman, but I meant

it, Percy. I can't help the way I was made, but I'll try to be a better person.'

'The main thing is to decide what to do next,' Nettie said firmly.

Lisette sighed, shaking her head. 'I was born a river gypsy, and it's in my soul. Maybe we could live in a boat again one day.'

'What about Don Julio?' Robert asked tentatively. 'You seemed to be very close. Wouldn't he help you?'

'Julio has a wife and children. We were simply amusing ourselves.' Lisette shot a sideways glance at Robert. 'I suppose you disapprove.'

He shrugged. 'It was nothing to do with me. You live your life as you please, Condesa.'

'Lisette,' she corrected, smiling. 'I am no longer a *condesa*.'

'And I am neither a wife nor a single woman,' Constance said angrily. 'What a fool I was to believe Duke. Now he's taken everything from me.'

Percy went down on one knee at her side. 'I'll take care of you, my love. We'll make a life for ourselves and you'll forget all this.'

'You are so good to me, Percy.' Constance wrapped her arms around him.

'There's still the question of money,' Nettie said firmly. 'We have to pay our fares and then we'll have to find accommodation.'

'My daughter — ever practical,' Robert smiled fondly. 'I wish I could help, but I have nothing.'

Byron turned to his mother. 'Is there anything of value left, Mama?'

'I have my jewels. At least they belong to me,

and they should be worth enough to get us to England.'

'I'll admit all this has come as a shock, but we have to be practical.' Percy rose to his feet. 'When we get to London I'll find work. My expensive education won't be wasted.'

'You were sent down, old boy,' Byron said, chuckling. 'That won't get you far.'

Percy cuffed him round the ear, but it was a playful gesture. 'I'll train to be a lawyer and you can be my clerk.'

'That's settled then.' Lisette rose to her feet, holding up her glass. 'We'll drink to the future. Here's to London and a new life.'

★ ★ ★

The sun was rising in a fireball next morning as they rode single file into the pine forest. Diego accompanied them, leading two donkeys laden with their luggage, which had been kept to a minimum. If Lisette had misgivings about leaving her extensive wardrobe, and the home she had created, she did not complain. Nettie suspected that perhaps the condesa's old life had begun to lose its sparkle, and that the gypsy in her heart had come to the fore.

This was the beginning of a journey that would be fraught with difficulties and danger, but Nettie felt almost ridiculously optimistic. She had not realised how much she missed London, despite the privations they had suffered during the hard times. The sights, the sounds, the familiar accents and even the stark contrast between the rich and the poor, all these things made up the city where she had been born and bred, and now she could not wait to get home.

They travelled for three days, stopping as they had before at small inns where Lisette acted the part of the *condesa*, and had the landlords fawning upon her and the servants eager to please such a grand lady.

When they reached Perpignan the horses were sold, Diego was paid off and they parted from him with genuine regret. Lisette, aided by Byron, dealt with a jeweller in a backstreet and persuaded him to purchase enough of her jewels to pay for train tickets that would take them all the way to Calais. Despite the fact that they were supposed to be economising, she insisted that they must travel first class, endearing herself even more to Robert, who approved wholeheartedly.

'I refuse to share a compartment with peasants stinking of garlic and tobacco smoke,' she said as Robert handed her into the carriage. 'And that person is taking a pig into third class. Either that or she has a very ugly child.'

Nettie exchanged amused glances with Byron, and Percy made pig noises, which made Constance giggle. To the astonishment of the porter who had been left to carry their luggage, they fell into their compartment collapsing on the richly upholstered seats in hysterics. Nettie wiped her eyes on her sleeve, wishing that she had thought to bring a hanky, but travelling light meant bringing only the barest of necessities, and their clothes were already travel-stained.

There were several changes, according to the

different railway companies that operated the lines, and they slept as best they could, either in the carriage or, at worst, on the hard wooden seats in the station waiting rooms. They arrived in Calais late one evening and Lisette insisted on taking rooms at a small hotel near the harbour, declaring that another night of interrupted sleep would be the death of her. No one believed that, but when they were shown to rooms containing feather beds, clean linen and the first opportunity to have a proper wash since they had left the castle, there was not a single protest. After a good meal and several glasses of wine, Nettie was ready for bed, and even though she had to share with Constance, she had no difficulty in falling into a deep and dreamless sleep.

Next morning Nettie was up early and was surprised to find Lisette and Byron already at breakfast in the small dining room. Lisette put down her cup and greeted Nettie with a genuine smile of pleasure.

'You're just in time to accompany Byron and me. The landlord said that there's a jeweller's shop not far from here. You can come with us, if you wish.'

'I will,' Nettie said eagerly. 'But it seems a shame that you have to sell all your jewels. I'm sure that Pa feels as awkward as I do about taking your money.'

'Nonsense. We're in this together. Enjoy your breakfast and we'll be off before the others wake up. They don't need to know.'

★ ★ ★

The jeweller's shop was so small that Nettie chose to wait outside, even though it had started to rain. She sheltered beneath the overhang, watching the raindrops evaporate in small hisses of steam as they hit the hot pavement. It was a summer shower and over quickly, leaving the air heavy and humid. Each breath felt laboured and clouds of flies swarmed around the detritus in the gutters and the steaming piles of horse dung on the cobbled street. Nettie turned with a start as the shop door opened and Lisette and Byron emerged from the dark interior, blinking as their eyes grew accustomed to the bright light.

'What's the matter?' Nettie demanded anxiously. 'Didn't he want to buy anything?'

'They're all fake,' Lisette said angrily. 'Talavera gave me jewels made of paste. They're the sort of imitation gems that actors wear on stage, and I was fooled by them.'

'But you sold some in Perpignan.'

'Apparently they were real. The diamond earrings and pearl necklace were the presents that Talavera gave me when I was the toast of the Parisian nightclubs. He cheated me, and I'm glad he's dead.' She marched off, with her head held high.

Nettie turned to Byron. 'What will we do now?'

'The jeweller bought a couple of things, and I think there is enough to settle the hotel bill. I'm not sure about the crossing to Dover. We might have to swim,' he added with a wry smile.

'We'd better follow her,' Nettie said hastily.

'She's very upset and I don't blame her.'

Byron proffered his arm. 'Come on, we'd better get back to the hotel before there's another downpour. We'll sort something out, so don't worry.'

They hurried after Lisette and caught up with her in the hotel dining room where Constance, Percy and Robert were just finishing their breakfast. Their smiles faded when they looked up and saw Lisette's grim expression. Their reactions to the news were predictable, but it was Robert who urged everyone to keep calm.

'We need to get back to England,' he said firmly. 'Once there we can make our way to London, or wherever we decide to go. I don't mind doing odd jobs in order to pay for necessities, and I'm sure that you two fit young men could turn your hands to some sort of work. We'll be all right once we get home.'

'Pa is right.' Nettie emptied her purse on the table. 'That is all I have.'

Robert emptied his pockets and the others followed suit. They pooled what little money they had, and, even after paying the hotel bill, there was just enough left to buy tickets for the next ferry to Dover.

'It will be second class, Condesa,' Robert said, smiling. 'There's no first-class travel for us this time.'

★ ★ ★

The white cliffs of Dover were fading into the misty purple dusk as the paddle steamer headed for the port, and it was almost dark by the time they disembarked.

'What do we do now?' Constance demanded as they picked up their luggage and started walking towards the town. 'I'm tired and I'm hungry.'

'We're all feeling the same,' Nettie said sharply.

Lisette gazed at the lights on a hill above the port. 'That looks like a splendid hotel. I could do with a bath and a decent meal.'

'We are broke, Ma,' Percy sighed. 'We can't afford a cup of tea, let alone a night in luxury.'

Lisette turned on him angrily. 'Either call me Maman or Lisette.' She handed her valise to Robert. 'You'll carry this for me, won't you, my dear? I am a little tired, but I refuse to sleep on another bench in a waiting room, or a shabby lodging house.'

'That's all very well,' Robert said gently, 'but how will we pay? We don't want to draw attention to ourselves by getting into trouble the moment we put our foot on home soil.'

'Leave that to me. It's not too far to walk.' She set off at a pace that made it necessary for the others to run in order to catch her up.

'Are you sure this is wise, Ma?' Byron asked warily. 'The jewels are virtually worthless. You heard what the man said.'

'Needs must when the devil drives. That's what your father used to say, Byron. Well, the devil is driving me on, and I intend to sup with him.'

Nettie laid her hand on Byron's arm. 'There's

no point in arguing. Your mother will do as she pleases.'

'I most certainly will.' Lisette marched on, leaving Robert to carry her bag as well as his, and the others followed.

They arrived at the hotel to find a party in progress. Gaslights bathed everything in a golden glow and all the windows were flung open to let in the cool night air. Lisette sailed up to the reception desk, but Nettie could not hear the conversation for the noise of the revellers in the next room. The party seemed to be in full swing, although it was late in the evening. Men and women in evening dress paraded through the large foyer, some of them taking seats by the window while others went outside. The scent of expensive cigar smoke floated in through the open door, and the sound of champagne corks popping was followed by laughter and the strains of an orchestra striking up a waltz.

Lisette's voice rose in a crescendo as she attempted to make herself heard, and it was obviously not going well with the harassed clerk. Percy and Byron went to her aid, but Lisette was by now in full spate like a river about to burst its dam.

'We've been travelling for days,' she said angrily. 'We've been buffeted about on the sea and now all I want is three rooms, a hot bath and a decent meal. Is this hotel incapable of providing that for a weary traveller?'

The clerk's response was lost in the general hubbub, but Lisette's vociferous refusal to accept that the rooms were fully booked had caught the attention of a tall, dark-haired young man in evening dress, who had been strolling across the foyer. He was strikingly good-looking and there was something familiar about him. Nettie was certain that she had seen him before, but when she caught his eye and he smiled, she was suddenly back in the Gaiety Restaurant, and she remembered their unfortunate first meeting. He came towards them, holding out his hand to Percy.

'Percy, old man. What the deuce are you doing down here in deepest Kent?'

'Rufus. It's good to see you.' Percy grasped his friend's hand and shook it enthusiastically.

Constance moved swiftly to stand beside Percy and she tugged at his sleeve. 'Won't you introduce us?'

'I'm sorry. I was so pleased to see a familiar face that I forgot my manners. This is my friend Rufus Norwood. We met at Cambridge.' He proceeded to make the necessary introductions and Rufus responded gallantly. He bowed over Lisette's hand, acknowledging her with a devastating smile, and he charmed Constance, who blushed and fluttered her eyelashes. He won Robert's approval by acknowledging him as an artist of some note, which Nettie thought at first was mere flattery, but Rufus added that a particular work was hanging in pride of place in the family home. Nettie could see that her father was pleased, and she herself was partly won over, but the memory of the rowdy party of young men and the arrogance that Rufus Norwood had shown at the restaurant in London, was hard to forget. When it came to Byron, the two young men shook hands and exchanged pleasantries, although there was reserve in Byron's attitude. Rufus, however, did not appear to notice.

'This is a splendid coincidence, Percy,' Rufus said, smiling. 'What are you doing here in Dover, anyway?'

'Just travelling through.' Percy shot an anxious glance at his mother. 'We're on our way to London.'

'And this man says there are no rooms vacant,' Lisette added, pouting. 'You seem to have influence here, Mr Norwood. Perhaps you could put in a good word for us.'

'I can do better than that, Condesa. You must be my guests. Norwood Hall is only a mile or two distant and you will be most welcome to stay with us.'

'I couldn't put you to so much trouble,' Lisette said coyly. 'But it is a very tempting offer. We've been travelling for days.'

'Then that's settled. I'll send a messenger on ahead to warn my father that we have company, and I'll have my carriage brought round to the front entrance.' He strode off, beckoning to one of the servants.

Lisette beamed at Percy. 'What a fortunate coincidence. He seems like a personable young man, and his family must be very wealthy.'

'His father owns a brewery, Mama. Mr Norwood started as a worker in an oast house when he was a boy, and went on to own the brewery.'

'Oh, well, I suppose nothing is perfect, but at

least we'll have a decent bed for the night.' Lisette turned to the clerk behind the desk. 'I wouldn't recommend this hotel to anyone. You have not been helpful.'

The man flushed uncomfortably and Nettie took pity on him. 'I'm sure you did your best,' she said softly. 'Thank you, anyway.'

He managed a weak smile and turned away to leaf through the hotel register.

Nettie moved closer to her father. 'Isn't this a wonderful coincidence, Pa? And to think that one of your paintings has found its way to Norwood Hall. I think that's splendid.'

'Indeed it is,' Robert said, grinning. 'Maybe I'll have found another patron, Nettie. I'm looking forward to meeting Mr Norwood senior.'

★ ★ ★

Rufus had chosen to abandon the party and had hired horses from the hotel stables so that he and Percy could ride, enabling the occupants of the carriage to travel in relative comfort. When they left the well-lit streets they were plunged into darkness as the vehicle negotiated the rutted country lanes. Nettie was squashed between Constance and Lisette, with Byron and her father seated opposite. They lapsed into silence after the first few minutes, and the drumming of the horses' hoofs and the rumbling of the wheels had a soporific effect. Robert was snoring gently and Constance had fallen asleep with her head on Nettie's shoulder, but they awakened with a start as the carriage drew to a halt and the light of half a dozen flambeaux flooded through the mud-spattered windows.

Nettie gazed out of the open carriage door and could not help being impressed. Norwood Hall was not large by the standards of the castle in Spain, but even in the darkness it stood out as a sizeable country house. It was set in large grounds just a short distance from a group of oast houses, and the brewery, which they had passed a short time before. Although it was late, lights shone from the windows and puffs of steam billowed from grilles low down in the building. The smell of hops and malt hung heavily in the still night air.

Nettie was the first to alight, followed by Lisette, who stood very still, sniffing the air with a look of disgust.

'What a revolting smell,' she said, turning up her nose. 'I never could abide beer of any sort. How do these people live with that stench?'

'It's money, Mama,' Byron said, chuckling. 'That is the smell of success.'

Lisette's reply was lost in a bluff greeting from their host. A middle-aged man, wearing a velvet smoking jacket and a matching cap with a long tassel, came hurrying towards them.

'Maurice Norwood, how do you do?' He seized Lisette's hand and raised it to his lips. 'My dear Condesa, Rufus arrived ahead of you and he told me of your dilemma. You must be exhausted after travelling so far. Do come in, all of you.' He proffered his arm to Lisette, who accepted graciously and allowed him to lead her into the house.

Nettie followed them with Constance at her side.

'Maybe Rufus's father is a widower,' she said, giggling. 'The *condesa* would like that.'

'Hush, they'll hear you.' Nettie controlled the urge to laugh with difficulty. Lisette seemed unable to resist the temptation to charm every eligible man she met; the portly brewer would stand little chance if she decided to use it to her advantage.

'I'll just make sure the horses are taken back to the hotel stables, Pa,' Rufus said cheerfully. 'We'll talk later, Percy.'

'The poor fellow looks done in, Rufus,' his father said sternly. 'There'll be plenty of time on the morrow.'

'We won't impose on your hospitality for a moment longer than necessary.' Lisette gave him her most winning smile and Nettie could see Maurice Norwood melting beneath her limpid gaze.

'You may stay here for as long as you like, Condesa. You are more than welcome.'

Nettie smiled to herself as she waited for the pleasantries to cease. Robert had joined in vociferously and Constance was also having her say. The only one to remain silent was Byron and he, too, was looking around the large entrance hall with its wainscoted walls and urns spilling over with garden flowers. It was homely rather than grand, and the wide staircase with carved oak banisters was well worn and had been polished to a glowing patina by brigades of housemaids for a century or more. It was the house of a country squire, as opposed to being the property of landed gentry, but it had a charm all of its own, and Nettie felt instantly at home despite the exhaustion that was threatening to overcome her.

The pleasantries over, the tired party were led into a large parlour where, despite the warmth of the summer evening, a log fire spat and sizzled as the sap oozed into the flames. A simple cold collation has been laid out on a table by the window, and two golden Labradors sat guard, drooling and sniffing the air.

'Out, boys,' Maurice said firmly, and the dogs obeyed reluctantly. 'Your luggage has been taken to your rooms, and you'll be shown to them as soon as you've taken some light refreshment. Unless, of course, you would like to retire straight away. You'll find everything waiting for you.'

Lisette clasped her hands together. 'You're too kind, Mr Norwood, I hope your wife won't object to us turning up uninvited.'

Nettie and Constance exchanged wry smiles, but Maurice Norwood did not seem to realise that he was being quizzed about his marital status.

He beamed at Lisette. 'Mrs Norwood goes to bed early, but she will be delighted to meet you in the morning. You will excuse me if I retire also. I rise at dawn and do a full day's work at the brewery. We're country people, and we keep country hours.'

'We appreciate your hospitality, sir,' Robert said hastily. 'And I understand from your son that you own a painting of mine.'

'Not now, Pa,' Nettie whispered. 'Let the poor man go to his bed.'

'Why yes,' Maurice puffed out his chest, which together with his portly belly was threatening to pop the buttons on his waistcoat. 'You will see it tomorrow, sir. It hangs in pride of place over the mantelshelf in our drawing room. I am quite an art lover.' He bowed out of the room, leaving them to fall on the food.

The brass clock on the mantelshelf struck midnight and Lisette yawned and rose gracefully from her seat. 'I'm exhausted. It's time I was in bed.'

Percy leaned over to ring the bell for the servant. 'I'm going to wait up for Rufus. We've a lot to catch up on.'

'I'm going to my room.' Constance dabbed her lips on a table napkin. 'To sleep in a proper bed again will be delightful. I'll swear there were bed bugs in that hotel in Calais.'

'It cost me nearly all the money I had,' Lisette said crossly.

The door opened and a maid rushed in, bobbing a curtsey. 'You rang, my lady?'

Lisette smiled. 'How charming. Yes, you may show me to my room.'

'And me,' Constance said, leaping to her feet. 'Come on, Nettie. You look worn out, and dark shadows beneath the eyes are not becoming.'

Nettie stood up. 'You're right, of course. I am tired. I'll see you all at breakfast, but we'll need to have a serious talk about what to do next. We can't stay here for ever.'

14

Robert stood in front of the ornately carved mantelshelf, gazing up at the painting of a young girl in an idyllic rural setting. 'You were only eleven then, Nettie,' he said proudly.

'I do remember sitting for it, Pa. But we were living in Plaistow and I don't think we ever ventured out of the city.'

Robert smiled benevolently. 'I used my imagination, Nettie. A background of grimy streets and ragged children would not have had the same appeal.'

Maurice shook his head. 'Poor child. You only have to look out of the window to see what you've missed. I grew up in a cottage not a stone's throw from the brewery. I count myself very fortunate to have had so much freedom.'

'We can't all reside in the country,' Robert said sharply. 'I had to make a living and London was the best place to sell my work. Where, as a matter of interest, did you purchase this one?'

'It weren't in London, that's for certain. I think I got it in a small gallery in Dover, as far as I can recall. I just had to have it.' He turned to Nettie, eyeing her closely. 'You've grown into quite a beauty, but you were obviously a charming child. I always wanted to have a little girl to make a fuss of, but our little angel was with us for a short time only. A long time after Rufus was born my wife gave birth to a baby girl,

245

but she survived only a few hours . . . '

'Maurice.' A shrill voice behind them made all three turn round to look at the small, plump woman who had burst into the dining room. Her cheeks were stained scarlet and her lips had disappeared into a thin slit. She might once have been considered pretty, but years of discontent had soured her expression and furrowed her brow. 'Who are these people? There are strangers in the parlour, too.'

'You were asleep when they arrived, my little dumpling, and I didn't like to wake you so early this morning.' Maurice hurried towards her, holding out his hands, but she brushed them aside.

'You haven't answered my question. Are they a travelling theatrical group? The woman said she is a *condesa*, whatever that means.'

'She is a Spanish noblewoman, Jane, my love,' Maurice said hastily. 'They needed shelter for the night and Rufus brought them here. Quite right, too.' He laid a tentative hand on her arm. 'Come and meet Robert. Mr Carroll is the artist who painted this picture, and this young lady is his daughter, Nettie. She is the little girl in the painting. If our baby girl had lived I like to think that she would have looked like that.'

'I don't want strangers to know of our personal tragedy,' Jane said in a low voice. 'There isn't a day goes by when I don't think of our little daughter.'

'I'm sorry, my dear. It was thoughtless of me.' Maurice took a brightly coloured paisley handkerchief from his breast pocket and blew his nose. 'Anyway, our little jewel is among the angels now.'

'We are not a guesthouse,' Jane said, frowning. 'We know nothing of these people.'

Maurice turned to Robert with an apologetic smile. 'My wife is very forthright.'

'At least she is honest,' Robert said mildly. 'I'm sorry if we have put you out, ma'am.'

'Thank you for your hospitality,' Nettie added. 'We'll be leaving as soon as possible'

'Now, now, don't be hasty.' Maurice shot a warning look at his wife. 'We don't often get visitors, least of all a titled personage.'

'We are not a charity, Maurice. People like that seldom pay their way. You've been in business long enough to know how things are.'

Nettie could see that Mrs Norwood was in no mood to compromise. 'We should go now, Pa.'

'Jane.' Maurice eyed his wife sternly. 'This is not the way we treat guests.'

She tossed her head. 'They weren't invited, Maury. We don't know who they are.'

Maurice slipped his arm around his wife's ample waist. 'The *condesa* is Percy's mother — you remember Percy, don't you? Charming chap, shared our son's room in the halls of residence for a while.'

'Yes, I suppose so,' Jane said grudgingly. 'But don't think this is a dosshouse, Mr Carroll. I know what you artistic people are like.'

'I'm afraid I don't know what you mean, ma'am.' Robert shot a sideways glance at Nettie, which she interpreted as a cry for help.

'You've been more than kind, Mrs Norwood,'

Nettie said quickly. 'You have a beautiful home and I quite understand your reservations. We are financially embarrassed at the moment, but perhaps there is something we can do to pay for our bed and board?'

Maurice threw up his hands. 'No, certainly not. I never heard of such a thing.'

Jane put her head on one side, her eyes darting from one to the other. She tucked a stray lock of mousy brown hair under her lace cap. 'Are you saying that you need money?'

'No, ma'am, of course not.' Robert glared at Nettie, shaking his head.

'I think we need to be honest, Pa.' Nettie looked from Maurice's flushed countenance to his wife's pale-lipped scowl. 'We're heading home to London and we've travelled all the way from Spain. It's been a long journey and the countess has had to sell her jewels to pay our fares. We're running out of money, but we are all ready and willing to work.'

'A fine lady like the countess ought not to toil in the fields like a farm worker,' Maurice said firmly.

Jane glared at him. 'Fine lady! Stuff and nonsense. That person is no better than she should be, if you want my opinion.'

'That's enough, Jane.' Maurice turned to Robert with an apologetic smile. 'My wife is a little upset. I shouldn't have mentioned our tragic loss. It still causes us much pain.'

Nettie could see that her father was about to say something he might regret, and she stepped in between them. 'The *condesa* has a most interesting story, ma'am. I'm sure she would be willing to share it with you, given the chance. As to the rest of us, we would willingly help you in the hop fields. I've heard that people flock here from London at this time of the year.'

'Think of Rufus, my love,' Maurice said softly. 'How would he feel if you turned his friend's family away in their hour of need?'

Jane shrugged. 'I knew there was more to it. Look at their clothes, Maury. They don't look like wealthy travellers.'

'Nettie has been very frank with us, Jane.' Maurice held his hand out to Robert. 'As for myself, I would like to commission you to paint a portrait of my dear wife, sir.'

Robert's mouth worked as if he were a clockwork automaton. 'I'd be honoured,' he said after a pause.

'Are you mad?' Jane demanded. 'You'll end up paying him.'

'But think how grand you'll look above the mantelshelf in the drawing room, my pet. You will be immortalised on canvas, and I believe that Mr Carroll is well known in the art world.'

'Well, I suppose so,' Jane said grudgingly. 'They can all stay but they must earn their keep, including the countess. We're short-handed in the hop garden. They can start immediately.'

★ ★ ★

'What!' Lisette cried, falling back on the sofa in the parlour. 'They want me, Condesa Talavera, to work in a field?'

249

'It's not too arduous,' Nettie said valiantly. 'We'll help you, and we will be paid for our efforts. Moreover, we're safe here. This is the last place that Wegg would think of looking for us, and it is a delightful spot. I went for a short stroll after our talk with the Norwoods. It's a beautiful part of the country.'

'Are you sure this is a good idea?' Robert turned to Nettie with an anxious frown. 'I know I agreed to it when that harpy was haranguing us, but on thinking it over, you'll be working with the sort of people I wouldn't want you to associate with,' he lowered his voice, 'and gypsies.'

His horrified expression brought a smile to Nettie's lips. 'I don't think the gypsies would be a problem, Pa. If they're prepared to work, that makes them just the same as us.'

'I don't know about that,' Robert said doubtfully. 'But if we remain here I will have to face Jane Norwood every day and paint a likeness that will both please her husband and flatter her. I think I would rather go to prison.'

Nettie reached up and kissed her father's thin cheek. 'Never mind, Pa. Think of the money, and the rest of us will work in the hop garden.'

'It's not fair,' Lisette said crossly. 'I had to leave my portrait behind, and now you're going to paint that virago.'

'I promise to do another likeness of you, Condesa.' Robert crossed his heart. 'It will be my pleasure. This is pure necessity.'

'And I'm not used to manual labour,' Lisette protested. 'I can't work in the fields.'

'I'll do your share, Condesa,' Nettie said eagerly. 'All you would have to do would be to sit in the shade and try to look as though you're doing something. If we stay here we'll be safe, and we're all together, that's the most important thing.'

'No one has asked me,' Constance said crossly. 'It would ruin my hands, and the sun would do dreadful things to my complexion. I'm not doing it.'

'You could wear a hat,' Nettie said unsympathetically. 'We can't stay here unless we work, and we can't get away from here unless we earn some money.'

Robert shook his head. 'You're forgetting Byron and Percy. We haven't told them or even asked their opinion. They're young men, Nettie. They have minds of their own.'

'Byron will do what is right.' Nettie made an effort to sound confident. 'I'm not so sure about Percy.'

'He'll agree with me,' Constance said, pouting. 'We're not meant to toil in the fields like common labourers.'

Lisette rose from the sofa and made for the door. 'I'm not happy about this, but I'll speak to my sons, although I doubt if they'll listen to me. Both of them are stubborn.'

'I'm coming with you, Condesa.' Constance followed her from the parlour, closing the door softly behind her.

'At least I brought my paints and brushes with me,' Robert said with an attempt at a smile. 'All I need is a canvas and I can start painting that woman's portrait. How her husband puts up with her is beyond my reckoning. The man must be a saint.'

Nettie patted him on the shoulder. 'If we all work hard we can save enough to move on.'

'You're right, as always. We must be thankful to be rid of Wegg, and now I'm free from Duke Dexter I'll never go back to my old ways.'

'You're a great artist, and one day you'll receive the recognition you deserve.'

Nettie looked round as the door opened, expecting to see the *condesa* returning with her sons, but it was Rufus who entered the room.

'Ah, Miss Carroll, just the person I was looking for.' He made a mock bow. 'My father tells me that you're thinking of helping with the harvest, and he suggested that you might like to see the hop gardens for yourself before you make a final decision.' He turned to Robert. 'You, I gather, have the onerous task of pleasing my mother. I must warn you that she is fiendishly critical.'

'I'll do my best,' Robert said stiffly. 'If we decide to stay.'

Rufus was suddenly serious. 'Percy has told me a little of the events that brought you here, sir. It seems to me that to remain here for a while might be in your best interests, but of course that is your decision.'

Nettie eyed him curiously. Her first impression of Rufus Norwood in their brief encounter at the Gaiety Restaurant had not been favourable. She had written him off as a spoiled young man with wealth that he had done nothing to earn and a high opinion of his own charms; seeing him at the party in Dover had confirmed her opinion. Now, however, he seemed to be a different person, and she was confused.

'Thank you, Mr Norwood. We're considering the offer carefully.' Robert shot a wary glance at Nettie. 'We're waiting to hear what the *condesa*'s sons think of the plan.'

'I know what Percy will say,' Rufus said confidently. 'I can't speak for Byron, but the offer is still there, Miss Carroll. The accommodation for the workers is far from luxurious, and maybe you ought to see what you'll be letting yourself in for.'

Nettie shrugged. 'We've probably stayed in worse, but I would like to see the hop garden.'

⋆ ⋆ ⋆

The late August sun beat down relentlessly on the forest of tall hop plants, which looked to Nettie's untrained eye like exotic green fruits hanging in bunches from trailing vines. The air was hot and heavy, filled with the bitter scent of the hops, as men, women and children worked feverishly to fill their baskets, for which, Rufus said, they would be paid by the bushel. The heat was intense, but no one seemed to mind, and the women chatted to each other, the Romany speaking in their own tongue, while others sang. An old woman caught Nettie's eye as she walked past and smiled. Children who were old enough worked alongside their parents, and the little ones played in the dust or slept in makeshift cradles made out of orange boxes.

Away from the hop garden there were rows of wooden huts. Washing lines were strung between them, hung with clothes drying in the sunshine, but the pervading smell from the privies was noxious.

'You get used to it,' Rufus said, chuckling. 'It's unpleasant, but we do treat the latrines with lime each day in order to prevent disease, and there is a pump to provide fresh water.'

'It all seems well organised,' Nettie acknowledged. 'The workers look happy enough.'

'They can earn a lot more in a week here than they would in their normal occupations, and they get the benefit of fresh air and sunshine. We provide fruit and vegetables from our kitchen gardens, but the rest is up to them. Some of the men go out shooting rabbits or they go down to the river to fish. If they have small children Mama gives them milk from our dairy.' Rufus met Nettie's surprised look with a smile. 'She's not so bad when you get to know her. My mother was once a hopper.'

'A hopper?'

'She came with her parents from Shoreditch and she was picking hops when she caught my father's eye — that's how they met. Pa had worked his way up to being a foreman in the oast house by the time they married, and she's been at his side through the hard times and helped him build the business into what it is today. Don't judge her too harshly, Miss Carroll.'

Nettie turned her head away. She could feel the blush colouring her cheeks and she hoped he

254

would put it down to the heat and not the wave of embarrassment that washed over her. Rufus had seen through her attempt to conceal the dislike she felt for his mother, and now she was ashamed.

'We'll work hard and earn our money, and we'll move on as soon as the harvest is over.' Nettie shot him a sideways glance. 'You don't seem convinced.'

He shrugged. 'Have you ever done manual labour, Miss Carroll? Has the *condesa* ever lifted anything heavier than a wine glass? Percy is a good chap, but he's not the most reliable person. He's more likely to fall asleep in the sun than to do a full day's work.'

'He's your friend.'

'He is, and the hop harvest is important to my parents, and to me.'

Nettie rounded on him. 'Have you ever done a full day's work here?'

'Yes, when I was younger I used to help with the harvest.'

'And now, no doubt, you enjoy spending your parents' hard-earned money.'

'I don't think that's any of your business.'

'I'm simply making a point, Mr Norwood. You reprimanded me just now for making a hasty judgement, and now it seems to me that you are doing exactly the same thing where we are concerned.' Nettie managed to keep her tone calm, but inwardly she was fuming and she walked off without giving him a chance to respond. She quickened her pace, curbing the desire to look round to see if he were following, but there was no sound of footsteps and she could hear him talking to one of the hoppers. A quick peek over her shoulder confirmed the fact that he had stopped and was chatting amicably to a young Romany woman. Nettie walked on, she was even more determined to prove Rufus Norwood's arrogant assumptions unfounded and unfair. She went to find her father and the *condesa* and report on the conditions under which they would be working.

★ ★ ★

The hut proved to be large, clean and very basic. Lisette was shocked to discover that they were all to share the same accommodation, and she insisted that the sleeping arrangements should be moved around so that the men slept in one half, separated from the women. Percy said he had spotted just the thing and went outside, returning moments later with a large piece of canvas, which he and Byron rigged up to divide the room and give the ladies privacy.

Constance gazed in disgust at the roughly constructed wooden cot where she was to sleep.

'That's not a bed.'

'It's better than sleeping on the floor.' Nettie picked up a ticking case stuffed with straw and tossed it to her. 'There's your mattress. You'll sleep well tonight, Constance.'

'It crackles and it's prickly. I won't get a wink of sleep.'

'I think we'll all be exhausted by the end of the day,' Nettie said grimly. 'We've got to prove ourselves and if we don't pick enough hops we'll be sent packing.'

Lisette sank down on her bed and groaned. 'This is dreadful. I think we should give up now and move on regardless. I can't believe that the workers live in these conditions.'

'You haven't seen some of the lodging houses in London where Pa and I rented rooms in the past,' Nettie said briskly. 'Come on, it's not so bad. We can't just get up and leave because we're virtually penniless. If we arrive in London without any money we'll be sleeping under the railway arches and this will seem like luxury.'

'Nettie's right.' Byron stuck his head round the corner of the canvas curtain. 'The sooner we get started the better. I'm prepared to work twice as hard if it will make life easier for all of you.'

'I'll do my bit,' Percy added, peering over the top and chuckling. 'You do look a dispirited bunch. Come on, ladies. It's not so bad. One day, Constance, we'll look back at this and laugh.'

She glared at him. 'I don't think it's at all amusing.'

'We've already lost time.' Nettie caught Byron's eye and smiled. 'I'll pick twice as much as you.'

'I wouldn't put money on it.' He lifted the stiff canvas so that she could duck underneath it and make her way to the door. 'Come on, Mother. You too, Constance. Let's make a start.'

Reluctantly, Lisette rose to her feet and followed Nettie, with Constance not far behind.

Byron caught up with Nettie outside. 'It's

going to be tough. Are you sure you want to go through with this?'

'I don't see that we have much choice,' Nettie whispered as she fell into step beside him. 'I just comfort myself with the thought that we might have been forced to walk to London, begging for food on the way. This is infinitely preferable.'

Byron chuckled. 'I'll ask you the same question at the end of the day. You might feel differently then.'

She responded with a smile. 'You know me, Byron. I don't complain; I get on with things. I just hope the other hoppers don't resent us for barging in on them and taking some of the work.'

Byron gazed at the forest of hop vines and shook his head. 'I think there's enough work here to keep us all busy. Let's get started.'

Nettie was about to reply when they were approached by the burly foreman. He shot a cursory glance at each of them in turn and then barked out a set of instructions. He spoke so quickly that Nettie only caught a few of his words in the Kentish dialect, but he thrust baskets at them and it was easy enough to copy the actions of the other hoppers. Nettie had expected some animosity from the people who were working industriously, but, apart from one or two who gave them black looks, the other workers were friendly enough and willing to answer questions. The women were openly curious and Nettie was aware of the appreciative glances of the younger men, and some of the older ones, too. Although they received swift reprimands from their wives and the work went on at a surprisingly fast pace.

They were allowed a break for their midday meal, and they would have gone hungry had not a maid from the house arrived bringing a basket covered with a white cloth, which she handed to Nettie. 'From Cook, miss.'

'What is this?' Nettie asked. 'We didn't order anything from the kitchen.'

The girl shrugged and backed away. 'I think Mr Rufus told her to put up something for you and your friends.'

Percy had been standing close by, having been told to use his height to cut down the strings of hops for them to pick. 'That sounds like him. He's a good chap, Nettie. Generous to a fault.'

Nettie was tempted to hand the food back to the girl, but her stomach was rumbling and she knew the others must be equally hungry. 'Thank Cook for us, please.'

'Yes, miss.' The girl raced off in the direction of the kitchens at the back of the main house.

'Ten minutes,' the foreman shouted. 'You've got ten minutes and then I want to see those fingers flying and the baskets heaped up.'

Percy was first to snatch the clean napkin off the basket and he grinned appreciatively. 'Good old Rufus. Look at this. We've got bread, cheese and pickled onions, and that looks like ginger cobnut cake. It's a local speciality — Rufus brought one at the beginning of the Michaelmas term. It was for him to share with his year, but he gave me a slice, too.'

'He's a bit older than you,' Nettie observed

casually. 'How did you become friends?'

'We were both in the rowing club, but we weren't selected for the racing crew, so we went to the pub instead, and then we shared a room for a while.'

'He's very generous.' Lisette glanced into the basket. 'Although it's not the type of food my cooks used to send to the table, I'm too hungry to care.'

Nettie said nothing as she helped herself to bread and cheese. She wondered how her father was getting on with Jane Norwood and a wry smile curved her lips. Perhaps painting Jane's portrait was Pa's punishment for his past misdeeds. With a patroness like Mrs Norwood, he was serving his sentence in the most unusual manner.

★　★　★

The ten minutes passed all too quickly and they went back to the work, which looked deceptively simple; it was hard on those unused to manual labour, and it was hot and dusty beneath the vines. After an hour or two Nettie was tired and sweating profusely and her clothes were sticking to her back. She glanced round, wondering how the other women managed to keep up such a pace, but they seemed cheerful enough and their chatter never ceased. When they weren't talking, they were singing and the children who were too small to work danced amongst them like grubby elves.

Nettie had to concentrate all her efforts on the

job in hand, and even then she was much slower than the other pickers. Constance and Lisette worked in short bursts, stopping to fan themselves and take sips of water, and if they complained it was in whispers. Percy and Byron worked with the men, pulling down the vines and emptying the baskets into larger containers ready to be weighed before being tipped into bins and taken to the oast house.

By the time the afternoon session ended Nettie was aching all over and her fingers were stained black from the hop juice, and bleeding from tiny cuts from the spiny stems. She rose stiffly, stepping aside as the other hoppers streamed towards their respective huts, laughing and talking, with the younger children and dogs gambolling on ahead.

'What will we have for supper?' Constance looked round as if hoping that the maid would appear again, bringing a basket from the kitchen.

'We can't depend on food sent from the big house.' Nettie turned to Percy. 'There's a river nearby — are you any good at fishing?'

'I haven't fished since I was a boy.'

Byron came up behind him. 'We haven't done badly considering it's our first day.'

'Are you handy with a fishing line?' Percy asked. 'It looks as if we have to find our own dinner tonight. Unless I throw myself on Rufus's mercy, which I don't want to do.'

'I am going to lie down. I've never worked so hard in my life,' Lisette said, sighing. 'This was not a good idea.' She wandered off in the direction of the hut.

'We must eat,' Nettie said firmly. 'I caught a glimpse of water through the trees, so we aren't far from the river. We'd better do something or we'll go hungry.'

'Maybe one of the men could lend us some hooks and lines. I had a chat with that fellow over there. He's seems friendly enough. I'll go and ask him.' Byron walked over to the man, who was tipping the last of his afternoon's work into a poke, and exchanged a few words. 'It's all right,' he called. 'Ben is going to lend us what we need. You go on and I'll collect the lines and follow you to the river.'

Percy took Constance by the hand and Nettie led the way, following a well-trodden path past the huts and into the cool shade of a spinney, through which the silver ribbon of water was clearly visible. They emerged once again into the sunlight and the river stretched out before them, curving snake-like through open countryside. Weeping willows dipped their leaves in the water, and dragonflies hovered over the surface, their wings beating so fast that they barely seemed to move. Percy uttered a triumphant yell and kicked off his boots before wading into the river and using his hands to scoop up water and toss it over his head, creating tiny rainbows in the still air.

'Come out,' Constance cried. 'You'll drown.'

'I can swim like a fish.' Percy demonstrated by diving into the water, disappearing from view for a few seconds and then surfacing in a shower of spray as he swam for the shallows. 'The water is so cool. You should try it, girls.'

'Don't be ridiculous.' Constance turned her back on him as he stood and made his way to the bank. 'We have more sense, and anyway, I can't swim.'

'Neither can I,' Nettie said wistfully. 'But the water does look inviting.' She glanced over her shoulder at the sound of footsteps on the gravel path and saw Byron coming towards them with crudely made fishing rods, just as Percy emerged from the river with waterweed clinging to his clothes.

'Percy, you fool. You've probably frightened all the fish for miles.'

Percy threw back his head and laughed. 'Don't be such a misery. You want to try it, Byron.'

Nettie could see that the brothers were about to argue and she stepped in between them. 'I don't know anything about fishing, but perhaps we ought to go downriver and try there, or I can see us going to bed tonight without any supper.'

15

That evening they sat round a campfire eating the trout they had caught and cooked over the flames. Byron was a townsman, lacking the necessary skills to provide food from the wild, but Percy had had a different upbringing in Catalonia, with freedom to roam as he pleased, and during his time at Cambridge he boasted about weekends spent with friends whose fathers owned large country estates. He knew how to gut fish and prepare it to be roasted on stones, heated in the fire, or cooked on a makeshift spit. The results varied from reasonably well done to slightly charred, but they were so hungry by the time the fish were cooked that they devoured every last morsel.

They had just finished their meal when Rufus joined them. 'I'm not too late, I hope. My mother is a stickler for punctuality at the dinner table, or I would have come sooner.' He placed the hamper he was carrying on the ground and handed out bottles of ale. 'The best from Norwood's Brewery.'

'I don't drink beer,' Lisette said huffily.

'I'll have yours then, Mama.' Percy went to take it from her but she shook her head.

'I'm thirsty, so I'll try it, but that doesn't mean I have to enjoy it.'

'You'll find it quite refreshing.' Percy took the

bottle, uncapped it and handed it back to her.

'I prefer wine,' Constance said, pulling a face.

'Then you should have found work in a vineyard. I'm afraid we only brew beer.' Rufus opened a bottle and passed it to her. 'Take a sip, Constance. It's not so bad.'

'I quite like ale.' Nettie took a drink and nodded. 'This is good. I could get used to this.'

'At last — a connoisseur,' Rufus said, chuckling. 'You're a woman after my own heart, Nettie.' He raised his bottle to her in a toast. 'You've survived the first day in the hop garden. I hope it wasn't too terrible.'

She shot him a wary glance and realised that he was teasing her. She smiled and relaxed. Perhaps it was the strong ale, or maybe it was the moon rising over the horizon that made her feel warm and safe. Its beams reflecting on the water turned the river to ripples of molten silver, and somewhere in the spinney a nightingale began to sing.

'I'm sorry,' Lisette said, breaking the spell as she scrambled to her feet, 'I don't think I'll ever get used to English beer. It isn't the drink for a lady. Anyway, I'm going to bed. Come with me, girls. I'm not walking through the woods on my own.'

'Would you like me to see you safely to the hut, Mama?' Byron asked politely.

It occurred to Nettie that he might have been speaking to a stranger and she felt a pang of sympathy for him. She knew how much he needed some show of affection from his mother, but so far their relationship had been cordial, if not overly warm. It seemed that Percy was still very much his mother's favourite, and it hurt Nettie to see Byron pushed aside. She longed to say something to Lisette, but she was afraid any intervention might make matters worse.

'No, you stay and chat,' Lisette said coolly, adding as an afterthought, 'Thank you, anyway, Byron.'

Constance rose to her feet, handing the bottle back to Rufus. 'I suppose beer is good, if you like that sort of thing.'

'Come along,' Lisette said impatiently. 'I'm tired.'

Nettie glanced at Byron and gave him an encouraging smile. 'I'll go with them. We'll be quite safe.' She hesitated for a moment, turning to Rufus. 'I haven't seen my father since this morning. Did he dine with you tonight?'

'My mother insisted on it.' Rufus's lips twitched as if he were suppressing a chuckle. 'Your father didn't have much choice, but a glass or two of our best ale seemed to ease talk at the table, and Mama was in fine fettle.'

Nettie had no answer for that and she hurried after Constance and Lisette as they made their way back to the hut.

★ ★ ★

Nettie slept reasonably well, and she was first to rise from her bed. Her first task was to fetch water from the pump, but as she stepped outside she found two dead rabbits, hanging from a nail in the hut wall. On the ground beneath them was a basket filled with onions, potatoes, carrots, parsnips and a turnip. The sight of dried blood on the animals' fur made her feel physically sick, and she covered her lips as bile rose to her throat.

'What's the matter, ducks? Never seen a dead coney afore?'

Nettie looked round and saw an elderly Romany woman, whose face was tanned and weathered so that it gleamed liked polished leather. Her shrewd brown eyes twinkled and Nettie recognised her as the woman who had smiled at her the previous day.

'Coney?'

'Rabbit, dear. Someone has been generous, and you can make a stew that will fill your bellies for a day or two.'

'I can make soup,' Nettie said shyly, 'but I don't know what to do with a dead rabbits.'

'I'll show you. It's early yet and not many are about. If you fetch water for me, I'll make a start on the coneys.'

'Thank you, I'd be very grateful.' Nettie hesitated. 'I'm Nettie, what's your name?'

'I'm Florica. Now hurry before the others rise and form a queue. We have to begin work early or we won't fill enough baskets today.'

Nettie did as she was asked and filled the two buckets to the brim. When she returned she found Florica seated on the ground outside the hut, having skinned the rabbits, and about to prepare them for cooking.

'You'll need a stew pot, Nettie.'

'We haven't got anything like that.'

'I have a spare one I can lend you, but I want it back, mind!'

'Of course. Thank you.'

'It's in my vardo.' Florica beckoned to a small child, who had appeared and was staring at them, sucking her thumb.

'Daria, fetch the old cooking pot for the young lady.'

The little girl backed away, still staring wide-eyed at Nettie, and then she turned and ran.

'Is she scared of me?' Nettie asked anxiously. 'She's a pretty child.'

'She's a bit shy of gorgios, but she'll be back. Now pay attention — this is how you gut a rabbit and cut it up for the pot. You can peel and chop the vegetables, while I do this.'

They worked quickly and in silence until the pot was full.

'How will I cook it?' Nettie asked anxiously. 'I mean, isn't it difficult without a range?'

'As soon as you finish for the day you must get the fire going and hang the pan on a tripod over the flames.' Florica nudged her, grinning. 'I know you haven't got such a thing, but I'm sure that handsome young master's son could find you something from the big house kitchens. I saw him follow you down to the river last evening. I think he's got his eye on you, missy.'

Nettie shook her head. 'No, you're mistaken. If Rufus Norwood fancies anyone it will be Constance. All the men fall for her.'

'Trust Florica to know better.'

Nettie jumped to her feet as Byron stepped

out of the hut. 'Thank you for your help, Florica,' she said hastily. 'If there's anything I can do for you, just say the word.'

'We all help each other.' Florica rose to her feet with surprising agility. 'But I'll take the rabbit skins, if you don't want them. When I've finished with them they'll make a pair of fur gloves for my grand-daughter, or a warm hat.'

'Oh, yes, please. I wouldn't know what to do with them.'

Florica snatched the skins and scuttled off in the direction of her caravan. Byron leaned over to examine the contents of the pot.

'Where did this come from?'

Nettie jerked her head in the direction of the gypsy caravan. 'I don't know who gave us the rabbits or the vegetables, but the gypsy woman loaned us the cooking pot, and she showed me how to prepare a rabbit stew.'

'That should be tasty. I'll look forward to my dinner tonight.'

'Have you any idea who might have done this?'

'Well, it wasn't me. I'm not much use when it comes to being a hunter or a fisherman.'

'You make a good fire,' Nettie said, smiling. 'And that's what we'll need later. We'll also need some sort of stand so that we can hang the pot over the flames.'

'I think that's a job for Percy. I've heard him talking to the female servants. You'd think he was courting them, by the way he behaves, but it seems to work and he's definitely a favourite below stairs. I wish I were half as charming as my brother.'

Nettie laid her hand on his arm. 'You are just as good as Percy — in fact you're the better man. He's nice, but he's a spoiled boy and you're someone who can be trusted.'

Byron smiled ruefully. 'How dull you make me sound, Nettie.'

She released him with a sigh. 'Oh, well. If you're determined to feel sorry for yourself I'll leave you to wallow. I'm going to walk to the village and see if I can buy some bread for breakfast, or we'll have to work on empty stomachs.'

Byron put his hand in his pocket and produced two pennies. 'This is all I have.'

'That will do. I have a penny so that should be able to get enough for a loaf and maybe a pat of butter.'

'I'll come with you.' Byron fell into step beside her. 'We'll have to hurry or we'll be late starting and the foreman won't be pleased.'

'You stay here, Byron. You're the fastest worker out of all of us. I'll hurry and be back before you know it.'

'Will you be all right on your own?'

'I don't think the big bad wolf will be lying in wait for me and I'm quite capable of finding the bakery, but thank you anyway.' She hurried on, but had gone only a short distance when someone called her name and she looked round to see Rufus emerge from the stables. He was dressed for riding and carried a crop.

'Where are you off to so early in the morning, Nettie?'

'I'm going to the village for some bread.'

'You'll have a wasted journey then. There is no bakery in the village, which is little more than a hamlet, but Cook makes very tasty bread,' he added with a twinkle in his dark eyes.

'Thank you, but I can hardly go begging at your kitchen door.' Nettie was about to retrace her steps and return to the hut when Rufus barred her way.

'Don't be so hasty. I know you're in a difficult position, but your situation and that of your friends is different from the other hoppers. They come every year and they know the score, but Percy is my friend, therefore he and his family deserve to be treated as guests.'

'No,' Nettie said firmly. 'We're working for your father now, and that puts us in another class altogether. I've already had one of the Romany women remark on the fact that you joined us at the river last evening.'

'It's none of their business.' Rufus frowned angrily. 'I do as I please.'

'That's just my point. You are in a privileged position — we aren't.' Nettie started to walk away, but paused and turned her head to give him a straight look. 'Do you know anything about two dead rabbits left outside our hut? There was also a basket of vegetables.'

'Rabbits are a pest and our head gardener likes to keep them under control. The kitchen garden provides us with all our needs, so I thought you might be able to use them.'

'Thank you, but without wanting to sound ungrateful, I think it best if we try to get by on our own. It really isn't fair on the other workers

— some of them are so poor that their children go barefoot. You'll have a rebellion from the other hoppers if we're seen to receive special treatment.'

Rufus shrugged. 'It's still summer. The children don't need shoes in the country.'

'And their clothes are in rags.'

'Only a fool would wear their Sunday best to pick hops.'

'Are you so blind to the lives of those less fortunate?' Nettie demanded angrily. 'These people work ten hours a day to bring in your harvest, out of which your father has made a fortune.'

'They get paid well enough. I believe that most take home more than they would earn in London.'

'But you know nothing about their lives or the hardships they endure.'

'We run a business, not a charity.'

Nettie faced him, arms akimbo. 'What do you do, exactly? You were at Cambridge with Percy, but you've graduated.'

He eyed her coldly. 'That's correct.'

'So now you live here, riding your horse, going to parties and entertaining your friends.'

'You say that as if it were a bad thing. I will join the family business, when I am ready.'

'Oh, well, that's all right then, I suppose. Anyway, it's none of my business.' Nettie was about to walk away but he caught her by the wrist.

'You are a stubborn young woman. I was trying to help, but it seems that I'm wasting my time.'

'Leave us alone,' Nettie said in desperation.

'All we want to do is earn enough money to get us back to London, and the way of life we knew. It wasn't easy, but we managed somehow. You've grown up in the lap of luxury, so you wouldn't understand.' She walked away without giving him a chance to answer.

★   ★   ★

After a long morning stripping the vines Nettie was beginning to wish that she had accepted Rufus's offer of bread. They had eaten nothing since the previous evening, and with only water to drink Nettie was feeling faint, and Constance and Lisette worked so slowly that they were in danger of being laid off by the foreman.

'I can't and won't work on an empty stomach.' Lisette stood up, shaking the dust and dried leaves from her grimy skirt. 'This is my idea of hell, and I refuse to do it any longer.'

Constance followed her example. 'I'm going to the hut to lie down,' she said crossly. 'I'm hot and hungry, and my hands are ruined. I wish I'd gone with Duke. At least he treated me like a lady.'

'He tricked you into marriage so that he could get his hands on your property,' Nettie countered. 'We have to work, or we'll starve.'

'Come along, Constance. We'll return to the hovel, where at least it's cool and there are no plant lice crawling all over us. If I can't eat, I won't work.' Lisette marched off with her skirts held above her ankles, and Constance hurried after her.

Nettie was expecting the foreman to roar at them, but he chose that moment to call ten minutes for the midday break, and she breathed a sigh of relief. She rose to her feet and moved swiftly to where Percy was finishing off a vine.

'We need food. It's going to be nigh on impossible to do an afternoon's work if we don't eat.'

Percy stood up, brushing a shower of greenfly from his clothes. 'I suppose you want me to whisper sweet nothings to Cook.'

'I refused help from Rufus earlier, and I regret that now, but we can't go on like this.'

'Leave it to me,' Percy said, frowning. 'I'll see what I can do.'

Byron emptied his full basket into a bin. 'Come to the hut and have a rest, Nettie. You look done in.'

'It's the heat and the dust, as well as these wretched little insects. They keep crawling down my neck. I'm just thankful they don't bite like fleas and bed bugs.' She walked slowly to the hut and found Lisette and Constance were already there and they were exclaiming excitedly over a basket of bread rolls and a slab of butter wrapped in a cabbage leaf.

'I can't believe it,' Constance said, grabbing a roll and breaking it in two. 'It's as if a good fairy heard our prayers.'

Lisette seized a roll and bit into it. 'I don't care where this came from, it's so good.'

Nettie helped herself and sat down on her bed to savour the bread and butter; this was not the time for false pride. It must have been Rufus who sent the food, most probably to prove her in the wrong, but at this moment she did not care, and she ate hungrily. Constance was about to snatch another roll, but Nettie sent her a warning glance.

'Don't forget Percy and Byron, and we ought to save some for our supper.'

Constance sat back, pouting. 'But I'm still hungry. I wish Duke would arrive on a white charger and carry me back to my house in Paris.'

'It's his house now, don't forget.' Nettie was in no mood to humour her. 'Anyway, I thought you were in love with Percy.'

'I am, of course, and Percy is the love of my life, but he can't provide for me.'

'That's where you're wrong.' Percy lifted the canvas flap and placed another basket on the floor at Constance's feet. 'I raced to the kitchen and persuaded Cook to give us enough flour, lard and salt to make bread for days to come. She's also promised to keep by any leftovers that would normally have gone to feed the pigs.' He seized a roll and buttered it generously.

'I won't eat the slops saved for swine,' Lisette said icily. 'But I would love a glass of wine now, and a siesta before supper.'

Byron ducked under the canvas and sat down beside Nettie. 'No chance of that, I'm afraid, Ma. We've only got a couple of minutes and we'll be back at work.' He grinned mischievously and placed a bottle of wine on the floor. 'This, however, is for tonight. Your pa caught up with me as I was filling the poke, Nettie. He gave me this and said that the portrait is taking shape.'

'Why didn't he come to see me?'

'He said he was expected in the dining room, so he didn't want to offend Mrs Norwood by being late, but he sends his love.'

'Maybe he's our guardian angel.' Lisette gazed longingly at the wine. 'A glass of that would make the afternoon seem less tedious.'

Nettie moved the bottle from Lisette's reach. 'Byron is right. This will keep until tonight, and we'll dine royally — at least I hope we will. I've never made rabbit stew before, but the salt will help to bring out the flavour. We just need a metal trivet or a tripod so that I can hang the pan over the fire.'

'That was the bell.' Byron put a roll in his pocket and stood up. 'It's time we were back in the hop garden.'

'Garden,' Lisette said bitterly. 'It's not like my beautiful garden at the castle.'

'It's bread and butter, Ma.' Percy helped her to her feet. 'And wine, tonight. Maybe this place isn't so bad after all.'

Byron held his hand out to Nettie. 'We'll get through this somehow, and when we reach London I'll see if my old employer will take me back. He offered to train me as an articled clerk, and maybe I should have accepted.'

Nettie smiled. 'You're a fair-minded man, Byron. I think you'd make a very good solicitor if you wanted to go that way.' She covered the basket with a cloth and stood up. 'But we'll need to pick a lot more hops before we have enough money to move on. Hopefully the police will have given up searching for my pa, but London is our home, and I can't see us living anywhere else.'

'Not even here?' Byron said casually.

'Hop picking?'

'No, I meant could you see yourself living in the big house?'

'What a strange question. There's little enough chance of that. What are you saying, Byron?'

'Nothing, really.'

'No, you meant something. Tell me.'

'I think Rufus Norwood is sweet on you, Nettie.'

She tucked the basket under her arm. 'Nonsense. We squabble every time we meet.'

Byron raised his eyebrows, saying nothing.

'You're being ridiculous,' Nettie added, tossing her head. 'Come on, or we'll be in trouble for being late.'

★ ★ ★

When it came to cooking the stew, Byron made up the fire and Percy, with his recently acquired talent for scrounging, produced a trivet, and the pot was hung over the flames and left to bubble gently for an hour. The meal was delicious and they sat round the campfire, savouring the stew to the last drop, which they mopped up with what remained of the bread. Byron and Percy drank the last two bottles of beer and Nettie, Lisette and Constance shared the wine. For the first time since they had left the castle, everyone seemed content and there were no complaints. Replete and exhausted from the day's toil, they remained where they were until the sun plummeted below the horizon and the shadows lengthened.

Lisette shivered and rose to her feet. 'I'm ready for bed.'

'Me, too.' Constance yawned and stood up, rubbing her eyes like a sleepy child. 'It's such hard work — I'm worn out.'

'Come along then. I don't like walking through the spinney on my own.' Lisette set off in the direction of the huts and Constance blew a kiss to Percy before trailing after her.

Nettie watched them go, stifling a sigh as she began clearing up after the meal. Neither Lisette nor Constance ever gave a thought to the work that went into making a fire or preparing food, let alone washing a cup or a plate.

'I suppose I'd better wash the pots in the river.'

Byron nudged Percy. 'We'll do that. You've earned a rest.'

She looked from one to the other. 'Are you sure? You won't simply go for a swim and forget about it, will you?'

'Certainly not,' Byron said firmly. 'And that goes for my brother, too.'

Percy nodded, and although Nettie was not sure she believed them, it was too tempting an offer to refuse. 'Thank you.' She stood up, gazing at the fiery sunset and the sky livid with gashes of scarlet and gold. 'I think I might go for a stroll along the river bank before I turn in.'

Byron was on his feet. 'Don't go too far.'

She laughed. 'I suppose you're afraid of losing

the only person in our hut who's a good cook.'

'And a good friend,' he said softly.

Nettie smiled and walked on. The air was balmy with a hint of dampness rising from the warm earth. The bitter scent of the willows mingled with the smell of the warm grass crushed beneath her feet, and the honeyed perfume of clover from the surrounding fields. Away from the cramped, noisy conditions in the camp the serenity and peace of the countryside calmed her worries, and she felt as if she had entered another world. As she skirted the bend in the river she came upon a pool where the water was so clear she could see the bottom where the pebbles gleamed like jewels in the last fiery rays of the sunset. She was hot and dusty after the day's work and she had the sudden urge to plunge in and allow the cool clear water to soothe her aching limbs.

She glanced over her shoulder, and as there was no one about, she gave in to temptation, undid the buttons on her gown and allowed it to slip to the ground, followed by her petticoat, and her stays. Wearing only her chemise, she stepped into the shallows. Placing one foot in front of the other, she went deeper and deeper until the water was up to her waist, and then she crouched down, ducking her head beneath the surface. Wishing she had learned to swim, she took her feet off the bottom, but sank immediately and had to struggle to regain her footing. She burst through the surface, shaking droplets from her long dark hair, and it was then she became aware that she was being watched. The wet cotton clung to her body, leaving little to the imagination and she crossed her arms instinctively to cover her breasts.

'Why are you spying on me?' she demanded angrily.

16

'What do you think you're doing?' Rufus glared at her, his slanting eyebrows drawn together in an ominous frown.

'What I do is none of your business.' Nettie shivered as a cool breeze skimmed the surface of the pool. 'Please go away.'

He stepped into the water, holding out his hand. 'The currents are dangerous, Nettie. You only have to take a step or two in the wrong direction and you could be swept away.'

She hesitated, gazing uncertainly at the swirling water beyond the trailing withies of the weeping willow. 'I can manage on my own.'

'A girl was drowned a little further downriver just a month ago. Let me help you from the water, and then I'll leave you to make your own way back.' Rufus glanced round at the deepening shadows. 'The light is fading fast. Take my hand, please.'

'Don't fuss, Rufus,' Nettie said crossly, but the river that had seemed so inviting minutes earlier now looked dark and menacing, with danger lurking in its depths. She was chilled to the bone and she felt herself slipping on the stones as an undercurrent tugged gently at first, but with increasing strength.

'Take my hand.' Rufus waded closer and she allowed him to help her to the bank without further protest. If she were to be honest it was a relief to feel solid ground and warm soil beneath her feet, but she was stiff with cold and shivering. Rufus took off his jacket and wrapped it around her shoulders.

'You need to get your clothes on before you catch a chill or worse. At this time of the year it gets cold quickly after dark.' He scooped up her discarded garments and handed them to her. 'Don't worry, I won't look.'

'I'm all right now, thank you,' Nettie said hastily. 'You don't have to wait for me.'

He turned his back on her. 'You might find it difficult to explain why you arrive in camp wearing my jacket. The hoppers are always looking for something or someone to talk about, and I imagine you and your companions must already be the subject of many campfire discussions.'

'I don't see why. We're just the same as everyone else.'

'If you think that, you're more naïve than I supposed. The people who come hop picking are the salt of the earth, but you have a countess and a very spoiled young French lady in your party.'

'That's not fair.' Stung by Rufus's last remark, Nettie went to stand beneath the trailing foliage of the willow before stepping out of her sodden chemise. She abandoned any attempt to put on her stays and wrapped them in a bundle with her wet clothing. At least her dress was warm and dry, and it was a relief to feel the life coming back to her numbed toes as she put on her stockings and boots. Maybe she had been foolish to go in the water — she most certainly would not make the same mistake again — but she had no intention of admitting her folly. She tapped Rufus on the shoulder and returned his damp jacket.

'Thank you for that.'

'I am on your side, you know.'

His face was in shadow, but there was a note of sincerity in his voice, and Nettie found it almost possible to believe him, but not quite. Each time she found herself warming to him she recalled the circumstances of their first two meetings. She had a vague suspicion that he saw her as a challenge, and his interest in her was simply due to pique — a man as handsome, charming and wealthy as Rufus Norwood could have his pick of young women, and he was obviously used to getting his own way. A spoiled only child, the darling of his overbearing mother, and the white hope of his adoring father, Rufus had never known what it was to want for anything, and she suspected that his will was very rarely crossed.

'If you walk on I'll follow you,' Nettie said coolly.

He turned on his heel and walked away, without saying a word, but he came to a sudden halt as they reached the spinney.

'Lights,' he said brusquely. 'It seems that your friends are out looking for you.'

Nettie glanced over his shoulder. 'I think it best if I go on alone.'

'Are you ashamed to be seen with me?'

'No, it's not that. If the other workers think we're being singled out for special treatment, maybe that's because you and Percy are friends, and I don't want to add to that.' She slipped past him. 'Thank you again. I am grateful.' She broke into a run, stopping only when she reached the trees.

Byron and Percy were searching the spinney, but their relief on finding her quickly turned to anger when she explained the reason for her dishevelled appearance.

'What the hell were you thinking off,' Byron demanded. 'Going in the water at this time of night and on your own was madness.'

'No harm came to me,' Nettie said defensively. 'I'm here now.'

'You might have drowned,' Percy added crossly. 'You could have been carried downriver by the current.'

'Well I'm quite safe and I didn't ask you to come looking for me.' Nettie was about to walk on when a shot rang out, followed by a loud groan. She spun round, peering into the gathering gloom. 'I think someone is hurt.'

'It's only one of the hoppers out shooting rabbits,' Byron protested as she headed into the darkness. 'Come back, Nettie. You'll get yourself shot.'

Ignoring his pleas for her to stop, Nettie ran back into the clearing and in the flickering light of Byron's lantern she saw Rufus, who had fallen to his knees, one arm hanging limply at his side and blood oozing through his shirtsleeve.

'Go back, all of you,' he said through gritted teeth. 'And whoever fired that shot had better show themselves.'

There was a scuffle in the undergrowth and the sound of booted feet running in the opposite direction.

'I'll get them, Rufus.' Percy raced after the culprit, leaving Nettie and Byron to help Rufus to his feet.

'It's nothing,' he said lamely. 'A few pellets of lead shot, that's all.'

Nettie undid his cuff and rolled back his sleeve, ignoring his protests. 'Hold the lantern higher, Byron. This looks nasty.'

'It's more blood than actual damage.' Rufus winced, and even allowing for the half-light Nettie could see that his face was ashen.

Byron passed the lantern to Nettie and hooked Rufus's good arm round his shoulders. 'Let's get you home. You need a doctor to take a look at those wounds.'

'Yes,' Nettie added anxiously. 'You've already lost a lot of blood.'

It was a long walk to the house for an injured man, and his steps were faltering by the time they reached the front entrance. Nettie hammered on the door until one of the maids answered the urgent summons. The girl stared at Rufus in horror, seemingly struck dumb.

'Let us in,' Nettie said firmly. 'Fetch your master and tell him there's been an accident. Don't alarm your mistress.'

The maid backed away. 'Yes, miss.'

'I can speak for myself,' Rufus staggered a few steps and sat down heavily on a spindly hall chair. 'Thanks, Byron.'

'Someone should be sent to fetch the doctor,'

Nettie said anxiously. 'Do you feel faint? Perhaps you ought to lie down.'

Rufus managed a weak smile. 'Don't fuss, Nettie.'

'At least you haven't lost your sense of humour,' Nettie said, trying not to laugh. He had echoed the words she had used when he offered to help her from the water, and had created a pact between them that kept her foolish escapade a secret.

'Why do you say that?' Byron asked suspiciously, but Nettie was saved from answering by Maurice, who came hurrying across the hall followed by the maid.

'Good God! What happened? Who did this to you, son?'

'I got in the way of someone out hunting rabbits, Pa,' Rufus said wearily. 'It's nothing, really. Just a few pellets in my arm. It could have been worse.'

'I'll sack whoever did this. I didn't give anyone permission to hunt on my land.' Maurice beckoned to the maid. 'Don't stand there gawping like a goldfish. Send one of the grooms for the doctor. Tell the old quack it's urgent.' He shooed the young girl away. 'Go on, hurry, girl.'

She ran, her small feet pitter-pattering on the marble-tiled floor.

Maurice turned to Byron. 'You, whatever your name is, you look like a strong fellow. Help me to get my boy upstairs.' He shot a glance in Nettie's direction. 'The drawing room is across the hall. Go and break the news to Mrs Norwood, but don't alarm her. Your pa is with her, so he'll be a calming influence.'

Nettie entered the drawing room and was suddenly conscious of her dishevelled appearance. Her father stood up, staring at her open-mouthed, and Jane Norwood peered at her through a lorgnette.

'What's this?' Jane demanded angrily. 'You can't barge into my parlour without a by-your-leave, and just look at you, girl. You look as if you've been dragged through a hedge backwards.'

A bubble of near hysteria rose in Nettie's throat. 'I — I'm sorry, Mrs Norwood, but I have some bad news.'

'What?' Jane's pale blue eyes bulged from their sockets and she leaped to her feet. 'Has something happened to my boy?'

'It was an accident, ma'am,' Nettie said gently. 'Someone was out shooting rabbits and — '

Jane threw up her hands and fell back into Robert's arms. He staggered beneath her weight and guided her back to her seat. 'Calm yourself, Mrs Norwood. Let Nettie speak.'

'It's not serious,' Nettie said, making an effort to sound calm. 'The doctor has been sent for.'

Jane fanned herself with her hand. 'Oh, my poor boy. I must go to him.'

'Your husband is with him.' Nettie looked to her father for help. 'It's his left arm that's injured. It could have been much worse.'

'Oh, no. Poor Rufus.' Jane covered her face with her hands and rocked to and fro. 'He'll be maimed for life.'

'Why don't you go and see for yourself, ma'am?' Robert asked gently. 'If Nettie says it's not serious, I believe her.'

'What does she know?' Jane shot a malevolent glance at Nettie. 'What was he doing to get himself shot, and how do you come into it?' She raised her lorgnette again, staring at Nettie as if she could see through her. 'Why aren't you dressed properly?'

'Yes, Nettie,' Robert added suspiciously. 'Why are you in such a state?'

A series of excuses flitted through Nettie's mind as she looked from her father's concerned face to Jane Norwood's tight-lipped look of disapproval. She decided that the truth, however far-fetched it might seem, was the best way. 'I went for a dip. It was such a lovely evening and I was hot and dusty after a day working in the hop garden.'

'Are you mad?' Jane demanded. 'A girl was drowned in the river just a short while ago.'

'Nettie! How could you?' Robert stared at her aghast. 'You can't even swim.'

'I was in a shallow pool when Rufus came upon me, purely by accident. I hadn't realised there was danger and he helped me out of the water.'

'Hussy!' Jane spat the word at her. 'I knew you weren't wearing any undergarments. You should be ashamed of yourself.'

'Forgive me, ma'am, but this isn't about me. The fact that your son was hit by stray shotgun pellets was an accident.'

Jane rose to her feet. 'I'm going to see my boy.

You will wait here with your father. I haven't finished with you, miss.' She stalked out of the room, leaving the door to close slowly in her wake.

Nettie eyed her father warily. 'Really, Pa, it had nothing to do with me.'

Robert moved swiftly to a side table and picked up a cut-glass decanter. He poured the amber liquid into two small glasses and handed one to Nettie. 'I know that, dear. It sounds like a fuss over nothing, apart from young Norwood getting shot — but that wasn't your fault.'

Nettie sipped the sherry. 'Mrs Norwood thinks I'm after her precious son, but that's not true.'

'She is the most difficult sitter I've ever had. She twists this way and that, and she talks incessantly about nothing in particular. I think longingly of those golden days in the castle when I was painting Lisette's portrait. It was a shocking thing to have to leave it behind.'

'I know, Pa. We've had hellish bad luck since we left London. I just hope we can settle down again safely when we return.'

Robert downed his drink in one and refilled his glass. 'I can't complain, my love. I'm being well looked after here. I'll say this for Maurice, he's a good host and we get on well together, but I don't know how he stands that woman. And yet,' he added thoughtfully, 'he seems devoted to her. People are very strange.'

Nettie was about to answer when the door opened and Maurice strode into the room. 'The doctor's away delivering a baby in the next village. He might be gone all night.'

'I'm sorry to hear that,' Robert said earnestly. 'Is there anything we can do?'

'My lady wife is distraught, and demanding that something must be done, but I'm at a loss.'

'The wounds should be cleaned,' Nettie said slowly. 'And I should think the shot needs to be removed as soon as possible.'

'Good girl. That's sensible.' Maurice grabbed a decanter and a glass. 'My boy will need a few tots of brandy to dull the pain. Come with me, missy.'

'Me?' Nettie stared at him in horror. 'I'm not a nurse. I don't know what to do.'

'You just told me what must be done. You'll need hot water, cloths, bandages and an instrument of some kind that will extract the pellets, and carbolic soap to clean the wounds. I'll send the maid to fetch what you need.'

'Tweezers,' Nettie said faintly. 'They might do the trick. Perhaps Mrs Norwood has some.'

'Good Lord, I don't know about such things. You'll have to ask her.'

'The condesa has all manner of things to do with her appearance. I'll go and ask her.'

'No. You must come with me,' Maurice said firmly. 'Robert, will you see if the good lady can help? And hurry, please.'

'Of course. Delighted to do something useful.' Robert drained his glass and set it down on the table. 'I'll be as quick as I can.'

'Come with me, Nettie.' Maurice hurried to open the door.

★ ★ ★

It took all Maurice's powers of persuasion to make his wife allow Nettie to attend to Rufus's wounds. The patient himself had been given a hefty dose of laudanum, and was lying on his bed with a glass of brandy in his hand, and a wry smile on his face.

'You're enjoying this, aren't you?' Nettie said in a low voice as his mother was tearfully ejected from the room.

'No one has made such a fuss of me since I broke my arm falling out of a tree. I was ten at the time and you'd think I'd broken my silly neck the way Mama carried on.'

Nettie dipped a cloth in a bowl of warm water and applied a little of the strong-smelling soap. 'This might hurt, but I have to clean the wounds.'

He took another sip of his drink. 'Go ahead. I'm sure you'll enjoy inflicting pain on me.'

'I need a steady hand — don't make me laugh.' Nettie bent her head over her work, using gentle strokes to wash away the dried blood. His upper arm was peppered with shot, but he had been quite a distance from the hunter and, as far as she could see, the pellets were not too deeply embedded. She looked up and met his gaze squarely. 'Wouldn't you rather wait for the doctor? I've never done this before.'

'I won't feel a thing,' Rufus said cheerfully.

'I wouldn't count on that if I were you.' Nettie washed the tweezers in carbolic soap and dried them on a clean cloth. 'Just say if it's too much to bear and I'll stop.'

'Can we get this over and done with, please? I

promise not to make a fuss.'

Nettie concentrated on the task in hand. The first few pellets came out easily and Rufus did not utter a sound, but she found that more disconcerting than if he had cried out, and she kept looking up to make sure he had not fainted from the pain. Each time he managed a smile, but there were lines etched on either side of his mouth, and, when having to dig deeper, she felt his body tense.

'I'm sorry,' she murmured. 'There are only a few more.'

Maurice handed his son another glass of brandy. 'Drink up, son. This will deaden the pain.'

'Thanks, Pa, but it's all right.' Rufus winced as Nettie probed for yet another piece of shot. 'One thing is for certain, now I know how much it hurts I'll never go out shooting rabbits again.'

'I agree,' Nettie said earnestly. 'We'll live on bread and vegetables from now on, or maybe a few fish, and I'll keep away from the river.'

Maurice patted Nettie on the back. 'You're doing a splendid job, my girl. You and your friends will eat with us every night from now on.'

'I don't think your other workers would appreciate that, sir.'

'I don't give a damn what they think or don't think. It's my business and Rufus is my son and heir. You might have saved his life tonight, young lady. You will be repaid in kind, and treated as respected guests.'

'Please don't go to any trouble on our account, although a few handouts from the kitchen would be most welcome — just to tide us over until we've learned how to look after ourselves, you understand. We're grateful for the work, sir.'

'All right, but I'll double your hourly rate — that should make things easier for you.'

'Well said, Pa.' Rufus winced as Nettie extracted the last pellet.

She washed the wounds again, patted them dry and applied the bandages. 'There you are. All done.'

'I'll have that brandy now, Pa.' Rufus raised himself on his good arm. 'Thank you, Nettie. You've done a splendid job. You should be a nurse.'

She smiled. 'That's the brandy talking. You won't be so complimentary when the effect wears off.'

'Well done, young lady.' Maurice patted her on the back. 'And you need to sleep, son. You've had a shock and you'll remain in bed until the doctor's seen you in the morning.'

'I'm not a child, Pa,' Rufus said wearily. 'I'll rest for a while, but then I'm getting up. I want to find the person who's going round taking pot shots.'

'You'll stay in bed even if I have to lock the door.' Maurice reached out to smooth a stray strand of hair from his son's forehead. 'You might still come down with a fever, so you'll do as you're told.'

Rufus pulled a face, lay back and closed his eyes. 'I'm twenty-two, Pa.'

'And I'm your father. What I say goes.'

Maurice shooed Nettie from the room, closing the door behind them. 'You did very well, Nettie. Thank you.'

'I hope he'll be all right, sir. I can't help feeling responsible. If I hadn't gone in the river this might not have happened.'

'The fault is with the person who doesn't know how to handle a shotgun. I'll have the perpetrator up before the magistrate, if he's caught. Anyway, you look a bit pale, my dear. Come downstairs and have a tot of something to ward off the chill, and then I'll see you safely back to your hut.'

They reached the entrance hall in time to see the maid open the front door and Percy entered, dragging a youth by the scruff of the neck. He gave the boy a shove that sent him sprawling on the floor at Maurice's feet.

'What's this?' Maurice demanded.

'Tell Mr Norwood what you did,' Percy said angrily. 'I caught this fellow red-handed. The shotgun belonged to his father, who claimed he didn't know the boy had taken it.'

'What's your name?' Maurice glared at the youth, who was cowering at his feet.

'Billy Coggins, sir. I never meant to shoot no one, sir.'

'He's just a boy,' Nettie said hastily. 'I'm sure it was an accident, Mr Norwood.'

Billy nodded. 'It were an accident — that's the truth, sir.'

'What's going on?' Jane Norwood emerged from the drawing room, followed by Robert. 'Who is this urchin?'

'There's no need to concern yourself, my love,' Maurice said hastily. 'I have the matter in hand.'

Jane pointed a trembling finger at the culprit. 'He's the one, isn't he? He's the young villain who nearly killed our son.'

'I never meant to hurt no one, ma'am.' Billy buried his face in his hands and sobs shook his body. 'Me dad will kill me.'

'That would serve you right,' Jane snapped. 'Send for the constable, Maurice. Have this lout arrested and thrown in prison.'

'He's very young, Mr Norwood,' Nettie said firmly. 'It really was an accident, and Rufus will recover in a day or two.'

Jane rounded on her. 'Keep out of this, miss. I suggest you return to your quarters, where you belong.'

Robert cleared his throat. 'Ahem, might I make a suggestion, Mrs Norwood?'

'Well, what is it?' Jane eyed him suspiciously. 'Say what you have to say.'

'As my daughter said, the boy didn't shoot your son on purpose. I've no doubt that he'll be in trouble with his father and the rest of his family.'

'Sack them all,' Jane cried passionately. 'We don't need ruffians like that creature on our land.'

Billy wiped his eyes on his sleeve. 'Please, missis, don't throw us out. We need the money.'

She bridled, eyeing him with a tight-lipped scowl. 'You should have thought about that before you shot my son.'

'The boy has a point,' Maurice said slowly. 'His family need the money and we need to get the harvest in. What's your father's name, boy?'

'Harry Coggins, sir.'

Maurice nodded. 'I know him. He's a good man and his family have been coming here for years. Get up, Billy. We'll let your father decide the punishment, since you took his gun without his permission.'

'He'll skin me alive, sir.'

'Very likely, and no less than you deserve. Firearms are to be treated with respect.' Maurice beckoned to Percy. 'You will see Nettie safely back to the hut, and I'll take this fellow to his father. If I know Coggins he'll be more severe than any magistrate, and the boy will have a lesson he won't forget.'

'I think you're being too soft on him. A spell in prison would do him the world of good,' Jane said angrily. She turned to Robert with an attempt at a smile. 'Pour me a glass of sherry wine, Mr Carroll. I feel I need sustenance after all this upset.'

'I think you'd better instruct your maid to wait on you, ma'am,' Robert said slowly. 'I'm done with being your lackey.'

Maurice stared at him in surprise. 'What did you say?'

'Pa is upset.' Nettie had seen the stubborn set of her father's jaw many times in the past. He was slow to anger, but she could see that he was silently fuming.

'Yes, Nettie. I am upset. I have seen a side of Mrs Norwood that I cannot condone. What's more, I don't wish to continue with our sittings. I'm sorry, Norwood, you're a decent fellow, but all things considered, and the fact that my daughter might well have been the victim this evening, I think our time here is at an end.'

'What are you doing, Pa?'

'I'm coming with you, my dear. My place is with you and my friends in the hut. We'll be leaving tomorrow.'

17

Nothing that Maurice could say would change Robert's mind.

'But the portrait,' Maurice said when all else had failed. 'You can't walk away and leave it unfinished, Robert. It's such a splendid likeness.'

Nettie stood by the open door, breathing in the cool night air. The chance meeting with Rufus in Dover had brought them here, but the prospect of leaving so abruptly was disturbing. She crossed her fingers, hoping that her father's professional pride might come to the fore, but he shook his head.

'I've put up with your wife's carping and criticism for days, Maurice. You're a decent fellow and you've been good to us, but the time has come to move on. I should never have accepted the commission in the first place.'

'Are you going to stand there and let him insult me, Maury?' Jane cried, mopping her eyes with her hanky. 'Let them go and good riddance.'

'Can I go, too, guv?' Billy pleaded. 'I promise never to touch me dad's gun again.'

Maurice fixed him with a menacing look. 'You deserve a beating, but that's up to Coggins.' He signalled to Percy, who was standing beside Nettie. 'Get him out of my sight and take him back to his hut. Tell Coggins what happened and let that be an end to the matter.'

'That goes for us, too. I'll sleep with my friends on our last night here.' Robert crossed the floor, ignoring the accusations that Jane hurled at him. He hesitated in the doorway. 'On second thoughts, I will honour my commitment. I'll take the canvas with me. I can finish it without any more sittings, and I'll return it to you when it's finished.'

'If you think my husband will pay you after what you've just said, you're very much mistaken,' Jane cried angrily.

'There will be no charge,' Robert said calmly. 'Never let it be said that Robert Carroll is not a gentleman. Consider it as payment for my board and lodging.'

Maurice walked over to them with a measured tread. He put his hand in his pocket and took out a leather pouch. 'I'm sorry to lose you, Robert, and I'm grateful to your girl for looking after Rufus. Take this as payment for the work your friends did in the hop garden. I may not be a gentleman, but I'm a man of honour and I pay my debts.' He thrust the pouch into Nettie's hand and went to comfort his wife.

★　★　★

They left next morning, setting off on foot. Nettie had expected Lisette and Constance to protest, but the fact that they would not have to spend the day stripping hop bines seemed to outweigh their reluctance to walk to the nearest railway station. Byron and Percy carried the heaviest cases, and Robert strode on ahead with the half-finished portrait clutched in one hand, and his bag of paints in the other. Nettie was left in charge of her father's small valise as well as her own, and she was thankful that they had been forced to travel light.

They had reached the brewery, which was about half a mile from the big house, when they were overtaken by the Norwoods' carriage and the coachman drew the pair of horses to a halt. He leaned over and beckoned to them.

'Mr Rufus sent word that I was to take you to the railway station.' He climbed down and opened the carriage door.

'That was very civil of him.' Robert helped Lisette in first, followed by Constance, leaving Nettie to the last. She found herself squashed against the squabs, seated opposite her father and Percy, while Byron opted to ride on the box with the coachman.

'Well, this is jolly,' Constance said brightly. 'I wasn't looking forward to a long walk.'

'It was kind of the young man to think of us,' Lisette added. 'But I, for one, am delighted to be away from that place. My hands are ruined, and I long for a hot bath with scented soap and soft towels.'

'I hope Rufus is feeling better,' Nettie murmured, more to herself than to the other occupants of the carriage.

Percy gave her a sympathetic smile. 'It was lucky for him that you knew what to do. He's a good chap, but I don't suppose I'll see him again after what happened last night.'

'The shooting wasn't Nettie's fault,' Constance said sharply. 'Now, if I'd turned a gun on Duke that would have been different. I would have intended to kill him.'

Percy reached out to take her hand in his. 'You have me to protect you now, *querida*.'

Lisette yawned, as if bored with the conversation. 'I, for one, am grateful to you, Robert. You certainly put that creature Jane Norwood in her place.'

'I don't know how I managed to hold my tongue during the sittings,' Robert said, sighing. 'She was difficult from the start — always wanting to jump up and see how far I'd got, and grumbling that she was stiff, or cold or simply bored.'

'And Mr Norwood is such a nice man,' Nettie added. 'You'd think she'd be grateful to have such a good husband.'

'To be fair, Mrs Norwood can be quite pleasant, when she's in a good mood.' Percy leaned back and gazed out of the window. 'But I imagine that's the last time I'll be invited to stay.'

'I'm sorry, Percy,' Nettie said slowly. 'If I hadn't gone in the water none of this would have happened, and now, because of me, you've lost a friend.'

He shook his head. 'It would have happened anyway. Things were different when we had money, but I can't compete with the Norwoods' wealth.'

'We won't always be poor,' Lisette said firmly. 'I rose from the gutter once, and I can do it again. We're on our way to London and I intend to prove that the pavements are made of gold. I am the Condesa Talavera, and I will do whatever it takes to restore our fortune.'

'I'm sure you will,' Robert said gently. 'But our first priority is to find somewhere to live, and as much as it pains me to admit it, somewhere that the police won't think of looking for me.'

Nettie smiled. 'I think I have the answer to that, Pa.'

He put his head on one side, eyeing her doubtfully. 'Really? And where is that?'

'In plain sight, Pa. Somewhere the police, if they are still after you, wouldn't think of looking.'

★   ★   ★

It was late afternoon by the time they arrived in Covent Garden. Robert had proved difficult to convince that moving back to their old lodgings, or somewhere in the vicinity, was a good plan, but eventually, and with unexpected backing from Lisette, Nettie had managed to persuade him. They had to live somewhere and Ma Burton would be prepared to overlook minor complications, such as their being on the run from the law, if the price was right.

Robert stood on the cobblestones, gazing up at the top storey where they had previously rented rooms. 'Someone might be living there already. Have you considered that possibility, Nettie?'

'Yes, of course, Pa. But I doubt if Pip and Ted will have moved on.' Nettie turned to Byron. 'They'll be at work now, but I know they'd be delighted to see you.'

'They might have taken in someone to help with the rent,' Byron said doubtfully. 'But it's worth a try, and to be honest it feels good to be home.'

Nettie stood on tiptoe to kiss him on the cheek. 'That's exactly how I feel. I didn't think I'd miss London so much, but it feels right to be here now.' She turned to Lisette, and Constance, who was clutching Percy's arm as if afraid to let him out of her sight. 'I'll go and brave Ma in her den.'

'I should accompany you,' Lisette said firmly. 'The old woman will consider herself fortunate to have a countess dwelling in one of her apartments.'

Robert restrained her as she was about to follow Nettie into the building. 'No, my dear. Allow Nettie to know best this time. You might have met your match in Ma Burton.'

'I'll be as quick as I can.' Nettie turned to Constance, who was obviously unimpressed by her surroundings. 'I know it's not what you were accustomed to, but we will be reasonably comfortable here, and I think it might be best if we say that you are the *condesa*'s daughter.'

'I don't see why I can't use my real name,' Constance said crossly.

'Do you want Duke to find you? We don't know where he is, but I'm certain he'll return to London eventually.'

Constance shook her head. 'No. I want to get my marriage to that villain annulled as soon as possible.'

'Then I'll tell Ma Burton that you're related to Lisette, and I'll throw in her title for good measure. That will impress the old harridan.' Nettie glanced at Byron, who winked and nodded.

'Do you want me to come with you, Nettie?'

'Yes, that's a good idea, Byron. Ma always had a soft spot for you.'

'I could charm her,' Percy said eagerly. 'My youthful good looks win over most ladies of a certain age.'

'You haven't met Ma Burton.' Nettie opened the front door and was met by the familiar smell of stale food, dry rot and cheap cologne.

★　★　★

'Well, well!' Ma Burton looked Nettie up and down, curling her lip. 'So you've returned to the scene of the crime, have you? The cops will be very interested to hear that.'

'So they came here looking for us, did they?' Nettie asked innocently.

'Not for you, missy. They was after your pa. He's been a bit of a naughty boy, so I've heard — passing off his daubs for real paintings.'

'It's true,' Nettie said airily. 'And there's good money in it. We haven't come back asking for favours, Ma.'

'No, indeed,' Byron added hastily. 'We've been abroad and made a tidy sum.'

Ma Burton eyed him suspiciously. 'Not by any honest means, I imagine.'

'What do you think?' Nettie winked and

tapped the side of her nose. 'We understand each other, don't we, Ma? And as Byron said, there's no need to worry about payment. The question is — have you rooms to let?'

Ma raised herself from her rocking chair by the range, and her plump body sagged like an old mattress as she waddled across the flagstone floor to take a tin box from one of the cupboards. She shook it and coins rattled.

'I want a month's rent in advance, plus a bit extra to keep me mouth shut. I'm a business-woman first and foremost, so pay up or get out and take your chances elsewhere.'

Nettie fingered the leather pouch that Maurice Norwood had given them. 'We need two rooms for Pa and me, and Byron will be pleased to share with his friends if they're still living here. Then there's the countess — she'll require a room for herself and one for her daughter.'

Ma slammed the tin down on the kitchen table, which was littered with the remains of several meals and empty beer bottles. 'Countess? You're pulling me leg.'

'No, Ma,' Byron said, grinning. 'You could, if you so wished, have the Condesa Talavera and her lovely daughter as lodgers.'

'Is she rich?'

Nettie sent a warning glance to Byron, who seemed to be getting carried away with his inventiveness. 'Have you ever heard of a poor aristocrat, especially a foreign one?'

'The nobs don't come knocking on me door too often, dearie.' Ma rattled the tin. 'But, as it happens I have a couple of rooms vacant. That

Mr Lorimer and his missis, they moved out a week ago. I think he was sent north by his newspaper, or maybe he wanted to get shot of her, the whimpering cow. She's gone to her parents in Hertfordshire, and good riddance — always complaining and sending that kid Biddy down here for hot water. I got fed up with them.'

'I'm sure the *condesa* would be pleased to rent their rooms.' Knowing Ma only too well, Nettie tried not to sound too enthusiastic in case the old spider put up the rent. 'And there's Pa and me?'

'I've had difficulty getting tenants for the attic rooms. People say the smell of the oil paint lingers on and makes them feel ill. You're welcome to it, but I'll have to charge you double, if you want me to keep me trap shut.'

Nettie had been expecting this and she shrugged. 'That's fair enough.'

'And your mates are still in residence,' Ma said, attempting a smile as she turned to Byron. 'I dare say they'll take you back, and you was always the one what came down to pay me. That Pip ain't half the man you are, Byron, me boy.'

'Thanks, Ma. I'll be glad to see my friends again.' Byron hesitated, eyeing her warily. 'My brother is recently down from Cambridge. He'll be staying for a while, if you could provide another bed or just a mattress. He's not too fussy.'

'I expect I could make an exception to me rules, seeing as how it's you, Byron dear.' Ma's eyes glittered greedily as she eyed the leather pouch. 'Let's see what you got, and then I'll say yea or nay.'

Nettie tipped coins onto the table, keeping a few back. She knew that she would have to bargain hard, but Ma had the upper hand and would almost certainly get the best of the deal.

Ten minutes later they joined the others, who were waiting impatiently in the narrow entrance hall.

'Well?' Lisette demanded. 'Have we somewhere to lay our heads tonight? Or do we sleep in the street?'

Nettie smiled tiredly; dealing with Ma Burton had always been an exhausting battle of wits. 'You and Constance can have the Lorimers' old apartment on the ground floor. It's the best in the house,' she added hastily.

'And I will doss down with my friends,' Byron said, smiling. 'And we can make room for my young brother.'

Percy pulled a face. 'Young in years, but old in wisdom.'

'And we have our old rooms back, Pa,' Nettie said triumphantly. 'Apparently the smell of your paints put prospective tenants off.'

'Excellent.' Robert picked up his bag of paints and the canvas and headed for the stairs. 'Give me the key, please, Nettie. I'll go on ahead.'

'And I'll take Percy up to inspect our rooms.' Byron handed a set of keys to Robert and he and Percy followed him up the narrow staircase.

'That leaves you to take a look at the Lorimers' apartment.' Nettie made an effort to sound cheerful, but she could tell by the looks on their faces that Lisette and Constance were not happy. She went to unlock the door and ushered them inside, silently crossing her fingers.

★   ★   ★

Lisette and Constance took their time to explore the rooms and Nettie waited for their comments. Not that they had much choice as, even allowing for Ma Burton's greed, the rent charged was still far cheaper than anything they could get in a more salubrious area. Nettie was beginning to lose patience when her father breezed into the parlour.

He gazed round with a nod of approval. 'It looks to be quite clean and tidy. Are they satisfied?'

Nettie was about to answer when Constance emerged from the bedroom, followed by Lisette.

'I suppose it will do,' Lisette said sulkily. 'Although it reeks of camphor and carbolic, and some other medicinal substances I can't put my finger on.'

'Mrs Lorimer was an invalid.' Nettie went to the window and opened it, but the gust of air smelled even worse than the room and she closed it again.

'It's very dark and dingy,' Constance said crossly. 'So different from the castle, or my home in Paris. I'm not sure I like London as I did when I was a child, but of course we had a lovely house and servants.'

A sudden crash coming from the bedroom made them all turn with a start.

'It might be a thief. Stay here.' Robert strode into the room and there were sounds of a scuffle. He reappeared dragging a young girl by the arm. 'I seem to recognise this child. Who is she, Nettie?'

'It's Biddy, Pa. The girl who used to work for the Lorimers.' Nettie moved swiftly to put her arm around the sobbing child. 'It's all right. Don't cry.'

'What is she doing here?' Lisette demanded. 'Were you stealing things, child?'

Biddy wiped her eyes on the sleeve of her shabby cotton blouse. 'No, missis. I ain't got nowhere to go. Mr Lorimer was going to put me in the workhouse, but I hid and I been here ever since.'

'You've been here alone for a week?' Nettie stared at her aghast. 'Have you had anything to eat since the Lorimers left?'

'I crept out at night, miss. Sometimes I found some squashed fruit or vegetables in the market hall, but I ain't had a proper meal since the master took the mistress to the country for her health.'

'Perhaps you should have gone to the workhouse,' Constance said casually. 'It seems to me you made a bad choice by staying here.' She turned to Nettie, eyebrows raised. 'What? Why are you looking at me like that? I only speak the truth.'

'If you knew what life was like in a workhouse you wouldn't say such things.'

'Have you ever lived in one?'

'No, but I've spoken to people who have, and I

309

know that it's a dreadful existence.'

Lisette gave Biddy a searching glance. 'What did you do for the people who lived here?'

Biddy puffed out her chest. 'I done everything, ma'am. She were a sick woman what never got up from the sofa unless it was to use the commode or go to lie on the bed. I waited on her hand and foot, so I did.'

'You might be glad of Biddy's help,' Nettie said in a low voice. 'She's small, but she's willing.'

'I'm blooming starving.' Biddy slumped down on the nearest chair. 'If I don't get food soon I'll die of hunger.'

'We all need to eat,' Robert said firmly. 'How much did Ma Burton extract from you, Nettie?'

'Nearly all of it, Pa.' Nettie handed him the pouch, which was much lighter than previously. 'She wanted twice the rent from us to buy her silence.'

Robert frowned. 'Knowing the old girl as I do, I suspect that she has as much to fear from the police as I do. However, I kept some money back for necessities.'

'We passed a pieman and someone selling baked taters.' Nettie held her hand out. 'I'll get what we need.'

'You should get Byron to help you. Where is the fellow?' Robert looked over his shoulder as if expecting Byron to materialise out of thin air. 'And Percy seems to have gone missing, too.'

'They went upstairs to see if Pip and Ted were at home.' Nettie turned to Biddy with an encouraging smile. 'Would you like to help me fetch the food?'

Biddy was already at the door. 'I got a big basket in the hall cupboard. I'm strong and I can carry anything you want.'

'A useful child,' Robert said, taking a handful of coins from his pocket and passing them to Nettie. 'Get pies for all of us, potatoes and watercress. Maybe you could fetch a jug of ale from the pub, too?'

'We need to keep some money, Pa. The summer is over, and soon we'll need coal and candles as well as food.'

'We'll worry about tomorrow when it comes,' Robert said vaguely. 'I'm going to our rooms, Nettie. The sooner I finish the portrait of that dreadful woman the better, and then I can begin a new canvas. I'll sell my work in the streets, if necessary.'

'And get yourself arrested.' Lisette threw herself down on the chaise longue. 'Well, I, for one, am not going to sit around doing nothing. I earned my living on the stage in Paris. Perhaps it's time for me to make my London debut.'

Nettie was about to leave the room, but she hesitated. 'If you mean it, Condesa, you might like to speak to Madame Fabron and her husband, who appear regularly at the Adelphi. I used to earn money doing a bit of sewing for Madame and her daughter, Amelie.' A vision of Amelie flirting boldly with Duke Dexter brought back memories of that fateful evening at the Gaiety Restaurant when Nettie had first met Rufus and Percy. So much had changed since

311

then that it felt as if she were recalling another life. The time they had spent in France and the somewhat surreal interlude in Catalonia had left their mark, but the memory that was indelibly etched on her heart was the brief time she had spent picking hops for the Norwoods. The distinctive smell of the vines, the hot sunshine, the singing of the families as they worked and the companionship they had shared made the recent past seem like the best of times, and now it was over. They had returned to the real world of crowded city streets and the daily struggle to survive.

She caught Biddy by the hand. 'Come along. Let's go and get that food. I'm hungry, too.'

★   ★   ★

That night Nettie slept in her old bed with the light from the streetlamp filtering through the moth-eaten curtains, and the familiar sound of drunks staggering out of the pubs, horses' hoofs on the cobblestones, and the rumble of carriage wheels. There were scuffles that turned into fights, followed by the thunder of footsteps, police rattles and then a period of quiet until the market opened in the morning.

Nettie rose early, determined to make the best of things. She took a bucket and made the all-too-familiar trip down several flights of stairs to the back yard. The pump was accessible, but only if she climbed over the discarded boxes, sacks and piles of rubbish that had accumulated over the years. She filled a bucket with water and was on her way upstairs when she met Pip on the second landing.

'It's good to see you, Nettie.' He leaned over to brush her cheek with a kiss. 'We were up half the night listening to Byron's tales of your adventures in France and Spain, and hop picking, too!'

'Yes, we've had quite a time of it, but we're home now, and I hope we can stay, but it might not be possible.'

'The police came here not long after you'd left, but we didn't tell them anything. We didn't know where you'd gone anyway, so they left us alone after that.'

'Let's hope they've given up looking for Pa,' Nettie said, sighing. 'It's Duke Dexter they really want, and we don't know what happened to him. He could be anywhere.'

Pip gave her a sympathetic pat on the shoulder. 'I've got to go now or I'll be late for the office, but we'll talk tonight over a fish supper. How does that sound to you?'

'Heavenly,' Nettie said with feeling. 'I've eaten all manner of strange and exotic dishes abroad, but I longed for something simple like fish and chips or eel pie and mash.' She stood aside to let Pip pass and he thundered down the stairs, leaping the last few and taking the next flight at a run. She hefted the heavy bucket up to the top floor and set it down in front of the empty grate, but without fuel for the fire there was no means to heat the water and, although it was still relatively warm, the prospect of a cold wash was not encouraging. She would have to persuade her father to spend what little money he had on coal and kindling, and then they would have to have a serious conversation as to how they were going to make ends meet during the coming winter. Perhaps she could find work in a shop or in a sewing room, although she knew her father would insist that he was going to sell more of his work, and no daughter of his was going to soil her hands toiling for someone else. It was an argument they had had many times in the past, and Nettie had always given in, hoping one day to get her book published. But the trials of her heroine were nothing when compared to the ups and downs of recent weeks, and she had not written a word while they were hop picking. She was so near the end of the story that it had been frustrating, but lack of privacy and exhaustion had prevented her from unpacking the manuscript.

There was no sound from her father's room and she decided to take advantage of the quiet moments to work on her novel. Belinda's story had taken a surprising turn when she was kidnapped by a handsome Spanish grandee. She had rebuffed his advances, but it had become clear that she was in danger of succumbing. The hero was now a dashing soldier who was making every effort to reach his love, but the Spanish noble was intent on enjoying his privileged life to the full and had planned Belinda's seduction down to the last detail. Would she escape unaided or would her soldier come to her rescue? Nettie took her manuscript from the bottom of her valise, sharpened her pencil and set to work. Now she had the added impetus of needing to support herself and her father. She closed her eyes and visualised the scene in the grand duke's castle. She began to write furiously as the words spilled onto the paper.

18

During the next couple of weeks Nettie wrote at every possible opportunity, although she managed to keep her work secret from everyone except Byron. He had been fortunate enough to get his old job back in the solicitor's office, although he said it was just luck, as his replacement had proved incompetent and unpopular and had been sacked. The senior solicitor had commended Byron on his work and had promised him the position of head clerk when the present incumbent retired at Christmas. Nettie suspected that this was not what Byron really wanted, but when questioned he merely smiled and said he considered himself fortunate to be given a second chance. Nettie was not convinced.

Robert had gone out every day with his pad and tin of charcoal, and had taken up a position in Trafalgar Square, where he sketched the likeness of anyone who was willing to pay a few pennies for his work. When he returned home he spent every evening putting the finishing touches to the portrait of Jane Norwood, and early one morning he called Nettie into the studio.

'It's completed,' he said wearily. 'What do you think, my dear? You are always my most honest critic.'

Nettie stood back, gazing at Jane Norwood's likeness captured for posterity in oils. 'It's excellent, Pa. You haven't flattered her, and she is no beauty, but you've given her dignity that I don't think she possesses.'

'I hope so, Nettie. I simply had to get that face down on canvas or it might have haunted me for the rest of my life.' Robert wiped his hands on a cloth.

'You've been kind to her under the circumstances,' Nettie said, laughing. 'She looks a little stern, but you can still see traces of the pretty young woman she must have been when Mr Norwood fell in love with her.'

'It's hard to imagine.' Robert turned his back on his work. 'However, it's done, and when the paint is dry I'll get Percy to deliver it for me. I don't care to listen to the woman's critical appraisal because I know she'll hate it. I just hope that Maurice is satisfied.'

'I'm sure he will be.' Nettie gathered up the gown she had been mending for Violet Fabron. 'I'll just take this to the theatre, Pa. Madame needs it for the play this evening.'

'She pays you a pittance, Nettie. If she hired a professional seamstress it would cost her double. You ought to ask her for more.'

'It wouldn't do any good. Madame is very careful with her money, but the little she gives me will be enough to buy our supper. I've found a street seller who makes really delicious pea soup and it's only a penny a cup.'

'To think that not so long ago we were living like lords at the castle,' Robert sighed, shaking his head. 'But it was bound to come to an end, and now I need a new canvas and some paints,

Nettie. How much money have you got?'

'Not enough, Pa. Maybe I can find more sewing work at the theatre. I'm going there now, so I'll ask around.'

'My next painting will sell,' Robert said firmly. 'I'm going to paint pretty pictures that the wives of well-off merchants will want to hang on their walls, but I can't work without the right equipment.'

'Don't worry, Pa. You'll get your canvas and paints even if I have to steal them.' Nettie hurried from the room, clutching Violet Fabron's elaborate costume. She raced downstairs and was in so much of a hurry that she almost bumped into Lisette and Constance, who were on their way out of the building.

'Where are you going in such haste?' Lisette demanded. 'You almost knocked us over.'

'I'm sorry, but Madame is waiting for this.'

'That wretched woman,' Lisette said angrily. 'I've tried several times to speak to her about a part in the play, but she refuses to talk to me. She muttered something about making an appointment to see the producer.'

'I wish we could afford to go to the theatre.' Constance fingered the embroidery on the satin gown. 'I'm so tired of being poor. Percy hasn't found suitable employment yet, and I can't afford to pay a lawyer to take my case so I'm still tied to Duke. I feel as if I'm living in a bad dream.'

Lisette glared at her. 'If you keep moaning like that I'll have to ask you to find somewhere else to live. I've lost everything, but you don't hear

318

me going on and on about it.'

'I have an idea,' Nettie said in desperation. 'Why don't you come to the theatre with me? The doorman is an old friend and he'll turn a blind eye, although I'm not supposed to take anyone with me. Anyway, once you're inside you can have a look around back stage, and maybe Madame will be a little more helpful, or perhaps one of the other cast members would be willing to speak to you.'

Lisette's downcast expression was wiped away in an instant. 'Yes, of course. I should have thought of asking you in the first place.'

'I suppose it might be diverting,' Constance said sulkily. 'I'm so bored and I hate this place. I almost wish I'd gone with Duke.'

'I'm sure you don't mean that, Constance,' Nettie said briskly. 'Follow me.' She let herself out of the building and set off for the Adelphi Theatre, where the doorman greeted her with a toothless grin. Nettie introduced Lisette by her title, which had the desired effect, and the doorman admitted them without an argument. Once inside, Nettie made for the main dressing room and was told that Madame Fabron was on stage. No one questioned Lisette or Constance, and Nettie took them into the auditorium where the dress rehearsal had just begun. They sat in the second row, behind the producer and Lisette, for once, was silent as she watched the performance, tapping her foot in time to the music and her lips moved as if she knew the libretto by heart.

Amelie Fabron had a big part, as did her

mother, but it became apparent that something was wrong when the orchestra played an introduction for the second time and no one appeared. Those who were already on stage peered into the wings.

The producer rose to his feet. 'What the devil is going on? Where is Miss Leslie?'

A flustered stage hand put in an appearance, shaking his head. 'I'm sorry, sir. Miss Leslie was taken ill. She's very poorly.'

Lisette jumped to her feet. 'I know the part. I played Madeleine in a production in Paris.'

'Sit down,' Nettie whispered. 'You can't do this.'

Lisette shot her an angry glance. 'Don't interfere. This might be my chance to prove myself.'

The producer turned to stare at her. 'Who are you?'

'I am Lisette Joubert. I was once the toast of Paris.'

He frowned. 'Well, Madam, I've never heard of you, so please sit down.' He turned his back on her. 'Where is the understudy?'

The stage hand clasped his hands nervously. 'She's sick, too, sir. They seem to have eaten a dozen oysters each for luncheon, so I was told.'

Violet Fabron moved to centre stage. 'We need to get on, sir. Maybe this person could stand in for now. Miss Leslie should recover in time for the opening night.'

'Very well.' The producer nodded. 'Miss Joubert will take the part, for now. Let's see how good her memory is.'

Lisette was on the stage almost before the words left his lips, and the orchestra stuck up once again.

Nettie clutched Constance's hand. 'I hope she's doing the right thing. I don't think I can watch.' She closed one eye, holding her breath as Lisette launched into the lyrics of the comic opera, and there was a general sigh of approval as her voice rang out loud and clear.

Lisette seemed to be in her element. She lived up to her boast and knew all the words, and instinctively followed the actions of the other players. When the scene ended she received a round of genuine applause and the producer was obviously impressed. He handed her down from the stage.

'You were right, Miss Joubert. You have obviously performed this part before.'

'As I told you,' Lisette said haughtily. 'I was famous once.'

'And what occurred to end such a promising career?'

'I married an Englishman and I left the stage. Both were a mistake.'

'If you are not otherwise employed, I could offer you the part of Miss Leslie's understudy. She has one at present, but the girl is unreliable. Would you be interested?'

Nettie and Constance exchanged anxious glances.

Lisette was silent for a moment and then she nodded graciously. 'I am free, as it happens, and I do love the Adelphi. I would be happy to accept, if the terms are suitable, of course.'

Nettie held her breath; Lisette was taking an awful chance, but the producer merely laughed and patted her on the shoulder.

'I think we can come to an agreement, Miss Joubert. Come to my office and we'll discuss the matter.' He proffered his arm and led Lisette backstage.

'She is rather good,' Constance said enviously. 'I wish I had a talent I could exploit like that.'

'The condesa has lived by her wits for a long time.' Nettie rose from her seat. 'I need to see Madame and collect my money, or we won't eat tonight.'

'Perhaps we ought to have gone with the condesa,' Constance said nervously. 'That man's intentions might not have been honourable.'

Nettie smiled. 'I think Lisette was well aware of that, and I'm sure she can handle herself in a difficult situation.' She lowered her voice. 'I think Violet Fabron and her daughter have a worthy rival. In fact, I wouldn't be surprised if the condesa ended up with the leading role.'

Constance glanced at the stage. 'Madame Fabron doesn't look too happy, and she's coming this way.'

Violet Fabron stood in front of the footlights, arms akimbo. 'What's your game, Nettie? Are you trying to put us out of business?'

Nettie shrugged. 'I don't know what you mean, Madame.'

'Yes, you do. You brought that painted creature to our lodgings, and now she's getting cosy with the producer. I've met her type before.'

'You were the one who encouraged the

producer to give her a chance,' Nettie said impatiently.

'Yes, but I thought she'd make a mess of it and I'd get the part.' Violet's eyes flashed angrily.

'You tell her, Ma.' Amelie rushed to her mother's side. 'I'm the next in line for Miss Leslie's part, if anything should happen to her. And who is that person? Is she an actress, too?' Amelie pointed at Constance. 'There's no work here for the likes of you.'

Constance sprang to her feet. 'I'm Mrs Marmaduke Dexter, a respectable married woman.'

'Duke? You're married to Duke Dexter?' Amelie threw back her head and laughed, and the chorus, who had lined up behind her, joined in until tears were running down their cheeks, leaving streaks in the greasepaint.

'You know my husband?' Constance's voice shook with emotion.

'Of course she doesn't,' Nettie said, glaring at Amelie. 'Mademoiselle Fabron is a respectable young woman. Her papa would be very angry if he thought that she was intimate with a man like Duke Dexter.'

Amelie shot a wary glance at her mother. 'No, of course not. It's hearsay.'

'And should be disregarded as such.' Nettie grabbed Constance by the arm. 'We're done here, anyway. Let's go.'

'I can't trust you any more, Nettie Carroll,' Violet said bitterly. 'I'll find another seamstress to alter my gowns, and you'd better keep that young person away from my Amelie — she's got a temper like a tigress when she's roused.'

Nettie hesitated, turning her head to give Violet a straight look. 'Maybe you ought to ask the tigress how she knows so much about Duke Dexter, and perhaps she'll recall an evening at the Gaiety Restaurant not so long ago.' Nettie guided Constance from the auditorium and out into the street, nodding her thanks to the doorman as they left the building.

'What was all that about?' Constance demanded. 'How did that person know Duke?'

'Duke has quite a reputation when it comes to young women.' Nettie shivered as a cold wind whipped at her skirts. She wrapped her shawl more tightly around her shoulders. 'Let's go home; I think it's going to rain.'

'No, you don't get out of it that easily.' Constance came to a sudden halt. 'I won't move from this spot until you tell me what that Amelie creature meant.'

'I don't know the full extent of their relationship, but not so long ago I was at the Gaiety with Byron, Ted and Pip. Duke was there with a group of people and Amelie was one of them.'

'Was she with him?'

'Yes, at least that's how it seemed. She was hanging on to his arm and flirting with him. I dare say it meant nothing to Duke.'

'I'll scratch her eyes out.'

Nettie stared at her in amazement. 'But you hate Duke. You're in love with Percy and you're going to marry him when your annulment is granted.'

'Yes, of course I hate Duke, but that doesn't mean that actress can claim him as one of her beaux. He's still my husband.'

'I don't think I'll ever fully understand you, Constance. It must be because you're French and you see things differently.' Nettie glanced up into the lowering clouds. 'I felt a drop of rain. We'd best hurry or we'll get soaked.'

'I do love Percy,' Constance said breathlessly as she quickened her pace in an attempt to keep up with Nettie. 'But he's a penniless boy, and Duke might be less than honest in his dealings, but he's rich and clever.'

Nettie opened the door to Ma Burton's lodging house and stepped over the threshold as the rain began to fall in earnest. 'What are you saying, Constance?'

'I don't know anything, any more. My life used to be boring, but safe, and now it's neither. One minute I'm engaged to a dashing young man who'll inherit a castle in Spain, and now I'm living in this dreadful place without a penny to my name, and no prospects. I wish I'd never left Paris.'

Nettie stared at her, frowning. 'Are you saying that you'd go back to Duke, given the chance?'

'Oh, I don't know. Maybe.'

Nettie was trying to think of a suitable answer when she heard heavy footsteps and a dragging sound emanating from the steps leading down to Ma Burton's lair in the basement. She waited, hardly daring to breathe. Ma rarely left her quarters and when she did it was always for something momentous. Nettie could not decide whether to retreat quickly, or to wait and find out what had caused the reclusive landlady to emerge into daylight.

Gasping for every breath, Ma Burton heaved herself up the last step. Leaning on her cane, she waddled across the entrance hall to face Nettie and Constance.

'Where was you?' she demanded. 'You've got a lot to answer for, young woman.'

'I don't know what you mean,' Nettie protested.

'You've brought trouble to my door. I should have known better than to let you and your friends take up residence. This is a respectable lodging house.'

'Respectable?' Nettie laughed. 'Your sons are notorious criminals, Ma. You deal in stolen goods — everyone knows that.'

'Wash your mouth out,' Ma said furiously. 'My boys are businessmen, and if they learn that you're spreading lies about me, they'll break every bone in your skinny body.'

'What sort of house is this?' Constance shot a nervous glance in Nettie's direction.

Ma curled her lip. 'You'll find out if my boys learn that you entertain people like Duke Dexter and Samson Wegg.'

'What are you talking about?' Nettie asked angrily.

'They're in the *condesa*'s parlour. I didn't want no one to see such as them hanging around my front door.' Ma moved a step closer to Nettie. 'Get them out of here and you and your pa can go, too. Unless, of course . . . '

326

Nettie stood her ground. 'Don't threaten me, Ma. I think I know enough about you and yours to put you away for a considerable length of time. As to the visitors — you can call the police if you wish, or get your boys to throw them out. In fact you'd be doing us a favour.'

'Well, you've got a cheek, miss.' Ma backed away. 'Get rid of them, that's what I say. Get them out of here, or there'll be trouble.' She made for the stairs with surprising speed and her booted feet clattered on the bare treads.

'Was she telling the truth?' Constance asked anxiously.

Nettie pushed past her and opened the door. 'There's only one way to find out.' She paused, giving Constance a steady look. 'But if Duke is here you'd better make up your mind which way to go.'

'What will I do?'

'That's entirely up to you.'

Nettie marched through the small entrance hall and let herself into the parlour. 'So it's true,' she said calmly. 'I never thought to see Duke Dexter and Samson Wegg in the same room, unless of course they were under arrest.'

Duke rose from the armchair by the empty grate. 'You've got nerve, Nettie Carroll. I'll say that for you.'

'How did you know we were here?' Nettie demanded angrily.

'My friend Wegg is a very good detective,' Duke said, grinning.

'He is not your friend, nor mine.'

'We neither like nor trust each other, do we,

Wegg?' Duke slapped him on the shoulder. 'But, having agreed that, we decided to work together to achieve our ends. I decided to sup with the Devil — no offence meant, Wegg.'

Wegg winked and nodded. 'None taken, Duke.'

'What do you want?' Nettie spoke calmly, but her heart was beating fast and she was ready for flight. 'What do you hope to achieve by coming here?'

'I've come for my wife, of course, and I want to see your father.'

Constance hung back, eyeing him warily. 'I'm not a piece of property, Duke.'

'I married you, didn't I?'

'You tricked me into marriage so that you could get your hands on my house and the gallery.'

'You married me for financial gain, so don't pretend that you were in love with me.'

'I never said I was, and I don't even like you. I doubt if any woman would love someone as selfish and callous as you.'

Wegg yawned. 'Can we put an end to this bickering? Tell them why we come here, Duke.'

'Yes, why are you here?' Nettie asked suspiciously. 'You are a criminal, Duke, and Wegg is a coppers' nark. I can't see how you two would ever get along.'

'Forget Wegg; I have business with Robert,' Duke said casually. 'I went upstairs and knocked on your door, but there was no answer.'

'He's probably gone out looking for commissions, but he wants nothing to do with you,

Duke. You're the cause of all our problems.'

'Hardly, my dear. Robert, as we know, is hopeless with money and always will be. I suspect that you are living hand to mouth, and unless something changes, you will end up old before your time, caring for a man who thinks only of himself.'

'I believe there's a saying for that,' Nettie said coldly. 'The pot calling the kettle black, springs to mind. Anyway, why are you back in London? You're a wanted man.'

'Marmaduke Dexter fell foul of the law, but Marc Gaillard is a respected businessman. I am here under that alias, and in the process of doing a deal that will make a fortune. I'm offering your father a chance to share my future prosperity.'

'You are the reason he turned to faking the works of others in the first place. Leave him alone.'

'You haven't heard the proposition yet, miss,' Wegg said, curling his lip. 'You might change your mind if you stop gabbing and listen, for a change.'

'Well, Duke, what have you got to say to that?' Constance sank down on the sofa. 'What is this brilliant plan of yours?'

'Yes, speak up or get out and leave us in peace,' Nettie said wearily. 'Although I doubt if you have anything to say that is worth hearing.'

The door opened before Duke had a chance to reply and Lisette burst into the room, but her smile faded when she recognised her uninvited guests.

'What on earth are you doing here, Duke? And

what is he doing here?' she added, glaring at Wegg.

'You get more beautiful every time I see you, Condesa,' Duke said smoothly. 'I was in town on business and I thought I would call in to see you.'

She tossed her head. 'Don't lie to me, Duke. You couldn't have known where we were, and I don't want either of you in my home.'

'I've come to claim my bride,' Duke said calmly.

'Your marriage was a sham.' Lisette placed a protective arm around Constance's shoulders. 'What has changed?'

Duke threw up his hands. 'Might we all sit down and discuss this like rational human beings?'

Wegg threw himself down on a chair by the window. 'I second that. Get on with it, boss.'

'Boss?' Nettie gazed from one to the other. 'What's going on, Duke?'

'Please sit down, ladies. There's no need to be anxious. My intentions are strictly honourable. Wegg and I have come to an understanding, and we are now working together.'

'That's right,' Wegg said, grinning. 'Duke made me an offer that I couldn't refuse, so we decided to bury the hatchet, so to speak, but not in each other's heads.'

'And Wegg now knows that I had nothing to do with the tragedy that befell his dear sister. She was a sweet girl, led astray by a villain, but not me. Wegg and I are now on the same side.'

'That I find hard to believe, but go ahead. I'm

sure we're all listening.' Nettie sank onto the sofa and was joined by Lisette and Constance.

Duke took a seat opposite them, resting his hands on his knees. 'I have decided to abandon my old ways. From now on I intend to become a respectable citizen.'

'And how will you accomplish that, Duke?' Lisette met his smile with a challenging lift of her chin. 'You've led this poor child astray, and you must have known that the Botticelli was a fake, but you didn't tell me, which leads me to wonder how much you made by selling my trinkets. You are a liar and a cheat.'

'All that is at an end. Perhaps I see myself getting older, a fugitive from the law and lacking the love of a family.'

Nettie almost choked. 'You're not serious.'

'Indeed I am, and that's why I want to see your father.'

'Leave my pa alone, Duke. You've been a bad influence on him and we're struggling, but I'd rather starve than see him going down that road again.'

For once Duke was not smiling. 'I promise you, Nettie, that I have no intention of asking Robert to do anything illegal. I have a business proposition to put to him, but it is completely above board.'

Constance jumped to her feet. 'Am I another business proposition, Duke? When were you going to get round to me?'

He stood up, taking her hands in his. 'My dear Constance, I have treated you badly, but all that will change.'

She snatched her hands free. 'I don't believe you. There's something you're not telling me, Duke. What is it?'

'I realised that I was jealous of that callow youth for whom you formed an attachment. It led me to lie about the house in Paris — it is yours, Constance. Your father signed the deeds over to you long before he went bankrupt.'

Constance sat down suddenly. 'The house is mine?'

He nodded. 'It is and always will be.'

'You could still take it from me?' She eyed him suspiciously. 'Is that a threat you intend to use on me?'

'No. Never.' Duke's serious expression melted into an amused smile. 'You have a mind as devious as my own. We are made for each other, Constance. I'm asking you to give me a chance to prove myself to you.'

Nettie shifted uncomfortably on the sofa. 'Perhaps you would like some time alone? This is between you and Constance.'

'No. Don't go,' Constance said hastily.

'You don't have to agree to anything he says.' Lisette patted Constance on the shoulder. 'Don't forget Percy. My son loves you, so don't break his heart.'

Constance rose slowly to her feet. 'I'm going to my room. I need to be alone.'

Duke moved swiftly to open the door for her. 'You will think about what I've just said?'

'I might, or I might not.' She walked into her room without looking at him.

'Well, boss, that didn't go too well, did it?'

Wegg snorted with laughter. 'You need to brush up on your wooing skills.'

'You can shut your mouth, Wegg. When I want your opinion, I'll ask for it.' Duke turned to Nettie, staring at her with a knotted brow. 'Will you speak to her for me? I know that Constance sets a lot of store by what you have to say.'

'It's nothing to do with me, Duke. I'm the last person you should ask for help.'

'I know you're angry with me, Nettie, but I intend to put things right for you and your father. When do you expect him to come home? I need to see him as soon as possible.'

'Why should I believe you, Duke? What could you offer my pa that would save his reputation and allow him to prove himself as the great painter he really is?' Nettie said angrily.

'That's right, Nettie.' Lisette nodded in agreement. 'You tell him straight, my dear.'

Duke bowed his head. 'I know I've upset many people, Condesa, and I am truly sorry.'

Wegg reached for his top hat and rammed it on his head. 'I've had enough of this, boss. You're overdoing the penitent sinner, if you ask me. I'm off to spy on the wife of a cuckolded husband. Let me know when you need my services again.' He jumped to his feet and headed for the door, where he paused. 'You'd better listen to him, miss. Duke Dexter has the golden touch when it comes to making money — whether it's on the right or the wrong side of the law. If I was you I'd take a chance. What have you got to lose?'

19

Robert listened attentively while Duke outlined his idea for a business collaboration, which, to Nettie's astonishment, sounded completely legal.

'Let me get this straight, Duke,' Robert said slowly. 'You want me to make copies of paintings by well-known artists to sell in your gallery.'

Duke sat back in the Windsor chair, grimacing. 'Is this the most comfortable seat you can offer me, Robert?'

'It's all we have,' Nettie said angrily. 'This isn't the castle in Spain, Duke. We are living in reduced circumstances, as you very well know.'

'And my business proposition will put an end to that.' Duke turned to Robert with a winning smile. 'Come on, old man. It will be easy — the paintings will simply be copies, with the full knowledge and assent from the original artists. They will, if still living, receive a percentage and you will be well paid.'

Robert was silent for a moment, frowning thoughtfully. 'But who will buy these copies, Duke? They won't be cheap.'

'They will cost far less than the originals, and the numbers will be strictly limited. I'm not insulting your artistic ability by asking you to turn out copy after copy, but I know how skilful you are, Robert.'

'Clever enough for the Botticelli to pass as an original,' Robert said, chuckling. 'It's a pity it ended up smashed over your head, but you deserved it.'

'Forget all that, my friend, and think to the future. There is a growing market amongst the well-to-do middle classes who wish to emulate their betters. In the future I dare say there will be a way to reproduce works of art in vast quantities, and attempts have already been made using lithography, but it is not the same as having a genuine oil painting hanging on the parlour wall.'

Nettie had been sitting on the window seat, listening avidly, but now she jumped to her feet. 'You don't have to do this, Pa. We can get by without you having to stoop to such depths.'

'My dear, I think anything is better than starving to death in a cold garret, and there's a long hard winter ahead.' Robert gave Duke a speculative look. 'Are you sure that this is all above board, Duke? I've had enough of being a fugitive, and I have to face facts. I can't even afford to buy paint and canvases unless I have an advance on a commission.'

'That will not be a problem, Robert. I will see that you have enough funds to buy materials, and an advance to cover your living expenses.' Duke rose to his feet and crossed the floor to examine the portrait of Jane Norwood. 'Who is this?'

'It's a long story,' Robert said, sighing. 'I painted Mrs Norwood in lieu of payment for my board and lodging. We stayed with the family for a while before we returned to London.'

'Tell him the truth, Pa. We had to work for the

335

Norwoods to pay our way. You painted Mrs Norwood's portrait while the rest of us worked in the hop garden.' Nettie faced Duke with a defiant gaze. 'That's how poor and desperate we were, and it was largely due to you. If Wegg hadn't traced us to Spain we might have remained with the *condesa* until Pa had earned enough money to get us home.'

'You wouldn't have received much help from the *condesa*. She was all but bankrupt, Nettie. I know that for a fact.' Duke gave her a pitying smile. 'You're a plucky young woman, and you deserve better than this.' He encompassed the attic room with a wave of his hand. 'Allow your father to earn a decent living from his talent as a copyist.'

'But he's a brilliant artist.'

'We must be realistic, my dear,' Robert said gently. 'Duke is right, and we can't live on the pittance you get for your sewing.'

'I've always said I would willingly work in a shop, or go into service if that would allow you to concentrate on your painting, Pa.'

'Doesn't that make you ashamed, Robert?' Duke walked towards the door. 'What sort of man relies on his daughter to pander to his vanity in such a way? I'll leave you to mull it over, but don't wait too long. I have other artists in mind, and the reopening of my gallery to organise.' He eyed Nettie speculatively. 'Maybe you could work for me? A pretty young woman to greet prospective customers might go down extremely well.'

'The police will arrest you the moment you

show your face,' Nettie said warily. 'You're a wanted man.'

'Not any more, my dear. Marmaduke Dexter died in Spain. Wegg has informed the Metropolitan Police of their suspect's death by drowning.'

'Why would they believe a man like Wegg?'

'Why wouldn't they?' Duke countered. 'He was working for them. They're not to know that he's thrown his lot in with me, and I am reborn as Marc Gaillard. I was always careful to do business in London through Pendleton, and my clients never met me face to face.'

'What would you do if he decided to peach on you?'

'Pendleton knows better than that, Nettie. He, like Wegg, is well paid for his efforts. I might include you on my staff, if you so wish?'

'Duke,' Nettie said icily, 'I would as soon go down a coal mine as work for you. Constance might have fallen under your spell once more, but not I.'

He shrugged. 'Oh, well, the offer is there, should you become desperate. As to you, Robert, think very carefully before you put pride before common sense.' He opened the door and left them staring after him.

Nettie turned to her father. 'Don't let him bully you into something you'll regret, Pa.'

'I know better than that after my last experience with Duke Dexter, but I think perhaps he has had a sound idea. We have to pay the rent, Nettie, because Ma Burton would relish the prospect of sending her sons to break my fingers one by one, and that would put an end to my artistic career altogether.' Robert rose from his chair. 'I'll catch him up and tell him that I'm more than interested.' He held up his hand as Nettie opened her mouth to protest. 'Don't fret, my dear, I'll go into the whole thing very carefully, but at the moment it seems like my one and only chance to put things right.'

★   ★   ★

When her father did not return, Nettie assumed that he must have gone to the gallery. Duke's idea was probably a good one when it came to profitability, but she knew that her father was worthy of acclaim in his own right. It seemed a waste of his talents to spend his time copying the works of others, but they could not continue as they were. It would be a hard decision to make, but they had to pay the rent and soon it would be winter, with all the hardships brought about by cold and damp. She took out her manuscript and tried to settle down to write, but she could not concentrate. Even though she was so close to finishing the story, a satisfactory ending evaded her, and she tucked it out of sight and went to find Constance. She, too, had a hard decision to make.

She found Constance alone in the parlour, listening to Lisette, who was in her bedroom, singing what seemed to be the entire libretto of the operetta. The glass shades on the gasolier rattled in their brass holders as Lisette's warbling soprano hit the high notes.

Constance shook her head. 'I don't think I can

stand much more of this, Nettie. She's giving me a headache.'

'At least she knows the words,' Nettie said, trying not to giggle. 'I can see her ousting the famous Cora Leslie as leading lady before long. Violet will be furious and so will Amelie.'

'From what I've seen of those two, it serves them right.' Constance rose from the sofa and went to peer out of the window. 'Where is Percy? He's been gone for ages.'

'I think he went to the law offices with Byron. He's just getting to know his brother,' Nettie said reasonably. 'There's nothing wrong with that, is there?'

'Percy has changed since we left Spain.'

'What do you mean?'

'He's not so attentive, and today he went off without a word, leaving me at the mercy of his mother. I daren't say anything in front of her or she'll get angry. He can do no wrong in her eyes.'

'I suppose that's natural, although it's a bit unfair on Byron. He's the one she should be making a fuss of, considering the fact that she abandoned him when he was so young.'

'Duke hasn't returned either. I simply don't understand men, Nettie. They make a fuss of you, and then they go away and leave you to cope on your own.'

'Perhaps you ought to find something to do,' Nettie suggested tentatively. 'How did you occupy your time in Paris?'

'I used to go for walks with Mademoiselle Menjou. Sometimes we went to art galleries or one of the parks, but what I liked most was going to the shops in the boulevard Haussmann, although I didn't have much money to spend on myself.'

Nettie eyed her thoughtfully. 'Don't take this the wrong way, but are you sure you want to marry Percy? I know he's handsome and charming, but he's poor and you've been used to living in what most of us think of as luxury.'

'I love Percy.'

'I'm sure you do.' Nettie chose her words carefully. 'But you married Duke, and he seems to have evaded the law. If you were to live as his wife you wouldn't want for anything.'

Constance's blue eyes darkened and filled with tears. 'But I don't love him.'

'Maybe you ought to talk to Percy. Tell him how you feel.'

'Yes, that's right. I'll do that.' Constance brushed away a tear and smiled. 'I still have my house in Paris. Perhaps Percy could find work and we could live there together.'

'I think Duke might object to that, and Percy would have to earn a very good salary to run such an establishment.'

Constance's smiled faded. 'I suppose Duke must have paid for everything after my parents died. I never gave it a thought.'

'And, even now, he must be giving the *condesa* something towards the rent and your food.'

'I'll go out and find work.' Constance sprang to her feet. 'Perhaps I could sell flowers on street corners; that doesn't look too hard.'

Nettie had a vision of Constance let loose amongst the women who fought each other daily in order to obtain the best blooms, and the ragged girls who snatched up the bruised and broken flowers to make into nosegays. Their shrieks and the language they used turned the morning air blue, and it was not uncommon to see one or two of the older women staggering around bloodied and bruised. It was not an easy way of earning a living.

'You would have to get up very early, before dawn even. I've heard the women screeching at each other. They're a rough lot, Constance. But if you think you could . . . '

'No, perhaps not,' Constance said hastily. She took her bonnet from a hook behind the door and put it on. 'I'll take a walk along the Strand. Maybe it would give me some ideas.'

Nettie shook her head. 'You wouldn't go out on your own in Paris, and London is no exception.'

'Why does that apply to me and not to you? I know you go out unchaperoned.' Constance's bottom lip trembled. 'It's so unfair. What am I to do?'

Nettie was struggling to think of a reply when the door opened and Percy breezed into the room.

'Ah, there you are, *querida*. I've come to tell you that Byron has found me employment. I'll be working alongside Pip as a law writer, which is a waste of my university education, but it's a start and I'll be paid for my labours.'

'Oh!' Constance stared at him blankly. 'What does a law writer do?'

'It's very important,' Nettie said quickly.

'Documents have to be copied, and there must be no errors. It needs someone with a good hand and a great deal of patience.'

'Exactly.' Percy puffed out his chest. 'At least I've found work. Aren't you pleased?'

'Does it pay well enough for us to rent a nice house with a garden?'

Nettie and Percy exchanged meaningful glances.

'Well,' Percy said slowly, 'not at the beginning, but I'll progress quickly. That I promise. And you are happy enough here with Mama, aren't you?' He cocked his head on one side, listening with a smile on his face as Lisette launched into yet another aria.

'I suppose so.' Constance sat down again, clutching her bonnet. 'You promised to take me to the zoological gardens today, Percy.'

'Did I? I'm sorry, my love. I forgot, but we'll do it another day. The chief clerk said that I could start work after luncheon, which is excellent. Don't you agree?'

'Of course, we do.' Nettie could see that Constance was in no mood to be encouraging. 'Maybe, instead, we could visit Sanger's Amphitheatre one evening. I believe the circus is quite amazing. You'd like that, wouldn't you, Constance?'

'I suppose so,' Constance said sulkily, 'but I'd prefer to watch a ballet or a pantomime.'

Percy shrugged. 'We could do that some time when I've made my fortune, but I have to go now. I don't want to be late and create a bad impression.'

'You said you would start after luncheon,' Constance said crossly. 'You could at least treat me to something nice to eat. I am so sick of baked potatoes or pea soup.'

'Yes, well, I'm afraid my money won't run to anything more appetising, *querida*.' Percy leaned over to drop a kiss on her forehead. 'When I get paid we will celebrate.' He shot a wary glance at Nettie. 'You'll see that she gets something to eat, won't you?'

'Of course. You go to work and we'll see you later.' Nettie shooed him out of the door. She turned to Constance, frowning. 'You behaved like a spoiled child just now. Percy was so pleased with himself and you couldn't even give him a smile.'

Constance covered her ears with her hands. 'I'm not listening to you or to Lisette and her singing. Go away, Nettie. Leave me alone.'

Nettie sighed and let herself out into the entrance hall. She was beginning to think that Constance and Duke deserved each other, and that Percy would be better off with someone who would support him and help him to make a career for himself. She was about to go upstairs when the front door opened and her father entered on a gust of cold air, bringing with it a flurry of dried leaves. Laden as he was with packages, Robert had to lean against the door in order to close it.

'Canvases, Nettie,' he said joyfully. 'Paints and some new brushes. I'm going to make our fortune, my dear, and to celebrate I'm going to take you to the Lamb and Flag for some of their steak and kidney pie. You need a good meal to put the roses back in your cheeks.'

'That would be lovely, Pa, but can we afford it?'

'Don't start that, Nettie. I'm in charge of our finances, and I say we need a good meal. I'll take my purchases upstairs, and then we'll be off. It's very chilly, by the way. You'll need to wrap up warm.' He started up the staircase, but as Nettie was about to follow him she was caught in the draught of the front door opening once again. She turned her head to see Violet Fabron rush in, followed by Amelie, and neither of them looked happy.

'Where is she, the bitch?' Violet demanded. It seemed to be a rhetorical question as she ignored Nettie and went to hammer on Lisette's door. 'Open up, I say. Come and face me, you sneaky serpent.'

'Whatever is the matter?' Nettie asked anxiously.

Amelie glared at her. 'Your friend, the *condesa*, has just been given Miss Leslie's part, which should be Ma's, by rights.'

'What happened to Miss Leslie?'

'She's run off with her sister's husband, or some such thing. I dunno, but she's out of the show, and the understudy was dead drunk, so she was passed over for the part. Ma should be the leading lady, not that foreign cow.'

Nettie looked for her father, but Robert had negotiated the stairs with surprising speed for a middle-aged man, carrying heavy parcels.

'Open up or I'll kick the door in,' Violet

344

screamed. 'Or I'll get my old man to do it for me.' She kicked the wooden panel at the foot of the door and yelped with pain. 'I'll scratch your eyes out.'

The door was wrenched open and Lisette stood there, wearing a thin silk dressing robe that outlined the voluptuous curves of her naked body, leaving little to the imagination. She took in the situation with a single glance and, as Violet advanced on her with her hands fisted, Lisette swung her arm and landed a punch that knocked Violet off her feet.

'What about you?' Lisette demanded, staring at Amelie. 'Do you want some of the same medicine? I was born and bred a water gypsy and I lived in the slums of Paris. No one gets the better of Lisette Joubert.' She slammed the door in Amelie's face.

Nettie did not wait to see Amelie's reaction. She hurried upstairs to fetch her bonnet and shawl. The *condesa* had proved beyond doubt that she was capable of standing up for herself.

★   ★   ★

A week passed with Robert rising from his bed early each morning with renewed energy. He left Nettie to light the fire while he went out to fetch coffee from a stall in Southampton Street, and hot rolls from a bakery in Drury Lane. Then, having breakfasted together, Robert took his sketchbook and charcoal and set off for the National Gallery, intending to make detailed sketches of the paintings that Duke wanted copied. He returned home at midday to work on each of the three canvases he had on separate easels, all depicting the same masterpiece. Nettie secretly thought it a travesty of her father's talent, but he seemed content to work hard, secure in the knowledge that these paintings were guaranteed a sale.

Ma Burton could not hide her disappointment when Nettie went to her basement den at the beginning of November to pay the rent in full with no excuses. Nettie had always suspected that Ma enjoyed bullying and threatening her tenants with eviction or a visit from her brutish sons. The mere mention of their names was enough to make even the poorest of the lodgers find all or part of the money owed. Now, however, there was no need to worry. The rent was paid and they had an ample supply of coal, kindling and candles. It could snow for all she cared, but they would not suffer as they had in winters past.

Best of all, she had finished writing her novel and, after a final read-through, she was preparing to take it to the publisher who had shown some interest in her previous attempt. It was exciting, even though the prospect of yet another rejection was daunting, but to gain financial independence was even more of a priority now. Her father's new-found prosperity was unlikely to last long. He had ordered a new jacket and trousers from a very expensive tailor, who had not quite made Savile Row, even though he had an illustrious clientele. Robert had tried to persuade Nettie to visit the modiste, insisting that she must dress according to their new status, but she had refused, telling him that she did not need a smart gown. Never one to take no for an answer, Robert went off on his own to purchase a fur-trimmed mantle and dashing hat to match. When Nettie protested that the outfit was too expensive, her father merely smiled and said that it was his pleasure to treat such a good daughter, and she must allow him to spoil her once in a while. She had not the heart to argue, although she knew she would regret it when they were down to their last candle and had run out of coal.

Constance was not sympathetic when she came upstairs to have a chat with Nettie that afternoon. 'I don't know why you're making such a fuss,' she said crossly. 'I would have opted for a new gown. Let your father worry about the money.'

'You wouldn't say that if you'd had to live as I have.' Nettie put her tea cup back on its saucer. 'I just wish that Pa was as good at business as he is at painting. It doesn't matter how much he earns, he simply spends more and gets into debt.'

'I hate penny-pinching.' Constance stared into the fire, frowning. 'I find it hard to say this, Nettie, but I don't think I love Percy. I did, when we were in Spain, but everything is so different now. My life is so dull. Lisette sleeps most of the day in order to be ready for the evening performance, and she expects me to wait on her hand and foot, even though Biddy is supposed to be her maid. I lose patience with the child, but she cries like a baby when she's scolded.'

'Poor little thing. She is very young, and she's had a hard life. You ought to be kind to her.'

'I know, but I can't help getting impatient, and I haven't seen Duke for over a week. Why doesn't he come to see me? We are supposed to be man and wife.'

'You sent him away. You told him you wanted nothing to do with him, as I recall, and you made it clear that you want an annulment.'

'I know all that, but we are still married, and he should take care of me.'

Nettie rose to her feet. 'This is ridiculous. If you've changed your mind and you want to be with your husband, for goodness' sake tell him, and let Percy know that you've had a change of heart.'

Constance shook her head. 'I don't love Duke.'

'You married him none the less. Maybe you don't need either of them and you would be better on your own?'

'Heavens, no!' Constance stared at her wide-eyed. 'I don't want to be an old maid.'

'Then choose one or the other.' Nettie reached for her bonnet. 'I'm going to the grocer's shop in Drury Lane to get something for supper. Do you want to come with me?'

'I suppose so. I've nothing better to do.' Constance raised herself from the Windsor chair. 'You could do with some comfortable furniture, and I don't know how you manage to put up with that awful smell of oil paint and turpentine. It would make me ill.'

'I'm used to it, and there are worse odours.' Nettie took her cape from the back of a chair and slipped it on. She opened the door to find Duke with his hand raised as if about to knock. 'Duke, this is a surprise, but I'm afraid my father is out.'

Duke frowned. 'I thought he would be working.'

'He is. He's gone to the National Gallery to check some details on the latest painting.'

'I'd like to see his progress. May I come in and have a look?'

Nettie stood aside. 'Of course. I was just going out, but Constance is here.' She turned to give Constance a meaningful look. 'I'm sure she will entertain you until I get back.'

'You can't leave me alone with a gentleman,' Constance protested.

'He is your husband, Connie. I think you two have a lot to talk about. I won't be long.' Nettie picked up her shopping basket and hurried from the room before Constance had a chance to argue.

She returned an hour later, having spent some time chatting to Mrs Sainsbury, the young wife of the shop owner in Drury Lane. Having made her purchases, Nettie walked home slowly in order to give Constance and Duke a chance to talk, but when she reached the top floor there was no sign of either of them. She unpacked her basket, but curiosity finally got the better of her and she went downstairs to knock on Lisette's door.

Biddy opened it and her small face split into a

grin when she saw Nettie. 'It's you, miss.'

'Yes, Biddy. I've come to see Miss Constance.'

'She ain't here, miss.'

Nettie stared at her, frowning. 'You mean she went out again?'

'That's right, miss. She went out with that nice Mr Duke. He come in with her and waited while she put on her bonnet and mantle, and he was ever so charming.'

'Where did they go, Biddy?'

'I think he said he would take her to a place where they sell cake and ice cream. Can't remember the name.'

'Was it Gunter's?'

Biddy frowned, 'Maybe, I dunno.'

'All right, thank you.' Nettie patted her on the shoulder. 'Don't worry about it. I'm sure Miss Constance will be back in time for supper.'

'Yes, miss. I hope so. I don't like being left here on me own when the missis goes to the theatre.'

'If you're scared you can always come upstairs to see me.'

Lisette emerged from her room, blinking sleepily. 'Biddy, I told you to go out and fetch me a cup of pea soup from the street seller. Where is it? I have to be at the theatre in half an hour.'

'It's my fault,' Nettie said hastily. 'I came to see Constance.'

'Shoo. Go now, you stupid child.' Lisette scowled at Biddy, who fled from the room. 'Where is Constance? She should be here to make sure the child does what she's told.'

'Biddy said that Duke took Constance to Gunter's.'

Lisette threw up her hands. 'It's all right for some. Here am I working hard to pay the rent and Constance does nothing but complain. Duke can take her off my hands, as far as I'm concerned. He's welcome to her.' She marched into her room and slammed the door.

Nettie shrugged and made her way back upstairs. Constance was old enough to know her own mind, and Duke was her husband. He had a perfect right to take her out to tea.

⋆ ⋆ ⋆

Later that evening, Robert had already gone to bed and Nettie was just about to undress when there was a loud knock on the door. She crossed the room and opened it to find Lisette, looking pale and exhausted, with traces of her stage make-up lingering on her face.

'Is she here?'

'Who do you mean?'

'Constance, of course. Have you seen her this evening?'

Nettie shook her head. 'She went out with Duke. That's the last time I saw her.'

'She hasn't come home.'

'It's very thoughtless of Duke to keep her out so late, but perhaps he took her to the theatre and supper afterwards.'

'She never has a good word to say about him, Nettie. What will Percy think?'

'I'm sure there's a reasonable explanation.'

'She's a selfish girl. I'll have words with her in the morning. Anyway, I'm going to bed and I'm locking the door. Maybe it will teach her to be more considerate.' Lisette marched off in the direction of the stairs.

Nettie closed the door and turned the key in the lock. Perhaps Constance had decided to accept Duke's overtures after all? There was nothing to be done at this late hour, but Constance would have a lot of explaining to do in the morning. Nettie made ready for bed, but she lay wide awake for a long time. The feeling that all was not right would not go away.

20

Nettie awakened early next morning. She could hear her father snoring gently in the next room, and she was careful not to make a noise and disturb his sleep. Her first task of the day was to fetch water from the pump in the back yard, and she made her way downstairs. The cold air took her breath away as she stepped outside, and the first light of dawn revealed a thin coating of frost on the pump and a skim of ice on the water in the stone trough. There were the usual sounds from the market, which was already in full swing. The clatter of cartwheels and the tramp of booted feet were as nothing compared to the chorus of raised voices of the porters, punctuated by bursts of raucous laughter. It was a normal beginning to each day, but the sound of someone sobbing their heart out in the privy was something out of the ordinary. Nettie stepped over the piles of detritus to knock on the door.

'Are you all right? Who's in there?'

'It's me,' a small voice whimpered.

'Biddy?' Nettie opened the door and found Biddy sitting with her head in her hands. Tears trickled between her fingers and her shoulders shook.

'What's the matter? Are you ill?'

Biddy shook her head.

'It's freezing out here. Come inside and you can tell me what's wrong.' Nettie turned away and waited. 'How long have you been in there?' she asked when Biddy finally emerged.

'I dunno, miss.'

'Well, it doesn't matter. We'll go upstairs and light the fire. I'll put the kettle on to boil and we'll have a nice hot cup of tea, and you can tell me what's upset you.'

Nettie led the way up to the attic rooms and settled Biddy in a chair with a blanket round her skinny shoulders while she lit the fire and placed the soot-blackened kettle on the trivet. She sat back on her haunches. 'Now then, Biddy. What's wrong?'

'The missis has thrown me out.' Biddy's pale eyes filled with tears. 'She says it's my fault that Miss Constance didn't come home last night.'

'Constance isn't back yet?'

'That's what I said, and it's my fault.'

'What nonsense. Your mistress had no right to put the blame on you. Anyway, I doubt if she meant what she said. She was probably worried, but Constance is with Mr Dexter. I'm sure he'll take care of her.'

'The missis meant it all right. She threw me bundle at me and told me to go to the workhouse. She says it's where I belong.' A fresh bout of sobbing racked Biddy's small body and Nettie moved to her side, giving her a hug.

'You will not go to the workhouse. That's a promise.' Nettie glanced round at the sound of her father's door opening. 'Sorry, Pa. Did we disturb you?'

Robert stood in the doorway, blinking owlishly. 'What's all the fuss about?'

354

Nettie stood up, placing her finger on her lips. 'Constance went off with Duke yesterday afternoon and hasn't returned. Lisette seems to blame the child and she's thrown her out. I found her in the privy, frozen to the marrow and sobbing like baby.'

'Constance is a flighty piece. She needs to make up her mind who or what she wants. I've no patience with her.' Robert stared at Biddy, frowning thoughtfully. 'I was going to ask you to take the portrait to the Norwoods for me, but I didn't want to send you to Kent on your own. However, now you've got the child for company I dare say it would be quite proper.'

'You want me to go to Norwood Hall?'

'I haven't got time to go gallivanting around the countryside, and I don't want to face Jane Norwood again. I'll pay for your tickets — first class, of course. Duke left the advance in my studio with a note telling me he's delighted with the progress of the paintings, and naming a sum for their completion. It's very generous, Nettie. There's money in reproducing the works of famous artists, and Duke handles all the details, so all I have to do is paint.'

'I'm glad it makes you happy, Pa.'

'And you, Nettie. It means that I can give you a better life. I'm not completely selfish.'

Nettie smiled and walked over to plant a kiss on her father's cheek. 'You are my pa and I love you.'

'So you will travel to Kent today? I'd like to think I pay my debts and Maury Norwood is a good chap.'

'Yes, Pa.' Nettie held her hand out, smiling persuasively. 'As you're so well off you might like to give me some money now. I'll go out and get some fresh rolls for breakfast.'

Robert put his hand in his pocket and drew out some coins. 'A large pat of butter would be most welcome, and maybe some marmalade or jam. I'm sure the child could do with feeding up; she's all skin and bone.'

Biddy looked up from the depths of the blanket. 'I could go for you, miss.'

'You'll stay here in the warm, Biddy. Pa will make a pot of tea and I'll be back in two shakes of a lamb's tail.'

'Wrap up well,' Robert said vaguely. 'It's cold this morning.'

Nettie seized her cape. 'You're getting quite considerate these days, Pa.' She left her father to take care of Biddy and was halfway down the stairs when she met Byron on the landing.

'You're up early,' she said, smiling. 'Are you so keen to get to work?'

'Percy's been up all night, looking for Constance. I'm going out to get coffee.' He gave her a searching look. 'You don't seem surprised. You knew, didn't you?'

'I only know that Duke took her to Gunter's yesterday afternoon, and she hasn't returned. But they are legally married, Byron. She has every right to be with him if she so chooses.'

'Percy doesn't think so. He went to the gallery last evening and he persuaded Pendleton to give him Duke's London address. They weren't there and the servants hadn't seen Duke since early yesterday morning.'

'Perhaps they went to a hotel?' Nettie said slowly. 'Duke can be very persuasive and Constance isn't happy living with Lisette.'

'Percy tried a few of the better hotels, but they either couldn't or wouldn't give out any information. The poor fellow is distraught, Nettie.'

'It's partly his fault,' Nettie said stoutly. 'I know he's been working hard, but Constance feels neglected.'

'She's a spoiled brat. In my opinion Duke's welcome to her, but Percy doesn't see it that way.'

'I am truly sorry for him, Byron, but I have other things to worry about. Pa wants me to go to Kent today and deliver Jane Norwood's portrait.'

'You shouldn't travel on your own. Anything might happen.'

'I'll have young Biddy with me. Pa seems to think that makes it quite respectable.'

'I'd come with you, but I have to go to work.'

'I wouldn't expect it of you. Go and get your coffee. I'll see you this evening when I return from Kent. Don't worry about Constance. I expect she'll turn up in her own good time.'

★ ★ ★

The journey to Kent was uneventful and Biddy seemed to have forgotten everything other than the excitement of travelling by train. When they arrived at their destination Nettie hired a pony and trap to take them to Norwood Hall. Seated on the box with Biddy beside her, Nettie took the reins and, feeling confident, she encouraged the horse to a brisk trot. The sun was shining, but it was bitterly cold and she was glad of her new fur-trimmed cape and hat. Biddy's eyes were sparkling and her cheeks had lost their normal pallor and were quite rosy. She cried out with excitement at each new sight, admitting freely that she had never seen a sheep or a cow before, and she might have landed in foreign parts, for all she knew of the countryside and farming. Biddy's childish enjoyment was catching and, despite worries about Constance, Nettie was beginning to feel quite light-hearted as she drove past the brewery with its distinctive smell of hops and roasting barley. When Norwood Hall came into view she forgot the exhausting business of hop picking, and remembered only the camaraderie of the hoppers and the evenings spent around the campfire. The sound of the river brought back mixed memories, and when she saw Rufus Norwood striding towards them, her heart began to beat faster and she felt the colour rush to her cheeks. This reaction was unexpected and she felt suddenly shy and at a loss for words, but he was smiling as he approached and he caught hold of the harness and brought the pony to a halt outside the front entrance.

'This is a pleasant surprise, Nettie. I wanted to thank you properly for tending to my wounds, but I had no way of knowing your address.'

'There was no need,' Nettie said shyly. 'It was

partly my fault anyway. If I hadn't gone into the river like that you wouldn't have been in the wrong place at the wrong time.'

'It was an accident, and the boy was dealt with by his father. I don't think he'll play with a shotgun again. But I did want to see you and I was hoping that Percy might contact me so that I could find out where you were living.' He swung Biddy from the driver's seat and placed her on the ground. 'Who is this young lady? We haven't met before.'

'I'm Biddy, sir.' Biddy bobbed a clumsy curtsey, almost toppling over in her attempt to be graceful.

'How do you do, Biddy?' Rufus bowed. 'I'm Rufus Norwood. It's a pleasure to make your acquaintance.'

Biddy blushed and giggled, staring down at her feet in total confusion.

Rufus helped Nettie to alight, calling out to a groom who had emerged from the stables and came at a run to hold the reins.

'I've brought your mother's portrait.' Nettie retrieved the package. 'It's almost dry, but my father said to handle it carefully, in case some of the thicker layers are still a little sticky.'

'My parents will be delighted. Your father is very talented and I could never understand why you needed to work in the hop garden, but I didn't like to ask questions.'

'I'm hungry, mister,' Biddy said plaintively. 'Are you going to give us something to eat?'

'Biddy, that's rude!' Nettie frowned at her. 'You wait to be invited in and you don't ask questions like that.'

'It's quite all right,' Rufus said, laughing. 'A girl after my own heart. Why should we not speak our minds?'

'Sorry, sir. I forgot me manners.' Biddy shot him a sideways glance, grinning as if she had found a soulmate.

'I'm sure we can find some suitable refreshment for you both.' Rufus ushered them up the steps and into the entrance hall. He summoned a maid to take Nettie's cape, but Biddy refused to give up her shawl, even though Nettie assured her that it would be returned when it was time to leave.

'I know what happens,' Biddy said in a low voice. 'They take people's duds and they don't get them back. I'll bet they end up in the pawn shop.' She glanced at the heavy, ornately carved furniture, wall hangings and pictures. 'That's how the toffs afford to live like this.'

Nettie glanced at Rufus, hoping that he was out of earshot, but she could tell by the amused look on his face that he had heard every word, and his lips quivered.

'Don't worry, Biddy,' he said solemnly. 'Your shawl is quite safe with Dora. She'll keep it until you're ready to leave.'

With the greatest reluctance Biddy peeled the knitted shawl from her shoulders. 'You'd better give it back,' she said through clenched teeth. 'It's the only one I got, and it's blooming taters outside.'

'Yes, miss.' Dora bobbed a curtsey.

Nettie could hear the maid giggling as she

sped towards the servants' quarters.

'That's settled then,' Rufus said hastily. 'I think my mother is in the morning parlour and she will want to see her portrait.' He turned to a manservant, who was hovering in the background. 'Send someone to the brewery to fetch my father, Mason. Ask him to come home immediately. There's a pleasant surprise awaiting him.'

'Yes, Mr Rufus. I'll go myself.'

'If you tell him that Miss Carroll has come all the way from London to see him, that should spur him on.'

'Yes, sir.' Mason bowed and backed away.

'And on your way out, please ask Cook to send some light refreshments to the morning parlour.'

Mason's answer was lost as he hurried off to pass on the message, and Rufus crossed the wide expanse of hallway to open a door on the far side.

'Mama, you have a surprise visitor.'

Nettie grasped the painting with both hands. Her last meeting with Mrs Norwood had been anything but friendly, and she had hoped that Mr Norwood might have been there to make things go smoothly. She glanced at Rufus and he gave her an encouraging smile.

Jane Norwood was seated at a table, frowning over an accounts book. She looked up and her smile froze. 'What is she doing here?'

Nettie stepped forward and laid the wrapped canvas on the table. 'My father couldn't come in person, ma'am, but he sent his best regards and hopes that the portrait meets your approval.'

Jane's expression changed subtly. She seized the package and began tearing off the paper.

'Perhaps we ought to wait for my father to arrive before you open it?' Rufus said cautiously.

'It's my portrait,' Jane said stonily. 'I will be the judge of whether it's satisfactory, or not, as the case may be.' She ripped off the last shred of paper and stepped back to examine the painting.

Nettie held her breath. It was probably her father's best work to date, and if it was not exactly flattering, it was a remarkable likeness. He had captured the very essence of the sitter's personality, omitting the bad-tempered traits that marred her expression.

Rufus went to stand beside his mother, as he studied the painting. 'I think it's excellent.'

'It makes me look older,' Jane said crossly. 'I don't like it.'

Biddy stepped forward before Nettie could stop her. 'I think you would be very pretty if you smiled more, missis.'

Jane stared at her open-mouthed. 'Who are you?'

'I'm Biddy, missis.'

'Biddy — you must have another name. Are you related to Miss Carroll?'

'They called me Biddy Tuesday at the orphanage. It was a Tuesday when they found me in a basket, left on their front step.'

'Good heavens!' Jane stared at her aghast. 'How old are you, Biddy?'

'I think I'm nine or thereabouts.'

Jane sat down suddenly, staring at Biddy, the

painting apparently forgotten. She shot an accusing look at Nettie. 'Why is the child with you? She's too young to be a servant.'

'That's not fair, missis,' Biddy said boldly. 'I ain't her servant. I come to look after her on the journey from London. I used to look after Mrs Lorimer while her old man was at work, but they moved away. Then the *condesa* took me on, but there's no pleasing some people, and she threw me out and Nettie found me in the privy. I might have frozen to death but for her.'

Jane turned to Nettie. 'Is this true?'

'Yes, Mrs Norwood. Biddy has been ill-used by almost all those who were supposed to have her welfare at heart.'

'I had a daughter once,' Jane said, sighing. 'She only lived for a few hours, but I still miss her.

'Don't think about it, Mama.' Rufus laid his hand on his mother's shoulder. 'It was a long time ago.'

'She would have been twenty now, my little Elizabeth.' Jane took a deep breath and rose to her feet. 'Are you responsible for this child, Miss Carroll?'

'I suppose I am, in a way. At least I hope I can do something for her.'

'I'm starving, missis,' Biddy said plaintively. 'A slice of bread would go down well, and butter if you can afford it.'

'I've sent for refreshments to be brought here, Mama.'

'A cup of tea and a slice of cake are not suitable for a growing child, Rufus.' Jane seized

Biddy by the hand. 'You will come with me and I will order cook to prepare something nourishing.' She looked Biddy up and down. 'As for those garments, I don't know where they came from, but I've been collecting clothes from my well-off acquaintances for the missionaries to take to Africa. I'm sure we can do much better than those thin rags.'

'Here, you can't steal me duds,' Biddy said suspiciously. 'I thought it was queer when that posh maid took me shawl. I want it back, missis. I didn't come here to give me clothes to people in Africa, wherever that is.'

Jane rolled her eyes. 'Ignorant as well as neglected. I am not taking your clothes for the missionary barrel, you silly girl. I am going to find you something much warmer and more suitable to a child of your age. Come with me. We'll get you fed first and then we'll sort out something for you to wear.'

'The portrait, Mama?' Rufus said hastily.

'Yes, very nice. I'm sure your father will like it.' Jane dismissed it with a wave of her hand. She paused in the doorway. 'You have no objections to me taking charge of the child, have you?'

'No. At least, I don't think so.' Nettie looked to Rufus for help. 'What are your intentions, Mrs Norwood?'

'I haven't thought it through, but this girl is not old enough to go into service, and she's so underfed it's a disgrace. I might keep her here with me until she is bigger and stronger. I'll send her to the village school, or I'll arrange for someone to give her lessons here. You'd like that, wouldn't you, Biddy?'

Biddy gazed up at her, shrugging. 'I dunno, missis. I think better on a full belly.'

'That's easy to fix.' Jane shooed her out of the room. 'Your father can deal with the painting, Rufus. I have better things to do.' She held the door open. 'Talk of the devil and he appears. You must sort out the fee for the portrait, Maury.' She swept past her husband, leaving him staring after her.

'Where is your mother going with that child?'

'It's a long story, Pa,' Rufus said, shaking his head. 'I'm not sure, but it looks as if we have an addition to the household.'

Maurice shrugged. 'Oh, well, if it keeps your mother happy I won't complain. I was on my way home and I met Mason halfway. He told me that you were here, Nettie. I'm so pleased to see you.'

'Pa would have come in person, Mr Norwood, but he's very busy. He sent his best regards and he hopes you like the portrait.'

Rufus held the painting up for his father's inspection and Maurice peered at it in silence. Nettie bit her lip as she waited for him to speak. He turned to her at last and she was shocked to see tears in his eyes.

'It's wonderful, Nettie. Your father has done Jane justice. He's captured everything I love about my wife.' He took a handkerchief from his pocket and blew his nose. 'I feel quite emotional.'

'Mama thinks it makes her look old,' Rufus said, chuckling.

'Your mother will never look old to me, son. I still see her as the pretty young girl who captured my heart more than twenty-five years ago. She is the stalwart spirit who kept me going through the hard times, and without her I would not have succeeded in business.'

Nettie looked away. His words had touched her deeply and she knew she would look at Mrs Norwood with completely different eyes. To inspire such devotion she must be a remarkable woman, and the shrewish exterior she presented to the world at large was merely a façade. Nettie knew she had judged Jane Norwood harshly and she was ashamed of taking her at face value. Perhaps Pa was a better judge of character when he saw a person through the eyes of an artist. Nettie looked again at the portrait, endeavouring to see it from Mr Norwood's point of view, and failing miserably. Maybe the old adage was true — love is blind.

Rufus was at her side and she realised that he had spoken to her. 'I'm sorry,' she murmured. 'I was far away.'

'My father wants to pay for the painting.'

'Oh, no, Mr Norwood,' Nettie said hastily. 'My father wouldn't hear of it. He wanted to give you something in return for your hospitality.'

Maurice laid the portrait down reverently as if it were a precious icon. 'It's too much, I always pay my way, Nettie.'

'You'll insult him if you offer money,' Nettie said firmly. 'We're in a much better position now than previously, sir. My father is working on several commissions at a time, for which he's being well paid.'

'I'm very glad to hear it, but there must be something I can do in order to show my appreciation.'

'Perhaps I can help.' Rufus went to open the door in answer to a timid knock, and the maid bustled in, carrying a tea tray, laden with plates of dainty sandwiches, cakes and biscuits. 'Thank you, Dora. That will be all.'

The maid placed the tray carefully on the table, and left the room, closing the door quietly behind her.

'What can you do, son?' Maurice asked, frowning.

'I thought I'd spend a few days in London, Pa. I want to see Percy, and I thought I might look into the possibility of opening an office in the city.'

'Whatever for? We do very well as we are.'

'But we could sell further afield, Pa. We need to modernise and advertise our products. You've seen the posters and billboards that some companies produce — I've been thinking of working along those lines. We're doing well, but we could do even better.'

Maurice stared at his son, open-mouthed. 'But, Rufus, I spent a fortune on your education to make a gentleman of you. I didn't think you were interested in the brewery.'

'My time at Cambridge opened my eyes to a much bigger world, Pa. My education won't be wasted, and I might not be interested in the brewing and bottling side of things, but the business of promoting the products, advertising and selling is what really excites me. Give me *carte blanche* and I could double or treble trade figures.'

'I don't know what to say. You've taken me by surprise.' Maurice turned to Nettie. 'You seem to get on well with my son — did he mention any of this to you?'

She shook her head. 'No, sir. We never spoke about such things.'

'Oh, well, I suppose it's not the most romantic of subjects.' Maurice pulled up a chair. 'Come and sit down, my dear. Do please help yourself, and forgive our ramblings.' He turned to his son. 'We'll speak of this later.'

'Yes, and you'll find I have a lot to say, but in the meantime I will see Nettie safely home. It's the least I can do.'

'Yes, of course you must.'

Nettie took a seat at the table and selected a sandwich. 'There really is no need. I have my ticket and I can look after myself.'

'Well, my dear, whatever you decide you must give your father my sincere thanks, and tell him how happy I am with the portrait. I hope to see him again very soon.'

Maurice was about to leave the room when his wife burst in, and she was smiling.

Nettie paused with the sandwich halfway to her lips. The pleasant expression transformed Mrs Norwood's normally tight-lipped appearance, taking years off her age.

'Jane? What is it?' Maurice asked anxiously.

'I've been talking to the child, Maury. She is

an orphan and she has no one. Miss Carroll has shown her kindness, but it seems that she is alone in that.'

'That's very sad, my dear.'

'It is, Maury.' Jane took a deep breath. 'I want to adopt Biddy. She can never take the place of our baby, but she is in desperate need of care and protection.'

Maurice steered his wife to a chair by the fire. 'Are you sure about this, my love? It's a big step and you hardly know the child.'

'I know enough, Maury. She's nine years old, and the most she can hope for is the workhouse, or some unscrupulous person might take her on as a skivvy, and she'll be worked to death or die of starvation.'

'It's a big step, Jane. We need to talk this over.'

'No, Maury. My mind is made up. We lost our daughter and now we have a chance to make another child happy. Please say you agree.'

21

Nettie looked from one to the other, hardly daring to breathe. There was little she could do for Biddy, but if Mrs Norwood was sincere, and she had no reason to doubt this, then Biddy would have the best possible chance in life.

'Very well,' Maurice said, smiling. 'You know that I can't refuse you anything, my love. And I can see this means a great deal to you.'

Jane leaped to her feet and threw her arms around her husband's neck. 'Thank you, Maury. You're a good man.'

'We'll give it a try at first, Jane. We'll see how it works out before we do anything that cannot be undone, like adoption.'

'It will be perfect,' Jane said earnestly. 'I know in my heart that it's the right thing to do.'

'We'll give it a few months, maybe a year, and if the child settles well and is open to education and willing to learn how to behave, then we'll adopt her legally. I can't say any fairer than that.'

'Have you asked Biddy what she wants, Mama?' Rufus pulled up a chair for himself and sat next to Nettie at the table. 'She might not want to live here.'

'Why would she not?' Jane demanded, once again on the defensive. 'Of course I've spoken to her about it. I'm not completely stupid, Rufus, even if I haven't had the advantage of a university education.'

'I'm sorry, Mama. I didn't mean it like that. It's just that Biddy's opinion is surely the one that counts. She's been raised in the city and she knows nothing about country living.'

'I've talked to her at length, and I've promised that she can attend the village school, where she'll make friends of her own age. To be honest I think she'd sell her soul for good food, a clean bed and a little kindness. She will have all those things here with us, Rufus.'

'I don't doubt that, Mama.' He picked up the teapot and filled two cups, handing one to Nettie. 'It seems that it's young Biddy's lucky day, but no one has asked your opinion. What do you think, Nettie?'

'I think, if Biddy is agreeable, that it would be a wonderful opportunity for her, in all ways. She's a good girl, and she deserves a chance in life.'

'Is there anyone I should contact regarding Biddy?' Jane asked anxiously. 'She said she was working for the condesa, but the woman had given her the sack. Is that correct?'

'Yes, that's what Biddy told me, and I don't doubt her.'

'Is the condesa she mentioned the same woman who was here for the hop picking?'

'Yes, and I have to say that she took Biddy in out of pity. The poor child was left behind when the people who employed her moved on without making any provision for her. Biddy has been passed from hand to hand as if she had no feelings and no say in the matter.'

'So there is nothing to stop us from having

371

Biddy to live here?'

'If she's happy then so am I.'

'What about her belongings? Could you send them to us?

'I'm accompanying Nettie to London, Mama,' Rufus said casually. 'I could fetch them for you.'

'That's kind.' Nettie met his earnest look with a smile. 'But I doubt if she has anything worth salvaging.'

'How shocking.' Jane shook her head, sighing. 'Our servants are much better treated.'

'I'm sure they are,' Nettie said earnestly. 'But I'd like a word with Biddy before anything is settled, if you don't mind.'

Jane gave her a curt nod. 'I'll see if she's finished her meal, and I'll send her to you.' She hurried from the room.

Maurice was about to follow her, but he hesitated. 'I enjoyed my time spent with your father, Nettie. I might visit London in the not-too-distant future, and I'd like to call on him.'

'I'll leave our address for you, sir,' Nettie said eagerly. 'Pa would love to see you.'

'If we do decide to open an office in London, I'll visit quite often, and I'm sure that goes for Rufus, too.' He hurried after his wife.

Nettie shot a sideways glance at Rufus, but he was looking thoughtful and showed no sign of having heard his father's last remark. He pushed back his chair and stood up.

'I'd better go and pack a bag. I've enjoyed being at home, but now I'm ready to spend time in town.'

'Yes, of course.' Nettie eyed him warily. 'I'd invite you to stay with us, but we are cramped as it is, and Percy sleeps on the floor of Byron's room. I'm afraid you would find it very uncomfortable.'

'I'll find somewhere to lay my head, so don't worry on my account.'

He was gone and Nettie found herself alone in the morning parlour. It seemed a shame to waste the food that Cook had prepared and she ate the sandwiches, and was about to choose a cake when Biddy rushed into the room.

'Look at me, Nettie. Mrs Norwood has found me this lovely dress. Someone had given it for the poor children in Africa, but it might have been made for me.' Biddy did a twirl to demonstrate the blue merino dress with a starched white collar and a silk bow at the neck. She lifted her skirts just enough to reveal a red flannel petticoat and striped stockings worn with a pair of old, but serviceable boots.

'You look very smart,' Nettie said, smiling. 'The dress and petticoat look like new.'

'I know, and Mrs Norwood said she would get her dressmaker to measure me up for even more clothes, and Cook gave me a plate of mutton stew and a big slice of seed cake. I ate so much I thought I would burst.'

Nettie laughed. 'That would be a tragedy.' She was suddenly serious and she leaned forward to clutch Biddy's hand. 'Tell me truthfully, do you want to stay here with the Norwoods? If you have any doubts at all you must say so, and I'll take you back to London today.'

'You're kind, Nettie. I like you, but I know you ain't got the room for me.'

'We would get around that if you didn't want to accept the Norwoods' offer. I want you to think very hard before you give an answer.'

Biddy folded her hands as if she were praying and closed her eyes. Nettie waited, knowing that to interrupt would be a mistake.

'Yes,' Biddy said at length. 'I'd like to stay here and go to school. I can't read nor write and I want to learn.'

'If, by any chance, you change your mind, you must tell Mr Norwood or Mr Rufus. They will contact me and I'll come and fetch you, but I doubt if that will happen. I think you'll be very happy here.'

Biddy flung her arms around Nettie's neck. 'I'll miss you, Nettie.'

'And I'll miss you, but you'll have a good home now and kind people to love and care for you.'

Nettie looked up as the door opened and Rufus beckoned to her.

'If you're ready, I've had the trap brought round to the front door.'

Biddy clung to Nettie in a moment of panic, but Nettie stroked her head, murmuring endearments. 'You can come and visit us, Biddy,' she said gently.

'You won't forget me, will you?'

'Of course not. Who could forget someone like you?' Nettie kissed her cheek before disengaging Biddy's clutching hands. 'Now, I have to go, but I can see Dora in the hall. She has a kind face and I'm sure she will look after you, as will everyone else in Norwood Hall.'

Rufus took Biddy by the hand. 'I'll only be gone a few days, and if you're not settled in when I return I promise to take you to Nettie in London. Does that sound about right?'

Biddy nodded. 'Yes, sir.'

'Good girl.' Rufus beckoned to Dora. 'I'm giving Biddy into your capable hands, Dora. I know you'll help to look after her and keep her company if she feels homesick for London.'

Dora nodded and took Biddy by the hand. 'Come with me, miss. The mistress is waiting for you in the drawing room, and your bedchamber is being made ready as we speak.'

'I have me own room?'

'Yes, of course. You're a lucky girl and you'll be treated like one of the family.' Dora led Biddy into the hall and their voices faded as they headed towards the drawing room at the back of the house.

'I hope she settles in well,' Nettie said anxiously.

'Don't worry on that score.' Rufus held the door open for her. 'And if she isn't happy I promise to bring her to you, but my mother is clearly besotted, and I think she'll care for Biddy as if she were her own child. Anyway, we should leave before the weather closes in on us.'

★ ★ ★

Nettie was apprehensive as they set off together less than an hour later. She had said her

375

goodbyes to Biddy and the Norwoods, and the prospect of travelling to London with Rufus was at once exciting and nerve-racking. Their brief acquaintance during the hop-picking season had ended after the shooting accident, and although she still felt responsible for his injuries he seemed to have put all that behind him. He took the reins and drove them to the railway station, leaving the pony and trap at the stables nearby. They waited a short time for the train and were lucky enough to get a compartment to themselves.

Nettie was suddenly and unaccountably shy, but after the first five minutes she relaxed and settled down to enjoy the journey. Rufus was totally at ease and he made her laugh with tales of his exploits at university with Percy. He admitted freely that he was not a top student, and what interested him now was building up his father's business and making it even more successful. Nettie listened to his ideas for promoting sales, and she could see the sense in what he was proposing. He seemed to have thought it through, and she had no doubt that his enthusiasm and energy would ensure his success. The conversation turned to matters that concerned her deeply, and she found herself telling Rufus about Duke's apparent change of heart and his determination to run a legitimate business. She described the work that her father was doing, and how he had applied himself to the task, putting his own artistic ambitions to one side.

Rufus listened intently, posing the occasional

question. When she came to a halt he turned the conversation to Byron. It was done so smoothly that Nettie barely noticed a change in the tenor of his voice, but she sensed his resentment of her friendship with Byron.

'You're very fond of him, aren't you?'

She looked up, startled by the personal nature of the question. 'Of course. We're like brother and sister. Anyway,' she added hastily, 'it's Percy we need to worry about.'

'How so?'

'I don't like telling tales, but I do think that Constance has treated him badly. I like Percy and I believe that he was sincere in his feelings for Constance, but I can't say the same for her, especially now.'

'I don't understand. What has changed?'

'I can't prove it, but I believe she went away with Duke. He took her out to tea one afternoon and they didn't return.'

'Do you think she went willingly?' Rufus eyed her thoughtfully. 'I hardly know Constance, and I don't know the extent of her feelings, but Percy was quite smitten. Do you think she was merely leading him on?'

Nettie shook her head. 'Oh, no. Constance may be a bit spoiled and sometimes she can be selfish, but I thought she was genuinely in love with Percy and he with her. That's why I can't understand how she could go off with Duke.'

'Percy has no money and it sounds as though Duke has plenty. Perhaps it was as simple as that?'

'You make Constance sound calculating and

mercenary. I can't believe that of her.'

'Your loyalty does you credit, but the only other explanation is that she was abducted against her will. Do you think Duke is capable of behaving in such a manner?'

'I believe anything of Duke Dexter. He led my father astray, and he lied to Constance once. I think he would stop at nothing to get what he wants.'

Rufus leaned back in his seat, frown lines wrinkling his brow. 'What would he gain, though? Constance isn't an heiress. She's pretty enough, but Duke's actions don't make sense — unless he's madly in love with the girl.'

'I suppose that's possible, but it does seem out of character. I never imagined that Duke could love anyone other than himself. He was charm itself to the *condesa* when he thought she owned the castle in Spain, but he disappeared quickly enough when he found out that was untrue.'

'Then you must draw your own conclusions and, as you said before, they are married. He has done nothing wrong according to the law.' He eyed her speculatively. 'You don't seem convinced.'

'No. I can't help worrying about her. Duke is devious and whatever his reasons for wanting to take Constance away from her friends, I don't think she went willingly.'

'Then you seem to have little choice.'

Nettie looked up, startled. 'What do you mean?'

'If Percy feels the same as you, then perhaps you ought to try and find Constance.'

'You think we should chase after them?'

'I suspect that's exactly what Percy will do, and if you need my assistance you only have to ask.'

'You would do that for your friend?'

'Of course, and I suspect that you had already decided to go after them. You just needed to talk it over with someone who was not emotionally involved.'

'You're right, but first there is something even more important that has to be done.'

Rufus raised an eyebrow. 'That sounds intriguing. Do you feel like confiding in me?'

'No, I'm sorry. It's a long-held secret and there's only one other person, apart from Constance, who knows about it.'

'Would that be Byron?'

'Yes. How did you guess?'

'It's obvious that he's in love with you, Nettie. Anyone could see that, although perhaps it comes as a surprise to you.'

'I told you, Rufus — we're old friends, that's all there is to it.'

'Really? I wouldn't be too sure about that.'

Nettie glanced out of the window. 'It's getting dark and I can see the lights of London. We're almost there.'

★   ★   ★

The train chugged into Charing Cross Station, expelling clouds of steam as it ground to a halt. The air smelled of smoke, soot and crowded humanity as people scurried about, heading for their chosen destinations with grim determination. Rufus insisted on hiring a cab, although Nettie insisted that it was only a short walk to Covent Garden, but it was dark and it had started to rain. The market was closed, and it was too early for the theatre crowds to arrive as they alighted from the cab outside the door of Ma Burton's lodging house. The pubs were open, but there were only a few hardened drinkers roaming the streets, and now the rain was falling steadily. The yellow beams of the gaslights danced on the puddles and turned the cobblestones to shimmering gold, but Nettie knew that this was simply an illusion, and the stench of rotting vegetable matter combined with horse dung and overflowing drains brought her back to the reality of living in the city.

Rufus paid the cabby and the Hansom clattered off, splashing through the surface water.

'You'd better come in.' Nettie opened the door and stepped inside. 'Percy should be home from the office by now, and if Pa has lit the fire I can make you a cup of tea.'

Rufus followed her into the entrance hall. 'So this is where you live?'

It was too dark to see his expression, but Nettie sensed his disapproval. 'It's not a bad place,' she said defensively.

He sniffed. 'Whatever that is, it stinks to high heaven.'

Nettie stifled a giggle. 'It'll be Ma Burton's attempts at cooking. She's the only one with a proper kitchen range. The rest of us have to manage with a trivet in front of the fire.'

'I hope whatever it is tastes better than it smells.'

Nettie was about to speak when the door to Lisette's apartment opened and the condesa stood in the doorway, resplendent in a fur-trimmed cloak.

'Nettie, you're home.' She raised the lantern she was holding a little higher. 'Mr Norwood, I wasn't expecting to see you here. What brings you to Covent Garden?'

'I have business in the city, ma'am.'

'You've obviously come to stay for a while.' Lisette stared pointedly at the valise Rufus was holding. 'I doubt if there's room for you with Byron and his friends.'

'It's not a problem, Condesa. There are plenty of hotels in London.'

'I'm just off to the theatre, but I have a spare room since Constance went away. You're welcome to use it, Mr Norwood, but you would have to look after yourself. I had to let my maid go; she was quite useless.'

Nettie stepped in between them. 'You'll be glad to know that Biddy has found a new home. I found her shivering in the cold in the privy where she must have spent the night, thanks to you.'

'I don't like your tone, Nettie.'

'I'm sorry about that, but it's the truth. You turned her out and it was lucky I found her when I did.'

'Where is she now? I'll give her another chance.'

'You mean you need a servant who will work for almost nothing.' Nettie could barely contain her anger. 'As it happens, Biddy has found a new home. I left her with Mr and Mrs Norwood and they intend to adopt her.'

'How fortunate for her,' Lisette said vaguely. 'Now, if you'll excuse me, I have to leave for the theatre.' She turned her attention to Rufus. 'My offer of the room still stands. I doubt if I'll see Constance again.'

Nettie followed her to the door. 'What do you mean by that? Do you know where she might have gone?'

'Not exactly, but she was always talking about a grand house on the River Seine. She said that Duke had given it to her as a wedding present, or some such thing.'

'I thought she hated the château.'

'Constance is forever changing her mind. But if I were Duke Dexter and I wanted to spirit my reluctant bride away from her friends, I think that's where I might take her.'

'Why didn't I think of that?' Nettie resisted the temptation to give her a hug. 'Condesa, you're brilliant.'

'No, my dear, I merely face facts. Now I must go or I'll miss curtain call.' Lisette swept out of the building as if she were exiting the stage after a performance.

'I think the *condesa* is right,' Nettie said thoughtfully. 'Whether Constance went willingly, or not, I think that's where Duke would have taken her.'

'What do you intend to do? If she went of her

own free will there's no point in following them, but if she was coerced into accompanying him, she might need help.'

'I couldn't put it better myself.' Nettie headed towards the staircase. 'I need to speak to Percy and I'm sure you want to see him, too. Follow me.' She led the way upstairs and came to a halt on the second floor outside the room shared by Byron and the others.

After a few seconds the door opened and Percy peered into the darkness. 'Nettie, you've come home. Your pa said you'd gone to the country and he didn't know when you'd be back.' His face lit up when he spotted Rufus standing behind her. 'This is a nice surprise. Come in, both of you.'

Nettie stepped into the room where a warm fug had built up as the friends grouped round the fire, eating fish and chips out of newspaper, and drinking beer. They jumped to their feet at the sight of her, and Byron hurried over to give her a hug, but his smile faded when he saw Rufus.

'What is he doing here? Did he bring you back to London?'

'I'm not a child, Byron. I can travel on my own if I choose. Rufus happened to have business in town and he wanted to see Percy.'

Byron glared at Rufus, who had walked over to join Ted and Pip by the fire. Percy handed him a bottle of ale and they seemed to have forgotten Nettie's existence.

'He could have done that at any time,' Byron

said in a low voice. 'Why did he choose to come today?'

Nettie met his angry gaze with a shake of her head. 'Ask him, not me. We travelled together, that's all. Now I've done my bit and I'm going upstairs to see what Pa wants for supper.'

'No, wait, please. I didn't mean to sound cross. It's dark and I was worried about you travelling on your own.'

'As you can see I wasn't alone, and Rufus was coming to London on business anyway, so he accompanied me on the journey. Are you satisfied now?'

'Yes, I'm sorry. Won't you come in and join us?'

'Maybe later. Pa will be wondering where I am.' Nettie walked towards the stairs and she did not look back. Byron's reaction had been both unreasonable and annoying. She had, until now, taken the relationship between them very much for granted. He was a dear friend, but she had never thought of him romantically. Rufus's comment on the train came back to her forcibly, and Byron's behaviour might be put down to jealousy, although he had once or twice tried to explain how he felt. Perhaps she had been too wrapped up in her own problems and those of her friends to listen properly? She would think about that later, but now she must make sure that her father had something to eat, because once he started working he was likely to forget about small details like food and drink. Tomorrow morning, first thing, she would take her manuscript to the publisher's office.

The clerk at Dorning and Lacey greeted Nettie with a welcoming smile. 'You've finished it then, Miss Carroll?'

Nettie nodded and laid the manuscript on the desk. 'I've tried to make it neater this time,' she said earnestly. 'But it's travelled a long way since I wrote the first sentence.'

'Really?' The woman adjusted her spectacles and turned to the first page. 'A good beginning. Let's hope Mr Dorning likes this one. Although, I have to say I read your first effort and I thought it showed great promise, but then I'm only a clerk.'

'But you're more like the women who would read my books,' Nettie said eagerly. 'I value your opinion.'

'Well, good luck. I'll put this on Mr Dorning's desk. He isn't in yet, but I'll be sure to point it out to him.'

'Thank you. I really appreciate it.' Nettie left the office feeling hopeful, but also nervous. She had worked under the most difficult of circumstances in order to produce the novel, and now it was in the hands of strangers. Surely it must feel like this when a mother sent her child off to boarding school for the first time? Nettie wished that she could stay with her manuscript and defend her work from the inevitable criticisms the publisher would make, but that was impossible. She quickened her pace as she set off for Covent Garden and home, but a sudden thought occurred to her and she changed direction, heading instead for Duke's gallery in Mayfair.

★   ★   ★

She thought at first that it was closed. There did not seem to be any activity inside, but she tried the door and found it opened easily. She went in and came face to face with Pendleton.

'Miss Carroll,' he said smoothly. 'I didn't expect to see you today.'

'I haven't come on business. I need your help, Mr Pendleton.'

'Really? I can't think how I might be of assistance to you, Miss Carroll.'

'I really need to find Mr Dexter.'

'I'm sure I don't know where he is, miss.'

Nettie managed a smile. 'I'm sure that's not true, Mr Pendleton. I know for a fact that Mr Dexter trusts and respect you more than anyone. You need not put it into words — a nod would do.'

Pendleton straightened his shoulders, looking down his nose at her. 'I wouldn't betray my employer's trust.'

'Of course not, and I wouldn't ask it of you. All I want to know is if Mr Dexter has gone to France. The flicker of an eyelid or a nod will do.'

Pendleton stiffened, saying nothing, but his left eyelid closed so slightly that its movement was almost imperceptible.

'Was his destination the château?'

22

Nettie took a cab home. It was sheer extravagance, but it was early afternoon and she needed to move quickly. She found her father at work, as usual, and having run up all three flights of stairs, she stopped to catch her breath.

'I think Duke has taken Constance to France,' she gasped.

'Really? Well, that's a surprise,' Robert said calmly. 'I thought she was sweet on Byron's brother.'

'She is, or at least she was. But I saw Pendleton this morning and he led me to believe that they'd gone to the château.'

Robert wiped his brush on his smock, adding to the rainbow hues already there. 'Well, I can't think of a lovelier spot. I could quite happily live in that ancient castle overlooking the river.'

'Pa, be serious. I can't just abandon Constance. She might have been taken against her will.'

'My dear Nettie, in my opinion Constance wouldn't think twice if the situation were to be reversed. That young lady puts herself first in everything. If Duke has made her a better offer I doubt if she would refuse.'

'I need to speak to Byron, but he's at work, and so is Percy.'

'I hope you don't intend to go gallivanting across the Channel again, my love. I need to finish these three paintings, and Duke is bound to return if only to collect them and pass them on to his clients.'

'I'm sure that Pendleton could do that, Pa. I think Duke is up to something.'

'Give the man a chance, my love. If Duke has decided to turn over a new leaf then we must respect him for making the change.'

Nettie sighed and left him to continue painting. She had hoped, if only for her father's sake, that Duke was trying to make an honest living, but she now had serious doubts. It would be just like Duke to sell the copies abroad as originals, and there had been something highly suspect in Pendleton's demeanour. The fact that the gallery appeared to be closed for business was another reason to wonder why Duke had suddenly decided to return to France. And why had Constance agreed to accompany him? Nettie needed to talk to someone who was not directly connected with the problem. Byron and Percy would be hard at work, as would Ted and Pip. There was just one other person who might give her a sensible answer, and if she hurried she might catch Rufus before he left the building.

Nettie hurried downstairs without stopping to take off her outdoor things, but as she reached the first-floor landing she was aware of raised voices coming from the entrance hall. Madame Fabron was screeching at someone and Amelie was adding her voice to the argument. As Nettie rounded the bend in the stairs she saw Lisette standing with her back to the wall. She was deathly pale, clutching her throat and making strangled attempts to speak.

'What's the matter?' Nettie cried as she raced down the remaining stairs and hurried to Lisette's side. 'Are you ill?'

'She won't sing again today, that's for sure.' Violet Fabron threw back her head and laughed. 'That's what you get for stealing my part in the show — now it's mine.'

'You tell her, Ma,' Amelie screamed.

'What's going on?' Ma Burton emerged from the door leading down to her basement lair. 'What's the commotion?'

'Mind your own business, you nosy cow,' Violet snarled. 'This is between me and her, the Frenchwoman.'

'What have they done to you?' Nettie asked, placing her arm around Lisette's trembling body.

'My throat,' Lisette rasped. 'They've poisoned me.'

'Poison, my eye,' Violet said angrily. 'I wish I had poisoned you, you bitch. You'll have a sore throat for a few days, that's all.'

'I can't say I blame you.' Ma Burton's chins wobbled up and down as a deep chuckle rumbled from her stomach to her lips. 'She's a stuck-up foreigner, and she owes me a week's rent.'

'Well, you won't get it now.' Violet preened herself. 'After that disaster at the matinee performance I doubt if she'll ever work on the London stage again.'

'I'll call the police,' Lisette said hoarsely. 'What did you put in the honey I take to ease a sore throat?'

'Oh dear, me hand must have slipped with the cayenne pepper,' Amelie said, laughing. 'Sorry, love. My mistake. Anyway, the audience loved it. They laughed till they cried.'

'So they did,' Violet said, nodding. 'But the producer didn't see the funny side. I was her understudy, but tonight I'll be the leading lady, and tomorrow and the day after. I'll be so good that the French bitch will get the boot, and you can toss her out on the street, for all I care, Ma.' She linked arms with her daughter and they sauntered into the street, their laughter echoing in the hallway even after they had gone.

'Serve you right for being a stuck-up cow,' Ma Burton said, wheezing with laughter. 'I wish I'd seen your face. Now you can clear off. I got another tenant lined up for your rooms, and you can send your fancy man packing, too. I don't hold with immoral goings-on in my house.'

'Mr Norwood is a respectable businessman,' Nettie said angrily. 'You can't throw the *condesa* out. We'll pay her rent if she's in arrears.'

'And where did you get the money from, I'd like to know?' Ma Burton stood, arms akimbo. 'You and your pa are the ones who normally pay late. Has he slipped off the straight and narrow again? Naughty, naughty.' Her smile faded. 'But if you're an hour behind with your rent, I'll send my boys to collect the money or take what they want. If you get my meaning.' She took a step backwards as the door to Lisette's rooms opened and Rufus emerged, his angry scowl directed at Ma.

'I heard what you said. Your boys will come off

worst if they try to intimidate either of these ladies. I don't know you, madam, but don't threaten my friends.'

'You don't frighten me, sonny. Take the old whore and get out of my house. I don't want her sort giving my respectable lodging house a bad name. I got a reputation to keep up, and that one is finished in the theatre. Madame Fabron will see to that.' Ma stomped off, head held high, her huge body rocking from side to side as she opened the cellar door, slamming it behind her.

Lisette clutched her throat. 'I may never sing again.'

'I'm sure your voice will return when the soreness goes away,' Nettie said anxiously. 'I could go to the shop and get some honey and a lemon or two. That might help.'

'Perhaps a few drops of laudanum in water would soothe the pain,' Rufus suggested warily. 'Maybe you should see a physician.'

'I can't afford to pay.' Lisette leaned against the wall, fanning herself with her hand. 'They did this to me. My throat was dry and I called for my usual glass of lemon and honey, and took a sip.' Tears rolled down her cheeks, streaking her stage makeup. 'I croaked like a frog — it was humiliating.'

'Save your voice, Condesa,' Nettie said gently. 'Come inside and lie down. I'll see if I can find some laudanum.'

Lisette allowed them to help her into her parlour where she stretched out on the sofa, covering her eyes with her hand. 'I'm ruined.'

Nettie found a bottle of laudanum in one of the cupboards and she added a few drops to a glass of water, which she handed to Lisette. 'Drink this. It will ease the pain.'

Lisette raised herself on her elbow and gulped down the liquid, wincing as if each swallow caused her pain. She lay back, handing the empty glass to Nettie. 'I'm finished in London.'

'I can't do anything here,' Rufus said quietly. 'I have a business appointment, Nettie. I have to go now.'

Nettie followed him to the door. 'Yes, of course. I'll look after the *condesa*.'

'Is she really a countess?'

Nettie noticed that his eyes crinkled at the corners and his generous mouth had a comical twist when he smiled. Despite the seriousness of the situation she found herself responding with a chuckle. 'No, although we were taken in at first. She lived with the count, but they never married.'

He nodded. 'She has had a colourful past, poor lady. I don't imagine this fiasco will do much for her reputation in the theatre, even though it wasn't her fault.'

'Maybe she would like to return to France,' Nettie said thoughtfully. 'She might want to come with me.'

'What did you say?' Rufus was about to leave, but he turned to give her a searching look.

'It's just something I learned this morning. I believe that Duke has taken Constance to the château, and I won't rest until I know whether or not she went willingly.'

'You told me they were married. I don't see the problem.'

'She wanted an annulment. They weren't properly married, if you know what I mean.'

'Even so, if they've been gone for a day or two, you might be wasting your time, Nettie.'

'It's not just that,' Nettie said hastily. 'Constance chose to marry Duke, but it's my father I'm worried about. I think Duke might have led him astray yet again. It's just a feeling and I can't prove it, but if Duke intends to sell the copies as original paintings, it is the same old story. Pa will be on the wrong side of the law, but Duke will be safe in France and, if I know him, he will deny everything, leaving Pa to take the consequences if the fraud is discovered.'

'When were you planning to leave?'

'You think it's the right thing to do?'

'I don't think you'll rest until you know the truth, but you mustn't go alone. Give me until four o'clock, and we'll go together.'

Nettie stared at him in amazement. 'You'll go to France with me? At such short notice.'

'I still have my passport in my wallet and my bag is not yet unpacked. We'll leave the moment I return.'

'But I should tell the others,' Nettie said doubtfully. 'Byron and Percy ought to know.'

'Leave them a note. They're grown men, they can follow us if they want to, but as I see it there's no time to waste. Now I have to go, but I'll be back as soon as I can.' He opened the front door and stepped outside onto the pavement, leaving Nettie staring into empty space.

'Nettie, fetch me some lemon and honey.' The *condesa*'s plaintive voice brought Nettie back to the present and she walked purposefully into the parlour. 'Do you really want to return to France, Condesa?'

Lisette lay back against the cushions. 'Yes, I've had enough of London. I was never happy here, and my sons are grown men — they don't need me.'

'Then pack your things. We're leaving for France as soon as Rufus returns.'

'But I have no money, Nettie. I've spent all my earnings on new clothes and shoes. I can't even pay the rent.'

'All the more reason to move on. I'm going upstairs to tell my father what's happening. He'll argue, but he'll understand when I explain why I have to leave now.'

★ ★ ★

It had been a rough crossing, followed by a tedious train journey from Calais. The upright wooden seats in third class were not the most comfortable way to travel, and the compartment was packed with farmers' wives on their way to market, complete with goats, and hens in rush baskets. The air was heavy with the mixed smells of hairy animals, garlic and French tobacco, and Lisette suffered a nagging cough, for which she sucked throat pastilles. They snatched food wherever they could, but Nettie was hungry and thirsty and, having listened to Lisette's hoarse voice complaining constantly, she was beginning to wish they had left the *condesa* in London. However Lisette's spirits soared when they arrived at the Gare du Nord and she hurried off to enquire about train times and the price of tickets to Beauaire.

Nettie looked up hopefully as Lisette hurried back to them. 'Well?' she said eagerly. 'Is there a train soon?'

'We've just missed one and there isn't another for several hours, at least not one that stops at Beauaire.' Lisette covered her mouth with her hand as a cough racked her body. 'I should have realised that. Heaven knows, I grew up here.'

'What do we do now?' Nettie looked from one to the other. 'It's too far to go by cab.'

'There is a train that goes as far as Vernon. If we can get there tonight we can perhaps hire horses or a cab to the château tomorrow morning. I think it will be too late to do so by the time we arrive this evening.'

'Then that's what we'll do,' Nettie said firmly. 'At least we'll be on our way and it will be cheaper than staying in Paris overnight. What do you think, Rufus?'

He nodded. 'I agree. I don't speak the language, so if you'll come with me, Condesa, we'll purchase tickets to Vernon.'

'I'm not a *condesa*,' Lisette said tiredly. 'It was silly of me to assume the title. Please call me Lisette.'

'Of course, if you wish, Lisette.' Rufus raised her gloved hand to his lips. 'We will get to the château somehow.'

'And the first thing I will do is to call on my

395

brother. I haven't seen Jean for so many years that I can't recall how many. I doubt if he would recognise me now.'

'He hasn't forgotten you,' Nettie said hastily. 'It was Jean who told Byron about you.'

Lisette chuckled. 'Nothing good, I imagine.' She tucked her hand into the crook of Rufus's arm. 'Let's get those tickets before we freeze to death on this draughty platform.'

★   ★   ★

The train stopped at every small station on the way to Vernon, but eventually they arrived in the small town on the banks of the River Seine, although it was dark and too late to hire any form of transport to take them on to the château. Lisette made enquiries at the ticket office and they were directed to a nearby inn, where they managed to book two rooms. It was not the most comfortable place to stay, and Nettie was certain that the bed linen was damp, but she was too tired to complain. She slept surprisingly well, considering she had to share a bed with Lisette, who not only talked in her sleep, but was extremely restless.

Nettie woke up next morning to the sound of animals being driven along the cobbled street below their window. She climbed out of bed and went to open the casement. Sheep and goats were being herded toward the market square, a corner of which was just visible if she craned her neck. The farmers shouted to each other and they had to raise their voices to make themselves heard above the sound of the animals bleating, and the background noise of steam whistles from the direction of the river. Nettie was reminded of Aristide and the time they had spent on his barge, and she smiled, remembering his colourful life and loves. He had formed a special relationship with her father, and she had no doubt that Pa would have been quite content to live the life of a bargee. She glanced over her shoulder to see if Lisette had awakened, but she was still sound asleep and it seemed a pity to disturb her. Nettie had a quick wash in the ice-cold water she poured from the flower-patterned jug into the cracked washbasin. She dressed with equal haste in an attempt to combat the chill in the room. Judging by the ashes that spilled from the grate and the thick coating of dust on the furniture, it appeared that housekeeping was not the landlord's first priority. Perhaps they could have had a fire lit for them had they been prepared to pay extra, but money was tight and Rufus held the purse strings. He was so different from her father in that respect: had Pa been in charge they would have had servants running round after them, even if it cost him his last penny.

Nettie smiled to herself as she left the room and tiptoed along the corridor to knock on Rufus's door. There was no response, and assuming that he was still asleep Nettie went downstairs and let herself out into the street.

She had intended to walk to the station and look up the timetable, but the narrow streets had all looked the same in the darkness and she found herself heading towards the river. A pale wintry sun had forced its way through banks of clouds, burning off the morning mist that hung over the water like a shroud. It was quieter here, away from the bustling marketplace and the only sounds were the rushing waters of the Seine and the cawing of rooks high up in the bare branches of the skeletal trees. The familiar scent of the river with just a hint of smoke from the funnels of the barges moored alongside a wooden landing stage brought back a flood of memories. Lines of washing, strung from stem to stern of several of the vessels flapped in the gusty wind like colourful flags, and the heady aroma of coffee and hot bread reminded her that she had not had breakfast. She was about to turn back when a sight that she had not thought to see again caught her eye. The bare body of a man shone pink and white in the early morning sunlight. He was balanced on the bulwark of a barge, standing with his back to her as he stared into the distance, and a plume of pipe smoke spiralled above his peaked cap. He was naked except for a red and white spotted bandana tied around his neck and a pair of neatly darned woollen socks on his feet. She cupped her hands around her mouth.

'Aristide Durand, is that you?'

He spun round, very nearly losing his balance, but he managed to save himself from toppling into the water. 'Nettie!' He stepped down from the bulwark and pulled on his trousers, slipping a thick fisherman's smock over his head without disturbing his cap or taking his pipe from his mouth. He strode across the deck, sending puffs of smoke into the air.

'Nettie, this is a surprise. Have you come all this way to see me?' He held out his hand and helped her to clamber aboard. 'You're cold. Come into the cabin and have some coffee. It should be ready now.'

'I can't stay long, Aristide. I left my friends at the inn.'

'Bring them here,' Aristide said, grinning. 'We can have breakfast together.' He led the way to the cabin, giving Nettie little alternative other than to follow him. The interior of the living accommodation was warm and welcoming. The brass was polished to a brilliant shine and the stove black-leaded until it gleamed. Everything was as clean and tidy as Nettie remembered, and she perched on the edge of the bunk, accepting a mug of black coffee sweetened with honey. Aristide sat opposite her, smoking his pipe and listening intently as she told him as briefly as possible of their trip to Spain, and their time spent in the Kentish hop garden. He was eager for news of her father, and he was suitably angry with Duke for the way in which he had behaved.

Nettie finished her coffee. 'I must go now, Aristide. It's lovely to see you again, but we have to get to the château as quickly as possible. I was on my way to the station to look up the timetable when I took the wrong road and ended up on the river bank.'

'It's market day, and a bad time for travelling,' Aristide said, shaking his head. 'The trains will be packed with farmers and their animals. Fetch your friends and I'll take you downriver. We'll get there by mid-afternoon if we leave soon. I have business in the town anyway, so it suits me well.'

Nettie rose to her feet. 'Are you sure it won't be putting you out?'

'You know me. I wouldn't offer if I didn't mean it.'

Nettie reached up to kiss his whiskery cheek. 'Thank you, Aristide.'

'The lady, this *comtesse*, is she very grand?'

'Lisette was a water gypsy, like yourself, before she took to the stage. She is very adaptable and I'm sure she'll be very grateful.'

Aristide grinned. 'I hope so.'

'You are wicked,' Nettie said, chuckling. 'She will put you firmly in your place if you don't behave.'

'I can't wait. Go and fetch the lady, Nettie. I'll make a fresh pot of coffee.'

★ ★ ★

When Nettie reached the inn she was met by the sight of Byron and Percy, who were arguing volubly with Rufus while Lisette tried to calm them down.

Percy was the first to spot Nettie. 'Where were you? Why didn't you tell us what you were planning?'

'Yes,' Byron added angrily. 'We've been worried sick. You should have waited for us, Nettie.'

'Calm down, everyone,' Rufus said sternly. 'This is getting us nowhere. Surely we've all got one aim and that is to find Constance and make sure that she isn't being forced into agreeing to do something against her will.'

'She would never have gone off with him voluntarily,' Percy said angrily.

'How did you know we were here?' Nettie looked from one to the other.

'We didn't.' Byron shook his head. 'The train only came this far and Percy asked the man in the ticket office if he remembered seeing you three. He said he'd sent you here.'

Percy shot an enquiring look in his mother's direction. 'Are you all right, Ma? We heard what happened to you in the theatre.'

Lisette nodded, holding her hand to her throat. 'I'm still hoarse, but it could have been worse. I hope Violet Fabron forgets all her lines, the bitch.'

'You're free from them now,' Nettie said sympathetically. 'But we have to concentrate on getting to the château as quickly as possible.'

'We've been told that it's market day.' Rufus glanced out of the window. 'There's no chance of hiring horses, but we could try the railway station.'

Byron shook his head. 'Not a chance, at least until midday. That's the next stopping train.'

'I have a better solution.' Nettie had to raise her voice in order to be heard. 'If you'll all stop talking at once, I'll tell you.'

★ ★ ★

It was almost an hour before they boarded Aristide's barge. Lisette had to make herself

401

presentable, even though it was going to be a trip on the river where no one would recognise her. Rufus paid the bill at the inn, and as Percy and Byron had not eaten since the previous evening, they visited a bakery on the way to the barge and purchased fresh bread. Lisette bargained hard for butter and jam from a farmer's wife in the market.

'You took your time, and there seem to be more of you now,' Aristide said sternly as he helped Nettie back on board, but his expression changed subtly when Nettie introduced him to Lisette. He proffered his hand. 'Madame Horton, it is an honour to have such a famous lady on board my humble vessel.'

She accepted his assistance, landing lightly on the deck. 'You may call me Lisette. I was born on one of these things, so I know the score, Monsieur Durand.'

'Aristide,' he said, raising her hand to his lips. 'As you will know, we river people don't stand on ceremony.'

Byron climbed on board, laden with their luggage. He dropped the bags on the deck and held out his arms. 'Aristide, my friend. It's good to see you again.'

'We will have a long talk when we get underway.' Aristide leaped nimbly ashore to release the mooring rope and was back on board before the barge moved an inch. 'There's coffee on the stove, and I see you've brought provisions. Excellent. Help yourselves.' He moved swiftly to man the tiller and steered the barge into mid-channel.

'How long will this take? Percy demanded. 'It's not the fastest form of transport.'

'We've been this way before and the quay is close to the centre of the town,' Byron said calmly. 'At a guess I think we should reach the château by late afternoon.'

'Come and have some food, you'll feel much better when you've eaten.' Nettie decided that someone must take charge, and she led the way to the cabin. They huddled together on the bunks and ate the bread, lavishly spread with butter and jam, and washed down with Aristide's strong coffee.

Lisette licked her fingers one by one. 'I haven't enjoyed breakfast so much since I was a child. There's something about being on the water that gives one an appetite.'

'Aristide will be pleased to hear you say that,' Nettie said, smiling. 'Funnily enough I was only thinking of him this morning, and it must have been fate that led me down to the jetty.'

Byron finished his coffee with an appreciative sigh. 'I feel better after that, and you're right, Mama. Food does taste better eaten like this. I think my water gypsy blood must have come to the fore during our trip downriver with Aristide.'

Lisette looked longingly at the remaining bread. 'It would be sheer greed to eat more. Anyway, that should be for our host. I think I'll take it to him.' She rose to her feet and left the cabin, taking the bread, butter and jam with her.

Nettie filled a bowl with hot water from the kettle and began to wash the mugs and plates. She glanced out of the open door and smiled.

'Look at them, Byron. Lisette and Aristide are chatting away like old friends. Who would have thought that they would get on so well?'

'Who indeed?' Byron followed her gaze. 'My mother certainly has a way with men. It looks as if Aristide has already fallen under her spell.'

Nettie smiled. 'Or maybe the *condesa* is charmed by the roguish bargee. I've seen how the local women fall at his feet. I don't know how he does it, but Aristide is a real ladies' man.'

'I hope his intentions are honourable. My mother has been badly used by the men in her life.'

'I think your mother can stand up for herself,' Nettie said wryly. 'I'd pitch her against Aristide any day, but it's Constance I'm concerned for.'

Percy had been staring out on deck, but he turned to them, frowning. 'I must get to her soon. If Duke is trying to force her to do anything against her will it's up to me to stop him.'

'I agree. The sooner we reach the château the better,' Nettie said earnestly. 'I just hope we're in time to save Constance from doing something she'll regret for the rest of her life.'

23

They arrived at Beauaire in the early afternoon. Lisette and Byron went directly to Jean Joubert's shop, accompanied by Aristide, who was eager to meet Lisette's brother. This left Nettie, Percy and Rufus to hurry on to the château. Nettie led them to the postern gate, hoping to find it unlocked, and as luck would have it, they walked into the cherry orchard unchallenged. It was surprisingly quiet and the only person they saw was an old man who was sweeping up the dead leaves.

'Act as if you've every right to be here,' Nettie said in a low voice. 'I don't know where the rest of the gardeners are, but it's usually much busier than this.'

'Where would we start looking for Constance?' Percy asked anxiously. 'I didn't realise that the château was so big.'

'It's more like a castle than any mansion I've ever seen,' Rufus added. 'You know the place, Nettie. You'd better lead on and we'll follow.'

'We'll try the room that Constance had on our previous visit.' Nettie hesitated as she was about to open the door that led to the servants' quarters. 'I think you'd better wait here. I might pass unnoticed on my own, and if I should happen to be seen, the staff will probably remember me.'

Rufus caught her by the arm as she was about

to enter the building. 'What should we do if you don't return?'

'Give me an hour, and if I haven't come back by then you must go and find Aristide. He's well in with the local police.' Nettie broke away from him and let herself into the stone passageway. She had not dared to look Rufus in the eye or he would realise that she had been lying. The only contact that Aristide had with the local gendarmerie was when he had been arrested, but Rufus was not to know that, and if it kept him and Percy from barging into the château it was worth a little white lie.

She walked quickly, dodging in and out of doorways when she heard footsteps, but as luck would have it she managed to get to the main part of the château without being spotted. The meandering corridors and stone staircases were confusing, but Nettie concentrated hard, noting artefacts that had caught her eye on her previous visit. There were crossed swords on the wall over a portrait of a military gentleman at the foot of the stairs that led to the rooms in the east wing. She remembered that the sun had awakened her every morning during her previous stay, and when she reached the first landing she recognised a particularly fine oak chest, carved with flowers and birds. It was not far now to Constance's room and Nettie breathed a sigh of relief, but she was not safe yet. Even if Constance was in the château, she could be anywhere. It was a chance, but one she had to take as she approached the bedroom door. She turned the handle gently, praying that the hinges would not shriek and give her away, but it opened silently and she peered inside.

Firelight flickered on the wall opposite, which must be a good sign, but just because the room was in use did not mean it was where she would find Constance. Emboldened, she pushed it open just enough to step inside and she could have shouted for joy when she spotted a familiar figure huddled in a huge armchair by the fire.

'Constance,' she called in a low voice. 'Constance, it's me, Nettie.'

Constance raised a tear-stained face, staring at her as if she were a ghost. 'Nettie?'

'Yes, I'm here.' Nettie rushed over to her and went down on her knees at her friend's side. 'Are you all right? You're not ill, are you?'

Constance shook her head and tears flowed freely down her pale cheeks. 'Oh, Nettie. I was never so glad to see anyone in my whole life.'

Nettie wrapped her arms around Constance's trembling body. 'I'm here now. Has he harmed you?'

'No, but he won't let me go. He says I'll stay here until I agree to live as his wife, if you know what I mean? I've held out so far, but I haven't eaten properly for two days. He only allows me to have water and some dry bread, as if I were a prisoner.'

Nettie rose to her feet, staring down at the hunched figure of the girl who had once been so full of spirit and energy. 'What has he done to you? And why is he treating you like this?'

'I don't know, Nettie. He's told so many lies and changed the story so often that I don't know what is true and what is false.'

'But you haven't given in to his demands?'

'No, but I knew I couldn't go on like this. I don't know how you got here, but please take me home.'

'Get dressed quickly. Rufus and Percy are waiting in the grounds.' Nettie helped Constance to her feet. 'Where are your things? We haven't much time?'

Constance pointed weakly to a mahogany clothes press. 'I don't want anything that Duke bought for me.'

'It doesn't matter what you wear just so long as you're warm. It's very cold outside and we'll be travelling on Aristide's barge.'

Constance nodded dully. 'All right, but we must hurry. They keep checking on me, although it's a saint's day and I think the servants are more interested in celebrating than in guarding me.'

Nettie went to the clothes press and took out a flannel petticoat and a dark blue woollen gown, which was the plainest and most practical garment she could find amongst the silks and satins. Together they managed to get Constance dressed and wrapped up in a fur-lined cloak. Nettie rifled through a chest of drawers and found gloves and stockings, and while Constance pulled on her hose Nettie searched the cupboards for a pair of leather boots.

'Now, you'll be warm enough in that outfit,' Nettie said triumphantly. 'All we have to do is get you to safety.' She went to open the door and looked both ways, beckoning to Constance.

'There's no one coming. Hurry.'

Constance was weak from lack of food, but she managed to keep up by clutching Nettie's arm and leaning on her. It did not make for a quick escape, although the sounds of merriment from the servants' hall were encouraging. Nettie thought they were safe, but a door opened and a young maidservant stepped out of the pantry. She stared at them wide-eyed, and for a horrible moment Nettie thought she was about to cry out. Constance put her finger to her lips, and she murmured something in rapid French, which the girl acknowledged with a faint smile before going on her way.

Nettie did not stop to ask what Constance had said to persuade the servant to keep quiet, and she opened the outer door, taking a deep breath of cold, frosty air. Constance swayed on her feet and Nettie had to support her or she would have fallen. She could see Rufus and Percy standing in the entrance to the kitchen garden, but the back yard stretched out before them with nowhere to hide.

'Try to walk, Constance,' Nettie said in desperation. 'It's not far now and you'll be away from here for ever.'

Constance made a valiant effort, but it was slow progress, and a shout rang out, echoing off the walls of the outbuildings.

'Stop there. Don't go a step further.'

Nettie glanced over her shoulder to see Duke striding across the cobblestones followed by a manservant.

'It's too late,' Constance whispered. 'I'm done for.'

'No, you aren't.' Nettie gave her a hefty shove. 'Run for it. I'll delay him for as long as I can.'

Constance stumbled, but she managed to right herself and she picked up her skirts and ran towards Percy, who hurried to meet her.

Nettie spun round to face Duke. 'Let her go. She doesn't want you.'

Duke's hand shot out and he grabbed Nettie by the arm, twisting it behind her back so that she cried out in pain. He held up his free hand, pointing at Rufus, who had started towards them. 'Keep back. This has nothing to do with you.'

Rufus came to a halt. 'Let her go.'

Duke tightened his grip, causing Nettie to wince with pain. 'It seems I have the trump card. What is your interest in Miss Carroll? Do I detect a romance?'

'Let me go, Duke,' Nettie said through clenched teeth. 'This is ridiculous. You're behaving like a fool.'

'Not so much of a fool. I have the upper hand, my dear, and I want what's mine. Constance is my wife.'

'You know you took advantage of her naivety and you tricked her into a sham marriage. I don't know what you hoped to gain by keeping her here against her will, but it's clear she doesn't want anything to do with you.'

'It's true that I saved Constance's father from bankruptcy, but I lied when I told her that I owned the gallery. I can't get my hands on any of it unless we are legally man and wife.'

'But you were prepared to forgo that pleasure when you thought that Lisette was a titled Spanish lady who owned a castle.' Nettie twisted her head to look him in the eye, and she could see that her barb had hit home.

'Let her go, Dexter.' Rufus took a step nearer, but Duke's manservant advanced on him, brandishing a shotgun.

Duke held up his hand. 'A fair swap is required here. Send Constance to me and I'll release Nettie.'

Rufus shook his head. 'She'll be safely out of the grounds by now. She'll have told Percy everything and he'll go to the police. It's only a matter of time before they come to arrest you.'

'On what grounds?' Duke demanded. 'In France I am known as Marc Gaillard, an honest art dealer. Duke Dexter is dead and the man the police want is Robert Carroll. He's the forger, and they only have to alert the police in London. The evidence is there, in his studio.' He laughed and relaxed his hold just enough to allow Nettie to break free from him. She backed away, glaring at him in disbelief.

'But you promised Pa that it was fair and square. You said that the copies you asked him to make were to be sold as such.'

'Your father is a fool, Nettie. The paintings he's been working on are my insurance. They will incriminate him, and I, Marc Gaillard, will deny all knowledge.' Duke took a step towards her, but Rufus was too quick for him. He snatched the gun from the servant's hand, aiming it at Duke.

'It would give me great pleasure to pepper you with shot, Dexter. It hurts, believe me, I know from experience, but the law will deal with you eventually.' He held his hand out to Nettie. 'Let's go.'

She hesitated. 'You disgust me, Duke. But you've taken advantage of my father for the last time. He trusted you and you've betrayed him yet again. Shame on you, that's all I can say.' She turned on her heel and walked away, heading for the kitchen garden and the path that led to the outside world. She did not stop until she reached the postern gate at the far end of the cherry orchard, where she found Percy holding Constance in his arms.

'Are you all right, Constance?' Nettie asked anxiously.

'She'll be fine when we get away from here,' Percy said stoutly. 'I'll never let her go again.'

'You go on ahead.' Nettie glanced over her shoulder and was relieved to see Rufus striding towards them.

'What about Duke?' Constance clutched Percy's hand. 'He's not likely to give up easily.'

'He can't touch you now,' Percy said gently. 'Can you walk, darling? You might be light as a feather, but I don't think I can carry you all the way to the quay.'

'I'm fine now I know you still love me,' Constance said shyly. 'I thought I had lost you, Percy.'

'Never. I'm afraid you'll have to put up with me and my family for a very long time. We'll have your marriage annulled and then I'll go down on one knee and propose.'

Nettie smiled. 'First things first. We have to get back to London, and I'm not sure we have enough money.'

Percy glanced over her shoulder. 'Here comes the man who can afford almost anything. Are you all right, Rufus? You don't look as if it came to fisticuffs.'

Rufus broke the shotgun and propped it up against the wall. 'I would have enjoyed shooting Duke Dexter, but in the end he gave up without a fight.' He eyed Nettie with a worried frown. 'Did he hurt you? If he did I'll gladly go back and give him what for.'

'He didn't break my bones, but I know how to fix Marmaduke Dexter or Marc Gaillard, whichever he likes to call himself,' Nettie said, chuckling.

'How so?' Rufus opened the postern gate and held it to allow Percy and Constance to pass.

'Samson Wegg,' Nettie said triumphantly. 'He and Duke were supposed to have settled their differences, but I didn't believe Wegg — he'll do anything for money.'

Nettie stepped out into the lane. Duke might have taken her father for being a gullible cat's paw, but now Duke Dexter was going to get his comeuppance. She would only have to put a word in the right quarter. Maybe Ma Burton and her shady contacts would come in useful after all.

They had to walk slowly for Constance's sake, but when they reached the market square they found Lisette, Jean, Aristide and Byron seated round an outside table, shielded from a sudden rainstorm by the canvas awning. They were about to tuck into steaming bowls of soup and Nettie sniffed the air, realising that she was extremely hungry. Constance was so pale she looked as though she might faint at any moment.

Byron rose to his feet. 'You've found her. Thank God for that. Come and sit down.' He pulled up three more chairs and everyone shuffled up to make room for them. Jean Joubert summoned a waiter and gave him an order, which when it came turned out to be three more bowls of soup, and a basket of warm bread rolls. They ate hungrily and drank wine, followed by coffee and calvados, which Jean recommended highly. Then it was time for explanations and everyone listened intently while Nettie told them what had happened at the château, with Lisette acting as interpreter for her brother. Nettie finished by praising Rufus for standing up to Duke, which did not go down too well with Byron, who was openly dismissive.

'I wouldn't have allowed you to venture into the château by yourself in the first place, Nettie,' he said, frowning.

'You were pleased enough to let her go with Percy and myself,' Rufus countered. 'I did what anyone would have done in the circumstances.'

'Nettie is a true friend.' Constance reached

414

across the table to pat Nettie's hand. 'I don't want to think about what might have happened had you not been so brave. Duke can be very nasty when he's put out.'

'Well, you won't be seeing him again.' Percy slipped his arm around her shoulders. 'I should have taken better care of you, Constance.'

Lisette rolled her eyes. 'So you are in love with a married woman, Percy. What are you going to do about it?'

Percy glanced at his brother. 'I was hoping that Byron would use his influence to get one of the solicitors to take Constance's case.'

'Of course I will,' Byron said earnestly. 'My job might not be the most exciting or the best paid, but it is important in its own way.'

'You speak too fast, Byron.' Jean shook his head. 'I understand only a little English.'

'I will teach you.' Lisette gave her brother a brilliant smile. 'I intend to stay here for a while, maybe permanently. I'm done with the theatre.'

Aristide moved his chair a little closer. 'That is the best news I have had this year. We will become good friends, I hope, Condesa.'

'Lisette,' she said firmly. 'No more *condesa*. I'm also done with pretending to be what I am not. Lisette Joubert is a water gypsy at heart.'

'I would enjoy your company on my barge, Lisette.' Aristide held his hand to his heart. 'It would be my honour and my pleasure to take you wherever you wanted to go.'

Lisette gave him a long look. 'I might take you up on that, Aristide. I feel the lure of the river calling to me.'

Nettie looked from one to the other. 'I must get back to London. I need to tell my father that Duke has tricked him into making more forgeries. I suspected it all along, and now I know I was right.'

'That man has a lot to answer for,' Byron said angrily. 'I'll see you safely home, Nettie.'

Rufus cleared his throat. 'I think you might need my assistance, old chap.'

'I suppose you mean financially.' Byron's eyes flashed angrily and his colour deepened. 'I suppose you enjoy throwing your money about.'

'Byron! That's not fair.' Nettie rose from the table. 'I can only think it's the wine talking. It's not like you to be so rude.'

Byron pushed back his chair and stood up. 'Not at all. I speak as I find, and I wonder why he has attached himself to our party. This is our business, not yours, Norwood. We don't need you or your money to get us home to London.'

Jean also rose to his feet. 'Come with me, *mon neveu*. We will talk together. Yes?' He looped his arm around his nephew's shoulders and they walked off slowly, Byron glancing over his shoulder and scowling at Rufus.

Aristide signalled to the waiter, who hurried to give him the bill. Aristide gazed at it, frowning. 'Monsieur Norwood, if you are sincere in wanting to help, perhaps you would settle with the waiter?'

Rufus smiled and nodded. 'Happy to do so, providing it doesn't offend anyone.'

Lisette nodded approvingly. 'Well said, Rufus. Don't allow my son's rudeness to upset you. I'm

416

afraid it's the green-eyed monster raising its ugly head.'

Nettie sighed. 'Byron doesn't own me. Why do men complicate matters?'

Percy helped Constance to her feet. 'Because we are men, my dear Nettie. Don't worry about my brother — he'll get over it.'

'There's nothing to get over,' Nettie said firmly. 'There was never an understanding between us, and Rufus is just a friend.' She fixed Rufus with a steady look. 'That's the truth, isn't it?'

'We should be discussing how we are going to get home,' Percy said urgently. 'It's one thing to report Dexter to the local gendarmerie, and quite another for them to act on it.'

'I agree.' Nettie glanced up at the darkening sky. 'I think it's going to rain again. Perhaps we should head back to the barge and we can decide what to do under cover. I need to get home as soon as possible.'

Aristide proffered his arm to Lisette. 'You are all welcome to stay on board. I could take you as far as Le Havre.'

'That sounds delightful,' Lisette said, smiling. 'I have no wish to return to London.'

'Your reputation might suffer if you come with me.' Aristide was suddenly serious.

'What reputation?' Lisette tucked her hand in the crook of his arm. 'I have none to lose.'

★ ★ ★

Lisette was adamant that she wanted to stay in France, although Byron and Percy did their best

417

to persuade her to return to London. Aristide and Jean promised to look after her, and were promptly put in their place by Lisette, who informed them that she was perfectly capable of managing her own affairs. Nettie could tell by the gleam in the *condesa*'s eyes that she was at the start of yet another adventure, and nothing would make her change her mind.

Nettie was eager to get home. She needed to convince her father that Duke had not changed, and that he intended to pass the copies off as original works of art. That done, she would feel free to seek Wegg's assistance in bringing Duke Dexter to justice. All this went through Nettie's mind during the train journey to Calais where they boarded the steam packet for Dover. It was a rough crossing and Constance was prostrate with seasickness and confined to the cabin, with Percy seeing to her needs as tenderly as any nursemaid. Nettie soon found her sea legs, but her problem was of a different kind, and she did her best to keep the peace between Byron and Rufus. She gave up after a while and went out on deck, leaving them seated in the saloon, glaring at each other. It was dark and the rough sea lashed the sides of the vessel, but Nettie took deep breaths of the salt-laden air as she clung to the ship's rail, watching the white-crested waves in awe. Already the scene that would begin her next novel was taking shape in her mind. She was so engrossed in her thoughts that she barely noticed the passing of time, but suddenly, in the distance, she could see the lights of Dover twinkling in the darkness.

The calm of the harbour was more than welcome, and the still waters gleamed silkily in the moonlight. Nettie turned her head as Byron came to stand at her side.

'I hope you don't intend to go on about Rufus,' she said sharply. 'Because I've had enough of you two squabbling like dogs over a bone.'

Byron chuckled. 'I wouldn't put it like that exactly.'

'You ought to listen to yourself when you're talking to him. What's got into you, Byron?'

He stared straight ahead, avoiding her direct gaze. 'You ought to know how I feel about you, Nettie. I thought we had an understanding, even though it's never been put into words, but now it seems that he's taken my place in your affection. He's everything I am not.'

Nettie laid her hand on his arm as it rested on the ship's rail. 'Don't say that, Byron. You know how fond I am of you.'

He turned his head, looking her in the eye. 'Perhaps that's not enough for me.'

'We've always been such good friends. Can't we go on like that?'

'No, we can't.' He grasped both her hands. 'I love you and I can't imagine my life without you, Nettie. This isn't a proposal because I know you'd turn me down this time, but I want you to think about it.'

'I don't know what to say.'

'Just promise to think about us. Could you love me as I love you? Please stop and give it some thought, because I don't want to go on for

419

ever as your best friend.'

Shaken by his sudden declaration and confused by the feelings it aroused in her, Nettie met his intense gaze with an attempt at a smile. Apart from her father, there had never been anyone in her life who had meant as much to her as Byron — until she met Rufus. Now the outlines were blurred and her emotions confused. 'All right, Byron,' she said slowly. 'I promise.'

He leaned over to kiss her cheek. 'Thank you.'

Approaching footsteps made Nettie glance over her shoulder and saw Constance and Percy coming towards them, followed by Rufus.

'Are you feeling better?' Nettie asked anxiously.

Constance gave her a bright smile. 'I am, and it's so good to be home. I know I am French, but I've always loved London.'

'And we will be married,' Percy said firmly. 'As soon as you're free from Dexter.'

'But how are you going to manage in the meantime?' Rufus looked from one smiling face to the other. 'Where will you stay, Constance? Have you thought of that?'

Nettie had not given any thought to the practicalities of bringing Constance to London.

'You could stay with us, Constance,' she said slowly. 'But I'm afraid you wouldn't be very comfortable.'

'I want to be with Percy.' Constance squeezed his arm, smiling up at him.

He shook his head. 'You know that's not possible, sweetheart. We have to do this properly.'

420

'Might I make a suggestion?' Rufus leaned against the ship's rail, gazing at the lights of Dover as the vessel entered the harbour mouth. 'We have to break our journey somewhere. I suggest we go to Norwood Hall.'

'We can't impose on your parents,' Nettie said hastily.

'Don't worry about my mother,' Rufus countered, chuckling. 'She'll be so pleased to see me that she'll welcome you all with open arms, and I'm sure you would like to see Biddy.'

'Yes, I would.' Nettie eyed him curiously. 'But there's something else. I can tell.'

'You know me so well,' he said, smiling. 'I think my parents would be most sympathetic if Constance were to tell them her story, and if I know my mother, she will be begging her to stay at Norwood Hall.'

'I wouldn't have to work in the hop garden, would I?' Constance demanded querulously.

'It's winter, my love,' Percy said gently. 'And it's a very generous offer, providing Mr and Mrs Norwood agree. I could visit you often, in fact I might be able to get a job in the brewery and then I could stay somewhere close by.'

Rufus nodded. 'That's a possibility. If I'm working in London my father will need someone to take my place.'

'I really need to go home and make sure that my father is all right,' Nettie said worriedly.

'He's a grown man. I think he can look after himself for a while longer, Nettie.' Rufus laid his hand over hers as it rested on the cold steel rail, and she felt the warmth seep into her veins.

Once again the Norwoods extended their hospitality to everyone. Jane appeared to have forgotten the traumatic accident when Rufus was shot in the arm, and she seemed a much happier person now that she had Biddy to fuss over. Biddy herself was a picture of health and happiness; she threw her arms around Nettie and dragged her upstairs to the room that had been decorated especially for her. There were dolls dressed in the latest fashion with smiles painted on their china faces, and piles of books waiting to be read. Biddy opened a cupboard to reveal shelves stacked with clothes and rows of slippers, buckled shoes and buttoned boots.

'Are you happy here,' Nettie asked, although she already knew the answer.

'I love Aunt Jane and Uncle Maury.' Biddy's eyes shone with emotion. 'They are so kind to me, and I go to the village school. I'm learning fast, Nettie, and Miss Swann — she's our teacher — says I could go far.'

'That's wonderful, Biddy.'

'What about you?' Biddy put her head on one side. 'Are you going to marry Rufus?'

'Biddy! What put that idea into your head?'

'I've seen the way he looks at you, and I've seen the way Byron glares at him. I think he's jealous.'

'You saw all that in the brief time we've been here?'

'Miss Swann says I'm very bright, and Aunt

Jane says I've been here before, although I don't quite know what that means.'

'It means you are too clever by half,' Nettie said, laughing. 'Come here and give me a hug. But you're quite wrong about Rufus, and I am very fond of Byron.'

Biddy nodded wisely. 'I know. It must be very difficult being grown up.'

'It's not easy.' Nettie dropped a kiss on Biddy's soft, sweet-smelling hair. 'Let's go downstairs and join the others, and you must come up to London sometimes. We'll go to the zoo and Madame Tussaud's Wax Museum.'

'And tea at Gunter's,' Biddy said eagerly. 'I heard Constance talking about it.'

'I'm sure that can be arranged, and if Constance stays here for a while she'll be able to tell you all about it, and maybe teach you some French as well.'

'Is Constance going to live here, then?'

'For a while, providing Mr and Mrs Norwood agree.'

Biddy's mouth drooped at the corners. 'I won't have to be her maid again, will I?'

'Certainly not. You are part of the family now, Biddy. You'll never be a servant again.' Nettie took her by the hand. 'Come on, let's go downstairs.'

Biddy led the way to the drawing room where Constance was the centre of attention. She was in the middle of relating her latest experience in the château and the Norwoods were obviously impressed.

Nettie and Biddy sat side by side on one of the

sofas, waiting for Constance to finish her narrative.

'So you see how it is.' Constance gazed at Jane with her hands clasped to her bosom. 'I am homeless yet again. I don't know if Duke was lying when he said that the house in Paris still belongs to me. I think he wants to confuse me, but all I know is that I'm desperate to have my marriage annulled.'

'You must stay with us until things are settled, my dear,' Jane said firmly. 'Isn't that right, Maury?'

Maurice nodded enthusiastically. 'Of course she must.' He turned to Percy. 'And you are interested in working for me, so my son says. Is that correct?'

'I would be more than willing to learn the trade, sir.' Percy reached out to clasp Constance's hand. 'I would work hard.'

Rufus slapped him on the back. 'Well said. That leaves me free to develop our London office. Between us we'll make Norwood's Brewery famous.'

'Don't forget the Honourable Miss Williams, Rufus,' Jane said slyly. 'I rather think she is a countrywoman and wouldn't take kindly to living in London after you're wed.'

Nettie shot Rufus a sideways glance, trying hard not to show the surprise she felt at his mother's sudden announcement.

'I think Lavinia Williams aims higher than someone like me, Mama,' Rufus said calmly. 'My relationship with that lady ended some time ago.'

'Not according to her, my dear.' Jane beamed

at him. 'She might be rather horsey and outspoken, but I believe she comes with a large dowry.'

'We were much younger when we had an understanding,' Rufus said hastily. 'The Honourable Miss Williams is looking for a titled husband with a landed estate, not a humble brewer.'

Nettie looked from one to the other, stunned by the sudden revelation. 'We should be going now. I don't want to miss the last train,' she said hastily.

'You must dine first, Nettie.' Maurice raised himself from his seat. 'Rufus, pour the sherry wine. We'll have a toast to our success as a family business.'

'I think we ought to eat now,' Jane said firmly. 'The young people have a train to catch.'

'Nonsense.' Maurice shook his head, smiling. 'You will all stay with us tonight and travel on in the morning after breakfast. I love a full house. Fill the glasses, Rufus. We're going to celebrate.'

'What are we celebrating, Maury?' Jane demanded suspiciously.

'Why, the good fortune of Norwood's Brewery, of course. We're building something big to pass on to Rufus and his children.' Maurice turned to Byron, who had been standing silently by the fireplace. 'I hear you're hoping to become a man of the law. I might be able to put work your way in the future.'

Byron smiled. 'Thank you, sir. But I'm just a clerk in a law office.'

'You will rise to greater heights, I'm sure.' Maury accepted a glass of sherry from his son.

'Here's to the future.'

Rufus handed a glass to Nettie. 'Don't worry about your father. We'll catch the first train to London in the morning.' He shot a sideways glance at Byron. 'I suppose you will be travelling with us.'

Byron shook his head. 'I should get back to London tonight. I might be in time to catch the last train if I leave now.'

Nettie was about to ask him to change his mind and stay, but things had changed subtly between them and she said nothing.

'Of course, my boy,' Maury said with a genial smile. 'I'll send for the carriage right away.'

* * *

Nettie said goodbye to Biddy next morning, promising to visit her as often as possible. Rufus had the carriage brought round to the front entrance to take them to the station. Now that they were alone and away from his domineering mother, Nettie tried to find out more about his romance with Miss Williams, but Rufus managed to evade her questions. He was a charming and amusing companion, and during the train journey back to London she found herself falling under his spell. His enthusiasm for his new business venture was infectious, and Nettie was deeply touched by the genuine affection in which he held his family. She had known him only a short time, but she was convinced of his sincerity, and she found herself more and more captivated. She did not refuse when Rufus

426

insisted on taking her out to luncheon at a smart restaurant before seeing her safely to the door of Ma Burton's lodging house. He raised her hand to his lips, holding her gaze with a teasing smile.

'I'll see you again very soon, but I have to find somewhere to stay.'

'Ma Burton will have a spare room now that Lisette has decided to stay in France.'

'That would suit me very well.'

'Would you like me to speak to her for you?'

He smiled, revealing even white teeth and his eyes twinkled. 'I think I can handle the lady. You go and see your father — he'll be wondering where you are.'

★　★　★

Robert was mildly pleased to see Nettie when she walked into his studio, and she realised she had worried unnecessarily; her father was so deeply immersed in his work that she doubted if he had even noticed her absence. The three copies of the famous paintings were finished and left to dry, and she knew that to destroy them would be as painful to him as if the cuts were in his own flesh. She sat with him by the fire and explained yet again that Duke had been using him. Robert listened but she could tell that he was not taking her seriously, and it was only when she gave her father a detailed account of the incident in the château that he sat up and took notice. Finally, and painfully, she managed to convince him that Duke Dexter was neither his friend nor a genuine sponsor. Duke was a criminal, and that was the harsh truth.

Robert rose to his feet and paced the floor, creating long shadows on the walls of their attic room.

'All that work,' he said sadly. 'All my time wasted. He won't pay me now, Nettie. I was banking on that money to pay the rent. We'll be thrown out onto the streets. My poor girl, what have I brought you to?'

Nettie jumped to her feet and gave him a hug. 'We've managed in the past, Pa. We'll get by somehow.'

'I don't know what to do,' Robert said, sighing heartily. 'Of course the canvases must be destroyed, although it will break my heart and it will leave us short when it comes to paying the rent. Ma Burton's boys will be certain to pay us a visit.'

24

Nettie knew that she must do something to save her father from himself. If she did not act now he would give in to Duke's demands and continue to be his puppet. Quite how Duke had evaded the law for so long was a mystery — he seemed to lead a charmed life — but he must be brought to justice, and there was only one person she could think of who might help her.

She had not quite believed Wegg when he said that all was well between him and Duke. Neither had she believed Duke when he disclaimed responsibility for the tragic death of Wegg's sister. It was a slim chance, but if she could find Wegg and put her case to him, she was almost certain that he would cooperate and together they could bring Duke to justice.

'I think I might have the answer, Pa,' she said softly.

'There's nothing I can do, Nettie. I will have to let Duke take these copies and do what he will with them. We have to eat, my love.' Robert stopped pacing and stooped to pick up a sealed envelope. 'I almost forgot. This came for you, Nettie. It was delivered by hand. I don't recognise the seal, but it looks important.'

Nettie snatched the envelope from her father and tore it open with trembling fingers. There could be only one explanation for the expensive hand-made paper and the imposing seal. She unfolded the letter and read it slowly, the words dancing around in front of her eyes.

'What is it, dear? You're very pale. Is it bad news?'

Nettie reread the short, handwritten note. She shook her head. 'No, Pa. It's wonderful. It's something I've wanted all my life. It's from Dorning and Lacey, the publishers. They've accepted my manuscript — they're going to publish my book.'

'What book?' Robert asked, scratching his head. 'What are you talking about, Nettie?'

'I've been writing in secret for almost as long as I can remember.' She leaped to her feet and danced him round the room. 'I'm going to be a published author, and they're paying me a handsome advance.'

Robert came to a standstill, staring at her wide-eyed. 'How much of an advance?'

Nettie hid the letter behind her back. The eager look in her father's eyes meant one thing only — her money would disappear like morning mist if he were to get his hands on it. She shook her head. 'I was exaggerating, Pa. They'll give me a certain amount, but it won't be much because I am an unknown. We should be able to pay the rent this month, and there might be enough to buy some coal and candles.'

'And a dinner out?' Robert said hopefully. 'With wine and perhaps a cigar?'

'I doubt it, Pa. But it's a start, and if I can polish up my first effort, they might publish that one as well.'

'Why didn't you tell me about this until now?'

'I hoped I'd be published one day, but I couldn't be sure.'

Robert slumped down in his chair by the embers of the fire. 'You must press for more money, Nettie. I'll go and see them — they'll take more notice of someone like me. You are very young and you're a female. Women have no place in business.'

Nettie resisted the temptation to argue. She knew from experience that nothing would change her father's attitude to women, and he always thought he was right. One thing was certain: he must never see the letter or be made aware of the handsome advance she had been offered. She nodded and smiled.

'I expect you're right, Pa.' She held out her hand. 'Have you any money? I'll go to the coffee stall and get us something to eat, if he's still there at this late hour.'

Reluctantly, Robert put his hand in his pocket and took out a handful of coppers. 'I was going to the pub for a pint of ale, but, of course you come first, my dear. If we share a mug of coffee and split a ham roll in two, I can still have a chat with my friends over a half or two.'

Nettie pocketed the money. 'I'll be as quick as I can.' She snatched up her cape and fur hat and hurried from the room with the letter still clutched in her hand. Her manuscript had been accepted and she was about to earn money, and she simply had to tell someone the good news. She ran down the stairs, but when she reached the ground floor she hesitated for a moment, and then hammered on the door of

Lisette's old rooms.

'Nettie? Is anything wrong?' Rufus stared at her, frowning.

'May I come in?' she said breathlessly. 'I've just had some wonderful news and I must share it with someone.'

'Of course.' He stood aside, and she hurried into the parlour where a fire burned in the grate, and candles had been lit in the wall sconces. It was warm and cosy, especially when compared to the austere chill of the attic rooms. The smell of medication that had lingered after the Lorimers had moved out was now replaced with the tasty aroma of fish and chips, a touch of vinegar and the tempting scent of hot coffee.

'I was just about to eat,' Rufus said, smiling. 'There's too much for one.'

Nettie thought of the ham roll she was to share with her father and the mug of coffee that would be cooling rapidly by the time she reached home, and her stomach growled with hunger. 'Thank you,' she said eagerly. 'If you're sure you can spare some.'

'Sit down and make yourself comfortable.' Rufus cut the large piece of fish in half and transferred it from the newspaper to a plate, adding a generous portion of chips. He passed it to Nettie as she took a seat opposite him. 'What was it that you wanted to tell me?'

She handed him the letter. 'Read it for yourself. I can hardly believe it, so tell me I'm not dreaming.'

He studied the document, looked up and

smiled. 'Congratulations! This really is something to celebrate, but you didn't tell me you were a writer.'

'I thought people would laugh at me. It's been my secret for such a long time, and I was beginning to think I would never get anything published.'

'This is a generous advance; they must think highly of you, and it's obviously a very good story.'

Nettie popped a piece of fried fish into her mouth. 'This is so tasty.'

'We should be eating out and toasting your success in champagne.'

'I'll only be a success if people buy my book,' Nettie said, spearing a chip on her fork. 'But now I can afford the rent, or at least I will when the publishers pay me.'

'If there's any delay I could lend you the money. You only have to ask.'

Nettie shook her head. 'Thank you, but Ma Burton will believe me if I show her the letter.'

'Why do you want to keep on good terms with that harpy? I've met many difficult people in my life, but she frightens me.'

'I need her help in order to track down a man who's borne a grudge against Duke for years. I think Samson Wegg would take great delight in seeing him get his comeuppance. All our problems have been caused by Duke Dexter and he belongs behind bars.' She bowed her head over her plate and concentrated on eating.

'Your father is a good artist, but a bad businessman.' Rufus held up his hand as Nettie opened her mouth to protest. 'I'm sorry, but it's true, and you've been forced to shoulder the burden of poor choices and his inability to handle his finances for far too long.'

Nettie knew what he said was true, but it was not an easy thing to admit. 'Even so, he's my father and I have a duty to look after him.' She pushed her plate away, and stood up. 'Thank you for the food, but I'd better be on my way. I was supposed to go out and fetch our supper, and Pa will still be hungry.'

Rufus rose to his feet and handed her the letter. 'I didn't mean to offend you, and I'm flattered that you chose to share your secret with me.'

Nettie eyed him warily. 'Byron knows about my writing. I should have gone to him first.'

'So why didn't you?' Rufus spoke softly but there was an intensity in his voice that made Nettie back away.

'I'm not a helpless little woman, Rufus. I don't need a man to guide me and I intend to make a success of my life. I'll look after Pa, who brought me up on his own. He may not be the best businessman in London, but he's my pa and I love him. I have to go now or the coffee stall will be closed.' She left before he had a chance to respond, and she hurried from the building, still clutching the precious letter in her hand.

The stall keeper was just about to pack up when Nettie arrived and he greeted her with a cheery grin. 'Haven't seen you around for a while, girl. I thought you'd got too grand for the likes of us.'

'I've been away, but I'm back for good now, Bert. Have you got a ham roll left?'

'You're in luck. Just the one? And a mug of coffee, of course. You can bring the empty back tomorrow. I trust you, Nettie.'

She waited while he filled the tin mug and added a spoonful of sugar. 'Ta, Bert. You're a toff.'

'Good night, girl. Don't speak to any strange men on the way home.'

Nettie quickened her pace and let herself into the house. There was no one about and she hurried up the stairs. She let herself into their living room.

'Pa, I've brought your supper. I'm sorry I took so . . . ' She gazed round at the empty room. The fire had gone out and there was no sign of her father. She checked his room, but it was in total darkness and the smell of oil paint and turpentine wafted out in a thick cloud. Nettie went back into the main room, and, having put the ham roll on the table, she sat down on the hearth to take advantage of the last warmth from the embers. She knew where he had gone — he would be in the Lamb and Flag, drinking ale with his friends.

★ ★ ★

Next morning Nettie was waiting outside the offices of Dorning and Lacey before they opened, and she was the first to enter when the clerk unbolted the door. She had to wait for almost an hour before anyone was prepared to speak to her, but she was ushered into the office of no lesser person than Mr Dorning, and they were joined by Mr Lacey. Nettie was quite overwhelmed by their praise for her novel and when they presented her with the contract she asked for time to read through it, receiving a pat on the back from Dorning. She studied the clauses in detail, and if she found anything difficult to understand she was not afraid to ask questions.

'I wish all our authors were as committed as you, Miss Carroll.' Mr Lacey handed her a pen and ink. 'Sign on the dotted line, if you please. Welcome to our company. Together we will make you a household name, equal to any of our famed lady novelists.'

Nettie signed and the two gentlemen also put their names to the document. She waited, hopefully, and then Mr Dorning produced a banker's draft for a sum of money that made her gasp. It was not huge but, having lived so long from hand to mouth, it seemed like a fortune. It was the first money she had ever earned, and there was no need for Pa to know exactly how much she had received. If she paid the rent first, and put some aside for housekeeping, she could in all honesty tell him that what remained was all she possessed. Smiling to herself, Nettie set off for home.

Ma Burton's beady eyes glittered like boot buttons when Nettie handed her the rent a week early. 'Did you rob a bank, girl?'

Nettie shook her head. 'No, this was money earned honestly.'

'Tell that to the marines,' Ma said, curling her lip.

'Believe it or not — it doesn't matter to me.'

'Not that it bothers me any. Let's hope there's more where that came from.' Ma was about to slam the door when Nettie put her foot over the threshold.

'I need a favour, Ma.'

'Do you indeed? There's a surprise. I suppose you're going to tell me that the cops are after your pa again.'

'No, but it's to do with Mr Wegg. I need to get in touch with him urgently.'

'Now that is a surprise. What's he done this time?'

'Nothing, Ma. I want to hire him to find someone.'

Ma's chins wobbled in unison as a deep chuckle shook her frame. 'Well, I never! Anyway, what makes you think I'd know where to find the old codger?'

'I know you have contacts, Ma.'

'That's true. My boys keep me up to date with what's going on round here, but it'll cost you.'

'I don't expect something for nothing.'

Ma winked and closed the door. Nettie removed her foot just in time to prevent it being bruised. Satisfied that the Burton boys would peach on their own mother if the price was right, Nettie headed for the stairs, intending to tell her father that she had signed the contract with Dorning and Lacey. She hesitated outside Lisette's door, wondering whether to apologise to Rufus for her abrupt departure the previous evening, and she was about to knock when the door opened.

'Nettie. How did it go with the publisher?'

His smile seemed genuine without a hint of reserve. Whether it was deliberate or not, Rufus had a way of making her feel attractive and desirable, and his warm glance set her pulse racing.

'I signed a contract and they want me to go through the manuscript they rejected, making a few alterations, and then they'll read it again.'

'That's wonderful news. I knew you could do it.'

'You did?'

'You are the same girl who was prepared to walk miles in order to fetch bread for your friends. You didn't flinch when you had to dig into my flesh to remove the lead shot. I knew you weren't going to give up easily.'

'Oh!' She stared at him nonplussed. 'It seems you know me better than I know myself.'

He chuckled and proffered his arm. 'I wouldn't assume so much, but I doubt if you've had breakfast and neither have I. Will you allow me to treat you to bacon and eggs, or a nice fat kipper?'

Nettie hesitated. 'I really ought to go upstairs and tell Pa he need not worry about the rent.'

'You have all day to do that, and I was going to ask for your help.'

'My help? In what way?'

'I think I've found suitable premises for our London office, and I've got my eye on a house in

Doughty Street, but I would value a second opinion.'

'You'll be moving on soon?' Nettie tried to keep the disappointment from her voice.

'Yes, of course. This was only a temporary measure. Will you come with me?'

His smile was disarming and she found it impossible to refuse. 'Of course I will, but could we have breakfast first? I'm absolutely famished.'

★ ★ ★

After a hearty breakfast in a nearby pub, Nettie and Rufus walked to Doughty Street where they met the agent who let them into the house. Nettie was immediately charmed by everything she saw, from the basement kitchen to the small attic rooms, suitable as the agent claimed for a cook/housekeeper and a maid of all work. The rest of the accommodation consisted of two large rooms on each floor as well as a much smaller one overlooking the tiny back garden. The drawing room and the dining room, which were situated at the front of the building, were very pleasant with tall windows making them light and airy, and polished wooden floors that needed only the addition of a carpet and some rugs to add a finishing touch.

'Do you intend to rent the whole house?' Nettie asked as they reached the ground floor after a thorough inspection of all the rooms. 'Surely it's too large for a single gentleman?'

'Perhaps I don't intend to remain single for much longer.'

439

A chill ran down her spine — so what his mother had said was true. 'You're engaged to be married?'

'Not yet. I haven't plucked up the courage to propose.'

'I wouldn't have thought you were shy.'

'I'm not, and maybe that's my problem. Perhaps I take too much for granted in assuming that the lady will accept my offer of love and protection.'

'Surely she has an inkling?' Nettie remembered only too well Jane Norwood's comment about the Honourable Miss Williams, the heiress and ideal bride for her son.

'I would hope so.'

Nettie eyed him warily. His expression gave nothing away, and she felt the colour rush to her cheeks. 'I really should be getting back,' she said hastily. 'I have a lot to do.'

'But what do you think of the house?'

'Quite charming. I'm sure if you bring the lady here it will help to persuade her. Now I must go, Rufus. Thank you for the breakfast, and good luck with the Honourable Miss Williams.'

Nettie went to open the front door and stepped outside into the pale wintry sunshine. She glanced up and down the tree-lined street and spotted a cab approaching.

Rufus hurried after her. 'Wait a moment. You have it all wrong. Let me take you home.'

'It's all right, thank you.' Nettie raised her hand to hail the cab. 'You're forgetting I'm a woman of means now. I can pay my own cab fare. Covent Garden, please, cabby.' She climbed into the hansom and settled down on the seat. She had maintained a calm exterior but inside she was fuming. Men like Rufus Norwood breezed their way through life without giving any consideration to the feelings of others. One minute he was being charming and making her feel that she was the most important person in the world, and then it turned out that he was simply using her to get a woman's perspective on the home he was preparing for the wealthy heiress that his parents wanted him to marry. She was too angry to feel upset — that might come later.

★ ★ ★

Robert was sitting disconsolately in his studio, facing a blank canvas. He looked up and managed a weary smile. 'What now, dear? Are we going to be evicted at the end of the week?'

Nettie opened her reticule and took out her purse. 'Hold out your hand, Pa.'

'Did they pay you?'

She placed a sovereign in his outstretched hand. 'That's for you, and I've settled up with Ma Burton. We're all right here for another month.'

'Thank you, Nettie, although it shames me to be dependent on my daughter. I should be supporting you, but I have no commissions now that I've been forced to sever my connection with Duke.'

'It had to happen, Pa. He needs bringing to justice.'

'I still find it hard to believe that he would cheat me. I really thought that he had changed his ways and I could trust him.'

'Didn't you wonder why he wanted such exact copies of famous works of art?'

'I took his word as a gentleman that what we were doing was above board, and now I need a new patron.'

'Then perhaps you'd better go out and look for one, Pa.' Nettie spoke more severely than she had meant to, but her patience was stretched to the limit.

Robert rose to his feet. 'Don't speak to me like that, Nettie. I am your father.'

'Yes,' she said angrily. 'And sitting up here feeling sorry for yourself won't get us anywhere. You have great talent, Pa.'

'No, Nettie. I am a brilliant copyist, if I say so myself, but I'm afraid I will never make the Royal Academy with my own work.'

Nettie was momentarily lost for words, but a knock on the door saved her from replying. She went to open it and Rufus stepped over the threshold without waiting to be invited. He doffed his top hat. 'I apologise for barging in, but I've come to see your father, Nettie.'

She turned her head away, unable to look him in the eye. 'He's in his room.'

Robert emerged from his studio. 'What can I do for you, Norwood? If it's a complaint about your mother's portrait, I'm afraid it was the best I could do.'

'No, sir. As far as I know both my parents were delighted with your work. I've come with a business proposition.'

Nettie was suddenly alert. 'What did you say?'

'As you know, I'm opening the London office, and my main job will be to promote and advertise my father's ales to a wider clientele. In fact I intend to make his beers and stouts known throughout the country.'

'How does that concern me?' Robert asked.

'I want posters printed to advertise our products. With colour lithography these can be very eye-catching, and I think you might be just the man to create the designs.' He turned to Nettie. 'And there should be memorable slogans to promote the different range of ales. I wonder if you might be interested in working on these with me. Of course, I would pay for both your services.'

'You are offering me a job?' Nettie said slowly. 'Is that what you've intended all along?'

He shook his head. 'No, not at all, but it came to me during my cab ride from Doughty Street. You and your father have experience of working in the hop garden. You've seen the brewery and tasted the ales. Who better to advertise Norwood's Brewery?'

'But I'm an artist,' Robert said mildly.

'And that's what we need. You would be paid well and you would have a studio of your own, when I've found a suitable office premises. What do you say?'

Robert glanced at Nettie. 'What do you think, dear?'

'I think it sounds like something you might enjoy, Pa.' Nettie chose her words carefully, avoiding meeting Rufus's gaze.

'And what about you, Nettie?' Rufus asked quietly. 'Writing slogans wouldn't take too much of your time, but I would value your help.'

Nettie shrugged. 'I suppose I could.'

'I accept your offer gladly, my boy.' Smiling broadly, Robert shook Rufus by the hand.

'Excellent. I think we ought to go out to dinner to celebrate.' Rufus turned to Nettie. 'I think there has been a slight misunderstanding between us.'

Nettie met his gaze with a cool glance. 'If you'll excuse me, it's been a long day and I have a headache.'

'Oh, come now, Nettie. Surely you won't pass up the opportunity for a glass or two of champagne and a tasty supper.'

'You go, Pa,' Nettie said firmly.

'I'm afraid my daughter won't be persuaded, but I am ready when you are, my boy.' Robert shrugged on his overcoat and placed his top hat on his head at a rakish angle. 'I'm ready.'

'I hope you feel better in the morning,' Rufus said in a low voice. 'But I really would like to clear up any misunderstanding between us, and I want to show you the new office. Will you come?'

His tone was persuasive and Nettie was too tired to argue. Her head had begun to ache and all she wanted now was to be left alone. She nodded. 'All right.'

'Excellent. If you could be ready by nine o'clock I'll be waiting for you downstairs.'

'Come along, my boy. I'm looking forward to this.' Robert held the door open and he followed

Rufus out onto the landing. 'Sleep tight, Nettie, my dear.'

She breathed a sigh of relief as the door closed on them and sat back on the sofa, staring into the fire. What a day it had been, starting with the exciting news that her book had been accepted by the publishers, and then breakfast with Rufus and their visit to his new home — but then it had all been spoiled. She should have known after her last visit to the Norwoods' home that Rufus would do anything to please his parents and ensure the success of the family business, even if it meant marrying an heiress.

Nettie leaned back against the cushions and closed her eyes. She was just drifting off to sleep when someone knocked on the door and Byron burst into the room.

'Congratulations, Nettie. I'm so proud of you,' he said, smiling. 'I met your father in the entrance hall and he told me about the book. I knew you could do it.' He held up a parcel wrapped in newspaper. 'He said you were feeling a bit poorly, so I thought some supper might make you feel better and I went to get fish and chips.'

Nettie stared at him dazedly, still half asleep. 'Did Pa tell you that Rufus has offered him a job?'

'He did indeed.' Byron sat down beside her and began to unwrap the package. 'This smells so good.'

'Did he tell you that I'm to work for Norwood's Brewery as well, writing slogans?'

'Are you mad?' Byron stared at her aghast.

'You've just had your book accepted by one of the most prestigious publishers in London and now you're going to write slogans for a brewery? How low can you stoop?'

'That's a horrible thing to say. I'm still going to write my stories, but if Pa is prepared to forgo his ambition as an artist and concentrate on a commercial venture, it seems only fair to support him.'

'Or perhaps you're more interested in helping Norwood to establish himself in his new venture?'

'Are you jealous, Byron? If so, you need not be. Rufus is about to become engaged.'

'Then I pity his bride-to-be. For a man who's supposed to have his heart set on marriage he seems to give you a great deal of attention.'

'That's not fair, Byron. I expected better from you.'

'I'm sorry, Nettie. I didn't mean to upset you. It's just that I care so much and I worry about you.'

Her anger melted at the sight of his downcast expression and she reached out to hold his hand. 'I'm not upset. You are my very best friend.'

'But that's all?'

'I can't think about it now, Byron. From now on I'm going to concentrate on my writing and taking care of Pa, as I have done ever since I can remember.' She squeezed his fingers. 'The fish and chips smell wonderful. Do you mind if we eat now? I'm starving.'

25

Robert had come in late the previous evening, waking Nettie from a deep sleep as he staggered across the room and tripped over the mat, diving headlong into his studio. She heard him grunt as he scrambled to his feet and he closed the door with a loud thud. Nettie had lain awake for a while but then sleep had claimed her once again, although she awakened early and was getting ready to meet Rufus. All was quiet in her father's room, and it seemed that he was sleeping off the excesses of the previous evening.

She lit the fire and put the kettle on the trivet, and was about to make a pot of tea when someone hammered on the door. She went to open it and Pip burst in, followed by two men dressed in funereal black. The tallest of the pair was stick-thin with a pale face and drooping ginger moustache. His companion was almost the exact opposite, small, plump, rosy-cheeked and fresh-faced as a boy, although a black eye patch and a scar running from the corner of his mouth to his chin gave him an oddly sinister appearance.

'I don't know what your pa's been up to, Nettie,' Pip said grinning. 'But I think Ma has sent her boys to sort him out. They knocked on our door by mistake.'

'It's all right, Pip. I know what this is about.' She glanced at the tall, thin man. 'I'm Nettie

447

Carroll, Mr Burton.'

He clicked his heels together and bowed. 'I am Francis Burton and this is my brother, Ernest. Ma said you needed our services.'

Pip whistled through his teeth. 'Good Lord, Nettie. Are you joining the gang?'

'Certainly not.' Nettie turned to the Burton brothers, trying hard to keep a straight face. They looked like a pair of undertakers and it was hard to imagine them as the vicious brutes their mother depicted. 'I need to find Samson Wegg,' she said softly.

'He's a bad man.' Ernest's voice was high-pitched like a girl's and he had a slight lisp.

Nettie shot a warning glance in Pip's direction as he snorted with suppressed laughter.

'Yes, I know that, but the person I want him to find for me is equally rotten, and I want him caught and brought to justice.'

Pip backed out of the room. 'I've got to get to work. I'll see you later, Nettie.' He went to stand in the doorway, seeming reluctant to leave her alone with the notorious criminals.

'We don't deal with the cops,' Francis said bluntly. 'We ain't their friends.'

'All I'm asking is for you to find Samson Wegg and ask him to contact me. I'll make it worth his while.'

'We don't do nothing for nothing.' Ernest's voice rose higher and his colour deepened. 'We ain't cheap.'

'If you can wait until my book is published I'll be able to pay you well enough,' Nettie said in desperation. Now that Pa had a chance to earn an honest living, it was even more important to see Duke safely behind bars.

'You write books?' Ernest asked eagerly. 'What sort of books do you write, miss?'

'I don't think you'd be interested,' Nettie said vaguely. She could see Pip hovering in the doorway and straining his ears to hear their conversation. She knew he would tease her mercilessly when he found out that she wrote novels.

'Do you think my brother is too stupid to read a book?' Francis demanded angrily.

'No, no, of course not. But my books would appeal more to ladies than to gentlemen. They are romances.'

Ernest clasped his hands together and his berry-bright eyes gleamed. 'I enjoy a good love story, but it must have a happy ending.'

'Sad stories are no good. They make him cry, and if my brother cries I get very angry.' Francis glared at Nettie and she backed away.

'My book isn't published yet, but if he wishes I'll allow Ernest to have a look at my first effort at novel writing. It was turned down by the publisher, but perhaps he can give me his opinion.'

'Really?' Ernest's lips twisted into a lop-sided grin. 'I'd like that, miss.'

'It's Nettie to my friends.'

'Don't let Ernie fool you,' Francis said darkly. 'My brother is a killer at heart and so am I.'

'I'd like a cup of tea,' Ernest said meekly. 'If it ain't too much trouble.'

'The kettle is almost boiling. I was making

some for myself anyway.' Nettie made the tea while Ernest sat on the sofa and read avidly.

Francis stood by the window, peering at the street below. He turned his head to stare at his brother. 'How long are you going to be, Ernie? We got other business to do.'

'Don't hurry me, Frank.' Ernest looked up at Nettie with a serious expression on his curiously child-like face. 'It's good, but I can see why it wasn't accepted, Nettie. I could make a few suggestions, if you don't mind.'

'Really?' She stared at him, torn between amusement and shock to think that an allegedly vicious killer could help when it came to romantic prose. 'I'd be interested to hear your views.'

'Would you?' His lips trembled. 'That's the nicest thing anyone's ever said to me. I'll have to tell Ma.'

'We got to go now, Ernie.' Francis moved away from the window. 'I just seen Jugs Malone stagger out of the pub and he's squaring up to a bunch of market porters. Looks like he's ready for a scrap.'

'But, Frank, I'm enjoying meself, and I was looking forward to a nice hot cup of tea.' Ernest sent a pleading look to Nettie. 'Do you have any biscuits or cake? I have a very sweet tooth.'

'Anyone would think you was a sissy to hear you talk, brother. If we don't get down there and stop him, Jugs will have a set-to and them porters are tough blokes — it could turn nasty, and we don't want the coppers to get their hands on him. He knows too much.'

'All right. I'm coming.' Ernest handed the manuscript back to Nettie with a sigh. 'May I come again? I'd like to finish the story and I'm sure I can help you to make it even better.'

'Of course. Come any time you like.'

He rose to his feet. 'And I like baldigarry biscuits.'

'He means Garibaldi,' Francis said curtly. 'You're an idiot, Ernest. I don't know why I put up with you. Come along or we'll be too late.'

'I'll tell Ma you're bullying me again, Frank.'

Ernest followed his brother from the room, leaving Nettie close to hysteria. They had lived under the threat of retribution from Ma Burton's gangster sons ever since they moved into the building, but meeting them in person had come as a shock. Still smiling, Nettie stood up and walked over to the window. She wanted to see Jugs Malone for herself, but her smile faltered as she saw the two Burton brothers throw themselves into the fight that had broken out on the pavement below. Nettie was not sure which one was Jugs, but Francis and Ernest were throwing punches that laid out a bunch of tough-looking market porters, leaving them prostrate on the ground. The sound of police whistles and running feet sent those who were still standing to flight, and two constables appeared as if from nowhere. Nettie moved away from the window. Perhaps Ma had not exaggerated after all? She looked round as the door opened and Byron rushed into the room.

'Are you all right, Nettie? Pip told me that Ma's boys were here.'

'Yes, they were, but they've gone now.'

'Those thugs have a bad reputation.'

'I'm unharmed, as you can see.'

'You shouldn't have anything to do with them,' Byron said, scowling. 'They're dangerous.'

'Ernest sat on the sofa reading the manuscript that the publishers rejected, and he was about to offer me some advice on how to improve it when his brother dragged him away.' Nettie's voice broke on a giggle. 'No, I'm serious, Byron. That's exactly what happened, and he was cross because he didn't get his cup of tea. Oh, yes, and he loves Garibaldi biscuits. Now does that sound like someone who's a danger to society?'

'You can't be too careful.'

'Thanks for worrying, but as you can see, I'm fine.' She sat down on the sofa and patted the empty space beside her. 'Tell me about work. I'm afraid I've neglected you with all that's been going on lately.'

He stood for a moment, looking down at her. 'Are you really interested in me? Or are you simply being kind?'

'Of course I want to know how you're doing. Nothing has changed.'

He sat down, leaving a space between them. 'Everything has changed, Nettie. You may not realise it, but it's obvious to me. Once I thought we would be together for ever, but now I realise that I was mistaken.'

'How can you say that?'

'You don't love me.'

'I do care about you, Byron.'

'It's not the same, is it?

'I don't know. Why are you saying these things?'

'Because they're true. After what you said yesterday I realised that you don't need me.'

'That's not true. I haven't changed.' She reached out to hold his hand. 'What are you trying to tell me, Byron? I can tell there's something on your mind.'

'I've decided that the law isn't for me. I was prepared to give it another go and work hard when I thought there might be a future for us, but I've always struggled with the dreary day-to-day routine, and when we were away on our travels I felt like a different man. I found my family and discovered my roots.'

Nettie met his intense gaze and a cold shiver ran down her spine. 'You're going away again, aren't you?'

He smiled and squeezed her fingers. 'I am more like my mother than I could have thought possible. Perhaps I'm a water gypsy at heart like my forebears? All I know is that I need to get away from London. I've given up my position at the law office and I intend to return to France. I'm going to join my mother and Aristide.'

'Are you sure that's what you want, Byron?'

'Absolutely certain.'

She stared at him, momentarily shocked into silence. A future without her dearest friend was unthinkable, but she could see how much it meant to him and she made an effort to hide her true feelings.

'I think that's the bravest thing I ever heard, and your mother will be delighted.'

Byron smiled ruefully. 'I wish things were different between us, Nettie, but I know when I'm beaten.'

She shook her head. 'You're not the loser. You'll be doing what you were meant to do, and I'm just glad you have the opportunity to follow your heart.' It hurt her to say so, but she knew she must not hold him back. 'What do the others say? Have you told them?'

'Not yet. You're the first to know, but Pip is set on becoming an articled clerk and Ted is getting engaged to Amelie Fabron. He always seems to go for flighty women, but he says he's in love with her and she returns the affection, so I wish him good luck.'

'He's welcome to a mother-in-law like Violet, but perhaps Amelie will make him a good wife, once she's settled down.'

'So we part as friends, Nettie?' Byron stood up, pulling Nettie to her feet.

'The very best of friends,' she said, fighting back tears.

He wrapped her in a warm embrace, and then he was gone.

Nettle stood silently, staring at the closed door. She could hear his footsteps pounding on the bare boards until the sound faded into a memory, and it felt like the end of an era. With Byron gone and her father working in an office somewhere in the city, life would never be quite the same. She missed Constance and Percy, but losing Byron would be the harshest blow of all. Working on her book had to be the answer to her problems, both emotional and financial. She would be independent and able to live her own life, but somehow the idea failed to thrill her, and literary success came a poor second to love.

She glanced at the clock on the mantelshelf, realising with a start that she was supposed to be meeting Rufus. She put on her bonnet, but checking her appearance in the mirror she was shocked to see how pale and drawn she looked. She pinched her cheeks to bring some colour to her face and forced her lips into a smile, but her eyes remained sad and soulful. Saying goodbye to Byron was the hardest thing she had ever done, but she must be happy that he had found his place in the world. She snatched up her cape and reticule and hurried downstairs, but there was no one waiting in the entrance hall, and she knocked on Lisette's door. Perhaps Rufus had given up and left for the office, mistaking her lateness for reluctance to accompany him? She knocked again and this time she heard footsteps and the door opened.

'Come in, Nettie.' Rufus ushered her into the tiny vestibule. 'There's someone I think you'll be interested to meet.'

Nettie followed him into the parlour, fearing the worst. She half expected to see his fiancée seated on the sofa, but to her astonishment she came face to face with Wegg, who was standing with his back to the fire. She turned to Rufus, unable to conceal her astonishment. 'How did you find this man?'

'I had a word with Ma Burton. She obliged, for a small fee.'

'You shouldn't have done that,' Nettie said in a low voice.

Wegg cleared his throat noisily. 'I can't think what you want with me, missy. I ain't your man, whatever it is you want, but this gent insisted I come here this morning.' He shot a malicious glance in Rufus's direction. 'Threatened me, he did, and used words what I never thought to hear from the lips of a toff.'

'Well, I'm very glad to see you, Mr Wegg, although I never thought I'd say so, but I'm desperate to find Duke Dexter. You are the only one I could think of who might be able to help.'

Wegg eyed her with a calculating grin. 'How much is it worth?'

Nettie hesitated, calculating how much she could afford, but Rufus stepped in between them.

'Name your price, Wegg. If it's too much you'll find yourself back on the street where you belong.'

'All right, mister. No need to be unpleasant.' Wegg frowned and his thick black eyebrows met over the bridge of his nose. He moved his fingers like a child learning how to count. 'Fifty sovs should do it, including expenses.'

'Fifty pounds! That's ridiculous,' Nettie said hastily.

'You seem very confident, Wegg.' Rufus eyed him suspiciously. 'You know where Dexter is, don't you?'

'What if I do? That's for me to know, and if I deliver him to you I expect to be paid.'

'Twenty pounds,' Rufus said firmly.

'Twenty-five,' Wegg countered.

Nettie shook her head. 'Ten pounds, and if, as I suspect, he's in London and you bring him to the Lamb and Flag at noon, I'll cancel my arrangement with the Burton brothers. I've just hired them to find you, and from what I've seen it's wisest not to offend Ma's boys.'

'Ten quid it is, but call them off and I'll bring Dexter to the pub. It just so happens I've been following him for reasons of me own, so I know where to find the cove.'

Rufus nodded. 'You'll get your money on delivery.'

Wegg backed towards the doorway. 'You'll be sure to call the hounds of hell off, won't you, miss? I ain't easily scared, but Ma's boys frighten the life out of me, as they do anyone who's had dealings with them.'

'Yes, I will.' Nettie had a vision of Ernest sitting on her sofa reading a romance, and if she had not seen the Burton brothers in action she might have laughed, but Wegg hurried from the room as if the devil himself was on his heels. She turned to Rufus with a questioning look. 'How did you find Wegg?'

'You mentioned his name and I made some enquiries. I have business contacts in the City, and I find it a good thing to keep on the right side of those high up in the Metropolitan Police. I called in a favour and tracked down Wegg to his rooms in Hanging Sword Alley.'

'You did all this for me and my father?'

'You're part of the company now, Nettie. I can't afford to lose valuable people. Together

457

we're going to make Norwood's Brewery a household name. I've found an investor who will put up the capital to allow us to expand and there'll be no stopping us.'

There was something in his tone that made Nettie suspicious. 'Does that person happen to be the heiress your mother mentioned?'

'It wasn't quite true what I said to my parents. Lavinia and I have had an understanding for a long time, although we were never officially engaged.'

'But you have an understanding?' Nettie said slowly.

He grasped her hand, holding it in a firm clasp. 'That was before I met you, Nettie.'

'What are you saying?'

'I bought the house in Doughty Street for us. It's you I want, Nettie.'

A cold shiver ran down her spine and she withdrew her hand. 'Are you asking me to become your mistress?'

'That's a harsh word, Nettie. I love you and I want to make you happy.'

'And you think that dragging my name through the mud would do that?'

'I don't see it like that, Nettie.'

'You have a strange way of looking at things, Rufus. You've just insulted me, and Lavinia could sue you for breach of promise.'

He shrugged and smiled. 'Only if I don't go through with the marriage. It's the one way I can raise enough capital to carry out my plans for modernisation of the brewery and set up the new office. You must understand that, Nettie.'

She was frozen with anger and she fixed him with a hard stare. 'So you plan to marry for money and you want us to live in sin?'

'You make it sound sordid, but I love you, and eventually I'm sure Lavinia will agree to a divorce and then you and I will be married.'

'You should be ashamed of yourself,' Nettie said icily. She met his startled gaze, wondering why she had allowed herself to be taken in by him.

He raised his hand and then dropped it to his side. 'It's not what I would have wanted. You must understand that, Nettie.'

'You would ruin the lives of two women in order to build your business. Think again, Rufus Norwood. I don't need you. I'm a free woman and I can support myself and my father.' Nettie stormed out of the room, but as she stepped into the entrance hall she almost bumped into Ma Burton.

'Fallen out, have you?' Ma said, chuckling. 'I suppose he's in a bad mood now, and he'll be even grumpier when I tell him I'm doubling the rent.'

'I need to get a message to your boys, Ma.' Nettie forced herself to sound calm, although inwardly she was fuming. 'Tell them I've found Wegg, but if Ernest still wants to read my novel he's more than welcome.'

'My Ernie is the clever one,' Ma said proudly. 'He could read and write when he was just a nipper, whereas my Frankie was always off somewhere, getting into bother, but they're good sons.' She waddled past Nettie and knocked on the door.

Nettie took the stairs two at a time, holding her skirts up above her ankles. She burst into her father's room and found him sitting up in bed, sipping a mug of tea.

'Softly, please,' he said in a low voice. 'My head aches.'

'I'm not surprised, Pa. The state you were in last night you deserve to suffer.'

'That's unkind, Nettie.'

'I'm not in the mood to be nice, Pa. I've just found out that Rufus is using us. He's going to marry an heiress, but he wants me to live with him as his mistress.'

'The cad!' Robert swung his legs over the side of the bed. 'Take my tea. I'll go downstairs and give him a piece of my mind.'

Nettie took the cup from him. 'No, don't do that. I was a fool to be taken in by him, but I've made my feelings perfectly clear. Rufus Norwood won't bother me again.'

Robert pulled up the bedcovers. 'Oh, well. That's good, my dear. I know I can always trust your good sense.' He eyed her warily. 'But there's something else. Out with it, Nettie.'

'I can't tell you what I have in mind, but I want you to meet me in the Lamb and Flag at midday. Will you be well enough to do that?'

'The hair of the dog is what I need.' Robert held his hand to his head. 'Give me my tea, and is there any seltzer in the cupboard? Get some for me, Nettie, please.'

'Only if you promise you'll meet me in the pub later.'

'Yes, I will. Now please get me some seltzer.'

Nettie was on her way to the pub when she heard her name called and she glanced round to see Ma Burton's boys hurrying after her.

'Where are you going?' Ernest demanded. 'This isn't the sort of place you should be on your own, miss.'

'It's all right, I'm meeting someone in the Lamb and Flag.'

'They don't call it the Blood and Bucket for nothing,' Francis said grimly. 'They used to have bare-knuckle fights there, and it ain't the place for a young lady like yourself, miss.'

'We're coming with you.' Ernest took Nettie by the hand. 'Might I come upstairs later, so that I can finish reading the story?'

She nodded. 'Of course you may.' There seemed little she could say that would deter them and Nettie walked on escorted by her two unusual-looking bodyguards.

The public bar was crowded and filled with smoke from the coal fire and the clay pipes smoked by the patrons. Through a blue haze Nettie could just make out Duke, who was standing at the bar with Samson Wegg, and Rufus. She was about to join them when her father hurried into the taproom.

'What's this all about, Nettie?' He glanced nervously at the Burton brothers. 'Are these men bothering you?'

'No, Pa. They were kind enough to escort me here.' Nettie took her father by the arm and propelled him towards the bar. 'There's

461

someone I want you to see.'

'Duke!' Robert came to a halt, staring open-mouthed. 'What are you doing here? And Wegg — what is this?'

Duke glanced anxiously at Ernest and Francis, who had stationed themselves behind Nettie.

'What are they doing here?'

'You know them, Duke?' Nettie stared at him in surprise.

'Everyone knows the Burton brothers,' Duke said grimly. 'Why did you bring me here, Wegg?'

Nettie took a step closer. 'I want you to tell my pa how you used him. Tell him how much you made out of his works, and how you deserted him and left him to struggle on his own.'

'I'm a businessman,' Duke protested. 'Your father knew what he was getting himself into.'

Robert shook his head. 'You promised me that the copies I made were sold as such. I was shocked when I saw the Botticelli in the condesa's home, especially when I realised that she thought she had the original.'

'Then you're a fool,' Duke said angrily. 'You deserve to be duped.'

Ernest fisted his hands. 'Shall I sort him out for you, Nettie?'

'Yes,' Francis added. 'Come outside, Dexter. We've been after you for some time.'

'I don't know what you're talking about.' Duke shoved Wegg forward. 'This fellow is the snitch. You'd best watch out, boys, or he'll set the cops on you and you'll end up in choky.'

'I'm a private detective,' Wegg said icily. 'You're the villain here, Dexter. I never believed your version of things, and this is where you get your comeuppance.'

'You're a cheat and a liar, Dexter. It's time you was taught a lesson you won't forget.' Ernest grabbed Duke by the collar and marched him out of the bar room to a round of applause.

'It seems that Duke is not a popular man around here,' Rufus said, chuckling. 'I'll buy you a drink, Wegg.'

Wegg glanced round furtively. 'Ta, maybe another time, but I've got things to do. I'm going, but first there's the matter of payment.'

'Suit yourself.' Rufus took a wallet from his inside pocket and selected a note, which he handed to Wegg. 'There. That's what we agreed.'

Wegg snatched the money, tipped his battered top hat and rushed out into the street.

Rufus turned to Nettie and her father with an ingratiating smile. 'What will you have? Ladies first.'

'No, thank you. I have something more important to do.' Nettie hurried outside and had to run to catch up with the Burton brothers as they marched Duke towards a narrow alleyway.

'Wait,' she cried breathlessly.

They came to a halt.

'You've relented,' Duke said with an ingratiating smile. 'I knew you wouldn't allow these thugs to beat up an innocent man.'

'I'll ask them to let you go on one condition.'

'Anything to oblige a beautiful lady.'

'Then you'll come with me to a law office in Lincoln's Inn, where you'll swear an affidavit that your marriage to Constance was never

463

consummated, and you'll agree to return all her property to her.'

'You're not serious?'

'Yes, I am. Either you come with me now or I let these nice gentleman do what they will with you.'

Ernest twisted Duke's arm behind his back. 'We'll come with you, to make sure this sewer rat does as you say. We don't like to see women used by men like him, do we, Frankie?'

Francis nodded. 'We most certainly don't. What do you say, Duke?'

Grimacing with pain, Duke nodded. 'Yes, I'll do it. Just stop twisting my arm.'

Nettie smiled triumphantly. 'Come along. It's not too far to walk.' She turned her head as she heard Rufus calling her name.

He strode up to them. 'Where are you going with those men?'

'It's none of your business, Rufus,' Nettie said firmly.

'You tell him, girl.' Ernest patted her on the shoulder. 'You stand up for yourself.'

'I need to talk to you, Nettie,' Rufus said in a low voice. 'You misunderstood what I was trying to say earlier.'

She looked him in the eye. 'No, I didn't, Rufus. It was crystal clear and I've been a deluded fool, as has my father. You'll find that we are not as gullible as you first thought.' She turned her back on him. 'Come on, gentlemen. We have more important things to do than to stand here gossiping.'

26

Later that afternoon after a successful meeting at the law office, Nettie returned home with the signed and witnessed affidavit in her reticule and a letter to Duke's bank in Paris, ordering the release of all Constance's properties.

Robert was at his easel, brush in hand. He stopped working and looked up, frowning. 'Where have you been, Nettie? I was worried.'

'You won't be seeing Duke again, Pa. He's duped you for the last time.'

'What have you done with him?'

'He's given up his rights to Constance's property, and I've got the papers that will help her to get her marriage annulled. I'm going to Kent to give them to her.'

'That's all very well, but what about Rufus? I thought you and he might make a go of it.'

'Didn't you hear anything I told you, Pa? Rufus is going to marry an heiress.'

'But we could still work for him, my love. I had a quick word with him after you left.'

'And you are happy to work for a man who would set your daughter up as his mistress?'

'I wouldn't put it like that, Nettie. Rufus said I was welcome to live with you in Doughty Street, and I'd have my own studio in the office. He does mean to marry you, eventually.'

'I'm sorry, Pa. I thought I was in love with Rufus, but I realise now that it was a huge mistake. He thinks of nothing other than making money.'

Robert laid his brush down. 'What are you saying, child?'

'I'm a woman now, in case you hadn't noticed. I've devoted myself to you and your welfare for as long as I can remember, and I kept my writing secret because I knew you would think I was being foolish to harbour any ambition for myself alone. I'm going away, and I'm afraid you'll have to manage on your own.'

'You want a change,' Robert said hastily. 'Of course, I understand that. When will you be back?'

'I don't know.' Nettie shook her head. 'Maybe not for a long time.'

Robert moved away from his easel, wiping his hands on his paint-spattered smock. 'You're leaving me?'

'For a while, Pa. It might be too late, but I must try to make amends to the one person who's always stood by me. I've treated him so badly that I wouldn't blame him if he never spoke to me again.'

'You're talking in riddles, my dear.'

'Yes, Pa. That's how it seems to me, too.' She stood on tiptoe to kiss his cheek. 'I'll always be your loving daughter, but you must allow me this chance to make a life for myself.'

He sighed. 'I know you'll do what you want, no matter what I say. Will you leave me some money to keep me going until Rufus pays me?'

'Yes, Pa. Of course I will.'

'What shall I do about supper?'

'I'm not leaving until the morning. I'm going to Kent first and I don't want to impose on the Norwoods by arriving late in the afternoon.'

'Is Rufus going with you?'

'No, Pa. I told you, I'm finished with Rufus Norwood. This has nothing to do with him.'

'Oh, dear. I'm more confused than ever.' Robert shook his head. 'As you're going away for a while it might be nice to go out for dinner. I fancy a nice juicy steak or some lamb chops, as I'll probably be living on tea and toast until you come home.'

★　★　★

Nettie arrived at Norwood Hall in the middle of the morning, having risen very early and taken a cab to the railway station. She had packed her valise with almost everything she owned, including the manuscript, which she had worked on during the train journey. Mason answered her knock on the door and he greeted her with a nod and a hint of a smile.

'Good morning, Mason. I've come to see Miss Constance. Is she at home?'

'I believe so, miss. If you'll wait here I'll go and enquire.' He left her standing in the familiar surroundings of Norwood Hall. Nettie looked round, trying to imagine what it would have been like to be mistress of this charming home, but somehow it had lost its appeal. She was still furious with Rufus for suggesting that she might accept such an indecent proposition — it had been the worst insult he could have given her

— but she was not here for Rufus. She had come to give Constance the papers that would set her free.

Mason reappeared. 'If you would come this way, miss?'

She followed him into the morning parlour, but to Nettie's dismay she saw that Constance was not alone. Jane was seated at the table, a pen held in her hand and writing paper spread out before her. Constance leaped to her feet, but a look from Jane Norwood made her subside back onto her chair.

'To what do we owe this honour, Miss Carroll?' Jane demanded coldly.

'Good morning, Mrs Norwood,' Nettie said politely. 'My business is with Constance. Might we have a moment, please?'

'You can say what you have to say in front of me.' Jane dipped her pin into the inkwell. 'I am too busy to listen to gossip.' She held her pen poised above the paper. 'I suppose you've come to crow about your engagement to my son?'

'Mrs Norwood!' Constance stared at her in horror. 'Nettie would never behave in such a manner.'

'Hold your tongue, girl. If my son intends to marry this person it is very much my business, and I'll say what I like.'

Nettie felt her temper rising, but she took a deep breath. 'I am not engaged to Rufus, Mrs Norwood. Nor do I intend to live with him in sin, as he has proposed.'

Jane threw the pen down on the desk, spattering the paper with blots. 'You are a vulgar young person. I won't listen to such talk.'

'It's true,' Nettie said calmly. 'Your son intends to marry the heiress, but he wanted me to live with him. I refused.'

'You're lying.' Jane stumbled towards the door. 'I'm going to fetch my husband. He'll have a few words to say to you.' She slammed out of the room, and there was a brief silence, broken by a cry from Constance as she rose from her seat and rushed over to envelop Nettie in a hug.

'The wicked old witch,' she breathed. 'Don't take any notice of her, Nettie. I've had just about enough of her and so has Percy. It was a terrible mistake coming here.'

'I've come with good news.' Nettie opened her reticule and took out the documents, handing them to Constance. 'These will set you free,' she said smiling. 'You will have your property restored to you, although I'm not sure about the château. I think Duke was renting it, but he tells so many lies it's hard to believe anything he says.'

'I wouldn't want the creepy old place, anyway.' Constance studied the affidavit and the letter to Duke's bank, and she did a little dance. 'This is wonderful. I can go home at last. I must tell Percy immediately.'

'Where's Biddy?' Nettie asked anxiously. 'I want to see her before I leave.'

'She's at school in the village.' Constance folded the documents and slipped them into the pocket of her skirt.

'Is she happy here? If not I'll take her with me.'

'She's settled in so well, and Jane is a different

person when she's with Biddy. Bringing her here was a stroke of genius, but you must stay and see her. She'll be so disappointed if you return to London without a word.'

'I'm not going to London,' Nettie said softly. 'I'm going to France.'

'To France?' Constance stared at her in surprise. 'Why?'

'I've been an utter fool. I sent Byron away and it was the biggest mistake of my life. I didn't realise how much he meant to me until he was gone.'

'He went back to France?'

'Yes, he said he was going to join Lisette and Aristide.'

'And now you're going there, too?'

'I don't know. I'm only certain of one thing and that is I want to ask Byron to forgive me for the way I treated him. That's why I'm going to France.'

'I'll come with you,' Constance said firmly. 'I just need to let Percy know and he'll be only too happy to get away from here. He hates working in the brewery and he's only stayed because we had nowhere else to go.'

'I must leave soon.'

'It won't take me long to pack, and I'll send Mason with a note for Percy.' Constance went to the table and retrieved the pen. She scribbled a quick note and rang the bell to summon a servant. 'I'm so excited. I'm going home.'

★ ★ ★

Within the hour Nettie, Constance and Percy were on their way to Dover, courtesy of Maurice, who put his carriage at their disposal. He had calmed his wife down and given Percy his blessing, saying that a career in brewing was not necessarily for everyone. Nettie had come away with the feeling that Maurice was not sorry to let Percy go. In fact, he seemed quite relieved and had paid him until the end of the month, with an extra bonus for good luck. No one could call Maurice Norwood a mean man. Even Jane had begun to thaw a little when she realised that Nettie was intent on going to France. All that remained was to say goodbye to Biddy, and they stopped briefly at the village school. There had been tears, but Nettie had promised faithfully to write and to come and see Biddy when she returned to England.

★　★　★

The journey to France passed in a haze as far as Nettie was concerned. She was desperate to see Byron again, but afraid that her treatment of him might have soured their relationship for ever. She had planned to head straight to the place where they had parted with Aristide, but Constance pointed out that he would have moved on, and she insisted that Nettie must stay with them.

They arrived at the Paris house to find Mademoiselle Menjou still in residence, but the cook and the only remaining maid had not been paid for some time, and were on the point of leaving. Constance managed to persuade them

471

to stay, promising to reimburse them as soon as she had cashed the banker's draft that Duke had been coerced into signing, and the maid was sent out to market to purchase food and necessities. Constance was delighted to be at home, but Mademoiselle Menjou shook her head when Constance asked for a room to be prepared for Percy.

'The young man cannot stay here, Constance,' Mademoiselle said in strongly accented English. 'It would not be proper.'

'But we're engaged to be married, Mademoiselle,' Constance protested, clutching Percy's hand as if she were afraid he might run away.

'You are still married to that other person.' Mademoiselle Menjou turned to Percy with a stern look. 'You understand, I'm sure.'

'Yes, of course.' Percy gave Constance a reassuring smile. 'I must find somewhere else to stay while we go through the formalities, my love.'

Nettie could see that Constance was close to tears. 'Is there living accommodation above the gallery?'

Constance brightened visibly. 'Yes, I believe so. That might do, for the time being.'

'Then I suggest you go and take a look,' Mademoiselle said stiffly. 'You will re-open the gallery, I suppose?'

Constance gazed wide-eyed at Percy. 'I don't know. I hadn't thought that far.'

'I must find paid employment,' Percy said slowly. 'But I don't know anything about works of art.'

'But my father does.' Nettie thought quickly. 'I know he's accepted a job with Rufus, but it's a waste of his talent. Maybe you could work together, Percy?'

He nodded. 'It's a thought, but first things first. Mademoiselle is right, I can't stay here, so let's go and take a look at this place.'

Mademoiselle Menjou took her hanky from her pocket and blew her nose. 'I thought you were gone for ever, Constance. This is too good to be true. If you'll excuse me, I'll go to my bedchamber and rest for a while. I'm quite overcome.' She sailed out of the room, wafting a hanky soaked in cologne in front of her.

'We'll go now, while there's still plenty of light,' Constance said happily. 'Will you come with us, Nettie?'

'I think I'll walk to the quay and see if anyone there has seen Aristide recently. I'm not sure how I'm going to find him and Lisette, but find them I will.'

'Not forgetting Byron,' Constance said with a mischievous smile. 'Tell the truth, Nettie.'

'He might not want to see me after the way I treated him, and I wouldn't blame him.'

'My brother is no fool. We'll help you to find him, Nettie.' Percy held his hand out to Constance. 'I'd much rather stay here, but Mademoiselle Menjou was right, it wouldn't do your reputation any good, and it won't be for long. We'll see a lawyer first thing in the morning and you'll soon be free from Dexter.'

Nettie walked with them part of the way and she went on to the quay where they had first met Aristide. It was a bitterly cold November afternoon and the watery sun had disappeared behind dark clouds. Frost sparkled on the grass in the gardens and the River Seine was the colour of gunmetal. The familiar scent of tobacco smoke and engine oil wafted from vessels moored alongside the quay, but there was no sign of Aristide's barge. Nettie tried out her French on one or two of the men who worked on the river, but either they could not understand her, or they had never met Aristide Durand. She returned to the house, despondent but even more determined to find Byron.

★   ★   ★

Percy settled into the apartment above the gallery and the word went round that it was opening, which encouraged artists to bring their works for sale. Nettie helped Constance to arrange the paintings and show them off to their best advantage.

Every day at noon, Nettie went to the quay to ask if anyone had news of Aristide, but the answer was always in the negative. She devoted all her free time to revising and rewriting the novel that had been rejected, and shortly before Christmas she borrowed the money from Constance and took the finished manuscript to London. She left it with the publisher and she was given the page proofs of her first novel to check for herself. It gave her an excuse to stay on for a couple of days and she had intended all along to visit her father. She had a proposition to put to him.

She found him in the cold attic room, wrapped in several layers of clothing and staring disconsolately into the embers of a fire. The coal scuttle was empty and the cupboards were bare.

'What have you been doing, Pa? Why aren't you at work?'

'I walked out, Nettie. That man is impossible. Nothing I did was right. I'm an artist and I was well known before I fell in with Duke.'

'It's freezing in here, Pa. You'll catch your death of cold.'

'The money ran out, Nettie. You will stay, won't you? I can't manage without you.'

'I'll stay tonight, because it's too late to travel and I have to work on the page proofs of my book, but tomorrow I'll take them back to the publishers, and then you and I are going to Paris.'

'But my home is here, in London.'

'And Constance needs your help to get the gallery up and running, Pa. Percy has tried but he knows nothing of art, and they're desperate. They need your help.'

'Well, if you put it like that, I suppose I could give it a try.'

'Get your coat on, Pa. We'll go out to supper tonight. I'm paying.'

Over their meal at the Gaiety Restaurant, Robert told Nettie that Wegg had finally got his revenge and Duke had been arrested and was awaiting trial. In a surprising act of good will, Duke had absolved Robert of involvement in his criminal activities, and this had been confirmed by a visit from a police officer. Nettie was relieved to hear that her father was now above suspicion, but he was without a sponsor, and under the influence of a bottle of good claret he grew more and more enthusiastic about working in the Paris gallery.

When they returned to their attic rooms Nettie sat by the window for a while, remembering times gone by, and she knew she must find Byron. The longer they were apart the more she missed him, and the thought of life without him was unbearable. The gaslight from the streetlamps played on the wet cobblestones, and a hansom cab drew up outside depositing Violet Fabron and her husband at the front door. Nettie had seen the posters outside the Adelphi, featuring Amelie as the leading lady. She sighed as she made herself ready for bed. Life recently seemed to have been governed by timetables: Channel crossings and waiting on cold draughty station platforms for trains, followed by long and often cramped and uncomfortable journeys. Perhaps this would be the last time she would have to travel, for a while at least. Life would go on exactly the same in Ma Burton's lodging house, but tomorrow Nettie would cross the Channel yet again, but this time it would be to follow her heart.

★ ★ ★

Safely back in Paris, Robert stayed with Percy in the apartment above the gallery and Nettie went to live with Constance and Mademoiselle

Menjou. The annulment was going through, and Constance announced that she and Percy would be married in the spring. Robert had already started on a painting, using the studio behind the gallery, but Percy had decided that art was not for him. He was taking lessons in French and, following in his father's foot-steps, had enrolled as a medical student. This left Robert as manager of the gallery, a position he seemed delighted to fill. It meant that he could spend his days chatting to fellow artists and he still had plenty of time for his art.

Nettie continued to visit the quays daily, never giving up her search for news of Aristide's barge, and she had begun work on a new story. Her first novel was published in April and her revised manuscript had been accepted. The publisher wrote to inform her that the advance sales were better than they had expected and she was now financially independent. She would have been overjoyed, but her lack of success in finding Byron overshadowed everything.

The annulment of Constance's marriage to Dexter was duly granted and their wedding took place in a small church not far from the house. It was a quiet affair, but that was how the happy couple wanted it, and after a wedding breakfast at home, they set off for a honeymoon in the warm south.

Nettie left her father and Mademoiselle Menjou sipping brandy on the terrace of the sunlit garden. It was a beautiful day and Nettie strolled through the tree-lined Paris streets with the sound of birdsong in her ears and an azure sky overhead. Every step she took reminded her of the time she had spent in Paris with Byron, and the longing to see him again and hear his voice grew stronger every day. She had not realised how much she relied on his warmth and sense of humour, his kindness and his companionship. But simple friendship was not what she wanted or needed now, and the only man she could imagine spending the rest of her life with might be anywhere in this large country.

She found herself heading automatically towards the river, and although she had not entirely given up hope, she had begun to think that Aristide must have changed his route. Perhaps Lisette had objected to his involvement with so many women, although Nettie could hardly believe that a glamorous woman like Lisette would form a deep attachment to someone like Aristide. However, it was all conjecture and although she still clung to the hope of finding them, she had nagging doubts.

The river sparkled in the sunlight and the water reflected the blue of the cloudless sky. The trees in the parks were bursting into leaf, and flowerbeds were overflowing with spring blooms. The Parisians had cast off their winter overcoats and capes and were sporting smart new jackets and gowns trimmed with lace. Parasols twirled and young lovers walked arm in arm. Nettie had come straight from the small reception, and was still wearing her wedding outfit with a smart new hat, trimmed with flowers and feathers, and she was vaguely aware of the admiring looks from gentlemen passersby. She came to a halt at the quay where she knew most of the bargees, and they greeted her like an old friend with grins and salutes. She strolled towards the café where they had first met Aristide, pausing to acknowledge one of her acquaintances.

He took the clay pipe from his mouth and exhaled a puff of smoke. 'Are you still looking for old Durand?'

'Yes, I am,' Nettie said wearily. 'I don't think I'll ever see him again.'

'You will if you go into the café. He's there, all right. Large as life and twice as ugly.'

'Thank you so much.' Nettie forgot everything as she picked up her skirts and ran. She burst into the shack, peering into the gloom. 'Aristide?'

He rose to his feet. 'Nettie.' He hurried towards her. 'You look so fine, I wouldn't have recognised you.'

'I've been searching for you for months. Is Lisette still with you?'

'She is, the little minx. What times we've had, Nettie. You wouldn't believe how much she's changed my life.'

'Oh, I think I would,' Nettie said, remembering the parties at the castle in Catalonia. 'And Byron?'

A sly grin twisted Aristide's lips. 'The poor boy is suffering from a broken heart. There's only one person who could make him smile again.'

'Where is he?'

Aristide pushed his cap to the back of his

head. 'Let me think. Lisette's gone shopping and that leaves Byron alone on the barge.'

Nettie did not wait to hear any more. She hurried from the café and raced along the quay until she came to the familiar barge. Nothing about it had changed, apart from a line of dainty women's undergarments hanging out to dry. Her heart did a massive leap against her ribcage when she saw Byron on the deck.

'Byron.' She hesitated, suddenly shy and unsure of her welcome. 'Byron.'

He looked up and his expression of astonishment was wiped away by a smile that melted her heart. He strode along the deck and leaped ashore.

'Nettie. Am I dreaming?'

She walked into his arms as if it were the most natural thing in the world. 'I've been in Paris since before Christmas. I've been trying to find you, but I didn't know where you were.'

He silenced her with a kiss that made her heart sing. He released her slowly. 'Does this mean that you've changed your mind?'

'I was a fool, Byron. You and I belong together, if you still feel the same, that is.'

He kissed her again and this time she was left in no doubt of his feelings.

'I've always loved you, Nettie. I still do, but I really thought I'd lost you.'

She brushed a stray lock of hair back from his forehead. 'I love you, too, Byron. You were always like part of me, and I suppose I took you for granted. It wasn't until I thought I would never see you again that I realised how I truly felt.'

'I've waited so long to hear those words.' His smile faded and he held her at arm's length. 'Could you live like a water gypsy? You look so grand and beautiful that I hardly dare ask it of you.'

'I could live anywhere if you were with me. I love the river, too. It will give me inspiration to write even better books.'

He went down on one knee. 'I'm not letting you go again. Will you marry me, Nettie?'

'Yes, gladly, happily and for ever, Byron. You and I will be water gypsies together.'

THE CHRISTMAS ROSE

Dilly Court

Standing on London's Royal Victoria Dock with the wind biting through her shawl, Rose Munday realises she's been abandoned by her sweetheart. She had risked everything to get to London but, stumbling through the pea soup fog, she has nowhere to go, and no one to turn to. Scared and alone, Rose steps straight into danger, only to be rescued by a woman of the night and her young sidekick, Sparrow. With all hope of her sweetheart's return fading, Rose fnds herself forging a new life with her unlikely companions. But a dangerous enemy threatens to ruin them all . . .

THE CHRISTMAS WEDDING

Dilly Court

Essex 1867. The first flakes of snow are falling when Daisy Marshall finds herself jilted at the altar. After losing her job as governess to the Carrington family, she is forced to leave London and everything she knows. Heartbroken, Daisy finds herself in the small coastal village of Little Creek in Essex. There she is warmly welcomed — but the village is poverty-stricken and hit by a cholera outbreak. Determined to help, Daisy makes new friends with earnest doctor Nicholas and dashing smuggler Jay — but also dangerous new enemies, who threaten to destroy everything she's built. Can Daisy save the village and find happiness in time for Christmas?